Romance

A coll
the wo

Thre

bestselling auth

LINDA
HOWARD

PRAISE FOR *NEW YORK TIMES* BESTSELLING
AUTHOR LINDA HOWARD:

"…a romance so hot readers will need to wear
asbestos gloves. Outstanding!"
—*Romantic Times BOOKreviews* on
Mackenzie's Pleasure

"*Raintree: Inferno* by Linda Howard is an exciting
and fast-paced novel… will keep readers
entertained from start to finish."
—*Romantic Times BOOKreviews*

"Linda Howard knows what readers want."
—*Affaire de Coeur*

"You can't read just one Linda Howard!"
—Catherine Coulter *New York Times*
bestselling author

100 Reasons to Celebrate

We invite you to join us in celebrating Mills & Boon's centenary. Gerald Mills and Charles Boon founded Mills & Boon Limited in 1908 and opened offices in London's Covent Garden. Since then, Mills & Boon has become a hallmark for romantic fiction, recognised around the world.

We're proud of our 100 years of publishing excellence, which wouldn't have been achieved without the loyalty and enthusiasm of our authors and readers.

Thank you!

Each month throughout the year there will be something new and exciting to mark the centenary, so watch for your favourite authors, captivating new stories, special limited edition collections…and more!

LINDA HOWARD

At His Mercy

Containing

**Mackenzie's Magic,
Heartbreaker
& Overload**

M&B™ and M&B™ with the Rose Device
are trademarks of the publisher.
Harlequin Mills & Boon Limited, Eton House,
18-24 Paradise Road,
Richmond, Surrey TW9 1SR

At His Mercy © by Harlequin Books S.A. 2008

Mackenzie's Magic, *Heartbreaker* and *Overload* were first published
in Great Britain by Harlequin Mills & Boon Limited.

Mackenzie's Magic © Linda Howington 1996
Heartbreaker © Linda Howington 1987
Overload © Linda Howington 1993

ISBN: 978 0 263 86687 2

025-1008

Printed and bound in Spain
by Litografía Rosés S.A., Barcelona

Mackenzie's Magic

LINDA HOWARD

The

Queens of Romance

Collection

MILLS & BOON
100
YEARS
pure reading pleasure

Dear Reader,

I love romance. I'm completely uninterested in the hearts-and-flowers aspect of it (my husband was greatly relieved to discover he had no obligations on St Valentine's Day), but I love *romance* itself, which focuses on the relationships that form the basis of society and civilisation. The importance of romance is often hidden behind the hearts-and-flowers symbolism, but the fact that it is such a bedrock of our human foundation is what causes it to often go unnoticed. When something has been there forever, one tends to take it for granted.

What I celebrate in my writing is the forming of those vital relationships, all the pitfalls and problems, the terrors and joys, and the astonishing ability of the human heart to form these life-giving connections even in the direst of circumstances. Love is the greatest joy, and the greatest pain, in life. Embracing it requires courage.

To me, romance books are all about that courage, the willingness to be vulnerable. They're about trust, and honour, all the old-fashioned concepts that are old but are never out of fashion. Each of these three books (*Mackenzie's Magic, Heartbreaker,* and *Overload*) is about trust and the triumph of love over the obstacle of fear.

Congratulations on your Centenary of Romance, which celebrates all that I love about romance. Romance – it's been with us forever, and it will forever be with us. How cool is that?!

Linda Howard

Linda Howard says that whether she's reading them or writing them, books have long played a profound role in her life. She cut her teeth on Margaret Mitchell and from then on continued to read widely and eagerly. In recent years her interest has settled on romantic fiction, because she's "easily bored by murder, mayhem and politics." After twenty-one years of penning stories for her own enjoyment, Ms Howard finally worked up the courage to submit a novel for publication – and met with success. This Alabama native is now a multi-*New York Times* bestselling author.

Chapter 1

Her head hurt.

The pain thudded against the inside of her skull, pounded on her eyeballs. Her stomach stirred uneasily, as if awakened by all the commotion.

"My head hurts." Maris Mackenzie voiced the complaint in a low, vaguely puzzled tone. She never had headaches; despite her delicate appearance, she possessed in full the Mackenzie iron constitution. The oddity of her condition was what had startled her into speaking aloud.

She didn't open her eyes, didn't bother to look at the clock. The alarm hadn't gone off, so it wasn't time to get up. Perhaps if she went back to sleep the headache would go away.

"I'll get you some aspirin."

Maris's eyes snapped open, and the movement made
her head give a sickening throb.

The voice was male, but even more startling, it had
been right beside her; so close, in fact, that the man had
only murmured the words and still his warm breath
had stirred against her ear. The bed shifted as he sat up.

There was a soft click as he turned on the bedside
lamp, and the light exploded in her head. Quickly she
squeezed her eyes shut again, but not before she saw a
man's broad, strongly muscled, naked back, and a well-
shaped head covered with short, thick dark hair.

Confused panic seized her. Where *was* she? Even
more important, who was *he?* She wasn't in her
bedroom; one glance had told her that. The bed beneath
her was firm, comfortable, but not hers.

An exhaust fan whirred to life when he turned on the
bathroom light. She didn't risk opening her eyes again,
but instead relied on her other senses to orient herself.
A motel, then. That was it. And the strange whumping
sound she had only now heard was the blower of the
room's climate-control unit.

She had slept in plenty of motels, but never before
with a man. Why was she in a motel, anyway, instead
of her own comfortable little house close by the stables?
The only time she stayed in motels was when she was
traveling to or from a job, and since she had settled in
Kentucky a couple of years ago the only traveling she'd
done had been when she went home to visit the family.

It was an effort to think. She couldn't come up with any
reason at all why she was in a motel with a strange man.

Sharp disappointment filled her, temporarily piercing

the fogginess in her brain. She had never slept around before, and she was disgusted with herself for having done so now, an episode she didn't remember with a man she didn't know.

She knew she should leave, but she couldn't seem to muster the energy it would take to jump out of bed and escape. Escape? She wondered fuzzily at the strange choice of word. She was free to leave any time she wanted...if she could only manage to move. Her body felt heavily relaxed, content to do nothing more than lie there. She needed to do something, she was certain, but she couldn't quite grasp what that something was. Even aside from the pain in her head, her mind felt fuzzy, and her thoughts were vague and drifting.

The mattress shifted again as he sat down beside her, this time on the side of the bed closest to the wall, away from the hurtful light. Carefully Maris risked opening her eyes just a little; perhaps it was because she was prepared for the pain, but the resultant throb seemed to have lessened. She squinted up at the big man, who sat so close to her that his body heat penetrated the sheet that covered her.

He was facing her now; she could see more of him than just his back. Her eyes widened.

It was *him*.

"Here you go," he said, handing the aspirin to her. His voice was a smooth, quiet baritone, and though she didn't think she'd ever spoken to him before, something about that voice was strangely familiar.

She fumbled the aspirin from his hand and popped

them into her mouth, making a face at both the bitter taste of the pills and her own idiocy. Of course his voice was familiar! After all, she'd been in bed with him, so she supposed she had talked to him beforehand, even if she couldn't remember meeting him, or how she'd gotten here.

He held out a glass of water. Maris tried to prop herself up on her elbow to take it, but her head throbbed so violently that she sank back against the pillow, wincing with pain as she put her hand to her forehead. What was wrong with her? She was never sick, never clumsy. This sudden uncooperativeness of her own body was alarming.

"Let me do it." He slipped his arm under her shoulders and effortlessly raised her to a sitting position, bracing her head in the curve of his arm and shoulder. He was warm and strong, his scent musky, and she wanted to press herself closer. The need surprised her, because she'd never before felt that way about a man. He held the glass to her lips, and she gulped thirstily, washing down the pills. When she was finished, he eased her down and removed his arm. She felt a pang of regret at the loss of his touch, astonishing herself.

Fuzzily she watched him walk around the bed. He was tall, muscular, his body showing the strength of a man who did physical work instead of sitting in an office all day. To her mingled relief and disappointment, he wasn't completely naked; he wore a pair of dark gray knit boxers, the fabric clinging snugly to his muscled butt and thighs. Dark hair covered his broad chest, and beard stubble darkened his jaw. He wasn't handsome, but he had a physical presence that drew the eye. It had drawn hers, anyway, since she'd first seen him two weeks ago, forking down hay in the barn.

Her reaction then had been so out of character that she had pushed it out of her mind and ignored it, or at least she had tried. She had deliberately not spoken to him whenever their paths crossed, she who had always taken pains to know everyone who worked with her horses. He threatened her, somehow, on some basic level that brought all her inner defenses screaming to alert. This man was dangerous.

He had watched her, too. She'd turned around occasionally and found his gaze on her, his expression guarded, but still, she'd felt the male heat of his attention. He was just temporary help, a drifter who needed a couple of weeks' pay in his pocket before he drifted away again, while she was the trainer at Solomon Green Horse Farms. It was a prestigious position for anyone, but for a woman to hold the job was a first. Her reputation in the horse world had made her a sort of celebrity, something she didn't particularly enjoy; she would rather be with the horses than putting on an expensive dress and adorning a party, but the Stonichers, who owned Solomon Green, often requested her presence. Maris wasn't a snob, but her position on the farm was worlds apart from that of a drifter hired to muck out the stables.

He knew his way around horses, though; she'd noticed that about him. He was comfortable with the big animals, and they liked him, which had drawn her helpless attention even more. She hadn't wanted to pay attention to the way his jeans stretched across his butt when he bent or squatted, something that he seemed to do a thousand times a day as he worked. She didn't want to notice the muscles that strained the shoulder seams of his shirts as he hefted loaded shovels or pitchforks. He had good hands, strong and lean; she hadn't wanted to notice them, either, or the intelligence in his blue eyes. He might be a drifter, but he drifted for his own reasons, not because he wasn't capable of making a more stable life for himself.

She'd never had time for a man in her life, hadn't particularly been interested. All her attention had been focused on horses, and building her career. In the privacy of her bed at night, when she wasn't able to sleep and her restless body felt too hot for comfort, she had admitted to herself the irony of her hormones finally being kicked into full gallop by a man who would likely be gone in a matter of weeks, if not days. The best thing to do, she'd decided, would be to continue ignoring him and the uncomfortable yearnings that made her want to be close to him.

Evidently she hadn't succeeded.

She lifted her hand to shield her eyes from the light as she watched him return the water glass to the bathroom, and only then did she notice what she herself was wearing. She wasn't naked; she was wearing her panties, and a big T-shirt that drooped off her shoulders. *His* T-shirt, specifically.

Had *he* undressed her, or had she done it herself? If she looked around, would she find their clothes haphazardly tossed together? The thought of him undressing her interfered with her lung function, constricting her chest and stifling her oxygen flow. She wanted to remember—she *needed* to remember—but the night was a blank. She should get up and put on her own clothes, she thought. She should, but she couldn't. All she could do was lie there and cope with the pain in her head while she tried to make sense of senseless things.

He was watching her as he came back to bed, his blue eyes narrowed, the color of his irises vivid even in the dim light. "Are you all right?"

She swallowed. "Yes." It was a lie, but for some reason she didn't want him to know she was as incapacitated as she really was. Her gaze drifted over his hairy chest and flat belly, down to the masculine bulge beneath those tight boxers. Had they really…? For what other reason would they be in a motel bed together? But if they had, why were they both wearing underwear?

Something about those sophisticated boxer shorts seemed a little out of place on a guy who did grunt work on a horse farm. She would have expected plain white briefs.

He turned off the lamp and stretched out beside her, the warmth of his body wrapping around her as he settled the sheet over them. He lay on his side, facing her, one arm curled under his pillow and the other resting across her belly, holding her close without actually wrapping her in his embrace. It struck her as a carefully measured position, close without being intimate.

She tried to remember his name, and couldn't.

She cleared her throat. She couldn't imagine what

he would think of her, but she couldn't bear this fogginess in her mind any longer. She had to bring order
to this confusion, and the best way to do that was to
start with the basics. "I'm sorry," she said softly,
almost whispering. "But I don't remember your name,
or—or how we got here."

He went rigid, his arm tightening across her belly.
For a long moment he didn't move. Then, with a
muffled curse, he sat bolt upright, the action jarring her
head and making her moan. He snapped on the bedside
lamp again, and she closed her eyes against the stabbing
light.

"Damn it," he muttered, bending over her. He sank
his long fingers into her hair, sifting through the tousled
silk as he stroked his fingertips over her skull. "Why
didn't you tell me you were hurt?"

"I didn't know I was." It was the truth. What did he
mean, hurt?

"I should have guessed." His voice was grim, his
mouth set in a thin line. "I knew you were pale, and you
didn't eat much, but I thought it was just stress." He
continued probing, and his fingers brushed a place on
the side of her head that made her suck in her breath as
a sickening throb of pain sliced through her temples.

"Ah." Gently he turned her in to him, cradling her
against his shoulder while he examined the injury. His
fingers barely touched her scalp. "You have a nice
goose egg here."

"Good," she mumbled. "I'd hate for it to be a bad
goose egg."

He gave her another narrow-eyed look, something he

had down to an art. "You have a concussion, damn it. Are you nauseated? How's your vision?"

"The light hurts," she admitted. "But my vision isn't blurred."

"What about nausea?"

"A little."

"And I've been letting you sleep," he growled to himself, half under his breath. "You need to be in a hospital."

"No," she said immediately, alarm jangling through her. The last thing she wanted was to go to a hospital. She didn't know why, but some instinct told her to stay away from public places. "It's safer here."

In a very controlled tone he said, "I can handle the safety. You need to see a doctor."

Again there was that nagging sense of familiarity, but she couldn't quite grasp what it was. There were other, more serious, things to worry about, however, so she let it go. She took stock of her physical condition, because a concussion could be serious, and she might indeed need to be in a hospital. There was the headache, the nausea… What else? Vision good, speech not slurred. Memory? Rapidly she ran through her family, remembering names and birthdays, thinking of her favorite horses through the years. Her memory was intact, except for… She tried to pinpoint her last memory. The last thing she could remember was eating lunch and walking down to the stables, but when had that been?

"I think I'm going to be okay," she said absently. "If you don't mind, answer a couple of questions for me.

First, what's your name, and second, how did we wind up in bed together?"

"My name's MacNeil," he said, watching her closely.

MacNeil. MacNeil. Memory rushed back, bringing with it his first name, too. "I remember," she breathed. "Alex MacNeil." His name had struck her when she'd first heard it, because it was so similar to the name of one of her nephews, Alex Mackenzie, her brother Joe's second-oldest son. Not only were their first names the same, but their last names both indicated the same heritage.

"Right. As for your second question, I think what you're really asking is if we had sex. The answer is no."

She sighed with relief, then frowned a little. "Then why are we here?" she asked in bewilderment.

He shrugged. "We seem to have stolen a horse," he said.

Chapter 2

Stolen a horse? Maris blinked at him in total bewilderment, as if he'd said something in a foreign language. She'd asked him why they were in bed together, and he'd said they had stolen a horse. Not only was it ridiculous that she would steal a horse, but she couldn't see any connection at all between horse thievery and sleeping with Alex MacNeil.

Then a memory twinged in her aching head, and she went still as she tried to solidify the confused picture. She remembered moving rapidly, driven by an almost blinding sense of urgency, down the wide center aisle of the barn, toward the roomy, luxurious stall in the middle of the row. Sole Pleasure was a gregarious horse; he loved company, and that was why his stall was in the middle, so he would have companionship on

both sides. She also remembered the fury that had
gripped her; she'd never been so angry before in her
life.

"What is it?" he asked, still watching her so intently
that she imagined he knew every line of her face.

"The horse we 'seem' to have stolen—is it Sole
Pleasure?"

"The one and only. If every cop in the country isn't
already after us, they will be in a matter of hours." He
paused. "What were you planning on doing with him?"

It was a good question. Sole Pleasure was the most
famous horse in America right now, and very recog-
nizable, with his sleek black coat, white star, and white
stocking on the right foreleg. He'd been on the cover
of *Sports Illustrated,* had been named their Athlete of
the Year. He'd won over two million dollars in his short
career and been retired at the grand old age of four to
be syndicated at stud. The Stonichers were still
weighing the offers, determined to make the best deal.
The horse was black gold prancing around on four
powerful, lightning-fast legs.

What *had* she been going to do with him? She stared
at the ceiling, trying to bring the hours missing from her
memory back to the surface of consciousness. Why
would she steal Sole Pleasure? She wouldn't have sold
him, or raced him—in disguise, of course—on her own.
She rejected those possibilities out of hand. Stealing a
horse was so foreign to her nature that she was at a loss
to explain having apparently done exactly that. The
only reason she could even imagine having for taking
a horse would be the animal was in danger. She could

see herself doing that, though she was more likely to take a whip to anyone mistreating one of her babies, or any horse at all, for that matter. She couldn't bear seeing them hurt.

Or *killed.*

The thought knifed through her, and suddenly she knew. Oh, God, she knew.

She jerked upright in bed. Instantly pain mushroomed inside her skull, the pressure almost blinding her for a second. She gave a gasping, almost soundless cry; a hard arm shot upward and closed around her, preventing her getting up, but it didn't matter anyway. She felt her muscles going slack, unable to support her, and she slumped over on him. The pain quickly subsided to a far more manageable level, but the moment of agony left her weak and shaking, collapsed on his chest, in his arms, her eyes closed as she tried to recover from the shock.

MacNeil gently turned so that she was flat on her back and he was half over her, one heavy, hairy, muscled leg thrown across her much slimmer ones, his arm under her neck, his broad shoulders blocking the light from her closed eyelids. One big hand covered her left breast, the contact brief and warm and electrifying, then moved up to her throat. She felt his fingers pressing against the artery there, then a soft sigh eased from him, and he briefly leaned down to press his forehead against hers, very gently, as if he were afraid the touch might hurt her. She swallowed, trying to control her breathing. That was the limit of her control, though, because there was nothing she could do about the speed at which her blood was thundering through her veins.

Only the thought of Sole Pleasure kept her focused. Maris gulped, opening her eyes and staring up at him. "They were going to *kill* him," she said in a stifled tone. "I remember. They were going to *kill* him!" Renewed rage bubbled in her bloodstream, giving force to the last sentence.

"So you stole him to save his life."

He said it much more as a statement than as a question, but Maris nodded anyway, remembering at the last second to limit herself to only a tiny movement of her head. The calmness of his voice again piqued her interest with its familiarity. Why wasn't he alarmed, indignant, or any number of other responses that could reasonably be expected? Maybe he'd already guessed, and she had only confirmed his suspicion.

He was a drifter, a man who routinely walked away from responsibility, but even though he'd guessed what she was doing, he had involved himself anyway. Their situation was highly precarious, because unless she could prove the charge she'd made, they would be arrested for stealing Sole Pleasure, the most valuable horse in the country. All she remembered now was the danger to the stallion, not who was behind it, so proving it could be a bit chancy.

Chancy...*Chance*. Chance and Zane. The thought of her brothers was like sunrise, bringing light to the darkness in her mind. No matter what was going on or who was behind it, all she had to do was call Zane, and he would get to the bottom of it. Maybe that had been her original plan, lost in the fog that obscured the past twelve hours. Get Sole Pleasure out of harm's way, contact Zane, and lay low until the danger was over.

She stared at the ceiling, trying to remember any other detail that would help clear up the situation. Nothing. "Did I call anyone last night?" she asked. "Did I say anything about calling one of my brothers?"

"No. There was no time or opportunity to call anyone until we got here, and you were out like a light as soon as you hit the bed."

That information didn't clear up the question of whether she had undressed herself or he had done it. She scowled a little, annoyed at how the physical intimacy of the situation kept distracting her from the business at hand.

He was still watching her closely; she felt as if his attention hadn't wavered from her for so much as a split second. She could sense him analyzing every nuance of her expressions, and the knowledge was unsettling. She was accustomed to people paying attention to her; she was, after all, the boss. But this was different, on an entirely different level, as if he missed nothing going on around him.

"Were you going to call your family for help?" he asked when she didn't say anything else.

She pursed her lips. "That would have been the most logical thing to do. I should probably call them now." Since Zane had left the SEALs, he was much easier to contact; Barrie and the kids kept him closer to home. And he would know how to get in touch with Chance, though the odds of Chance even being in the country weren't good. It didn't matter; if she needed them, if she made the call, she knew her entire family would descend on Kentucky like the Vikings swooping down on a medieval coastal village—and heaven help those who were behind all this.

Maris tried to ease herself away from him so that she could sit up and reach the phone. To her amazement, he tightened his grip, holding her in place.

"I'm okay," she said in reassurance. "As long as I remember to move slowly and not jar my head, I can manage. I need to call my brother as soon as possible, so he can—"

"I can't let you do that," he said calmly.

She blinked, her dark eyes growing cool. "I beg your pardon?" Her tone was polite, but she let him hear the steel underlying it.

His lips twitched, and a ruefully amused look entered his eyes. "I said I can't let you do that." The amusement spread to his mouth, turning the twitch into a smile. "What are you going to do, fire me?"

Maris ignored the taunt, because if she couldn't prove Sole Pleasure was in danger, neither of them would have to worry about a job for some time. She lay still, considering this sudden change in the situation, possibilities running through her mind. He was too damn sure of himself, and she wondered why. He didn't want her to call for help. The only reason she could come up with was that he must be involved, somehow, in the plot to kill Sole Pleasure. Maybe he was the one who'd been hired to do it. Suddenly, looking up into those blue eyes, Maris felt the danger in him again. It wasn't just a sensual danger, but the inherent danger of a man who had known violence. Yes, this man could kill.

Sole Pleasure might already be dead. She thought of that big, sleek, powerful body lying stiff, never to move again, and a nearly crippling grief brought the sheen of tears to her eyes. She couldn't control that response, but she allowed herself no other. Maybe she was wrong about MacNeil, but for Sole Pleasure's sake, she couldn't take the chance.

"Don't cry," he murmured, his voice dropping into a lower note. He lifted his hand to gently stroke her hair away from her temple. "I'll take care of things."

This was going to hurt. Maris knew it, and accepted the pain. Her father had taught her to go into a fight *expecting* to get hurt; people who didn't expect the pain were stunned by it, incapacitated and, ultimately, defeated. Wolf Mackenzie had taught his children to win fights.

MacNeil was too close; she was also lying flat on her back, which took away a lot of her leverage. She had to do it anyway. The first blow had to count.

She snapped her left arm up at him, striking for his nose with the heel of her palm.

He moved like lightning, his right forearm coming up to block the blow. Her palm slammed into his arm with enough force to jar her to the teeth. Instantly she recoiled and struck again, this time aiming lower, for his solar plexus. Again that muscular forearm blocked her way, and this time he twisted, catching both of her arms and pinning them to the pillow on each side of her head. With another smooth motion he levered himself atop her, his full weight crushing her into the bed.

The entire thing took three seconds, maybe less. There had been no explosion of movement; anyone watching might not even have realized a brief battle had taken place, so tight had been the movements of attack and response, then counterattack. Her head hadn't even been unduly jarred. But Maris knew. Not only had she been trained by her father, she had also watched Zane and Chance spar too often to have any doubts. She had just gone up against a highly trained professional—and lost.

His blue eyes were flinty, his expression cold and remote. His grip on her wrists didn't hurt, but when she tried to move her arms, she found that she couldn't.

"Now, what in hell was that about?" His voice was still calm, but edged with an icy sharpness.

Then it all fell together. His control, his utter self-confidence, the calmness that seemed so familiar. Of course it was familiar—she saw it constantly, in her brothers. Zane had just that way of speaking, as if he could handle anything that might happen. MacNeil hadn't hurt her, even when she had definitely tried to hurt *him*. She couldn't have expected such concern from a thug hired to kill a horse. The clues were there, even those sexy gray boxers. This was no drifter.

"My God," she blurted. "You're a cop."

Chapter 3

"Is that why you attacked?" If anything, those blue eyes were even colder.

"No," she said absently, staring up at his face as if she'd never seen a man before. She felt stunned, as if she really hadn't. Something had just happened, but she wasn't sure what. It was like the way she'd felt when she first saw him, only more intense, primally exciting. She frowned a little as she tried to pin down the exact thought, or sensation, or whatever it was. His hands tightened on her wrists, drawing her back to the question he'd asked and the answer he wanted, and reluctantly she gathered her thoughts. "I just now realized that you're a cop. The reason I tried to hit you was because you wouldn't let me call my family, and I was afraid you might be one of the bad guys."

"So you were going to try to take me out?" He looked furious at the idea. "You have a concussion. How in hell did you expect to fight me? And who taught you those moves, anyway?"

"My father. He taught all of us how to fight. And I could have won, against most men," she said simply. "But you—I know professional training when I see it."

"So the fact that I know how to fight makes you think I'm a cop?"

She could have told him about Zane and Chance, who, even though they weren't cops, had many of the same characteristics she'd noticed in him. She didn't, though, because she wasn't one hundred percent certain their organization or agency or whatever it was was exactly squared away with either the State or Justice Department. Instead, she gave MacNeil a secret little smile. "Actually, it was your shorts."

He was startled out of his control, his blue eyes widening. "My *shorts?*"

"They aren't briefs. They're not white. They're too sexy."

"And that's a dead giveaway for being a cop?" he asked incredulously, color staining his cheekbones.

"Drifters don't wear sexy gray boxers," she pointed out. She didn't mention the interest she could feel stirring in those sexy gray boxers. Perhaps, under the circumstances, she shouldn't have mentioned his underwear. Not that his reaction was unexpected, she thought. She was barely clothed, and he wore even less. She could feel the hard, hairy bareness of his legs against hers, the pressure of his hips. Just minutes before, she had thought his touch carefully controlled, so that there was no intimacy, despite his closeness. She didn't feel that way now. It wasn't just his arousal; there was something *very* intimate in the way he held her beneath him, as if their brief battle had startled him out of his careful control and provoked him into a heated, purely male response. She took a deep breath as an unfamiliar excitement made her heart beat faster, made every cell in her body tingle with life. The secret part of her, the wildness that she had always known was there but which no man had ever before managed to touch, shivered in fierce satisfaction at the way he held her.

"Cops don't necessarily wear them, either."

Her comment about his shorts had definitely disturbed him. She smiled again, her dark eyes half closing in sensual delight as she absorbed the novel sensation of having a hard male body on top of her—an extremely *aroused* male body. "If you say so. I've never seen one undressed before. What kind of cop are you, specifically?"

He was silent for a moment, studying her face. She didn't know what he saw there, but the set of his mouth eased, and if anything, he settled even more heavily against her. "Specifically, FBI. Special agent."

A *federal* agent? Startled out of her sensual preoccupation, she gave him a puzzled look. "I didn't think stealing a horse was a federal crime."

He almost smiled. "It isn't. Look, if I let go of your hands, are you going to try to kill me again?"

"No. I promise," she said. "Besides, I wasn't trying

to kill you, and even if I had been, I'm not as good as you are, so you don't have to worry."

"I can't tell you how reassuring that is," he said dryly, but he released her hands and shifted his position a little, propping himself over her on his forearms. The change forced his hips more firmly against hers, forced her thighs slightly apart to accommodate the pressure. She caught her breath. His interest had grown, to the point that there was no politely ignoring it. But he *was* ignoring it, not in the least embarrassed by his body's response to her.

Maris took another deep breath, delighting in the way the simple action rubbed her breasts against the hard, muscled planes of his chest, making her nipples tingle. Oh, God, that felt so good. She would gladly lie in his arms and do nothing more than *breathe,* if they didn't have a stolen champion horse stashed somewhere and someone presumably on their trail, trying to kill both them and the stallion.

But they did have a stolen horse hidden away, and a big problem on their hands. She focused her thoughts, and despite the fact that she was lying helplessly pinned beneath him, she fixed him with a dark, penetrating gaze. "So why was a federal special agent mucking out my stables?"

"Trying to find out who's been killing horses and collecting the insurance money on them—boss." He added the last word in a dry tone, responding to her arrogant claiming of the Solomon Green stables as her own.

She ignored the not-so-subtle teasing, because she'd

heard it so often from her family. What she loved, she claimed; it was as simple as that. She drew her head back deeper into the pillow and gave him a frankly skeptical look. "Insurance fraud rates a special agent?"

"It does when it involves kidnapping, crossing state lines and murder."

Murder. So she'd been right: Someone *was* trying to kill them. Had this someone hit her on the head, or had she gained the goose egg by a more mundane method, such as falling?

"What brought you to Solomon Green?"

"A tip." One corner of his mouth curved slightly. His face was so close to hers that she could see the tiny lines created by the movement, as if he smiled easily. "Law enforcement agencies couldn't operate without snitches."

"So you knew Sole Pleasure was in danger?" She didn't like that. Anger began to smolder in her dark eyes. "Why didn't you tell me? I could have been on guard without causing any suspicion. You didn't have a right to gamble with his life."

"All of the horses are insured. Any of them could have been targeted. Sole Pleasure should have been their least likely target, because he's so well-known. His death would raise a lot of questions, attract a lot of attention." He paused, watching her carefully. "And, until last night, you were on my list of suspects."

She absorbed that, her only reaction a slight tightening of her mouth. "How did last night change your mind? What happened?" It was both frustrating and frightening, not being able to remember.

"You came to me for help. You were so angry you could barely speak, and you were scared. You said we had to get Sole Pleasure out of there, and if I didn't want to help, you'd manage on your own."

"Did I say who was after him?"

He gave a slight shake of his head. "No. Like I said, you were barely speaking. You wouldn't answer any questions. I thought at the time you were too scared, and once we had the horse safe, I was going to give you a little time to settle down before I started questioning you. Then I noticed how pale and shaky you were, maybe a little shocky from the adrenaline crash. You wanted to go on, but I made you stop here. You conked out as soon as we got in the room."

That reminded her again of both the interesting question of whether she had undressed herself or he had done it for her and his rather irritating assumption that he could *make* her do anything. She frowned when she realized that he could back up that assumption with action; her current position proved it. He hadn't hurt her, but physically she was still very much under his control.

Her frown deepened as she grew more annoyed with herself than before. She was doing it again, letting her attention drift. She could keep letting herself get side-tracked by her undeniable attraction to him, or she could keep her mind on the problem at hand. Sole Pleasure's life, and perhaps her own, depended on doing whatever she could to help this man.

There was no question which was most important.

"The Stonichers," she said slowly. "They're the only

ones who would benefit financially from Sole Pleasure's death, but they'd make more by syndicating him for stud, so killing him doesn't make sense."

"That's another reason I didn't think he was in danger. I was watching all the other horses. The insurance on them wouldn't be as much, but neither would their deaths cause much of a stir."

"How did I find you?" she asked. "Did I come to your room? Call you? Did anyone see us, or did you see anyone?" His room was one of ten, tiny but private, in a long, narrow block building the Stonichers had built specifically to house the employees who were transient and had no other quarters, as well as those who needed to be on-site. As the trainer, Maris was important enough to have her own small three-room cottage on the premises. The foaling man, Mr. Wyse, also had his own quarters, an upstairs apartment in the foaling barn, where he watched the mothers-to-be on video monitors. There were always people around; someone had to have seen them.

"I wasn't in my room. I'd been in the number two barn, checking around, and had just gone out the back door when you rode by on Sole Pleasure. It was dark, so I didn't think you'd seen me, but you stopped and told me I had to help you. The truck and trailer that brought in that little sorrel mare this afternoon were still sitting there, hooked up, so we loaded Sole Pleasure in and took off. If anyone saw us, I doubt they could even have seen there was a horse in the trailer, much less recognized it as Sole Pleasure."

It was possible, she thought. The number two barn

was where the mares who had been sent to the farm for
breeding were stabled. Night came early in December,
and the horses were already settled down, the workers
relaxing or at supper. The truck and trailer didn't belong
to Solomon Green, and everyone knew they had
brought in a mare that afternoon, so no one would think
anything of the rig leaving, except the driver, who had
decided to spend the night and start back at dawn the
next day. And Sole Pleasure was exceptionally easy to
load; he never made a fuss and, in fact, seemed to enjoy
traveling. Loading him wouldn't have taken more than
a minute, and then they would have been on their way.

"I didn't have a chance to call my family," she said,
"but did you call anyone while I was asleep?"

"I went out to a pay phone and let my office know
what was going on. They'll try to run interference for
us, but they can't be too obvious without blowing the
operation. We still don't know who's involved in the
ring—unless you've remembered something else in the
past few minutes?"

"No," she said regretfully. "My last clear memory is
of walking down to the stables yesterday afternoon. I
know it was after lunch, but I don't know the exact time.
What little else I remember is just flashes of being
angry, and scared, and running to Pleasure's stall."

"If you remember anything else, even the smallest
detail, tell me immediately. By taking the horse, we've
given them the perfect opportunity to kill him and
blame it on us, or at least they'll see it that way, since
they don't know I'm FBI. They'll be after us hot and
heavy, and I need to know who to expect."

"Where's Pleasure now?" she asked in alarm, putting her hands on his shoulders and pushing. She squirmed under him, trying to slip free of his weight so that she could get up, get dressed and get to the horse. It wasn't like her to be so lax about a horse's comfort and security, and though she had watched MacNeil enough to know that he was conscientious with the animals, the final responsibility was hers.

"Calm down. He's all right." MacNeil caught her hands, once more holding them down on the pillow. "I've got him stashed in the woods. No one's going to find him. I couldn't make it easy for them. Leaving him in the parking lot, where anyone could get at him, would have made even a fool suspicious. They're going to have to come to us in order to find him."

She relaxed against the pillows, reassured about Pleasure's safety. "All right. What are we going to do now?"

He hesitated. "My original plan was to find out what you knew, then put you somewhere safe until we had everything settled."

"Where were you going to put me, in the trailer with Pleasure?" she asked, a slight caustic edge to her voice. "Well, too bad. I can't tell you what I know, and you need to keep me handy in case I do remember something. You're stuck with me, MacNeil, and you aren't putting me anywhere."

"There's only one place I'd like to put you," he said slowly. "And I already have you there."

Chapter 4

It wasn't a surprise, given all the evidence at hand.

Pure male possessiveness was in Alex MacNeil's attitude, in every line of his body, staring plainly down at her from those sharp blue eyes.

Maris knew she wasn't mistaken about that look. She had grown up seeing it in her father's eyes every time he looked at her mother, seen the way he stood so close to her, touched her, a subtle alertness in every muscle of his body. She had also seen it innumerable times in her five brothers, first with their girlfriends and later, for four of them, with their wives. It was a look of desire, heated and potent.

It was both scary and exhilarating, startling her, and yet at the same time it was as if she had known, from the moment she first saw him, that there was something between them and eventually she would have to deal with it.

That was why she'd been at such pains to avoid him, not wanting the complication of an involvement with him, or having to endure the resultant gossip among the other employees. She had dated, some, but she had instinctively shied away whenever a boy or man showed signs of becoming too involved, possessive. She'd never had much time or patience for anything that interfered with her concentration on her horses and her career, nor had she ever wanted to let anyone that close to her.

She had a strong private core that she'd never let anyone touch, except for her family. It seemed to be a Mackenzie trait, the ability to be alone and be perfectly content, and even though all her brothers except Chance had eventually married and were frighteningly in love with their wives, they had married *because* they were in love. Maris had always been content to wait until that once-in-a-lifetime love happened to her, too, rather than waste time by flinging herself without thought into a brief affair with any man who just happened to have the right physical chemistry with her.

The chemistry was there with MacNeil, all right. The proof of it, on his part, was pressing urgently against the soft notch of her legs, tempting her to open her thighs wider and allow herself to feel that rigid length full against her loins. The fact that she wanted to do so was proof of the right chemistry on her part. She should move away, she knew she should, but she didn't. There wasn't a cell in her body that wanted to move, unless it was closer into his embrace.

She stared up into his beard-stubbled face, into blue eyes that were hard and darkened by sharp desire, a desire he was ruthlessly containing. Her own eyes were dark, bottomless pools as she met that sharp gaze. "The question is," she said slowly, "what are you going to do about it?"

"Not very damn much," he muttered, shifting restlessly against her. His jaw tightened at the sensations resulting from that movement, and his breath sighed out between his teeth. "You have a concussion. You have a killer headache. We have an unknown number of unknown people looking for us, so I have to keep my mind on the situation, instead of thinking about getting into your little panties. And even if you said yes, damn it, I'd have to say no, because the concussion could be causing mental impairment!" The last sentence was raw with frustration, ground out as if every word hurt him.

She lay very still beneath him, though her instinct was to part her thighs and cradle him against her, pulling him into her soft heat. Her eyes went as dark as night, softening, something mysterious and eternal moving there. "My headache is better." Her voice was low, her gaze drawing him in. "And I'm not mentally impaired."

"Oh, God," he groaned, resting his forehead against hers and closing his eyes. "Two out of four."

Maris moved her hands, and he immediately freed them. She laid her palms against his shoulders, and he tensed, waiting for her to push him away, knowing it was for the best but dreading the loss of contact. She didn't push. Instead, she curved her hands over the powerful muscles that cushioned the balls of his shoulder joints, trailed her fingers over the curve of his collarbone and finally flattened her hands against the hard planes of his chest. His crisp black chest hair tickled her palms. His tiny flat nipples hardened to pinpoints, intriguing her. His heartbeat was hard and strong, throbbing beneath her touch.

She was amazed, a little taken aback, by the intensity of the desire that shook her. No, not just desire—*need*. Need, hot and strong. She had seen sexual attraction all her life, at the most basic level in her horses and the other animals on the ranch, and in her own family as something powerful and tender and somehow both straightforward and complicated at the same time. She didn't underestimate the compelling power of sex. She had seen it, but she'd never before *felt* it, not this heat and ache, this emptiness that could be filled only by him, this melting sensation deep inside. She had always thought that if she ever felt this way it would be associated with love, and love was impossible here, because she didn't know him, not really. She knew his name and his occupation, but nothing about the type of person he was, and it was impossible to love a stranger. Be attracted, yes, but not love.

But her sister-in-law Barrie had once said that within five minutes of meeting Zane she had known the kind of person he was, and loved him. They had been strangers, but extraordinary circumstances had forced them into an intimate situation and shown them facets of each other's characters that otherwise would have taken months for them to discover.

Maris considered her own situation and the stranger who was so intimately sharing it with her. What had she learned about him since awakening—or regaining consciousness—in his arms?

He wasn't pushing her. He wanted her, but he wasn't pushing. The circumstances weren't right, so he was waiting. He was a patient man, or at least a man who knew how to be patient when he had to be, something that was entirely different. He was intelligent; she would have seen that days—weeks—ago, if she had let herself study him. She wasn't certain, but she thought that an FBI special agent had to have a law degree. He had some working medical knowledge, at least about concussions. He was evidently strong-willed enough to have gotten her to do something she didn't want to do, though, of course, with a concussion she wouldn't have been at her best. He had taken care of her. And most of all, despite the fact that she had slept almost naked in his arms, he hadn't taken sexual advantage of her.

That was quite a list. He was patient, intelligent, educated, strong-willed, caring and honorable. And there was something else, the subtle quality of danger and controlled power. She remembered the quiet, authoritative tone of his voice, the utter confidence that he could take care of any problem that might arise. In that he was like her brothers, particularly Zane and Chance, and they were two of the most dangerous men she could imagine.

She had always known that one of the reasons she'd never fallen in love was that so few men could compare favorably with the men in her family. She had been content to dedicate herself to her career, unwilling to settle for less than what she knew a man could be. But Alex MacNeil was of that stamp, and her heart lurched. Suddenly, for the first time in her life, she was in danger of falling in love.

And then, looking into those eyes so blue it was like drowning in the ocean, she knew. She remembered the change inside herself, the quiet recognition of her mate.

"Oh, dear," she said softly. "I have a very important question to ask you."

"Shoot," he said, then gave a wry shrug of apology at his word choice.

"Are you married, or otherwise involved with anyone?"

He knew why she was asking the question. He would have had to be dead not to feel the electricity between them, and his state of arousal proved that he was far from it. "No. No involvements, period." He didn't ask the same question of her; the background check he'd run on all the employees at Solomon Green had given him the basic information that she was single and had no record of prior arrests. In the time he'd worked at the farm, from the questions he'd asked, he had also found out that she didn't date any one man on a steady basis. The other guys had kidded him about having the hots for the boss, and he'd gone along with the idea. Hell, it was true, so why not use it as part of his cover?

Maris took a deep breath. This was it, then. With the directness with which she faced life, and the fey quality with which she saw things so clearly, she gave him a tiny smile. "If you aren't already thinking of marrying me," she said, "you'd better get used to the idea."

Mac kept his expression still, not allowing it to betray the shock that was reverberating through him. *Marriage?* He hadn't even kissed her yet, and she was talking marriage!

A sane man would get up and get his mind back on the business at hand, which included keeping them alive through the next few hours. A sane man wouldn't continue to lie here with this woman in his arms, not if he wanted to preserve his enjoyable single state.

He wanted her, no doubt about that. He was familiar with desire, having indulged that particular urge since the age of fourteen, and knew how to ignore it when indulgence would interfere with work. The work was absorbing, and he'd thrown himself into it with the cool, incisive intelligence that he also used to govern his personal life. He'd always been the one in control in his relationships, the one who called an end to things whenever he thought a woman was beginning to cling, to expect more from him than he was willing to give. It wasn't fair to string a woman along and let her hope when there was no hope, so he always simply ended the affair before it got to the tears-and-recriminations stage.

But then, he'd never met Maris Mackenzie before.

He didn't get up. More disturbing, he didn't laugh and say the concussion must have impaired her mentally after all. She was small, delicately built, even fragile, so it was ridiculous for him to dread making her angry or, even worse, hurting her feelings. He wanted to continue holding her, wanted to cradle her close to him and protectively cover her, keep her safe from the danger that would erupt around them within the next couple of hours, shield her from everything—except himself. He wanted her open to him, vulnerable, naked, completely at his disposal. He wanted to sink into those beguiling, mysterious black eyes and forget everything but the feverish delight of thrusting into her.

The sharp turn of events had thrown him off balance, that was all. Until last night, she and everyone else at Solomon Green had been on his list of possible suspects, and he had refused to let himself dwell on the heat that ran through him every time her slight, disconcertingly female body came within sight. Hell, she hadn't even had to be in sight; the thought of her had slipped into his consciousness at odd times during the day and disturbed his sleep at night.

He had resented his inability to ignore her as easily as she ignored him. She had a very still, intense quality about her, a focus that bespoke a will of iron. She was as absorbed in her job as he was in his, to the point that he'd thought she didn't even know he existed as a person, much less as a man. The idea had been strangely disturbing. He'd needed to blend in, but instead he'd found himself wanting to stand out, so that she would look at him with recognition in her eyes instead of a blank stare. Night after night he'd lain alone and thought about her, resenting both the fact that he couldn't seem to stop and the fact that she was oblivious to him. He wanted her to be as aware of him as he was of her, wanted to know that she, too, twisted on lonely sheets and thought of him in bed with her.

He wanted her with an intensity that infuriated him. Everything about her appealed to him, and that was surprising in itself, because there was nothing overtly sexual about her manner. She was pure business; she never flirted, never played favorites with the men under her authority, never made a suggestive remark, didn't go out of her way to make herself more attractive. Not that she had to; he couldn't have been more aware of her than if she made a practice of parading naked in front of him.

He knew exactly how her jeans clung to her curvy little ass, had imagined more than once gripping those round cheeks in his hands and lifting her into his thrust. He'd studied the shape of her high, round breasts underneath the flannel shirts she wore and, considering the slightness of her build, driven himself crazy thinking about how tight she would be when he slid into her. He'd had all the normal, heated sexual thoughts. But he'd also found himself absorbed in the satiny texture of her skin, as flawless as if she didn't spend countless hours outdoors. No woman should have skin like that, as pure as a child's, and so translucent he could see the fragile blue veins in her temples. He would look at her pale brown hair, bleached by the sun into streaks of ashy blond, and think of how it would trail across his arm like a fall of silk. Her eyes were as black as night, fey and unfathomable, tempting a man to try to plumb those mysterious depths.

Desire, like heat, was measured in degrees, and ran the gamut from lukewarm to vaporization. She had long since turned him to steam, he thought; it was nothing short of a miracle that he'd held her in his arms all night and done nothing more than that, even though all she was wearing was a pair of skimpy, blood-pressure-raising panties and his own T-shirt, which was so large on her that it kept slipping down to reveal one silky shoulder.

This was desire, all right—and more. It was want carried to a higher degree than he'd ever before experienced, a fever that refused to cool, a need he hadn't let himself satisfy. Until last night, he hadn't even let himself talk to her, even though he'd known he should, to see what, if anything, he could find out from her. Oddly enough, she had seemed to avoid him, too, though he'd noticed immediately that Ms. Mackenzie was a hands-on trainer who knew everyone working under her and was on easy terms with them. She was pure magic with the horses and a tyrant when it came to their care, but a benevolent tyrant, and everyone from the stable hands to the riders seemed to treat her with varying degrees of respect and adoration. It was out of character for her to avoid him, but that was exactly what she'd done.

It had made him suspicious. It was his job to be suspicious, to notice anything out of the ordinary, and her behavior toward him had made him wonder if something about him had made *her* suspicious, put her on guard. With his background, he was familiar with horses, which had made him the logical choice for the job, and he'd tried to blend in. Still, he was always aware that his training had permanently changed him, and a sharp eye might be able to spot the little things that forever set him apart from others: the extraordinary alertness, so that he was aware of every little detail of the activity going on around him; his sharp, fast reflexes; his unconscious habit of placing himself in positions that could be defended.

And she had spotted those details, known what they meant. He didn't at all like the swiftness with which she had sized him up and said, "You're a cop," even if her actions of the night before had already convinced him that she wasn't involved in the ring that killed racehorses and collected the insurance money. She saw too much, with those black eyes of hers, and now she was looking at him as if she could see into his soul.

Honesty prodded at him. Even though every hormone in his body was roaring at him not to do anything to jeopardize his current position, to stay right where he was, on top of her and all but between her legs, he ground his teeth and said what he knew he had to say.

"Marriage? You must be hurt worse than I thought, since you're delirious."

She didn't take offense. Instead, she curled her arms around his neck and gave him that small, inscrutable, damnably *female* smile again. "I understand," she said gently. "You need time to get used to the idea, and you have a job to do. This can wait. Right now, you have to catch some damn horse killers."

Chapter 5

She needed to clear her head, needed some time away from him so that her nerves would settle down. Maris pushed lightly against his shoulders; he hesitated, but then rolled to the side, freeing her from his weight. The loss of that heavy pressure, the vital heat, was so unexpectedly painful that she almost reached out to pull him over her again. One glance at the straining fabric of his shorts told her that he might not be able to withstand any more temptation, and while her entire body yearned for him, she wanted to be able to fully enjoy their first time together. She had a concussion, and there were an unknown number of people after them who would likely try to kill them, as well as Sole Pleasure—powerful distractions, indeed.

Gingerly she sat up on the side of the bed, being very

careful to hold her head as still as possible. The aspirin
had helped; the pain was still there, but it didn't throb
as sickeningly as it had before. She eased into a
standing position and was relieved when the room
remained stable.

Instantly he was on his feet beside her, his hand on
her arm. "What are you doing? You need to rest as
much as possible."

"I'm going to take a shower and get dressed. If I'm
going to be shot at, I want to be on my feet and wearing
clothes when it happens." God, he was big, and there was
all that naked flesh right in front of her. She took a deep
breath, fighting the urge to press herself against him, to
find out exactly where her head would fit against his
shoulder now that they were standing up. His body was
so beautiful, his shoulders wide and powerful, his arms
and legs thick with muscle. How silly she'd been to
avoid him all these weeks, when she could have been
getting to know him! Silently she mourned those wasted
days. She should have realized sooner why her reaction
to him had been so sharp, why she'd felt that odd sense
of fright.

This was the man with whom she would spend the
rest of her life. No matter where her career had taken her,
home had always been a mountain in Wyoming, and
Alex MacNeil was going to change that. Her home
would be with him, wherever he was, and an FBI special
agent could be assigned anywhere. Though her life
would never be completely without horses, he might be
assigned to a city, where she wouldn't be able to find a
job as trainer. She had never before met a man whom she

would even consider putting ahead of her horses—but she looked at him and instinctively thought, *No contest.*

He was hers. She was his. She recognized it at every level of her being, as if she were vibrating to a resonance that only he produced.

But danger surrounded them, and she had to be prepared.

He had been watching her face with that narrow-eyed, intensely focused way of his. He didn't release her, but drew her closer, his arm circling her narrow waist. "Forget whatever you're thinking. You don't have to do anything but stay out of the way."

His nearness was too tempting. Maris leaned her head on his chest, rubbing her cheek against the hairy roughness as an almost painful tenderness filled her. "I won't let you do this alone." His nipple was right there, only a few inches from her mouth, and as irresistible as catnip to a kitten. She moved those few inches, and her tongue darted out, delicately licking the flat brown circle.

He shuddered, his arm tightening convulsively around her. But his gaze was grim and determined as he cupped her chin with his other hand and gently lifted her face. "It's my job," he said in the even, quietly implacable tone she had heard before. "You're a civilian, and you're hurt. The best way you can help me is by staying out of the way."

She smiled in wry amusement. "If you knew me better, you wouldn't say that." She was fiercely, instinctively, protective of those she loved, and the thought of letting him face danger alone made her blood freeze in

horror. Unfortunately, fate had decreed that she love a
man whose profession was putting himself between the
lawless elements in society and those he had sworn to
protect. She couldn't demand that he quit his job any
more than her family had demanded that she quit the
dangerous work of gentling unbroken horses. He was
what he was, and loving him meant not trying to change
him.

She straightened away from him. "I'm still going to
shower and dress. I still don't want to face anyone in
just my panties and a T-shirt…." She paused. "Except
you."

He inhaled sharply, his nostrils flaring, and she saw
his hand flex as if he wanted to reach for her again.
Because time had to be growing short, she stepped
away from him, away from temptation, and gathered up
her clothes. Just as she reached the bathroom door a
thought occurred to her, and she stopped, looking back
at him. *Was* he alone? Though Zane and Chance never
talked about their assignments, they had sometimes
discussed techniques, back in their training days, and
she had absorbed a lot. It would be very unusual for an
FBI agent to be working without backup.

"Your partner should be close by," she said. "Am I
right?"

His eyebrows lifted in faint surprise; then he smiled.
"In the parking lot. He got into position an hour or so
after we got here. No one's going to take us by
surprise."

If his partner hadn't been on watch, Maris realized,
MacNeil never would have relaxed his guard enough to

be in bed with her or let himself be distracted by the sexual attraction between them. Still, she was certain he hadn't slept but had remained awake in case his partner signaled him.

"What's his name? What does he look like? I need to be able to tell the good guys from the bad."

"Dean Pearsall. He's five-eleven, skinny, dark hair and eyes, receding hairline. He's from Maine. You can't miss the accent."

"It's cold out there," she said. "He must be frozen."

"Like I said, he's from Maine. This is nothing new to him. He has a thermos of coffee, and he lets the car run enough to keep the frost off the windshield, so he can see."

"Won't that be a dead giveaway, no frost on the car?"

"Only if someone knows how long the car has been there, and it isn't a detail most people notice." He picked up his jeans and stepped into them, never taking his eyes off her as he considered the somewhat startling workings of her nimble brain. "Why did *you* think of it?"

She gave him a sweet smile, her mother's smile. "You'll understand when you meet my family." Then she went into the bathroom and closed the door.

Her smile faded immediately once she was alone. Though she fully realized and accepted the wisdom of not interfering with a trained professional and his partner, she was also sharply aware that plans could go wrong and people could get hurt. It happened, no matter how good or careful someone was. Chance had been wounded several times; he always tried to keep it from their mother, but somehow Mary always sensed when he'd been hurt, and Maris did, too. She could feel it deep inside, in a secret place that only those she loved had managed to touch. She had been almost insane with fear that time when Zane was nearly killed rescuing Barrie from terrorists in Libya, until she saw him for herself and felt his steely life force undiminished.

It had happened to Zane, and he was the best planner in the business. In fact, expecting things to go wrong was one of the things that made Zane so good at what he did. There was always a wild card in the deck, he said, and she had to be prepared for it, no matter how it was played.

Her advantages were that she was trained in self-defense, was a very good shot, and knew more about battle tactics than anyone could expect. On the other hand, her pistol was in her cottage, so she was unarmed, unless she could talk MacNeil into giving her a weapon. Considering how implacable his expression had been, she didn't think she had much chance of that. She was also concussed, and though the headache had lessened and she was feeling better now, she wasn't certain how well she could function if the situation called for fast movement. The fact that her memory hadn't returned was worrisome; the injury could be more severe than she'd initally thought, even though her other symptoms had lessened.

Who had hit her? Why was someone trying to kill Sole Pleasure? Damn it, if only she could remember!

She wrapped a towel around her head to keep her

hair dry and stood under a lukewarm spray of water, going over and over the parts she remembered, as if she could badger her bruised brain into giving up its secrets. Everything had been normal when she went back to the stables after lunch. It had been after dark, say around six or six-thirty, when she stumbled across MacNeil. Sometime during those five hours she had learned that Sole Pleasure was in danger and either surprised someone trying to kill him or confronted the person beforehand and earned herself a knock on the head.

It didn't make sense, but the Stonichers had to be behind the threat to their prize stallion, because they were the only ones who could benefit financially from his death. Since they would make much more by syndicating him for stud, the only way killing him made any sense at all was if he had some problem that would prevent them from syndicating him.

It wasn't a question of health; Maris had grown up around horses, loved them with a passion and devotion that had consumed her life, and she knew every detail of the well-being of her charges. Sole Pleasure was in perfect health, an unusually strong, fast horse who was full of energy and good spirits. He was a big, cheerful athlete who ran for the sheer love of running, sometimes mischievous but remarkably free of bad habits. She loved all her horses, but Pleasure was special to her. It was unthinkable that anyone would want to kill him, destroy forever that big, good-natured heart and matchless physical ability.

The only thing she could think of that would interfere with his syndication, the only possible reason anyone would grab for insurance money rather than hold out for the much larger fortune to be gained from syndicating him, was if the fertility tests had proved him sterile.

If that was the case, the Stonichers might as well geld him and race him as long as he was healthy. But injuries happened to even the hardiest animals, and a racing career could be ended in a heartbeat. The great filly Ruffian had been on the way to victory, well ahead of her male opponent in a special match race, when an awkward step shattered her leg and she had to be put down. Given the uncertainties of winning purses on the track and the given of insurance money, if Sole Pleasure was sterile, the Stonichers could conceivably be going for the sure thing and have hired someone to kill him.

She didn't want to think it of them. Joan and Ronald Stonicher had always seemed like decent people to her, though not the kind with whom she would ever be close friends. They were Kentucky blue bloods, born into the life, but Ronald particularly seemed to be involved in raising horses only *because* he'd inherited the farm. While Joan knew the horses better and was a better rider than her husband, she was a cool, emotionally detached woman who paid more attention to social functions than she did to the earthy functions in the stables. The question was, could they deliberately kill a champion Thoroughbred for the insurance money?

No one else was in a position to collect, so it had to be them.

They wouldn't do it themselves, however. Maris couldn't imagine either one of them actually doing the deed. They had hired someone to kill Pleasure, but who? It had to be someone she saw every day, someone whose presence near the horses wouldn't attract attention. It was likely one of the temporary hands, but she couldn't rule out a longtime employee; a couple hundred thousand would be terribly tempting to someone who didn't care how he earned it.

She turned off the shower and stepped out, turning the situation around and around in her head. By the time she was dressed, one thought was clear: MacNeil knew who the killer was.

She opened the door and stepped out, almost stumbling over him. He was propped against the countertop in the small dressing area, his arms crossed and his long legs stretched out, patiently waiting in case she became dizzy and needed him. He, too, had dressed, and though he looked mouth-wateringly tough and sexy in jeans, flannel shirt and boots, she regretted no longer being able to see him in nothing more than tight-fitting boxers.

Maris jabbed a slender finger at his chest. "You know who it is, don't you?"

He looked down at the small hand so imperiously poking him, and one dark brow lifted in bemusement. He probably wasn't accustomed to being called to account by someone he could have picked up with one hand. "Why do you think that?" he asked in a mild voice, but even so he stood so that he towered over her, silently reestablishing his dominance.

It might have worked if she hadn't grown up watching her petite mother rule over a household populated by brawny males. She was very much her

mother's daughter; it never occurred to her to be intimidated. Instead she poked him harder.

"You said a tip led you to Solomon Green. Obviously the FBI has been working on this for a while, so
just as obviously you have to have a list of suspects
you're watching. One of those suspects is now working
at Solomon Green, isn't he? That's what tipped you
off." She scowled up at him. "Why did you say I was a
suspect, when you know darn good and well—"

"Hold it." He held up a staying hand, interrupting
her. "You *were* a suspect. Everyone was. I know who
my main suspect is, but he isn't working alone. This
ring has to have the collusion of a lot of people. The
owners are the main ones to profit, but any of the employees could also be in on it."

She didn't like to think any of her people would be
involved in murdering a horse for profit, but she had to
admit it was possible. "So you followed him there and
you've been watching him, trying to catch him in the
act so you'll have proof against him." Her dark eyes
caught fire. "Were you going to let him actually kill a
horse, so there would be no doubt?"

"That isn't the outcome we'd like," he said carefully,
watching her. "But we're aware that could be the
scenario."

Her eyes narrowed. She wasn't fooled by his formal
"official speak," used by both the military and law-en-
forcement organizations. Reading between the lines,
she knew that while he might not like letting a horse be
harmed, he'd been willing to let it happen if that was
what it took.

She wasn't thinking of slugging him; she was angry, but not foolish. He's already proven he was more than a match for her. Still, the expression on her face must have made him think she was about to try again to take him down, because his hand came up in one of those lightning-fast movements and caught her wrist, holding it against his chest.

She drew herself up to her full five feet almost three inches and lifted her chin. "I refuse to sacrifice a horse. Any horse."

"That isn't what I want, either." He gently cupped her stubborn chin, his fingertips tracing over the satiny skin of her jaw. "But we can't make our move until they do something conclusive, something we can make stick in the courts. We have to tie everything together in a knot some slick lawyer can't undo, or a murderer is going to walk. This isn't just about horses and insurance fraud. A stable hand was killed, a kid just sixteen years old. He must have stumbled across something the way you did, but he wasn't as lucky. The next morning there was a dead horse in the stall and the kid was missing. That was in Connecticut. A week later his body was found in Pennsylvania."

She stared at him, her dark eyes stark. The Stonichers might just be after the money, but they had aligned themselves with people who were truly evil. Any regret she might have felt for them vanished.

MacNeil's face was like stone. "I won't move too soon and blow the investigation. No matter what, I'm going to nail these bastards. Do you understand?"

She did. Completely. That left only one thing to

do. "You refuse to compromise the case, and I won't
let Pleasure be hurt. That means you'll have to use
me as the bait."

Chapter 6

"Absolutely not." The words were flat and implacable. "No way in hell."

"You have to."

He looked down at her with mingled exasperation and amusement. "Sweetheart, you've been the boss for so long that you've forgotten how to take orders. I'm running this show, not you, and you'll damn well do what I tell you to do, when I tell you to do it, or you're going to find yourself handcuffed and gagged and your sweet little ass stuffed in a closet until this is over."

Maris batted her long eyelashes at him. "So you think my ass is sweet, huh?"

"So sweet I'll probably be biting it before too much longer." The concept appealed to him; she could tell by the way his eyes darkened. She was rather taken by it, herself. Then he shrugged the moment away and grinned. "But no matter how good you taste or how fast you flutter those eyelashes, you aren't going to change my mind about this."

She crossed her arms and offered him an irrefutable fact. "You need me. I don't know what I saw or who hit me. It could have been one of the Stonichers, or it could have been whoever they hired. But they don't know that I can't remember, and they don't know about *you,* so they think I'm the biggest threat to them."

"That's exactly why you're staying out of sight. If it's one of the Stonichers holding the gun, I can't predict how he or she will act. Give me a professional killer any day, rather than an amateur, who's likely to panic and do something really stupid, like shooting you in front of a bunch of witnesses."

"God forbid you should have to deal with anyone who would get rattled by committing murder," she said, sweetly sarcastic, and he gave her another of those patented narrow looks of his. She continued with her argument. "They're probably surprised that I haven't already called the cops on them. By now they're figuring I was either hurt more than they'd thought at first and I'm lying unconscious somewhere, or that I've realized I have no proof to take to the cops, so I have no excuse for stealing a priceless horse. Either way, they want me. I'm the perfect patsy. They can kill Pleasure, make it look like I did it, and then kill me. Everything's tied up nice and clean, and who knows, the insurance policy may even pay double indemnity, which is more money in everyone's pocket. Nothing will make them commit faster than seeing me."

"Damn it, *no*." He shook his head in exasperation. "I can't believe the way your mind works. You must read a lot of thrillers."

She glared at him, affronted. Her argument was perfectly logical, and he knew it. That didn't mean he liked it. It didn't even mean he would agree with it; she was fast learning that she could add *protective* to the list of his characteristics. And *stubborn*. God forbid she should forget stubborn.

"Sweetheart…" He smoothed his hands over her shoulders, an unfamiliar, tender ache in his chest as he felt the delicacy of her bones. He tried to think of the words that would convince her to leave this business to him and Dean. It was their job; they were trained for it. She would be in the way, and worrying about her would drive him crazy. God, she evidently thought she was seven feet tall and made of pig iron, but he could see how pale she was, how carefully she moved. She wasn't normally fragile, despite the slightness of her build; he'd seen her ride, effortlessly controlling stallions that most men would have trouble handling, so he knew she was strong. She was also alarmingly valiant, and he didn't know if his nerves could stand the stress.

"Look at it this way," she said. "As long as they don't know where Pleasure is, I'm safe. They need me to get to him."

He didn't argue, didn't try to convince her. He just shook his head and said, "No."

She gave his forehead an experimental rap with her knuckles, a puzzled look on her face.

He drew back a little, blinking in surprise. "What are you doing?"

"Seeing if your head's made out of wood," she retorted, her exasperation showing through. "You're letting your emotions interfere with your job. I'm your best bet—so use me!"

Mac stood motionless. He couldn't have been more stunned if this delicate fire-eater had suddenly lifted him over her head and tossed him through the window. *He* was letting his emotions interfere with the job? That was the last thing he'd ever imagined anyone would say to him. What made him so good at his job was his ability to divorce himself from the emotions that could hamper his actions. He'd always been the one who kept his head, who remained cool no matter how tense the situation. He might have some sleepless nights afterward, he might sweat bullets, but while the job was going down he was an iceman.

He couldn't be emotional about her; it wasn't logical. Okay, so he'd had the hots for her since he'd first seen her. Chemistry happened. With her, it had happened in a big way. And he liked her; he'd learned a lot about her since she had practically commandeered him the night before. She was quick-thinking, had a sense of humor, and was too damned gutsy for his peace of mind. She also responded to his slightest touch, her soft body melting against him, with a sheer delight that went to his head faster than a hit of whiskey.

He frowned. Only the fact that she was concussed

had kept him from taking her, and even then, it had been a near thing. Never mind that they were waiting for a killer to come after them, that he had deliberately left a trail that was just difficult enough to keep from being obvious. He never should have undressed last night; he knew that. But the fact was, he had wanted to feel her against his skin, and so he'd taken off everything but his shorts and slipped into bed with her. Dean would beep him when anyone showed up; if Mac had timed it right, he figured it would take another hour at least before anything happened, but still he should have been dressed and ready in case something went wrong. Instead, he had been on top of her, between her legs, and thinking that only two thin layers of cotton were keeping him from her. It would have taken him maybe five seconds to get those two layers out of the way, and then he would have been inside her and to hell with anything else.

But none of that was emotion. That was liking, and a powerful lust. So she had this crazy idea, after spending only a few hours with him—and being asleep most of that time—that they were going to get married. Just because she felt that way didn't mean he did, and he sure as hell wasn't going to let himself be buffaloed into something like marriage, no matter how hard he got whenever she was anywhere around.

The thought of using her as bait almost made the top of his head come off, but that wasn't emotion, it was common sense.

"You're concussed," he finally said. "You're moving like a snail, and you don't need to be moving at all.

You'd be more of a hindrance than a help, because I'd
have to watch you, as well as myself."

"Then give me a weapon," she replied, her tone so
unruffled that he wasn't sure he'd heard right.

"A weapon?" he echoed incredulously. "Good God,
you think I'm going to arm a *civilian?*"

She straightened away from his grasp, and his palms
ached from the loss of contact. All of a sudden her
black eyes weren't bottomless at all, they were cool and
flat, and the recognition of what he was seeing jolted
him.

"I can handle a pistol as well as you, maybe better."

She wasn't exaggerating. He'd seen that look in the
eyes of snipers, and in the eyes of some fellow agents
who had been there, done that, and had the guts to do
it again. He had seen it in his own eyes, and he'd understood when some women had shied away from him,
frightened by the dangerous edge they sensed in him.

Maris wouldn't shy away. She looked delicate, but
she was pure steel.

He could use her. The thought flashed into his brain,
and he couldn't dismiss it. Policy said that no civilians
should be involved if it could be avoided, but too many
times it *couldn't* be avoided. She was right; she was his
best bet, and he would be a fool if he compromised the
investigation by not using her. It wrenched every
instinct he had to do it, but he had to put his feelings
aside and concentrate on the job.

Damn it, he thought in surprise, he *had* been letting
his emotions cloud his thinking. That wasn't a good sign,
and he had to put a stop to that kind of idiocy right now.

"All right," he said swiftly, wheeling around to get their jackets. He jerked his on and began stuffing Maris into hers. "Time's short, so we have to move fast. First we need to get the stallion out of the trailer and hidden somewhere else, then position the trailer so that whoever comes can't see that he isn't in it. Then we come back here. You drive the truck, I'll be hidden in the truck bed, under some blankets or something." He turned out the bathroom light and began ushering her toward the door. "We'll post Dean down the road, where he can see them arrive. He'll leave then and get into position at the trailer. He'll give us warning. You leave by the back way just as they arrive, let them get a glimpse of the truck. They follow."

They reached the door. MacNeil turned out the lights and took a small radio out of his pocket, keying it. "Is everything clear?" he asked. "We're coming out."

"What?" His partner's voice was startled. "Yeah, everything's clear. What's up?"

"Tell you in a minute."

He slipped the radio back into his pocket and un-chained the door. He paused then, looking down at her. "Are you sure you can do this? If your head is hurting too much, let me know now, before it goes any further."

"I can do it." Her voice was calm, matter-of-fact, and he gave a short nod.

"Okay, then." He opened the door, and cold air slapped her in the face. She shivered, even though she was wearing her thick down jacket. The weather bureau had been predicting the arrival of a cold front, she remembered. She had watched the noon news and weather yesterday; perhaps that was why she now had this thick jacket instead of the flannel-lined denim jacket she had been wearing yesterday morning. She was glad she had changed coats, because the temperature now had to be in the twenties.

She looked around as she left the cozy warmth of the motel room. The motel office and the highway were on her right. MacNeil took her arm and steered her to the left, circling her behind a late-model pickup truck that was covered over with frost. "Hold it a minute," he said, and left her hidden by the truck's bulk while he went around to the driver's side. He opened the door and leaned in. She caught the faint metallic jingle of keys; then the motor started and settled into a quiet idle. She noticed with approval that the interior light hadn't come on, which meant he had taken care of that little detail earlier.

Interior lights. As he closed the truck door with a barely audible click, the neon light from the motel sign slanted across his high cheekbones, and a door opened in her mind.

She remembered the way his face had looked last night as he drove, the grimness of his expression highlighted by the faint green glow from the dash.

She remembered the desperation with which she had hidden her condition from him. She had been afraid to let him know how weak she was, how terribly her head hurt, that she was vulnerable in any way. He hadn't said much, just driven in dark silence, but even through her pain she had felt the physical awareness running between them like a live electrical wire. If she showed any vulnerability, she'd thought, he would be on her.

That was why he'd come with her, not because he was concerned about Sole Pleasure.

Her thinking had been muddled by the knock she'd taken on the head. She had been terrified for Pleasure's safety, trying to think of the best way to protect him, and she hadn't been certain she could trust MacNeil. She had taken a big chance in asking for his help; he had given it without question, but afterward she'd been too unbalanced by the concussion and the strength and unfamiliarity of her own sensual awareness of him to think straight.

She had wound up exactly where she was afraid she would, under him in bed. And he hadn't done a darn thing, except make her fall in love with him.

"Come on," he said softly, not looking at her. In fact, he was looking at everything except her, his head swiveling, restless eyes noting every detail of their surroundings.

The early morning was dark and silent, so cold that their breath fogged into ice crystals. No stars winked overhead, and she knew why when a few white flakes began drifting soundlessly to the ground. A cold breeze sliced through her jeans, freezing her legs.

He led her across to a nondescript tan Oldsmobile that was backed into a parking slot between a scraggly bush, the motel's attempt at landscaping, and a Volvo station wagon. She walked carefully, and her headache obliged by remaining bearable.

He opened the rear door of the four-door car and put her inside, then he got into the front, beside his partner. Dean Pearsall was exactly as MacNeil had described him, thin and dark, as well as definitely puzzled. "What the hell's going on?"

Briefly MacNeil outlined the plan. Pearsall's head swiveled, and he looked over the seat at Maris, doubt plain in his expression.

"I can do it," she said, not giving him time to voice that doubt.

"We have to work fast," MacNeil said. "Can you get the video equipment set up?"

"Yeah," Pearsall replied. "Maybe. We're cutting it damn close, though."

"Then let's not waste any more time." MacNeil popped open the glove box and removed a holstered pistol. He took it out, checked it, then slid it back into the holster before handing it back to Maris. "It's a .38 revolver, five shots, and there's a round under the hammer."

She nodded and checked the weapon herself. A faint smile eased the grim line of his mouth as he watched her; he wouldn't have taken someone else's word on the state of a weapon's readiness, either.

"There's a Kevlar vest on the seat beside you. It'll be way too big for you, but put it on anyway," he instructed.

"That's your vest," Pearsall said.

"Yeah, but she's going to wear it."

Maris slipped the revolver into her coat pocket and grabbed the vest. "I'll put it on in the truck," she said as she opened the door and slid out. "We have to hurry."

The snowflakes were still drifting down, ghostly in the predawn quiet. Their footsteps crunched on the gravel as she and MacNeil crossed the parking lot to the truck. The defroster had cleared the bottom half of the windshield, and that was enough for him to drive.

He didn't turn on the headlights until they were on the highway and he could tell there was nothing in sight in either direction except for the tan Oldsmobile, which had pulled out behind them. Then he hit the switch, and the green dash lights illuminated his face just as they had earlier.

Maris shrugged out of her coat and into the Kevlar vest. It was heavy and far too big, so big it covered her hips, but she didn't waste her time arguing about wearing the cumbersome garment, because she knew MacNeil would never give in on this.

"I remember driving with you last night," she said.

He glanced at her. "Your memory's back?"

"Not all of it. I still don't remember who hit me on the head, or taking Pleasure. By the way, don't you think you should tell me?"

He grunted. "I don't know who hit you. There's a choice between at least three people, maybe more."

"Ronald and Joan are two. Who's the one you followed to Solomon Green?"

"The new vet. Randy Yu."

Maris was silent. That name surprised her; she would have thought of a lot of other people before she would have come up with the vet's name. She'd been impressed with his skill, and he'd never shown anything but the utmost care for his four-legged patients. He was a quarter Chinese, in his middle thirties, and with the strength a veterinarian needed. If he was the one she'd tangled with, she was surprised she'd managed to get away from him with no more than a bump on the head. Of course, whoever she'd fought with wouldn't have expected her to know how to fight, much less fight hard and dirty.

"It makes sense," she said, thinking about it. "A quick injection, Pleasure dies of cardiac arrest, and it looks like natural causes. Not nearly as messy as a bullet."

"But you ruined that plan for them," MacNeil said, harshness underlying the calm of his tone. "Now they'll be planning to use bullets—for both you *and* the horse."

Chapter 7

Sole Pleasure wasn't happy. He didn't like being alone, he didn't like being cramped in a small trailer for so long, and he was both hungry and thirsty. MacNeil had backed the horse trailer deep into a section of woods, so deep she didn't know how he'd managed it, and Pleasure didn't like the unfamiliar surroundings, either. He was a horse accustomed to open pastures, roomy stalls, noise and people. As soon as they got out of the truck they heard his angry neighing and the thud of one of his rear hooves repeatedly kicking against the back of the trailer.

"He'll hurt himself!" Maris hurried to the trailer, moving faster than she should have for the sake of her head, but if Pleasure managed to break his leg, he would *have* to be put down. "Easy, baby, easy," she crooned as she unlatched the back gate, the special note she used for her horses entering her tone. The kicking stopped immediately, and she could almost see the alert black ears swiveling to catch her voice.

"Hold it." MacNeil's hand came down on top of hers as she started to open the gate. "I'll get him out. He's fractious, and I don't want him bumping you around. You stand over there and keep talking to him."

She gave him a considering look as she moved to the side. Really, the man was acting as if this were the first time she'd ever been hurt. Anyone who worked with horses could expect to be kicked, bitten, bruised and bucked off—though she hadn't been thrown since she'd been a kid. Still, she'd collected her share of injuries: Both arms had been broken, as well as her collarbone. She'd had a concussion before, too. What was the best way to handle an overprotective man, especially after you were married?

Exactly the way her mother handled her father, she thought, grinning. By standing her ground, talking rings around him, and distracting him with sex, and by choosing her battles and sometimes actually letting him have his way. This was one of the times to not kick up a fuss. She would ignore him later, when the stakes were greater.

MacNeil skillfully backed the big stallion out of the trailer; Pleasure came eagerly, happy to have company again, relieved to be unconfined. He showed his happiness by dancing around and playing, shoving MacNeil with his head and generally acting like any four-year-old. All things considered, Maris was just as happy not to be on the receiving end of those head butts, or to have to control all that power as he danced around. He would have been quieter for her—the horses found her especially soothing—but any jolt right now wasn't fun.

MacNeil led Pleasure away from the trailer, the stallion's hooves almost soundless on the thick pad of pine needles and decomposing leaves that carpeted the forest floor. He tied the reins to a sapling and patted the animal's glossy neck. "Okay, you can come over now," he called to Maris. "Keep him happy while I reposition the trailer."

She took control of the stallion, calming him with her voice and hands. He was still hungry and thirsty, but he was such a curious, gregarious horse that his interest in the proceedings kept him occupied. Dean Pearsall had stopped the Oldsmobile farther back, positioning the car so its headlights lit the area. MacNeil got in the truck and put it in reverse, leaning out the open door to check his position as he backed the truck up to the trailer. He was good at it; it took some people forever to get the trailer hitch in the right position, but MacNeil did it on the first try. Pretty good for an FBI agent, Maris thought. He was a fed now, but he'd obviously spent a lot of time around horses in the past.

It was snowing a little more heavily now, the head-light beams catching the drifting flakes as they sifted through the bare branches of the hardwoods. The pines were beginning to acquire a dusting of white. MacNeil maneuvered the trailer around, threading it through the trees, repositioning it so that it directly faced the narrow trail they'd made and anyone coming down it wouldn't be able to see that Pleasure wasn't inside. There were high, narrow side windows in the trailer, but none in front.

As soon as the trailer was in position and MacNeil had unhooked the truck and pulled away, Pearsall went to work, squirming underneath the trailer and setting up a video camera so that it couldn't easily be seen but would still have a good angle on anyone approaching the trailer.

MacNeil turned to Maris. "While Dean's working, let's get Pleasure tucked away back in the woods." He checked the luminous hands on his watch. "We need to be out of here in five minutes, ten tops."

The trailer contained blankets that had been used to cover the mare who had been brought to Solomon Green the day before. Maris got the darkest one and spread it across Pleasure's broad back. He liked that, swaying his muscular rump as if he were doing the hootchie-cootchie, and blowing in the particular way he did when he was pleased. She laughed, the sound quiet and loving, as she reached up to hug his big neck. He lipped her hair, but gently, as if he'd somehow realized by the way she moved that she wasn't quite up to speed.

"This way." MacNeil's voice held an odd note as he handed a flashlight to Maris, then untied the reins and began leading Pleasure deeper into the trees. He curved his other arm around Maris, holding her close to his side as they walked. Between the oversize Kevlar vest and her thick down jacket, he couldn't feel *her,* so he slipped his hand under the coat, under the vest, resting it on the swell of her hip. "How are you feeling?" he asked as they picked their way through the dark woods, stepping over fallen limbs and evading bushes that clutched at their clothes.

"Okay." She smiled up at him, letting herself lean closer into the heat and strength of his big body. "I've had a concussion before, and though this one isn't any fun, I don't think it's as bad as the first one. The pain is going away faster, so I don't understand why I can't remember what happened."

Her bewilderment was plain, and his fingers tightened on her hip. "A different part of your brain is affected, I guess. And parts of your memory are already coming back, so by tomorrow you'll probably remember everything."

She hoped so; these blank holes in her life were unsettling. It was just a matter of a few hours now, as she regained partial memory of things that had happened both before and after she was hit, but she didn't like not knowing everything that had happened. She remembered driving with MacNeil, but why couldn't she remember arriving at the motel?

Only one way to find out what she wanted to know. "Did I undress myself?"

Glancing up, she saw him smile at the abrupt change of subject. His voice deepened, evidence of the way the memory affected him. "It was a joint effort."

Maybe she would have been embarrassed an hour ago, but not now. Instead she felt a sort of aroused contentment fill her at the thought of him pulling off his T-shirt and putting it on her, the soft cotton still warm from his body.

"Did you touch me?" The whispered words were like heated honey, flowing over him, telling him how much she liked the idea.

"No, you were too out of it." But he'd wanted to, he thought. God, how he'd wanted to. He helped her over a fallen tree, supporting her so that she wouldn't stumble, but he was remembering how she'd looked sitting on the side of the bed, wearing nothing but her panties, her eyes closing, her pale hair floating around her delicate, satiny shoulders. Her breasts were high, firm, small but deliciously round, her nipples like dark pink little crowns. His right hand clenched on the reins; his palm was actually aching to touch her now, to fill his hand with that cool, richly resilient flesh and warm it with his loving.

"Well, darn," she said sedately, and in the glow of the flashlight he saw the welcome in her night-dark eyes.

He inhaled deeply, reaching for control. They had no time for any delay, much less one that would last an hour. An hour? He gave a mental snort. Who was he kidding? He was so worked up that five minutes was more like it, and that was only if his self-control turned out to be a lot stronger than it felt right now.

"Later," he promised, his voice a rough growl of need. Later, when this was settled and his job done. Later, when he could take the time with her that he wanted to take, behind a locked door and with the telephone off the hook. Later, when she felt better, damn it, and wasn't dealing with a concussion. He figured it would be two days, at least, before her headache was gone—two long, hellish days.

He stopped and looked back. They had gone far enough that he could no longer see the headlights through the trees. A small hollow dipped just ahead, and he led Sole Pleasure into it. The hollow blocked the wind, and tall trees leaning overhead protected him from the light snow. "You'll be okay here for a couple of hours," he told the horse as he tied the reins to a low, sturdy branch. Pleasure would be able to move around some, and if there were any edible leaves or stray blades of grass, he would be able to graze within a small area.

"Be good," Maris admonished the horse, stroking his forehead. "We won't be gone long. Then we'll take you back to your big, comfortable stall, and you can have your favorite feed, and an apple for dessert." He blew softly, then bobbed his head up and down in agreement. She didn't know how many actual words he understood, but he definitely understood the love in her voice, and he knew she was telling him good stuff.

MacNeil took the flashlight from her hand and settled his arm around her again as they walked back to the truck. Pleasure neighed his disapproval of being left alone, but soon the trees blotted out the sound and there was only the rustle of their feet in the leaves.

"You know what to do," he said. "They won't follow you too closely on the highway, because they won't want to make you suspicious. Let them see where you leave the road, but then drive as fast as you can, to give yourself as much time as possible. They'll be able to follow the tracks. Pull up to the trailer, get out of the truck and get into the trees. Don't waste time, don't look back to see what I'm doing. Get into a protected place and stay there until either Dean or I come for you. If anyone else shows up, use that pistol."

"You need the vest more than I do." Worry gnawed at her. He was sending her out of harm's way, while he would be right in the middle of it, without protection.

"They might pull in before you're completely out of sight and get a shot off at you. The only way I'll let you do this is if you're wearing the vest."

There that stubborn streak was again, she thought. Streak? Ha! He was permeated with it. She was beginning to think that if she scratched his skin, stubbornness would ooze out instead of blood. Living with him was going to be interesting; as he'd noted, she was used to being the boss, and so was he. She looked forward to the fights—and to the making up.

Pearsall was waiting for them when they got back. "Everything's ready," he said. "There's a six-hour tape in the camera, and the battery pack is fully charged. Now, if we can just get back into position before the bad guys show up, we're set."

MacNeil nodded. "You leave first. We'll let you get out of sight before we follow. Radio if you see anything suspicious."

"Give me an extra minute so I can swing through the motel parking lot to make sure there aren't any new arrivals. Then I'll pull back and take up position." Pearsall got into the car and backed out, his headlights bobbing through the trees.

Darkness settled around them as they listened to the sound of the car fading in the distance. MacNeil opened the passenger door of the truck and put his hands on

Maris's waist, lifting her onto the seat. In the darkness, his face was only a pale blur. "Whatever happens, make sure you stay safe," he growled, and bent his head to her.

His lips were cold, and firm. Maris wound her arms around his neck and opened her mouth to him as he deepened the kiss, slanting his head for better contact. His tongue wasn't cold at all, but hot and strong, and her entire body tightened with excitement as she leaned closer to him. It wasn't enough; with the pleasure came frustration. She swiveled on the seat to face him, parting her legs so that he stood between them, pressed hard against her as the kiss changed yet again, into something fierce with need.

It was their first kiss, but there was no tentativeness, no searching. They already knew each other, had already made the inner adjustment to the hot ache of physical desire, and accepted the hunger. They were already lovers, though their bodies hadn't yet been joined. The pact had been made. Invisible strands of attraction had been pulling them together from the first, and the web was almost complete.

He tore his mouth away from hers, breathing hard, his breath fogging in the cold air. "No more," he said, the words strained. "Not now. I'm as hard as a rock already, and if we—" He broke off. "We have to go. Now."

"Have we given Dean enough time?"

"Hell, I don't know! All I know is that I'm about ten seconds away from pulling your jeans off, and if we don't go now, the whole plan is blown."

She didn't want to let him go. Her arms didn't want to release their hold on him, her thighs didn't want to loosen from around his hips. But she did it, forced herself to open her embrace, because she could feel the truth pushing against her.

In silence he stepped back, and she turned in the seat so that she faced forward. He closed the door, then walked stiffly around the truck to climb in under the steering wheel, a look of acute discomfort on his face.

She wasn't good for his sanity, he thought as he started the truck and put it in gear. She made him forget about the job and think only about sex. Not sex in general, but sex in particular. Sex with her. Again and again, holding that slim body beneath him until he was satisfied.

He tried to imagine being sated with her, and he couldn't. Alarm tingled through him. He tried to think of some of the other women he'd slept with over the years, but their names wouldn't come to mind, their faces eluded him, and there was no concrete memory of how any of them had felt. There was only her mouth, her breasts, her legs. Her voice, her body in his arms, her hair spread across the pillow. He could imagine her in the shower with him, her face across the table from him every morning, her clothes hanging beside his in the closet.

The most frightening thing was that it was so damn easy to imagine it all. The only thing that frightened him more was the thought that it might not happen, that he was actually using her in a setup where she could be hurt, despite all the pains he was taking to keep her safe.

They left the cover of the woods, and he eased the

truck across the rutted ditch and onto the highway. No headlights appeared in either direction. Fat snowflakes swirled and danced in the beams of their own head-lights, and the low clouds blocked any hint of the ap-proaching dawn.

The radio remained silent, meaning Dean hadn't seen anything suspicious. After several minutes the lights of the motel sign came into view, and a few seconds after that they passed the Oldsmobile, pulled off on the side of the road and were facing back the way they'd come. It looked unoccupied, but Mac knew Dean was there, watching everything. No vehicle could approach the motel without being seen.

He pulled into the parking lot and backed into a slot, so that she could get out faster. He left the engine running, though he killed the lights. He turned to face her. "You know what to do. Do exactly that and nothing else. Understand?"

"Yes."

"All right. I'm going to get into the back of the truck now. If the fools start shooting early, hit the floorboards and stay there."

"Yes, sir," she said, this time with a hint of dryness.

He paused with his hand on the door handle. He looked at her and muttered something under his breath. Then she was in his arms again, and his mouth was hard, urgent, as he kissed her. He let her go as abruptly as he'd grabbed her, and got out of the truck. Without another word, he closed the door, then vaulted lightly into the truck bed, where he lay down out of sight and waited for a killer to appear.

Chapter 8

The motel was located where a small side road entered the main highway. The highway ran in front of the motel, the secondary road along the right side. Dean had checked out the little road as soon as he arrived and found that it wandered aimlessly through the rural area. No one looking for them was likely to arrive by that route, because it went nowhere and took its time getting there. The Stonichers and/
or their hired killer would be on the highway, checking motels, following the faint but deliberate trail Mac had left. The plan was for Maris to let their pursuers catch a glimpse of her as she drove around the back of the motel and onto the secondary road. She would turn left, then right, onto the highway. They would notice immediately that she wasn't pulling the horse trailer, so

instead of trying to cut her off, they would hang back and follow her, expecting her to lead them to Sole Pleasure.

At least Mac hoped that was how it worked. If Yu was the only one following them, that was how it would go down. Yu was a professional; he would keep his head. If anyone else was with him, the unpredictability factor shot sky-high.

It was cold in the back of the truck. He had forgotten to get any blankets to cover himself, and the snow was still falling. Mac huddled deeper into his coat and tried to be thankful he was out of the wind. It wasn't working.

The minutes dragged by, drawn out agonizingly by his tension as he waited. Dawn finally began to penetrate the cloud cover, the darkness fading to a deep gray, though true daylight was at least an hour away. Traffic would begin picking up soon, making it difficult for Dean to spot their tail. People would begin leaving the motel, complicating the traffic pattern even more. And better light would make it more difficult for Maris to hide in the woods.

"Come on, come on," he muttered. Had he made the trail *too* difficult?

Right on cue, the radio clicked. Mac keyed it once in reply, then gave a single rap on the back of the cab to alert Maris, who had shifted into position behind the wheel.

The radio clicked again, twice this time. Quickly he rapped twice on the cab. Maris put the truck into gear and eased out of the parking slot. She was turning the corner behind the motel when headlights flashed across the cab as a vehicle pulled into the lot, and Mac knew the lure had been cast. In a few seconds they would know if the bait had been taken.

Maris kept the truck at an even pace. Her instinct was to hurry, but she didn't want whoever was following them to know they'd been spotted. The car hadn't turned the corner behind them by the time she pulled onto the secondary road, so if it *was* them, they were hanging back, not wanting her to spot them.

She stopped at the stop sign, then turned right onto the highway. Watching her rearview mirror as she turned, she saw the car easing out from behind the motel. Its lights were off now, and its gray color made it difficult to spot in the faint light; she wouldn't have noticed it at all if she hadn't been looking for it.

They were driving Ronald's gray Cadillac. Maris had only seen it once or twice, because she usually dealt with Joan, who drove a white BMW. The driveway wasn't visible from the stables, and she seldom paid attention to the comings and goings at the big house. All that interested her was at the stables.

Still, she wondered that they would drive one of their personal cars at all, until she realized that it didn't matter. Sole Pleasure was their horse, and no crime had been committed. If she had called the police, it would have been their word against hers that a crime had even been attempted, and no one in the world would believe the Stonichers were willing to kill a horse worth over twenty million dollars.

Dean's Oldsmobile was nowhere in sight. Maris

hoped she was giving him the time he needed to drive the car deep enough into the woods that it couldn't be seen and to work his way into position on foot.

Watching the mirror, she saw the Cadillac turn onto the highway behind her. Without its headlights on, and with the swirling snow cutting visibility, she could barely make out the gray bulk. They would be able to see her much better than she could see them, though, because her lights were on; that was why they were hanging back so far, because they were unable to judge how visible they themselves were.

Their caution was working for her and against them. The distance would give her a few extra seconds to get out of the truck and hide, a few seconds longer for Dean to get set, a few seconds longer that Mac was safe. She tried not to think of him lying on the cold metal bed, unprotected from any stray bullets except by a thin sheet of metal that wouldn't even slow down a lead slug.

It was only a few miles to the place where she would leave the road and drive into the woods. A couple of times the snow became so heavy that she couldn't see the Cadillac behind her. The white flakes were beginning to dust the ground, but it was a dry, fluffy snow that swirled up with every breath of wind, and the passage of the truck blew it off the highway.

She maintained a steady speed, assuming they could see her, even though she couldn't see the Cadillac. She couldn't do anything that would make them suspicious. Finally she passed the mile marker that told her she was close, and she began braking, looking for the tire ruts where they'd driven before. *There*. She steered the truck off the highway, bouncing across the ditch faster than, for the sake of her head, she wanted to, but she didn't want to go any slower than she already was. Now that they had seen her leave the highway, she wanted to go as fast as she could, to gain a few more of those precious seconds.

Her headache, which had lessened but never disappeared, increased in severity with each bounce. She ignored it, gritting her teeth against the pain, concentrating on steering the truck on the narrow, winding path MacNeil had already blazed through the trees. She couldn't begin to imagine how difficult it must have been to do this with the trailer in tow, but it was a testament to both his stubbornness and skill that he had.

The Cadillac wouldn't be able to take the bumps and holes as fast as the truck did; it was too low to the ground. More seconds gained.

A bare limb scraped over the windshield, then her headlights caught the dark bulk of the trailer, almost concealed among the trees. Now. She parked the truck in the exact position MacNeil had decreed, killed the lights so the glare wouldn't blind the camera hidden under the trailer, then slipped out the door and walked swiftly to the trailer and then beyond it. She cut sharply to the left, stepping in places where the snow hadn't sifted down. She left no tracks as she removed herself from the scene so he could do his job without worrying about her.

She'd caught movement in her peripheral vision as she walked away, a big, dark shape silently rolling over the side of the truck bed to conceal himself behind one of the tires. At least he would have *some* protection, she thought, trying to console herself with that. His mind might be easier now, but hers certainly wasn't. He needed the vest she was wearing; she would never forgive herself if he was killed because she'd agreed to take his vest. It would have been better to remove herself entirely, even if it meant they wouldn't be able to get any solid evidence against the Stonichers. The FBI would get another crack at Randy Yu, but she would never find another MacNeil.

She'd gone far enough. She stopped, her back against a big oak. Snowflakes drifted silently down in the gray dawn, settling in a lacy cap on her unprotected head. She leaned her aching head against the tree and closed her eyes, listening, waiting, her breath almost halted, her heart barely beating, waiting.

Mac waited, his eyes never leaving the rutted trail. They might drive right up to the truck, but if Yu was in charge, they would probably get out of the car and come the rest of the way on foot. He and Dean were prepared for both circumstances. The underbrush was thick; if they tried to force their way through it, they would make a lot of noise. The best thing to do was to walk up the trail, staying close to the edges. Maris had parked the truck so that they could bypass it only on the driver's side; the tailgate on the passenger side was right up against the bushes. Anyone coming along that trail would be funneled into the camera's view and duly recorded on tape.

After what seemed an interminable length of time,

he heard a twig snap. He didn't move. His position, crouched by the right front tire, was secure; he couldn't be seen until they walked in front of the truck, but by then they would have looked into the cab and seen it was empty, and wouldn't pay any more attention to the truck. They would be looking instead at the trailer, and at Maris's small footprints in the thin layer of snow, leading right up to it.

There were other sounds now, rustles from careless feet, more than one pair; the brushing sounds of clothing, the harshness of someone who was slightly winded trying to regulate their breathing. They were close, very close.

The footsteps stopped. "She isn't in the truck." The whisper was barely audible, sexless.

"Look! Her footprints go right up to the trailer." It was another whisper, excitement making it louder than the first.

"Shut…up." The two words were hissed between clenched teeth, as if they had already been said more than once.

"Don't tell me to shut up. We have her cornered. What are you waiting for?"

Though still whispering, the speaker's voice was so forceful that it was almost as audible as if he—or she—had spoken aloud. The mike might have caught it, Mac thought. With enhanced sound-extraction techniques, which the Bureau had, he was certain the words were now on tape. The only problem was, they hadn't exactly been damning.

"You hired me to do a job. Now stay out of my way

and let me do it." There was fury evident now, in both words and tone.

"You're the one who bungled it the first time, so don't act as if you're Mr. Infallible. If you'd been half as smart as you seem to think you are, the horse would already be dead and Maris Mackenzie wouldn't suspect a thing. I didn't bargain on murder when I hired you."

That should do it, Mac thought with grim satisfaction. They had just talked themselves into a prison sentence.

He tightened the muscles in his legs, preparing to step out and identify himself, pistol trained and ready. A crashing, thudding noise behind him made him freeze in place. He looked over his shoulder and almost groaned aloud. A big, black, graceful horse was prancing through the trees toward them, proudly shaking his head as if wanting them to admire his cleverness in getting free.

"There he is! Shoot him!" It was a shout. Pleasure's unexpected appearance had started them out of caution. Almost instantaneously there was the sharp crack of a shot, and bark exploded from the tree just behind the horse.

Damn amateurs! He silently cursed. Pleasure was behind him; if he stood up now, he would be looking straight down the barrel, caught between the shooter and the target. He couldn't do anything but wait for the next shot to hit the beautiful, friendly stallion, who had evidently caught their scent and pulled free so he could join the party.

Dean realized Mac's predicament and stepped from

concealment, pistol braced in both hands. "FBI! Drop your weapons on the ground——*now.*"

Mac surged upward, bracing his arms across the hood of the truck. He saw Randy Yu, his hands already reaching upward as his pistol thudded to the ground. You could always trust a professional to know how to do things. But Joan Stonicher was startled by Mac's sudden movement, and she wheeled toward him, her eyes wide with panic and rage. She froze, the pistol in her hand and her finger on the trigger.

"Ease off, lady," Mac said softly. "Don't do anything stupid. If I don't get you, my partner will. Just take your finger off the trigger and let the gun drop. That's all you have to do, and we'll all be okay."

She didn't move. From the excellent viewpoint he had, Mac could see her finger trembling.

"Do as he says," Randy Yu said wearily. The two agents had them caught in an excellent cross field. There was nothing they could do, and no sense in making things worse.

Pleasure had shied at the noise of the shot, neighing his alarm, but his life had been too secure for him to panic. He trotted closer, his scooped nostrils flaring as he examined their familiar scents, searching for the special one he could detect. He came straight for Mac.

Joan's eyes left Mac and fastened on the horse. He saw the exact instant when her control shattered, saw her pupils contract and her hand jerk.

A shrill whistle shattered the air a split second before the shot.

A lot of things happened simultaneously. Dean

shouted. Randy Yu dropped to the ground, his hands covering his head. Pleasure screamed in pain, rearing. Joan's hand jerked again, back toward Mac.

And there was another whistle, this one earsplitting.

Maris stepped from behind a tree, her black eyes glittering with rage. The pistol was in her hand, trained on Joan. Joan wheeled back toward this new threat, and without hesitation Mac fired.

Chapter 9

He was mad enough to murder her, Maris thought.

She was still so enraged herself that it didn't matter. Fury burned through her. It was all she could do to keep from dismantling Joan Stonicher on the spot, and only the knowledge that Pleasure needed her kept her even remotely under control.

The woods were swarming with people, with medics and deputies and highway patrol officers, with onlookers, even some reporters already there. Pleasure was accustomed to crowds, but he'd never before been shot, and pain and shock were making him unruly. He'd wheeled at Maris's whistle, and his lightning reflexes had saved his life; Joan's bullet had gouged a deep furrow in his chest, tearing the muscle at an angle but not penetrating any internal organs. Now it took all of

Maris's skill to keep him calm so she could stop the bleeding; he kept moving restlessly in circles, bumping her, trying to pay attention to her softly crooning voice but distracted by the pain.

Her head was throbbing, both from Pleasure's skittishness and from her own desperate run through the woods. She'd heard him moving through the trees, and in a flash she'd known exactly what had happened, what he would do. How he'd gotten free didn't matter; he had heard and smelled them, and pranced happily to greet them, sure of his welcome. She'd known he would catch her scent on MacNeil's clothes and go straight to him. It had been a toss-up which of them would be shot first, MacNeil or Pleasure. All she could do was try to get there in time to draw the horse's attention, as well as everyone else's.

For one awful, hellish moment, when Pleasure screamed and she saw Joan swing back toward MacNeil, she'd thought she'd lost everything. She had stepped out from the trees, moving in what felt like slow motion. She couldn't hear anything then, not even Pleasure; she hadn't been able to see anything except Joan, her vision narrowing to a tunnel with her target as the focus. She hadn't been aware of whistling again, or of taking the pistol from her pocket, but the weapon had been in her hand and her finger had been smoothly tightening on the trigger when Joan jerked yet again, panicked, this time aiming at Maris. That was when Mac had shot her. At such close range, just across the hood of the truck, his aim had been perfect. The bullet had shattered her upper arm.

Joan would probably never have use of that arm

again, Maris thought dispassionately. She couldn't bring herself to care.

The entire scene had been recorded, complete with audio. The camera had playback capability and Dean had obliged the sheriff by playing the tape for him. Both Yu and Joan were nailed, and Yu, being the professional he was, was currently bargaining for all he was worth. He was willing to carry others down with him if it would lighten his sentence.

It had stopped snowing, though the day hadn't gotten any warmer. Her hands were icy, but she couldn't leave Pleasure to warm them. Blood glistened on his black chest and down his legs, staining his white stocking, splattering on the snow-frosted leaves and on Maris. She whispered to him, controlling him mostly with her voice, crooning reassurance and love to him while she held his bridle in one hand and with the other held some gauze the medics had given her to the wound on his chest. She had asked a deputy to contact a vet, but as yet no one had shown up.

Yu could have seen to the horse, but he hadn't offered, and Maris wouldn't have trusted him, anyway. It was he who had hit her on the head. As soon as she saw him again she had remembered that much, remembered his upraised arm, the cold, remorseless expression in his dark eyes. Other memories were still vague, and there were still blank spots, but they were gradually filling in.

She must have gone to the big house to see Joan about something. She didn't know why, but she remembered standing with her hand raised to knock, and freezing as Joan's voice filtered through the door.

"Randy's going to do it tonight. While everyone's eating will be a good time. I told him we couldn't wait any longer, the syndicates are pushing for a decision."

"Damn, I hate this," Ronald Stonicher had said. "Poor Pleasure's been a good horse. Are you certain the drug won't be detected?"

"Randy says it won't, and it's his can on the line," Joan had coolly replied.

Maris had backed away, so angry she could barely contain herself. Her first concern had been for Pleasure. It was the time when the stable hands would either be eating or have gone home for the night. She couldn't delay a moment.

Her next memory was of running down the aisle to his stall. She must have surprised Randy Yu there, though she didn't remember actually coming up on him. She remembered enough to testify, though, even if she never remembered anything else, and assuming her testimony was needed. The tape was solid evidence.

Another vehicle joined the tangle, and a roly-poly man in his late fifties, sporting a crew cut, got out of a battered pickup truck. He trudged wearily toward Maris, clutching a big black bag in his hand. Finally, the vet, she thought. Dark circles under his eyes told her that he'd probably been up late, possibly all night, with an ailing animal.

Tired or not, he knew horses. He stopped, taking in Pleasure's magnificent lines, the star on his forehead, the bloodstained white stocking. "That's Sole Pleasure," he said in astonishment.

"Yes, and he's been shot," Maris said tersely. Her

head was throbbing; even her eyeballs ached. If Pleasure didn't settle down soon, her head would likely explode. "No internal organs affected, but some chest muscle torn. He won't settle down and let the bleeding stop."

"Let's take care of that problem, first off. I'm George Norton, the vet hereabouts." He was working as he spoke, setting down the bag and opening it. He prepared a hypodermic and stepped forward, smoothly injecting the sedative into one of the bulging veins in Pleasure's neck. The stallion danced nervously, his shoulder shoving her once again. She clenched her teeth, enduring.

"He'll quiet down in a minute." The vet gave her a sharp glance as he peeled away the blood-soaked gauze she'd been holding to the wound. "No offense, but even with the blood, the horse looks in better shape than you do. Are you all right?"

"Concussion."

"Then for God's sake stop letting him bump you around like that," he said sharply. "Sit down somewhere before you fall down."

Even in the midst of everything that was going on, as the medics readied Joan for transport, Mac somehow heard the vet. All of a sudden he was there, looming behind her, reaching over her shoulder for Pleasure's bridle. "I'll hold him." The words sounded as if he were spitting them out one at a time, like bullets. "Sit down."

"I—" She'd started to say "I think I will," but she didn't have a chance to finish the sentence.

He assumed she was about to mount an argument, and barked out one word. *"Sit!"*

"I wasn't going to argue," she snapped back. What did he think she was, a dog? Sit, indeed. She felt more like lying down.

She decided to do just that. Pleasure was going to be all right; as soon as he quieted and let the vet do his work, the bleeding would stop. The torn muscle would have to be stitched, antibiotics administered, a bandage secured, but the horse would heal. Even though the truck and trailer were stolen, under the circumstances she couldn't imagine that there would be any problem with using them to transport Pleasure back to Solomon Green. Until the vet was finished and Pleasure was loaded in the trailer, she intended to stretch out on the truck seat.

Wearily she climbed into the cab. The keys were still in the ignition, so she started the engine and turned on the heater. She took off her coat, removed the Kevlar vest and placed it in the floorboards, then lay down on the seat and pulled the coat over her.

She almost cried with relief as the pain immediately began easing now that she was still. She closed her eyes, letting the tension drain out of her, along with the terror and absolute rage. She might have killed Joan. If the woman had shot Mac, she would have done it. Enveloped in that strange vacuum of despair and rage, she had been going for a head shot. She hadn't even thought about Pleasure, not in that awful moment when Joan turned on Mac. She was glad she hadn't had to pull the trigger, but she knew she would have. Knowing her own fiercely protective nature was one thing, but this was the first time she had been faced with the true extent of it. The jolt of self-knowledge was searing.

Mac had already faced this; it was in his eyes. She had seen it in her father, in her brothers, the willingness to do what was necessary to protect those they loved and those who were weaker. It wasn't easy. It was gut-wrenching, and those who were willing to stand on the front lines paid for it in a thousand little ways she was only beginning to understand. She hadn't had to take that final, irrevocable step, but she knew how close it had been.

Her mother also had that willingness, and a couple of her sisters-in-law. Valiant Mary, intrepid Caroline, sweet Barrie. They had each, in different circumstances, faced death and seen the bottom line. They would understand the wrenching she felt. Well, maybe Caroline wouldn't. Caroline was so utterly straightforward, so focused, that Joe had once compared her to a guided missile.

The door by her head was wrenched open, and cold air poured in. "Maris! Wake up!" Mac barked, his voice right over her. His hand closed on her shoulder as if he intended to shake her.

"I am awake," she said, without opening her eyes. "The headache's better, now that I'm still. How much longer will it be before I can take Pleasure back?"

"*You* aren't taking him anywhere. You're going to a hospital to be checked out."

"We can't just leave him here."

"I've arranged for him to be driven back."

She could hear the effort he was making to be calm; it was evident in his careful tone.

"Are things about wrapped up here?"

"Close enough that I can leave it with Dean and take you to a hospital."

He wouldn't let it go until a doctor had told him she was all right, Maris realized, and with a sigh she opened her eyes and sat up. She understood. If their situations were reversed, she would be doing the same thing.

"All right," she said, slipping on her coat. She turned off the ignition and picked up the Kevlar vest. "I'm ready."

Her willingness scared him. She saw his eyes darken, saw his jaw clench. "I'll be okay," she said softly, touching his hand. "I'm going because I know you're worried, and I don't want you to be."

His expression changed, something achingly tender moving in his eyes. Gently he scooped her into his arms and lifted her from the truck.

Dean had brought the Oldsmobile out of its hiding place. Mac carried her to it and deposited her on the front seat as carefully as if she were made of the most fragile crystal. He got in on the driver's side and started the car; the milling crowd in front of them parted, allowing them through. She saw Pleasure, standing quietly now. The bandage was in place, and the wild look was gone from his eyes. He was watching the activity with his characteristic friendly curiosity.

As they drove by, Dean lifted his hand to wave. "What about Dean?" Maris asked.

"He'll get transport. It isn't a problem."

She paused. "What about you? When do you leave? Your job here is finished, isn't it?" She didn't intend to let him get away, but she wasn't sure exactly how much he understood of their situation.

"It's finished." The words were clipped. The look he

gave her was one of restrained violence. "I'll have to do the paperwork, tie up some loose ends. I may have to leave tonight, tomorrow at the latest, but I'll be back, damn it!"

"You don't sound happy about it," she observed.

"Happy? You expect me to be *happy?*" His jaw clenched. "You didn't obey orders. You stepped right out into the open, instead of staying hidden the way you were supposed to. That idiot woman could have killed you!"

"I was wearing the vest." She pointed that out rather mildly, she thought.

"The damn vest only improves the odds, it isn't a guarantee! The issue here is that you didn't follow the plan. You risked your life for that damn horse! I didn't want him hurt, either, but—"

"It wasn't for Pleasure," she said, interrupting him. "It was for you." She looked out the window at the snow-dusted pastures they were passing.

It was quiet in the car for a moment.

"Me?" He was using that careful tone again.

"You. I knew he'd go straight to you, that he'd catch my scent on your clothes. At the very least he would distract you, bump you with his head. It was even possible he'd give away your position."

Mac was silent, absorbing the shock of the realization that she was willing to risk her own life to protect his. He did the same thing on a fairly regular basis, but it was his job to take risks and protect others. But he'd never before felt the terror he'd known when he saw Maris draw Joan's attention, and he hoped he never felt it again.

"I love you," she said quietly.

Damn. Sighing inwardly, Mac kissed his bachelorhood goodbye. Her courage stunned him, humbled him. No other woman he'd known would have put herself on the line the way Maris had done, both physically and emotionally. She didn't play games, didn't jockey for control. She simply knew, and accepted; he'd seen it in the soft depths of her black eyes, an instinctive inner knowledge that few people ever achieved. If he didn't snatch her up, it would be the biggest mistake of his life.

Mac didn't believe in making mistakes.

"How long does it take to get married in Kentucky?" he asked abruptly. "If we can't get it done tomorrow, we'll go to Las Vegas—assuming the doctor says you're all right."

He hadn't said he loved her, but she knew he did. She sat back, pleased with the situation. "I'm all right," she said, completely confident.

Chapter 10

"Getting married in Las Vegas seems to be a tradition in my family," she mused the next day as her new husband ushered her into their suite. "Two of my brothers have done it."

"Two? How many brothers do you have?"

"Five. All of them older." She smiled sweetly at him over her shoulder as she walked to the window to look out at the blazing red sunset. It was odd how completely connected to him she felt, when they hadn't had time to talk much, to share the details of their lives. Events had swept them along like gulls before a hurricane.

The emergency room doctor had pronounced her concussion mild and told her to take it easy for a day or so. He had agreed with her that, if she had been going to lapse into a coma, she would already have done so. Over the course of the day her memory had completely returned, filling in the blank spots, so she knew she was okay.

Reassured, Mac had driven her back to Solomon Green and turned his attention to the job, ruthlessly clearing up details and paperwork so he could concentrate on the business of getting married. While she slept, he and Dean had worked. He had arranged for time off, checked into the details of marriage in Kentucky, decided it couldn't be done fast enough to suit him and booked them on a flight to Las Vegas.

Ronald Stonicher had been arrested for conspiracy to commit fraud; he'd had no idea his wife and Randy Yu planned to kill Maris, too, and was shattered by what had happened. Joan had undergone surgery on her arm, and according to the surgeon the nerve and tissue damage was extensive; he expected her to regain some use of the arm, but she would never again be able to write with her right hand, or eat, do or anything else requiring precise movements. Randy was spilling his guts to the feds, implicating a lot of people in the horse world in the scheme to kill off horses for the insurance money. He hadn't been charged with killing the sixteen-year-old boy. Evidently he had some information on it, though, and was holding that in reserve to bargain for an even bigger break on the charges.

Maris had called her mother, briefly filled her in on what had happened and told her she was getting married. "Have fun, baby," Mary had told her daughter. "You know your father will want to walk you down the aisle, so we'll plan another wedding for Christmas.

That gives me three weeks. There shouldn't be any problem."

Most people would have screamed in panic at the thought of organizing a wedding in three weeks. Mary saw no problem, and from experience Maris knew that while other people might have problems accomplishing what her mother wanted, in the end she would have her way.

Mac had phoned his family, which consisted of his mother, stepfather and two half-sisters. They would be joining the Mackenzies in Wyoming for the wedding at Christmas.

During the ceremony an hour before, Maris had learned that her husband's full name was William Alexander MacNeil. "A few people call me Will," he told her afterward, when she mentioned how difficult it was for her to think of him as Alex. "Most people call me Mac." Since in her mind she had already begun shortening MacNeil to Mac, that suited her fine.

"*Five* older brothers?" Mac asked now, walking up behind her and slipping his arm around her waist. He bent his head to nuzzle her pale hair.

"Five. Plus twelve nephews and one niece."

He chuckled. "Holidays must be lively."

"*Riotous* would be a better word. Wait until you see."

He turned her in his arms. "What I can't wait to see is my wife, in bed with me."

She clung to his neck as he lifted her and carried her into the bedroom. His mouth closed on hers as he lowered her to the bed, and the aching passion that had subsided but never vanished surged back at full force. He crushed her into the mattress in his need, but at the same time he tried not to be rough as he eased her out of her clothes.

She squirmed against him, pulling at his clothes, the roughness of the fabric against her nakedness driving her crazy. Mac drew back, staring down at her delicate body with open hunger. He was breathing hard, obviously struggling for control, his eyes hard and glittering with lust. Gently he shaped her breasts with his hand, each in turn, rubbing his thumb over her nipples and bringing them to aching hardness.

"Hurry," she whispered, reaching for his belt.

He laughed a little, though there was no humor in the sound; instead, it was raw with need. He shed his clothes, kicking them away, and rolled on top of her. A groan of deep satisfaction tore from her throat as his heavy weight settled on her, and she opened her legs to cradle him close. She wanted him with a ferocity that would brook no delay, wanted him as she had never wanted or needed anything else in her life.

Mac positioned himself, then framed her face with his hands and kissed her as he slowly pushed into her body. Her flesh resisted, and she gasped, surprised by the painful difficulty. She had expected all her riding to have eased the way, but the lack of a barrier had in no way prepared her for his size.

He lifted his mouth, staring down at her as realization dawned. He didn't say anything, didn't ask any questions, but something hot and primitive flared deep in his gaze. As gently as possible, he completed his penetration, and when he was fully home inside her he waited, waited until the tension left her and her body softened beneath him, around him. Then he began moving, a slight rocking at first that did no more than nudge him back and forth, but enough to make her gasp again, this time with sensual urgency, and lift herself to him.

He took exquisite care with her, restraining the power of his thrusts, maintaining a slow, easy pace even when anticipation clawed at him, making him groan aloud with each movement. She clung to him, desperately searching for her own ease, trying to take him as deep inside her as possible, because instinct led her to that satisfaction. She cried out, overwhelmed by the sheer glory of this dance and struggle they shared, by the generosity of his loving.

She surged upward, unable to bear it a moment longer, and everything inside her shattered with a burst of pleasure so intense that she lost herself, sucked down in the whirlpool of sensation, a mindless creature knowing only the feel of his body, and hers. And she felt him join her, convulsing, thrusting, hotly emptying.

He cradled her afterward, stroking her with shaking hands as if to reassure himself she was real, that both of them were still whole.

"How did this happen?" he asked roughly. He tilted her chin so he could look into her face, and she saw that the glitter in his eyes was wetness now, not lust. "How could I love you so much, so fast? What kind of magic did you use?"

Tears burned her own eyes. "I just loved you," she said, the words simple. "That's all. I just loved you."

The mountain was wreathed with snow, and her heart lifted when she saw it. "There," she said, pointing. "That's Mackenzie's Mountain."

Mac stared with interest at the massive bulk. He'd never known anyone before who owned an entire mountain, and he wondered about the people, and the way of life, that had nurtured this magical creature beside him. In the two days they had been married, he had come to wonder how he'd ever existed without her. Loving her was like becoming whole, when he hadn't even known anything was missing. She was so delicate and fairylike, with her pale hair streaming over her shoulders and her great black eyes that held all the knowledge of centuries of women, but he'd learned that she was strong, and that the heart of a lion beat beneath her lovely breasts.

His *wife!* The unexpected marvelousness of it kept waking him in the middle of the night to look at her, to wonder at how fast it had happened. Only three days before, she had awakened in his arms and politely said, "I'm sorry, but I don't remember your name," and the realization that she'd been hurt had jarred him down to his toes. Only three days, and yet now he couldn't imagine sleeping without her, or waking without seeing her sleepy urchin's grin as she curled into his arms.

He had only five days off, so they had to make the best of it. Yesterday they had made a fast trip to San Antonio, where he had introduced her to his family. Both of his sisters had arrived with their broods of kids, three each, husbands in tow, but after the crowd Maris was accustomed to, she hadn't turned a hair at any of it. His mother had been absolutely thrilled that he'd married at last, thrilled at the prospect of a Christmas wedding on top of a snow-covered mountain in Wyoming. Having gotten the telephone number from Maris, her mother had already called his mother, and they'd evidently become fast friends, judging from the number of times his mother referred to what Mary had said.

Today they were in Wyoming, and Mac wondered why he was getting a tight feeling in the pit of his stomach. "Tell me about your brothers," he murmured. "All five of them." He knew something about older brothers, being one himself.

She smiled, her eyes going soft. "Well, let's see. My oldest brother, Joe, is a general in the air force—on the Joint Chiefs of Staff, as a matter of fact. His wife, Caroline, has doctoral degrees in physics and computer science, and they have five sons.

"My next-oldest brother, Mike, owns one of the largest cattle ranches in the state. He and Shea have two sons.

"Next is Josh. He was a navy fighter pilot, aircraft carrier, until a crash stiffened his knee and the navy grounded him. Now he's a civilian test pilot. His wife, Loren, is an orthopedic surgeon. They have three sons."

"Do any of your brothers have anything but sons?" Mac asked, fascinated by the recital, and growing more worried by the minute. He tried to focus on the mundane. He thought he remembered Maris saying she had a niece, but perhaps he'd been mistaken.

"Zane has a daughter." There was a different note in Maris's voice and he raised his eyebrows in inquiry, but she ignored him. "He and Barrie also have twin sons, two months old. Zane was a Navy SEAL. Barrie's an ambassador's daughter."

A SEAL. He wondered how much worse this could get.

"Then there's Chance. He and Zane might as well be twins. They're the same age, and I think their brains are linked. Chance was in Naval Intelligence. He isn't married." She deliberately didn't mention what Zane and Chance did now, because it seemed safer not to.

"I wonder," Mac murmured to himself as he steered their rented four-wheel-drive up the mountain, "why I expected you to have a normal family."

She lifted delicate brows at him. "You're a special agent with the FBI," she pointed out. "There isn't one of those standing on every street corner, you know."

"Yeah, but my *family* is normal."

"Well, so is mine. We're just overachievers." Her smile turned into a grin, the urchin's grin that had laced itself around his heart and tightened the bonds every time he saw it. He stopped the Jeep in the middle of the road and reached for her. His kiss was hard, urgent with hunger. Her eyes were slumberous when he released her. "What was that for?" she murmured, her hand curling around his neck.

"Because I love you." He wanted to tell her one last time, in case he didn't survive the coming confrontation. She might think her family would welcome him with open arms, but he had a much better understanding of the male psyche and he knew better. He put the Jeep in gear again, and they resumed their drive up the snow-covered road.

When they topped the crest and saw the big ranch house sprawling in front of them, Maris said happily, "Oh, good, everyone's here," and Mac knew he was a dead man. Never mind that he'd married her before sleeping with her; he was an unknown quantity, and he was making love to their darling every night. She was the only daughter, the *baby,* for God's sake. He understood. If he lived, and he and Maris ever had a daughter, there was no way in hell he was going to let some horny teenage boy anywhere near his little girl.

He looked at the array of vehicles parked in front of the house, enough vehicles to form a good parade, and wondered if they would give chase if he turned around and headed back down the mountain.

Well, it had to be done. Resigned, he parked the Jeep and came around to open the door for Maris, clasping his hands around her narrow waist and lifting her to the ground. She took his hand and led him up the steps, all but running in her eagerness.

They stepped into warmth, into noise, into confusion. A very small person wearing red overalls suddenly exploded from the crowd, racing forward on chubby legs and shrieking, "Marwee, Marwee," at the top of her lungs. Maris laughed and dropped to her knees, holding out her arms in time to catch the tiny tornado as she launched herself forward. Mac looked down at the little girl, not much more than a baby, and fell in love. He lost his heart. It was that simple.

She was beautiful. She was perfect, from the silky black hair on her round little head to her crystal-blue eyes, dimpled cheeks, rosebud mouth and dainty, dimpled hands. She was so small she was like a doll, and his arms ached to hold her. Little kids and babies had never affected him like this before, and it shook him.

"This is Nick," Maris said, rising to her feet with her niece in her arms. "She's the one and only granddaughter."

Nick reached out a tiny hand and poked him in the chest, in a movement so exactly like Maris's that Mac couldn't help grinning. "Who dat?" the little angel asked.

"This is Mac," Maris said, and kissed the soft, chubby cheek. Nick solemnly regarded him for a moment, then stretched out her arms in the manner of someone who is absolutely sure of their welcome. Automatically he reached out and took her, sighing with pleasure as the little body nestled against his chest.

Mac became aware of a spreading silence in the room, of what looked like an entire football team of big men getting to their feet, menace in every movement, in the hard faces turned toward him.

Maris looked at them, her face radiant, and he saw her eyes widen with surprise at their militant stances.

He eyed the competition. His father-in-law had iron gray hair and the black eyes Maris had inherited, and looked as if he ate nails for breakfast. His brothers-in-law looked just as lethal. Expertly Mac assessed each one, trying to pick out the most dangerous one. They all looked like bad asses. The one with the graying temples and the laser blue eyes, that would be the general, and damn if he didn't look as if he went into combat every day. *That* one would be the rancher, whipcord lean, iron hard, a man who faced down Mother Nature every day. The test pilot…let's see, that would be the one standing with his feet apart in the instinctive cocky stance of someone who cooly gambled with death and never blinked an eye.

Then Mac's gaze met a pair of deadly, icy eyes. *That one,* he thought. That was the most dangerous one, the one with the quiet face and eyes like blue-gray frost. That one. He would bet a year's pay that was the SEAL. But the one who moved up to stand beside him looked just as lethal, despite the almost unearthly handsomeness of his face. That would be the one in naval intelligence.

He was in big trouble. Instinctively he moved, depositing Nick in Maris's arms and stepping in front of them both, shielding them with his body.

Six pairs of fierce eyes noted the action.

Maris peeked around his shoulder, assessing the situation. *"Moth-er!"* she called urgently, stressing both syllables as she brought in reinforcements.

"Maris!" There was utter delight in the soft voice that came from what Mac assumed was the kitchen, the cry followed by light, fast footsteps. A small, delicate woman, no bigger than Maris and with the same exquisite, translucent skin, burst into the room. She was laughing as she grabbed her daughter, hugging her and doing the same to him, even though he stood rigidly, not daring to take his eyes off the threat looming in front of them like a wall.

"Mom," Maris said, directing her mother's attention across the room. "What's wrong with them?"

Mary took one look at her husband and sons and put

her hands on her hips. "Stop that right now," she ordered. "I refuse to have this, do you hear?"

Her voice was sweetly Southern, as light as a breeze, but Wolf Mackenzie's black eyes flickered to her. "We just want to know a little about him," he said in a voice as deep and dark as thunder.

"Maris chose him," Mary replied firmly. "What else could you possibly need to know?"

"A lot," the one with the quiet, lethal eyes said. "This happened too fast."

"Zane Mackenzie!" a pretty redhead exclaimed, stepping out of the kitchen and eyeing him in amazement. "I can't believe you said that! We got married after knowing each other for *one day!*" She crossed the no-man's-land between the two battle lines, hugged Maris and turned to glare at her husband.

So he'd been right, Mac thought. That was the SEAL. It would look good on his tombstone: He Was Right.

"This is different," said the general, a perfect clone of Wolf Mackenzie except for his light blue eyes. He, too, looked as if nails were a regular part of his diet.

"Different, how?" asked a crisp voice, and a stylish blonde stepped out of the kitchen. She pinned a sharp green gaze on the six men. "You're all suffering from an overdose of testosterone. The main symptom is an inability to think." Marching forward, she aligned herself on Mac's other side. Something that was both heated and amused lit the general's eyes as he looked at his wife.

Another bruiser, the test pilot, said, "Maris is—"

"A grown woman," another feminine voice said, interrupting. A tall, curvy woman with chestnut hair and serene blue eyes took up a position beside the blonde. "Hi, I'm Loren," she said to Mac. "The one who just spoke is Josh, my husband, who usually exhibits better sense."

"And I'm Shea, Mike's wife." Another reinforcement arrived. She was dark haired, and sweetly shy. She stood beside Loren, crossed her arms over her chest and calmly looked across at her husband.

The two sides looked at each other, the men glaring at their turncoat wives, the women lined up protectively beside Mac. He was a little stunned to find himself surrounded by this perfumed wall of femininity.

Caroline gave her husband glare for glare. "Every one of us was welcomed with open arms when we married into this family, and I expect you to extend the same courtesy to Maris's husband—or else!"

Joe considered the challenge, his pale blue eyes glittering as he cocked his head. "Or else, what?" he asked, his deep voice silky and full of something that might have been anticipation.

Silence fell in the room, even the kids were quiet as they watched their parents. Mac looked at the six women ranged on either side of him, and his face softened into tender amusement. "It's okay," he said. "I understand."

"I'm glad you do, because I don't," Maris growled. "It's a—"

"Don't say it's a man thing," Mary warned, interrupting, and he bit back the words.

"No, ma'am," he said meekly.

Wolf's dark face lightened, and his lips twitched. Those two words were very familiar to him.

Nick squirmed to get down, and Maris leaned over to deposit her on her feet. The little girl patted Mac on the knee and said, "Mac," with great satisfaction in her tone. She trotted across to her father, holding up her arms to be picked up. Zane leaned down and lifted her, settling her on one brawny arm. "Dat's Mac," she said, pointing. "I wike him."

Suddenly that hard, deadly face softened into a smile, and a big hand smoothed a silky tendril of hair away from her face. "I noticed," he said dryly. "He took one look at you and turned into your slave, just like the rest of us. That's what you really like, isn't it?"

Her little head bobbed up and down, very definitely. Zane chuckled as he shot an amused glance across the room at her mother. "I thought you would."

From somewhere down the hall came a baby's wail. "Cam's awake," Barrie said, and immediately abandoned Mac to go to her baby.

"How does she *do* that?" Chance asked of the room in general. "They're only two months old. How do you tell twins apart by their cries?"

The females, Nick included, had won. The tension in the room dissipated, smiles breaking out as Chance followed his sister-in-law down the hall, intent on finding out if she'd been right. Before he walked out he winked at Mac, in a moment of male understanding. The crisis had come and gone, because when it came down to it, the Mackenzie men were unwilling to distress their women. The women had liked Mac on sight, and that was that.

Barrie was back in only a moment, a squirming bundle in her arms. Chance followed her, expertly holding another one. "She was right," he announced, shaking his head in bewilderment.

Mac looked at the two tiny faces, finding them as identical as if they were mirror images. It was impossible to tell them apart even by looking at them; how in hell did Chance know if she was right or not?

"Cameron," Barrie said, indicating her burden and smiling at his skeptical look. "Chance is holding Zack." She also carried two small, milk-filled bottles.

"How do you know?" He shook his head, still looking for any distinguishing difference in the babies.

"Cameron's the most impatient, but Zack is more determined."

"You can tell that in their *cries?*"

"Well, of course," she said, as if anyone should be able to do the same.

Nick was climbing up on her father's shoulder, gripping his hair for leverage. "Wook, Unca Dance," she exclaimed, standing upright and releasing her safety hold.

Zane reached up and snagged his daughter off his shoulder. "Here, swap with me," he said, and he and Chance exchanged kids. Zane settled the baby in the crook of his arm and took one of the bottles from Barrie, expertly slipping the nipple into the rapacious little mouth.

Chance balanced Nick on his hands, firmly holding her feet while she straightened and crowed with delight at her achievement. "Chance," he coaxed. "My name is Chance. *Chance.*"

Nick placed her little hands on each side of his face, leaning close to peer into his eyes and impress him with her seriousness. "No," she said with great finality. "*Dance.* Oo say it wrong."

The room exploded with laughter at Chance's expression. He eyed the pint-size dictator in his hands, then shook his head and gave up. "Are you sure you want to marry into this family?" He directed the question at Mac.

Mac looked at Maris and winked. "Yeah," he said.

Zane was watching him while the baby took the bottle, his calm eyes measuring. "Maris said you're an FBI special agent," he said, and something in his tone must have alerted Maris.

"No," she said firmly, pushing Mac toward the kitchen. "You can't have him. Being in the FBI is enough. You absolutely can't have him."

Mac found himself borne along on the tide of women, because they all wanted to discuss the wedding, but before he left the room he looked back. His gaze met Zane's...and Zane Mackenzie smiled.

"Welcome to the family," he said.

Epilogue

"**Y**ou so *pwetty*," Nick sighed, her big blue eyes rapt as she propped her elbows on Maris's knee and stared at her aunt. The entire process of preparing for a wedding had fascinated the little girl. She had intently scrutinized everything as the women of the household had painstakingly made hundreds of tiny net bags, filled them with bird seed and tied them with ribbons. She had stood on her tiptoes, clinging to the table's edge, and watched as Shea, who made wonderful cakes, practiced making dozens of roses from icing before decorating Maris's wedding cake. Before long the practice roses had all borne evidence of a tiny, investigative finger. Once Nick had determined they were edible, they'd gradually disappeared, and her little face wore telltale smears.

Maris's gown held her absolutely enthralled. The

long skirt, the lace, the veil, everything about it entranced her. When Maris had tried it on for the final fitting, Nick had clasped her hands under her chin and with shining eyes had said, "Oo a *pwincess!*"

"You're pretty, too, darling," Maris said. Nick was her flower girl. Zane had muttered about inviting disaster, and since Nick wasn't quite three years old, Maris was prepared for anything, including an outright refusal to perform her role. At the rehearsal the night before, however, Nick had strutted down the aisle with her little basket of rose petals and proudly strewn them, aware that every eye was on her. Whether she would do so when watched by a huge crowd was another question, but she was undeniably adorable in her long, blush pink dress, with ribbons and flowers in her silky black hair.

"I know," Nick replied matter-of-factly, and left her post at Maris's knee to return to the mirror to admire herself. It was something she had done every five minutes since Barrie had dressed her.

Barrie and Caroline were the acknowledged fashion mavens of the Mackenzie family, and they had taken over the arrangement of Maris's hair and the application of her makeup. They were astute enough to keep things simple, rather than overwhelming Maris's dainty face and frame with big hair and layers of makeup. Barrie had finished her hair and retired to a rocking chair to nurse the twins before the ceremony started. She supplemented their feedings with a bottle, but breast milk kept them contented longer, and she didn't want to have to feed them again in the middle of the reception.

Mary had quickly realized that the Mackenzie house, as large as it was, simply couldn't hold the crowd that was invited to the wedding. Because Christmas was on a Wednesday, the church in Ruth had held its Christmas service on Sunday, freeing it for the ceremony. The nine-foot-tall Christmas tree still stood in the corner, its multitude of white lights twinkling. Holly and evergreen needles still decorated the windowsills, filling the church with a wonderful aroma. White lights outlined the arched doorway, the windows, the sanctuary and the steps leading up to it. Rows of white candles lent their mellow glow to the church. None of the overhead lights would be on, but the tree, the Christmas lights and the candles combined to give the setting a magical aura.

This was Christmas Eve, a time when most of the occupants of Ruth would normally have been at home either having their private celebrations or preparing for them the next day. This year they were attending a wedding. From the private room off the vestibule Maris could hear the swell of noise as more and more people arrived.

Mary stood quietly, a sheen of tears in her slate blue eyes as she watched her daughter prepare for her wedding. It didn't matter that Maris and Mac were already married; this was the wedding that counted. This was her beloved daughter who looked so delicate and beautiful in her silvery white gown, a color that turned Maris's pale, ash brown hair to a darker shade of silver. She remembered the first time she had seen her daughter, only seconds old, so tiny and lovely and already staring around with big, solemn black eyes, her father's eyes. She remembered the tears that had sheened Wolf's own black eyes as he'd taken Maris in his arms and hugged the little scrap to his chest as if she were the most precious thing he'd ever seen.

There were thousands of other memories. Her first tooth, her first step, her first word—predictably, "horsie." Maris sitting on a pony for the first time, her eyes huge with delight while Wolf kept a protective arm around her. Maris, a little shadow dogging her father's footsteps just as her older brothers had done. Maris in school, fiercely joining in any fight the boys had gotten into, her little fists flying as she rushed to their defense, utterly ignoring the fact that the boys were twice her size. Maris sobbing when her old pony had died, and her radiant joy when, the next Christmas, Wolf had given her her first "real" horse.

There had been Maris's first date, and Wolf's scowling, prowling nervousness until his baby was safely back under his roof. One of Mary's favorite memories was of Zane and Josh and Chance pacing along with their father; if Joe and Mike had been there, they would have been pacing, too. As it was, the poor boy who had been so brave as to take Maris out had been terrified when the four Mackenzie males met them on the front porch on their return and had never asked her out again. They had gotten better about it over the years, but Maris must have forgotten her first date or she wouldn't have been so surprised at their reaction to Mac when she'd brought him home. *Men.* Mary loved her men, but really, they could be so overbearing. Why, they *liked* Mac, once they'd gotten over their bristly protectiveness. If Maris didn't watch out, Zane would have Mac recruited into whatever it was he and Chance—

Zane. Mary stopped short in her thoughts, looking around the room. All three of his children were here, with Barrie. Usually he was tending to at least one of the babies, or riding herd on Nick. That meant Zane was free and unencumbered, and she was sure it wasn't by accident.

"Zane's free," she announced, because she thought Maris really ought to know.

Her daughter's head snapped up, and her lovely eyes caught fire. "I'll skin him alive," she said wrathfully. "I will *not* have Mac gone for months on end the way Chance is. I just got him, and I'm not letting him go."

Barrie looked startled; then she, too, realized the significance of having all three children with her. She shook her head in rueful acknowledgment of her husband's canniness. "It's too late to do anything about it now. He's had plenty of time to have a private talk with Mac, and you know Zane—he planned it perfectly."

Maris scowled, and Caroline drew back with the eye shadow brush in her hand. "I can't do this with your eyebrows all scrunched up," she admonished. Maris smoothed her expression, and Caroline went back to work. "I don't believe in letting hormone-driven men interfere in a woman's wedding. You can skin him alive tomorrow. Ambush him when he least expects it."

"Zane always expects everything," Barrie said, grinning. Then she looked at her daughter, who was twirling and dancing in front of the mirror, admiring herself. "Except Nick," she added. "He wasn't prepared for her."

"Was anyone?" Loren murmured, smiling fondly down at the little girl. Nick, hearing her name, stopped her pirouetting to favor them all with an angelic smile that didn't fool them for one second.

"Mac's besotted with her," Maris said. "He didn't turn a hair even when she polished his boots with the Magic Marker."

"An indication of true love if I've ever seen it," Caroline said dryly. She touched the mascara wand to Maris's already dark lashes, then stood back to admire her handiwork. "There! Mac would be crazy to leave you and go running around half-civilized countries where there's no sanitation and no shopping." Caroline's philosophy in life was to be comfortable, and she went to extraordinary lengths to accomplish it. She would gladly walk miles to find the perfect *comfortable* pair of shoes. It made perfect sense to her, since her work often required her to be on her feet for hours; how could she possibly concentrate if her toes were cramped?

"I don't think Mac would care about the shopping," Shea said. She picked Nick up and whirled around the room with the giggling little girl, humming a lively tune.

There was a knock on the door, and John poked his head inside. "It's time," he said. His pale blue gaze fell on Caroline. "Wow, Mom, you look great."

"Smart guy," she said approvingly. "I'll let you stay in my will."

He grinned and ducked out again. Maris stood, sucking in a deep breath. It was time. Never mind that they'd been married for three weeks already; this was a *production,* and practically the entire town was on hand to witness it.

Shea set Nick on her feet and got the basket of rose petals from the top of the closet, where they'd put it to keep Nick from scattering the flowers around the room. They'd already picked up the velvety petals once, and once was enough.

Barrie laid Zack beside Cameron. Both babies were sleeping peacefully, their little bellies full. Right on time, one of Shea's teenaged nieces arrived to watch them while Barrie attended the wedding.

The music began, their cue to begin entering the sanctuary.

One by one they began filing out, escorted by the Mackenzie men to their reserved seats. Zane's big form filled the doorway. Maris said, *"No,"* and he grinned as he held his hand out to Barrie.

"Just a minute." Barrie stooped in front of Nick, straightening the ribbons in her hair and at last placing the basket of flower petals in the eager, dimpled little hands. "Do the flowers just the way you did them last night, okay? Do you remember?"

Nick nodded. "I fwow dem aroun' on de fwoor."

"That's right, sweetheart." Having done all she could, Barrie stood and went to Zane, who slipped his arm around her waist and briefly hugged her close before they left to take their places.

Wolf came to the door, severely elegant in a black

tuxedo. "It's time, honey," he said to Maris. His black eyes were tender as he wrapped his arms around her and rocked her back and forth, the way he had done all her life. Maris laid her head on her father's chest, almost overwhelmed by the sudden rush of love for him. She'd been so lucky in her parents!

"I was beginning to wonder if you'd ever forget about horses long enough to fall in love," he said, "but now that you have, I feel like we haven't had you long enough."

She chuckled against his chest. "That's exactly how I knew." She lifted her head, her eyes shining with both tears and laughter. "I kept forgetting about Sole Pleasure and thinking only about Mac. It had to be love."

He kissed her forehead. "In that case, I'll forgive him."

"Poppy!"

The imperious small voice came from the vicinity of his knee. They looked down. Nick was tugging on Wolf's pant leg. "We dotta *huwwy*. I dotta fwow fwowers."

As usual, her mangled English made him laugh. "All right, cupcake." He leaned down and took her free hand, to keep her from darting ahead of them and "fwowing fwowers" before they were ready.

He and Maris and Nick made their way into the vestibule, and Maris leaned down to kiss Nick's cheek. "Are you ready?" she asked.

Nick nodded, her slanted blue eyes wide and shining with excitement, and she clutched the flower basket with both hands.

"Here you go, then." Gently Maris urged Nick forward, into the center aisle. The church glowed with candlelight, and hundreds of smiling faces were turned toward them, it seemed.

Nick stepped out into the limelight like a Miss America taking her victory walk. She bestowed smiles to the left and the right, and she daintily reached into the basket for a rose petal. One. She held it out and let it drift downward. Then she reached for another. One by one she distributed the rose petals on the carpet with dainty precision, taking her time, even stooping once to adjust a petal that had fallen too close to another one.

"Oh, God." Beside her, Maris could feel Wolf shaking with laughter. "She's enjoying this too much. At this rate, you won't get to walk down the aisle until midnight."

People were turning and looking, and laughing at Nick's concentration on the task. Barrie buried her head in Zane's shoulder, lost in a helpless fit of giggling. Zane was grinning, and Chance was laughing out loud. Mac, standing at the altar, was beaming at the little imp who had so won his heart. The pianist, looking around, saw what was taking so long and gamely continued playing.

Tickled to be the center of attention, Nick began improvising. The next rose petal was tossed backward, over her shoulder. The minister choked, and his face turned red as he tried to hold back his guffaws.

She twirled on her tiptoes, flinging rose petals in a circle. Several flew out of the basket, and she frowned, stooping to pick them up and return them to the basket.

I can't laugh, Maris thought, feeling it bubbling inexorably upward. *If I laugh, I'll laugh until I cry, and it'll ruin my makeup.* She put her hand over her mouth to hold the mirth inside, but it didn't work. Her chest constricted, her throat worked and suddenly laughter burst joyously out of control.

Nick stopped and turned to look, beaming at them, waiting for them to tell her what a good job she was doing.

"*Fwow*—I mean, *throw* them," Maris managed to say between whoops.

The little head tilted to one side. "Wike dis?" she asked, taking a handful of petals from the basket and flinging them upward.

At least it was a handful, and not just one. "Like that," Maris said in approval, hoping it would speed the procedure.

It did. Another handful followed the first one, and Nick's progress down the aisle picked up speed. At last she reached the end, and bestowed an absolutely radiant smile on Mac. "I fwowed dem all," she told him.

"You did it just right," he said, barely able to speak for laughing. Her mission accomplished, she strutted to the pew where Zane and Barrie sat, and held up her arms to be lifted to the seat.

Relieved, the pianist launched into the familiar strains of "Here Comes the Bride," and at last Wolf and Maris began their stately walk down the aisle. Everyone rose to their feet and turned to watch, smiling.

Because time had been so short, there were no bridesmaids or groomsmen, no maid of honor or best man, so only Mac awaited Maris at the altar. He watched her approach, his hard face relaxed in a tender expression, his blue eyes still shining from his laughter. As soon as she stopped beside him, he gently took her hand in his, and behind them, they heard his mother give a teary, joyful little gasp.

Because Maris and Mac were already married, they had decided to skip the part about "who gives this woman." Wolf leaned down and kissed his daughter's cheek, hugged her tenderly, then shook hands with Mac and took a seat beside Mary.

"Dearly beloved," the minister began; then there was another gasp behind them. Recognizing Barrie's voice, Maris wasn't surprised when a little body slithered between her and Mac, taking a stance directly in front of them.

"I do it, too," Nick chirped, her little voice audible in every corner of the church.

Glancing over her shoulder, Maris saw Zane start to rise to retrieve his errant offspring. She shook her head, smiling. He winked and sank back into his seat.

So Nick stood pressed against their legs while the minister performed the service. They could feel her quivering with excitement, and Mac subtly gathered her closer to him so he would have a better chance of grabbing her if she started to do something startling, such as peek under the minister's cassock. She was already eyeing the garment with some curiosity. But she was content for the moment, completely taken with the ceremony, the candles, the twinkling Christmas tree, the beautiful clothes. When the minister said, "You may now kiss the bride," and Mac did so, Nick merely tilted her head back to watch.

"What's the best way to handle her when we leave?" Mac whispered against Maris's lips.

"Pick her up and hand her to Zane as we pass," she whispered back. "He'll be expecting it."

The pianist launched into the familiar stirring strains. Mac swooped Nick up with one arm, put the other around Maris, and they hurried up the aisle to the accompaniment of music, laughter, tears and a round of applause. As they passed the second pew, a tiny girl in a long dress was deftly passed from one pair of strong arms to another.

The reception was a long, glorious party. Maris danced endlessly with her husband, her father, all her brothers, several of her nephews, her brothers-in-law and an assortment of old friends. She danced with the sheriff, Clay Armstrong. She danced with Ambassador Lovejoy, Barrie's father. She danced with Shea's father and grandfather, with the ranchers and merchants and gas station attendants. Finally Mac claimed her again, holding her close and swaying to the music as he rested his cheek against hers.

"What did Zane say to you?" she demanded suddenly.

She felt him grin, though he didn't lift his head. "He said you'd know."

"Never mind that. What did he say?"

"You already know what he said."

"Then what did *you* say?"

"That I'm interested."

She growled. "I don't want you to spend months out of the country. I'm willing—barely—to let the FBI use you on investigations, but I don't like it. I want you with me every night, not thousands of miles away."

"That's exactly what I told Zane. Remember, I don't have to do what Chance does." He held her closer, dropping his voice to an intimate murmur. "Has your period started yet?"

"No." She was only two days late—but two days was two days, and she was normally very regular. It was possible her system had been disrupted by the concussion and the stress of everything that had happened, so she wasn't making any announcements yet. "Would you mind if I am pregnant so soon?"

"Mind?" He kissed her ear. "When we might get our own Nick?" His shoulders quivered under her embrace. "I didn't think she was *ever* going to get rid of those damn flower petals."

"She's one of a kind, I hope." But she leaned against him, feeling her breasts, her entire body, tighten with desire. If she wasn't already pregnant, she likely would be soon, given how often he made love to her.

They danced in silence for a moment, then Mac said, "Pleasure should have arrived by now."

She had to blink back tears, because Mac had given her the most wonderful gift for Christmas. With Sole Pleasure's worth hugely reduced now that the racing world had been rocked with news of his very low sperm count, the syndication offers had evaporated. It was *possible* Pleasure could sire a foal, but it was such a small possibility as to be negligible. He still had worth as a racehorse, and Ronald Stonicher might have gotten more for him than Mac had offered, but huge legal expenses had been staring him in the eye, and he'd jumped at the chance to sell the horse. Maris had worried so about Pleasure's future that Mac had made the offer for him without telling her, because he didn't want her to be disappointed in case the deal fell through.

"Dad can hardly wait to ride him," she said. "He's said several times that he envied me because I got to work with Pleasure."

They fell silent, simply enjoying the feel of being in each other's arms. Their wedding hadn't been a stately, solemn affair—Nick had seen to that—but it had been perfect. People had laughed and enjoyed themselves, and everyone for years would smile whenever they thought of Maris Mackenzie's wedding.

"It's time to throw the bouquet!"

The cry went up, and they swung around to see a crowd of giggling teenage girls gathering for the tradition, flipping back their hair, throwing sidelong glances at the older Mackenzie boys. There were more mature women there, too, giving Chance measuring looks.

"I thought you were supposed to throw it when we're ready to leave?" Mac said, amused.

"Evidently they can't wait."

She didn't mind hurrying things up a little; after that dance, she was ready to be alone with her husband.

Nick had been having the time of her short life, stuffing herself with cake and mints, and being whirled around the dance floor in the arms of her father, her grandfather and all her uncles and cousins. When she saw Maris get the bouquet that had so fascinated her earlier, with all the "pwetty" flowers and lace and ribbons, she squirmed away from Sam's grip on her hand and moved to where she had a better view of the situation, her little head cocked to the side as she intently watched.

Maris climbed on the dais, turned her back and threw the bouquet high over her shoulder. Cries of "Catch it! Catch it!" filled the reception hall.

Almost immediately there was a collective cry of alarm. Maris whirled. The crowd of girls and women was rushing forward, eyes lifted, intent on the bouquet sailing toward them. And directly in front of them, also concentrating on the bouquet as she darted forward, was a tiny figure in pale pink.

There was a surge of black-clad bodies moving forward as seventeen males, one MacNeil and sixteen Mackenzies, from six-year-old Benjy up to Wolf, all leapt for the little girl. Maris caught a glimpse of Zane's face, utterly white as he tried to reach his baby before she was trampled, and somehow she, too, was running, leaping from the dais, heedless of her dress.

Two crowds of people were moving toward each other at breakneck speed, with Nick caught in the middle. One of the teenage girls looked down, saw Nick and emitted a shrill scream of panic as she tried to stop, only to be shoved forward by the girl behind her.

Chance had been standing back, avoiding any contact with that wedding bouquet business, but as a result, his movements were less impeded. He reached Nick two steps ahead of Zane, scooping her up, enfolding her in his arms and rolling with her out of harm's way. Zane veered, putting himself between Chance and anyone who might stumble over him, and in another second there was practically a wall of boys and men protecting the two on the floor.

The bouquet hit Chance in the middle of the back.

Carefully he rolled over, and Nick's head popped out of the shield he'd made with his arms. "Wook!" she said, spying the bouquet. "Oo caught de fwowers, Unca Dance!"

Maris skidded to a stop beside them. Chance lay very still on the floor, with Nick on his chest. He glared up at Maris, his light, golden-hazel eyes narrow with suspicion. "You did that on purpose," he accused.

The MacNeils and the Mackenzies moved forward, smiles tugging at stern mouths. Maris crossed her arms. "There's no way I could have arranged this." She had to bite her lip to keep from laughing at his outraged expression.

"Hah. You've been doing spooky stuff all your life."

Nick leaned over and grasped one of the ribbons of the bouquet, pulling it toward her. Triumphantly she deposited it on Chance's chest. "Dere," she said with satisfaction, and patted it.

Zane rubbed the side of his nose, but he was less successful than Maris at hiding his grin. "You caught the bouquet," he said.

"I did not," Chance growled. "She hit me in the back with it!"

Mary walked up and stood beside Wolf, who automatically put his arm around her. Slowly a radiant smile spread across her face. "Why, Chance!" she exclaimed. "This means you're next."

"I—am—not—next." He ground the words out, sitting up with Nick in his arms. Carefully he put her on her feet, then climbed to his own. "Trickery doesn't count. I don't have time for a wife. I like what I do, and a wife would just get in the way." He was backing away as he talked. "I'm not good husband material, anyway. I—"

A little hand tugged on his pant leg. He stopped and looked down.

Nick stretched on tiptoe, holding the bouquet up to him with both hands. "Don't fordet oor fwowers," she said, beaming.

* * * * *

Heartbreaker

LINDA HOWARD

Chapter One

She found the paper while she was sorting through the personal things in her father's desk. Michelle Cabot unfolded the single sheet with casual curiosity, just as she had unfolded dozens of others, but she had read only a paragraph when her spine slowly straightened and a tremor began in her fingers. Stunned, she began again, her eyes widening with sick horror at what she read.

Anybody but him. Dear God, anybody but him!

She owed John Rafferty one hundred thousand dollars.

Plus interest, of course. At what percent? She couldn't read any further to find out; instead she dropped the paper onto the littered surface of the desk and sank back in her father's battered old leather chair, her eyes closing against the nausea caused by shock, dread and the particularly sickening feeling of dying hope. She had already been on her knees; this unsuspected debt had smashed her flat.

Why did it have to be John Rafferty? Why not some impersonal bank? The end result would be the same, of course, but the humiliation would be absent. The thought of facing him made her shrivel deep inside, where she protected the tender part of herself. If Rafferty ever even suspected that that tenderness existed, she was lost. A dead duck…or a sitting one, if it made any difference. A gone goose. A cooked goose. Whatever simile she used, it fit.

Her hands were still shaking when she picked up the paper to read it again and work out the details of the financial agreement. John Rafferty had made a personal loan of one hundred thousand dollars to her father, Langley Cabot, at an interest rate two percent lower than the market rate…and the loan had been due four months ago. She felt even sicker. She knew it hadn't been repaid, because she'd gone over every detail of her father's books in an effort to salvage something from the financial disaster he'd been floundering in when he'd died. She had ruthlessly liquidated almost everything to pay the outstanding debts, everything except this ranch, which had been her father's dream and had somehow come to represent a refuge to her. She hadn't liked Florida ten years ago, when her father had sold their home and moved her from their well-ordered, monied existence in Connecticut to the heat and humidity of a cattle ranch in central Florida, but that had been a decade ago, and things changed. People changed, time changed…and time changed people. The ranch didn't represent love or a dream to her; it was, simply, all she had left. Life had seemed so complicated once, but it was remarkable how simple things were when it came down to a matter of survival.

Even now it was hard to just give up and let the inevitable happen. She had known from the beginning that it would be almost impossible for her to keep the ranch and put it back on a paying basis, but she'd been driven to at least *try*. She wouldn't have been able to live with herself if she'd taken the easy way out and let the ranch go.

Now she would have to sell the ranch after all, or at least the cattle; there was no other way she could repay that hundred thousand dollars. The wonder was that Rafferty hadn't already demanded repayment. But if she sold the cattle, what good was the ranch? She'd been depending on the cattle sales to keep her going, and without that income she'd have to sell the ranch anyway.

It was so hard to think of letting the ranch go; she had almost begun to hope that she might be able to hold on to it. She'd been afraid to hope, had tried not to, but still, that little glimmer of optimism had begun growing. Now she'd failed at this, just as she'd failed at everything else in her life: as daughter, wife, and now rancher. Even if Rafferty gave her an extension on the loan, something she didn't expect to happen, she had no real expectation of being able to pay it off when it came due again. The naked truth was that she had no expectations at all; she was merely hanging on.

Well, she wouldn't gain anything by putting it off. She had to talk to Rafferty, so it might as well be now. The clock on the wall said it wasn't quite nine-thirty; Rafferty would still be up. She looked up his number and dialed it, and the usual reaction set in. Even before the first ring sounded, her fingers were locked so tightly around the receiver that her knuckles were white, and her heart had lurched into a fast, heavy pounding that made her feel as if she'd been running. Tension knotted her stomach. Oh, damn! She wouldn't even be able to talk coherently if she didn't get a grip on herself!

The telephone was answered on the sixth ring, and by then Michelle had braced herself for the ordeal of talking to him. When the housekeeper said, "Rafferty residence," Michelle's voice was perfectly cool and even when she asked to speak to Rafferty.

"I'm sorry, he isn't in. May I take a message?"

It was almost like a reprieve, if it hadn't been for the knowledge that now she'd have to do it all over again. "Please have him call Michelle Cabot," she said, and gave the housekeeper her number. Then she asked, "Do you expect him back soon?"

There was only a slight hesitation before the housekeeper said, "No, I think he'll be quite late, but I'll give him your message first thing in the morning."

"Thank you," Michelle murmured, and hung up. She should have expected him to be out. Rafferty was famous, or perhaps notorious was a better word, for his sexual appetite and escapades. If he'd quieted down over the years, it was only in his hell-raising. According to the gossip she'd heard from time to time, his libido was alive and well; a look from those hard, dark eyes still made a woman's pulse go wild, and he looked at a lot of women, but Michelle wasn't one of them. Hostility had exploded between them at their first meeting, ten years before, and at best their relationship was an armed standoff. Her father had been a buffer between them, but now he was dead, and she expected the worst. Rafferty didn't do things by half measures.

There was nothing she could do about the loan that night, and she'd lost her taste for sorting through the remainder of her father's papers, so she decided to turn in. She took a quick shower; her sore muscles would have liked a longer one, but she was doing everything she could to keep her electricity bill down, and since she got her water from a well, and the water was pumped by an electric pump, small luxuries had to go to make way for the more important ones, like eating.

But as tired as she was, when she was lying in bed she couldn't go to sleep. The thought of talking to Rafferty filled her mind again, and once more her heartbeat speeded up. She tried to take deep, slow breaths. It had always been like this, and it was even worse when she had to see him face to face. If only he wasn't so big! But he was six feet three inches and about two hundred pounds of muscled masculinity; he was good at dwarfing other people. Whenever he was close, Michelle felt threatened in some basic way, and even thinking of him made her feel suffocated. No other man in the world made her react the way he did; no one else could make her so angry, so wary—or so excited in a strange, primitive way.

It had been that way from the beginning, from the moment she'd met him ten years before. She had been eighteen then, as spoiled as he'd accused her of being, and as haughty as only a teenager standing on her dignity could be. His reputation had preceded him, and Michelle had been determined to show him that *she* couldn't be lumped with all the women who panted after him. As if he would have been interested in a teenager! she thought wryly, twisting on the bed in search of comfort. What a child she'd been! A silly, spoiled, frightened child.

Because John Rafferty *had* frightened her, even though he'd all but ignored her. Or rather, her own reaction had frightened her. He'd been twenty-six, a *man*, as opposed to the boys she was used to, and a man who had already turned a smallish central Florida cattle ranch into a growing, thriving empire by his own force of will and years of backbreaking work. Her first sight of him, towering over her father while the two men talked cattle, had scared her half to death. Even now she could recall her sudden breathlessness, as if she'd been punched in the stomach.

They'd been standing beside Rafferty's horse, and he'd had one arm draped across the saddle while his other hand was propped negligently on his hip. He'd been six feet and three inches of sheer power, all hard muscle and intensity, dominating even the big animal with his will. She'd already heard about him; men laughed and called him a "stud" in admiring tones, and women called him the same thing, but always in excited, half-fearful whispers. A woman might be given the benefit of the doubt after going out with him once, but if she went out with him twice it was accepted that she had been to bed with him. At the time Michelle hadn't even considered that his reputation was probably exaggerated. Now that she was older, she still didn't consider it. There was just something about the way Rafferty looked that made a woman believe all the tales about him.

But even his reputation hadn't prepared her for the real man, for the force and energy that radiated from him. Life burned hotter and brighter in some people, and John Rafferty was one of them. He was a dark fire, dominating his surroundings with his height and powerful build, dominating people with his forceful, even ruthless, personality.

Michelle had sucked in her breath at the sight of him, the sun glinting off his coal-black hair, his dark eyes narrowed under prominent black brows, a neat black mustache shadowing the firm line of his upper lip. He'd been darkly tanned, as he always was from hours of working outside in all seasons; even as she'd watched, a trickle of sweat had run down his temple to curve over his high, bronzed cheekbone before tacking down his cheek to finally drip off his square jaw. Patches of sweat had darkened his blue work shirt under his arms and on his chest and back. But even sweat and dirt couldn't detract from the aura of a powerful, intensely sexual male animal; perhaps they had even added to it. The hand on his hip had drawn her gaze downward to his hips and long legs, and the faded tight jeans had outlined his body so faithfully that her mouth had gone dry. Her heart had stopped beating for a moment, then lurched into a heavy rhythm that made her entire body throb. She'd been eighteen, too young to handle what she felt, too young to handle the man, and her own reaction had frightened her. Because of that, she'd been at her snooty best when she'd walked up to her father to be introduced.

They'd gotten off on the wrong foot and had been there ever since. She was probably the only woman in the world at odds with Rafferty, and she wasn't certain, even now, that she wanted it to be any different. Somehow she felt safer knowing that he disliked her; at least he wouldn't be turning that formidable charm of his on her. In that respect, hostility brought with it a certain amount of protection.

A shiver ran over her body as she lay in bed thinking about both him and what she'd admitted only to herself: she was no more immune to Rafferty than the legion of women who had already succumbed. She was safe only as long as he didn't realize how vulnerable she was to his potent masculinity. He would delight in taking advantage of his power over her, making her pay for all the cutting remarks she'd made to him over the years, and for all the other things he disliked about her. To protect herself, she had to hold him at bay with hostility; it was rather ironic that now she needed his goodwill in order to survive financially.

She had almost forgotten how to laugh except for the social sounds that passed for laughter but held no humor, or how to smile except for the false mask of cheerfulness that kept pity away, but in the darkness and privacy of her bedroom she felt a wry grin curving her mouth. If she had to depend on Rafferty's goodwill for survival, she might as well go out to the pasture, dig a hole and pull the dirt in over herself to save him the time and trouble.

The next morning she loitered around the house waiting for him to call for as long as she could, but she had chores to do, and the cattle wouldn't wait. Finally she gave up and trudged out to the barn, her mind already absorbed with the hundred and one problems the ranch presented every day. She had several fields of hay that needed to be cut and baled, but she'd been forced to sell the tractor and hay baler; the only way she could get the hay cut would be to offer someone part of the hay if they'd do the cutting and baling for her. She backed the pickup truck into the barn and climbed into the hayloft, counting the bales she had left. The supply was dwindling; she'd have to do something soon.

There was no way she could lift the heavy bales, but she'd developed her own system for handling them. She had parked the truck just under the door to the hayloft, so all she had to do was push the bales to the open door and tip them through to land in the truck bed. Pushing the hay wasn't easy; they were supposed to be hundred-pound bales, which meant that she outweighed them by maybe seventeen pounds…if she hadn't lost weight, which she suspected she had, and if the bales weighed only a hundred pounds, which she suspected they didn't. Their weight varied, but some of them were so heavy she could barely move them an inch at a time.

She drove the truck across the pasture to where the cattle grazed; heads lifted, dark brown eyes surveyed the familiar truck, and the entire herd began ambling toward her. Michelle stopped the truck and climbed in back. Tossing the bales out was impossible, so she cut the twine there in the back of the truck and loosened the hay with the pitchfork she had brought along, then pitched the hay out in big clumps. She got back in the truck, drove a piece down the pasture, and stopped to repeat the procedure. She did it until the back of the pickup was empty, and by the time she was finished her shoulders were aching so badly the muscles felt as if they were on fire. If the herd hadn't been badly diminished in numbers from what it had been, she couldn't have handled it. But if the herd were larger, she reminded herself, she'd be able to afford help. When she remembered the number of people who used to work on the ranch, the number needed to keep it going properly, a wave of hopelessness hit her. Logic told her there was no way she could do it all herself.

But what did logic have to do with cold reality? She had to do it herself because she had no one else. Sometimes she thought that was the one thing life seemed determined to teach her: that she could depend only on herself, that there was no one she could trust, no one she could rely on, no one strong enough to stand behind her and hold her up when she needed to rest. There had been times when she'd felt a crushing sense of loneliness, especially since her father had died, but there was also a certain perverse comfort in knowing she could rely on no one but herself. She expected nothing of other people, therefore she wasn't disappointed by any failure on their part to live up to her expectations. She simply accepted facts as they were, without any pretty dressing up, did what she had to do, and went on from there. At least she was free now, and no longer dreaded waking up each day.

She trudged around the ranch doing the chores, putting her mind in neutral gear and simply letting her body go through the motions. It was easier that way; she could pay attention to her aches and bruises when all the chores were finished, but the best way to get them done was to ignore the protests of her muscles and the nicks and bruises she acquired. None of her old friends would ever have believed that Michelle Cabot was capable of turning her dainty hands to rough, physical chores. Sometimes it amused her to imagine what their reactions would be, another mind game that she played with herself to pass the time. Michelle Cabot had always been ready for a party, or shopping, or a trip to St. Moritz, or a cruise on someone's yacht. Michelle Cabot had always been laughing, making wisecracks with the best of them; she'd looked perfectly *right* with a glass of champagne in her hand and diamonds in her ears. The ultimate Golden Girl, that was her.

Well, the ultimate Golden Girl had cattle to feed, hay to cut, fences that needed repair, and that was only the tip of the iceberg. She needed to dip the cattle, but that was something else she hadn't figured out how to manage by herself. There was branding, castrating, breeding…. When she allowed herself to think of everything that needed doing, she was swamped by hopelessness, so she usually didn't dwell on it. She just took each day as it came, slogging along, doing what she could. It was survival, and she'd become good at it.

By ten o'clock that night, when Rafferty hadn't called, Michelle braced herself and called him again. Again the housekeeper answered; Michelle stifled a sigh, wondering if Rafferty ever spent a night at home. "This is Michelle Cabot. I'd like to speak to Rafferty, please. Is he home?"

"Yes, he's down at the barn. I'll switch your call to him."

So he had a telephone in the barn. For a moment she thought enviously of the operation he had as she listened to the clicks the receiver made in her ear. Thinking about his ranch took her mind off her suddenly galloping pulse and stifled breathing.

"Rafferty." His deep, impatient voice barked the word in her ear, and she jumped, her hand tightening on the receiver as her eyes closed.

"This is Michelle Cabot." She kept her tone as remote as possible as she identified herself. "I'd like to talk to you, if you have the time."

"Right now I'm damned short of time. I've got a mare in foal, so spit it out and make it fast."

"It'll take more time than that. I'd like to make an appointment, then. Would it be convenient for me to come over tomorrow morning?"

He laughed, a short, humorless bark. "This is a working ranch, sugar, not a social event. I don't have time for you tomorrow morning. Time's up."

"Then when?"

He muttered an impatient curse. "Look, I don't have time for you *now*. I'll drop by tomorrow afternoon on my way to town. About six." He hung up before she could agree or disagree, but as she hung up, too, she thought ruefully that he was calling the shots, so it didn't really matter if she liked the time or not. At least she had the telephone call behind her now, and there were almost twenty hours in which to brace herself for actually seeing him. She would stop work tomorrow in time to shower and wash her hair, and she'd do the whole routine with makeup and perfume, wear her white linen trousers and white silk shirt. Looking at her, Rafferty would never suspect that she was anything other than what he'd always thought her to be, pampered and useless.

It was late in the afternoon, the broiling sun had pushed the temperature to a hundred degrees, and the cattle were skittish. Rafferty was hot, sweaty, dusty and ill-tempered, and so were his men. They'd spent too much time chasing after strays instead of getting the branding and inoculating done, and now the deep, threatening rumble of thunder signaled a summer thunderstorm. The men speeded up their work, wanting to get finished before the storm hit.

Dust rose in the air as the anxious bawling increased in volume and the stench of burning hide intensified. Rafferty worked with the men, not disdaining any of the dirty jobs. It was *his* ranch, his life. Ranching was hard, dirty work, but he'd made it profitable when others had gone under, and he'd done it with his own sweat and steely determination. His mother had left rather than tolerate the life; of course, the ranch had been much smaller back then, not like the empire he'd built. His father, and the ranch, hadn't been able to support her in the style she'd wanted. Rafferty sometimes got a grim satisfaction from the knowledge that now his mother regretted having been so hasty to desert her husband and son so long ago. He didn't hate her; he didn't waste that much effort on her. He just didn't have much use for her, or for any of the rich, spoiled, bored, *useless* people she considered her friends.

Nev Luther straightened from the last calf, wiping his sweaty face on his shirt sleeve, then glancing at the sun and the soaring black cloud bank of the approaching storm. "Well, that's it," he grunted. "We'd better get loaded up before that thing hits." Then he glanced at his boss. "Ain't you supposed to see that Cabot gal today?"

Nev had been in the barn with Rafferty when he'd talked to Michelle, so he'd overheard the conversation. After a quick look at his watch, Rafferty swore aloud. He'd forgotten about her, and he wasn't grateful to Nev for reminding him. There were few people walking the earth who irritated him as much as Michelle Cabot.

"Damn it, I guess I'd better go," he said reluctantly. He knew what she wanted. It had surprised him that she had called at all, rather than continuing to ignore the debt. She was probably going to whine about how little money she had left and tell him that she couldn't *possibly* scrape up that amount. Just thinking about her made him want to grab her and shake her, hard. Or better yet, take a belt to her backside. She was exactly what he disliked most: a spoiled, selfish parasite who'd never done a day's work in her life. Her father had bankrupted himself paying for her pleasure jaunts, but Langley Cabot had always been a bit of a fool where his beloved only child had been concerned. Nothing had been too good for darling little Michelle, nothing at all.

Too bad that darling Michelle was a spoiled brat. Damn, she irritated him! She'd irritated him from the first moment he'd seen her, prissing up to where her father had stood talking to him, with her haughty nose in the air as if she'd smelled something bad. Well, maybe she had. Sweat, the product of physical work, was an alien odor to her. She'd looked at him the way she would have looked at a worm, then dismissed him as unimportant and turned her back to him while she coaxed and wheedled something out of her father with that charming Golden Girl act of hers.

"Say, boss, if you don't want to see that fancy little thing, I'd be happy to fill in for you," Nev offered, grinning.

"It's tempting," Rafferty said sourly, checking his watch again. He could go home and clean up, but it would make him late. He wasn't that far from the Cabot ranch now, and he wasn't in the mood to drive all the way back to his house, shower, and then make the drive again just so he wouldn't offend her dainty nose. She could put up with him as he was, dirt, sweat and all; after all, she was the one begging for favors. The mood he was in, he just might call in that debt, knowing good and well she couldn't pay it. He wondered with sardonic amusement if she would offer to pay it in another way. It would serve her right if he played along; it would make her squirm with distaste to think of letting him have her pampered body. After all, he was rough and dirty and worked for a living.

As he strode over to his truck and slid his long length under the steering wheel, he couldn't keep the image from forming in his mind: the image of Michelle Cabot lying beneath him, her slim body naked, her pale gold hair spread out over his pillow as he moved in and out of her. He felt his loins become heavy and full in response to the provocative image, and he swore under his breath. Damn her, and damn himself. He'd spent years watching her, brooding, wanting her and at the same time wanting to teach her in whatever way it took not to be such a spoiled, selfish snob.

Other people hadn't seen her that way; she could be charming when she chose, and she'd chosen to work that charm on the local people, maybe just to amuse herself with their gullibility. The ranchers and farmers in the area were a friendly group, rewarding themselves for their endless hard work with informal get-togethers, parties and barbecues almost every weekend, and Michelle had had them all eating out of her hand. They didn't see the side of her that she'd revealed to him; she was always laughing, dancing…but never with him. She would dance with every other man there, but never with him. He'd watched her, all right, and because he was a healthy male with a healthy libido he hadn't been able to stop himself from responding physically to her lithe, curved body and sparkling smile, even though it made him angry that he responded to her in any way.

He didn't want to want her, but just looking at her made him hungry.

Other men had watched her with hungry eyes, too, including Mike Webster. Rafferty didn't think he'd ever forgive her for what she'd done to Mike, whose marriage had been shaky even before Michelle had burst onto the scene with her flirtatious manner and sparkling laughter. Mike hadn't been any match for her; he'd fallen hard and fast, and the Webster marriage had splintered beyond repair. Then Michelle had flitted on to fresher prey, and Mike had been left with nothing but a ruined life. The young rancher had lost everything he'd worked for, forced to sell his ranch because of the divorce settlement. He was just one more man Michelle had ruined with her selfishness, as she'd ruined her father. Even when Langley was deep in financial trouble he'd kept providing money for Michelle's expensive life-style. Her father had been going under, but she'd still insisted on buying her silks and jewels, and skiing vacations in St. Moritz. It would take a rich man to afford Michelle Cabot, and a strong one.

The thought of being the one who provided her with those things, and the one who had certain rights over her because of it, teased his mind with disturbing persistence. No matter how angry, irritated or disgusted he felt toward her, he couldn't control his physical response to her. There was something about her that made him want to reach out and take her. She looked, sounded and smelled expensive; he wanted to know if she tasted expensive, too, if her skin was as silky as it looked. He wanted to bury his hands in her sunlit hair, taste her wide, soft mouth, and trace his fingertips across the chiseled perfection of her cheekbones, inhale the gut-tightening fragrance of her skin. He'd smelled her the day they'd first met, the perfume in her hair and on her skin, and the sweetness of her flesh beneath it. She was expensive all right, too expensive for Mike Webster, and for the poor sap she'd married and then left, certainly too expensive for her father. Rafferty wanted to lose himself in all that richness. It was a pure, primitive male instinct, the reaction of the male to a ready female. Maybe Michelle was a tease, but she gave out all the right signals to bring the men running, like bees to the sweetest flower.

Right now Michelle was between supporters, but he knew it wouldn't be long before she had another man lined up. Why shouldn't he be that man? He was tired of wanting her and watching her turn her snooty little nose up at him. She wouldn't be able to wrap him around her finger as she was used to doing, but that would be the price she had to pay for her expensive tastes. Rafferty narrowed his eyes against the rain that began to splat against the windshield, thinking about the satisfaction of having Michelle dependent on him for everything she ate and wore. It was a hard, primitive satisfaction. He would use her to satisfy his burning physical hunger for her, but he wouldn't let her get close enough to cloud his mind and judgment.

He'd never paid for a woman before, never been a sugar daddy, but if that was what it took to get Michelle Cabot, he'd do it. He'd never wanted another woman the way he wanted her, so he guessed it evened out.

The threatening storm suddenly broke, sending a sheet of rain sluicing down the windshield to obscure his vision despite the wipers' best efforts. Gusts of wind shoved at the truck, making him fight to hold it steady on the road. Visibility was so bad that he almost missed the turn to the Cabot ranch even though he knew these roads as well as he knew his own face. His features were dark with ill-temper when he drove up to the Cabot house, and his disgust increased as he looked around. Even through the rain, he could tell the place had gone to hell. The yard was full of weeds, the barn and stables had the forlorn look of emptiness and neglect, and the pastures that had once been dotted with prime Brahman cattle were empty now. The little society queen's kingdom had dissolved around her.

Though he'd pulled the truck up close to the house, it was raining so hard that he was drenched to the skin by the time he sprinted to the porch. He slapped his straw hat against his leg to get most of the water off it, but didn't replace it on his head. He raised his hand to knock, but the door opened before he had a chance. Michelle stood there looking at him with the familiar disdain in her cool, green eyes. She hesitated for just a moment, as if reluctant to let him drip water on the carpet; then she pushed the screen door open and said, "Come in." He imagined it ate at her guts to have to be nice to him because she owed him a hundred thousand dollars.

He walked past her, noting the way she moved back so he wouldn't brush against her. Just wait, he thought savagely. Soon he'd do more than just *brush* against her, and he'd make damned certain she liked it. She might turn her nose up at him now, but things would be different when she was naked under him, her legs wrapped around his waist while she writhed in ecstasy. He didn't just want the use of her body; he wanted her to want him in return, to feel as hungry and obsessed as he did. It would be poetic justice, after all the men she'd used. He almost wanted her to say something snide, so he'd have a reason to put his hands on her, even in anger. He wanted to touch her, no matter what the reason; he wanted to feel her warm and soft in his hands; he wanted to make her respond to him.

But she didn't cut at him with her tongue as she usually did. Instead she said, "Let's go into Dad's office," and led the way down the hall with her perfume drifting behind her to tease him. She looked untouchable in crisp white slacks and a white silk shirt that flowed lovingly over her curvy form, but he itched to touch her anyway. Her sunny pale-gold hair was pulled back and held at the nape of her neck with a wide gold clip.

Her fastidious perfection was in direct contrast to his own rough appearance, and he wondered what she'd do if he touched her, if he pulled her against him and got her silk shirt wet and stained. He was dirty and sweaty and smelled of cattle and horses, and now he was wet into the bargain; no, there was no way she'd accept his touch.

"Please sit down," she said, waving her hand at one of the leather chairs in the office. "I imagine you know why I called."

His expression became even more sardonic. "I imagine I do."

"I found the loan paper when I was going through Daddy's desk the night before last. I don't want you to think that I'm trying to weasel out of paying it, but I don't have the money right now—"

"Don't waste my time," he advised, interrupting.

She stared up at him. He hadn't taken the chair she'd offered; he was standing too close, towering over her, and the look in his black eyes made her shiver.

"What?"

"This song and dance; don't waste my time doing the whole bit. I know what you're going to offer, and I'm willing. I've been wanting to get in your pants for a long time, honey; just don't make the mistake of thinking a few quickies will make us even, because they won't. I believe in getting my money's worth."

Chapter Two

Shock froze her in place and leeched the color from her upturned face until it was as pale as ivory. She felt disoriented; for a moment his words refused to make sense, rotating in her mind like so many unconnected pieces of a puzzle. He was looming over her, his height and muscularity making her feel as insignificant as always, while the heat and scent of his body over-whelmed her senses, confusing her. He was too close! Then the words realigned themselves, and their meaning slapped her in the face. Panic and fury took the place of shock. Without thinking she drew back from him and snapped, "You must be joking!"

It was the wrong thing to say. She knew it as soon as she'd said it. Now wasn't the time to insult him, not when she needed his cooperation if she wanted to have a prayer of keeping the ranch going, but both pride and habit made her lash back at him. She could feel her stomach tighten even as she lifted her chin to give him a haughty stare, waiting for the reaction that was sure to come after the inadvertent challenge she'd thrown in his teeth. It wasn't safe to challenge Rafferty at all, and now she'd done it in the most elemental way possible.

His face was hard and still, his eyes narrowed and burning as he watched her. Michelle could feel the iron control he exerted to keep himself from moving. "Do I look like I'm joking?" he asked in a soft, dangerous tone. "You've always had some poor sucker supporting you; why shouldn't it be my turn? You can't lead me around by the nose the way you have every other man, but the way I see it, you can't afford to be too choosy right now."

"What would *you* know about being choosy?" She went even whiter, retreating from him a few more steps; she could almost feel his impact on her skin, and he hadn't even moved. He'd had so many women that she didn't even want to think about it, because thinking about it made her hurt deep inside. Had those other women felt this helpless, this overwhelmed by his heat and sexuality? She couldn't control her inborn instincts and responses; she had always sensed her own weakness where he was concerned, and that was what frightened her, what had kept her fighting him all these years. She simply couldn't face being used by him as casually as a stallion would service a mare; it would mean too much to her, and too little to him.

"Don't pull away from me," he said, his voice going

even softer, deeper, stroking her senses like dark velvet. It was the voice he would use in the night, she thought dazedly, her mind filled with the image of him covering a woman with his lean, powerful body while he murmured rawly sexual things in her ear. John wouldn't be a subtle lover; he would be strong and elemental, overwhelming a woman's senses. Wildly she blanked the image from her mind, turning her head away so she couldn't see him.

Rage lashed at him when she turned away as if she couldn't bear the sight of him; she couldn't have made it any plainer that she couldn't bear the idea of sleeping with him, either. With three long strides he circled the desk and caught her upper arms in his lean, sinewy hands, pulling her hard against him. Even in his fury he realized that this was the first time he'd touched her, felt her softness and the fragility of her bones. His hands completely encircled her arms, and his fingers wanted to linger, to stroke. Hunger rose again, pushing aside some of the anger. "Don't turn your nose up at me like some Ice Princess," he ordered roughly. "Your little kingdom has gone to hell, honey, in case you haven't noticed. Those fancy playmates of yours don't know you from Adam's housecat now that you can't afford to play. They sure haven't offered to help, have they?"

Michelle pushed against his chest, but it was like trying to move a wall. "I haven't asked them to help!" she cried, goaded. "I haven't asked anyone for help, least of all *you*!"

"Why not me?" He shook her lightly, his eyes narrowed and fierce. "I can afford you, honey."

"I'm not for sale!" She tried to pull back, but the effort was useless; though he wasn't holding her tightly enough to hurt, she was helpless against his steely strength.

"I'm not interested in buying," he murmured as he dipped his head. "Only in renting you for a while." Michelle made an inarticulate sound of protest and tried to turn her head away, but he simply closed his fist in her hair and held her still for his mouth. Just for a moment she saw his black eyes, burning with hunger, then his mouth was on hers, and she quivered in his arms like a frightened animal. Her eyelashes fluttered shut and she sank against him. For years she'd wondered about his mouth, his taste, if his lips would be firm or soft, if his mustache would scratch. Pleasure exploded in her like a fireball, flooding her with heat. Now she knew. Now she knew the warm, heady taste of his mouth, the firm fullness of his lips, the soft prickle of his mustache, the sure way his tongue moved into her mouth as if it were his right to be so intimate. Somehow her arms were around his shoulders, her nails digging through the wet fabric of his shirt to the hard muscle beneath. Somehow she was arched against him, his arms locked tight as he held her and took her mouth so deeply, over and over again. She didn't feel the moisture from his clothing seeping into hers; she felt only his heat and hardness, and dimly she knew that if she didn't stop soon, *he* wouldn't stop at all.

She didn't want to stop. Already she was coming apart inside, because she wanted nothing more than to simply lie against him and feel his hands on her. She'd known it would be like this, and she'd known she couldn't let it happen, couldn't let him get close to her. The feeling was so powerful that it frightened her. *He* frightened her. He would demand too much from her, take so much that there wouldn't be anything left when he moved on. She'd always known instinctively that she couldn't handle him.

It took every bit of inner strength she had to turn her face away from his mouth, to put her hands on his shoulders and push. She knew she wasn't strong enough to move him; when he released her and moved back a scant few inches, she was bitterly aware that it was by his own choice, not hers. He was watching her, waiting for her decision.

Silence filled the room with a thick presence as she struggled to regain her composure under his unwavering gaze. She could feel the situation slipping out of control. For ten years she had carefully cultivated the hostility between them, terrified of letting him discover that just looking at him turned her bones to water. She'd seen too many of his women with stars in their eyes while he gave them his attention, focusing his intense sexual instincts on them, but all too soon he'd moved on to someone else, and the stars had always turned into hunger and pain and emptiness. Now he was looking at her with that penetrating attention, just what she'd always tried to avoid. She hadn't wanted him to notice her as a woman; she hadn't wanted to join the ranks of all those other women he'd used and left. She had enough trouble now, without adding a broken heart, and John Rafferty was a walking heartache. Her back was already to the wall; she couldn't bear anything else, either emotionally or financially.

But his gaze burned her with black fire, sliding slowly over her body as if measuring her breasts for the way they would fit his hands, her hips for the way his would adjust against them, her legs for the way they would wrap around him in the throes of pleasure. He'd never looked at her in that way before, and it shook her down to her marrow. Pure sexual speculation was in his eyes. In his mind he was already inside her, tasting her, feeling her, giving her pleasure. It was a look few women could resist, one of unashamed sexuality, carnal experience and an arrogant confidence that a woman would be ultimately satisfied in his arms. He wanted her; he intended to have her.

And she couldn't let it happen. She'd been wrapped in a silken prison her entire life, stifled first by her father's idealistic adoration, then by Roger Beckman's obsessive jealousy. For the first time in her life she was alone, responsible for herself and finding some sense of worth in the responsibility. Fail or succeed, she needed to do this herself, not run to some man for help. She looked at John with a blank expression; he wanted her, but he didn't like or even respect her, and she wouldn't like or respect herself if she let herself become the parasite he expected her to be.

Slowly, as if her muscles ached, she eased away from him and sat down at the desk, tilting her golden head down so he couldn't see her face. Again, pride and habit came to her aid; her voice was calm and cool when she spoke. "As I said, I don't have the money to repay you right now, and I realize the debt is already delinquent. The solution depends on you—"

"I've already made my offer," he interrupted, his eyes narrowing at her coolness. He hitched one hip up on the desk beside her, his muscled thigh brushing against her arm. Michelle swallowed to alleviate the sudden dryness of her mouth, trying not to look at those powerful, denim-covered muscles. Then he leaned down, propping his bronzed forearm on his thigh, and that was worse, because it brought his torso closer, forcing her to lean back in the chair. "All you have to do is go ahead and accept it, instead of wasting time pretending you didn't like it when I touched you."

Michelle continued doggedly. "If you want repayment immediately, I'll have to sell the cattle to raise the money, and I'd like to avoid that. I'm counting on the sale of the cattle to keep the ranch going. What I have in mind is to sell some of the land to raise the money, but of course that will take longer. I can't even promise to have the money in six months; it just depends on how fast I can find a buyer." She held her breath, waiting for his response. Selling part of the land was the only plan she'd been able to devise, but it all depended on his cooperation.

Slowly he straightened, his dark brows drawing together as he stared down at her. "Whoa, honey, let's backtrack a little. What do you mean, `keep the ranch going'? The ranch is already dead."

"No, it isn't," she denied, stubbornness creeping into her tone. "I still have some cattle left."

"Where?" His disbelief was evident.

"In the south pasture. The fence on the east side needs repair, and I haven't—" She faltered at the growing anger in his dark face. Why should it matter to him? Their land joined mostly on the north; his cattle weren't in any danger of straying.

"Let's backtrack a little further," he said tightly. "Who's supposed to be working this herd?"

So that was it. He didn't believe her, because he knew there were no cowhands working here any longer. "I'm working the herd," she threw back at him, her face closed and proud. He couldn't have made it any plainer that he didn't consider her either capable or willing when it came to ranch work.

He looked her up and down, his brows lifting as he surveyed her. She knew exactly what he saw, because she'd deliberately created the image. He saw mauve-lacquered toenails, white high-heeled sandals, crisp white linen pants and the white silk shirt, damp now, from contact with his wet clothes. Suddenly Michelle realized that she was damp all along the front, and hectic color rose to burn along her cheekbones, but she lifted her chin just that much higher. Let him look, damn him.

"Nice," he drawled. "Let me see your hands."

Instinctively her hands curled into fists and she glared at him. "Why?"

He moved like a striking rattler, catching her wrist and holding her clenched hand in front of him. She pulled back, twisting in an effort to escape him, but he merely tightened his grip and pried her fingers open, then turned her palm to the light. His face was still and expressionless as he looked down at her hand for a long minute; then he caught her other hand and examined it, too. His grip gentled, and he traced his fingertips over the scratches and half-healed blisters, the forming calluses.

Michelle sat with her lips pressed together in a grim line, her face deliberately blank. She wasn't ashamed of her hands; work inevitably left its mark on human flesh, and she'd found something healing in the hard physical demands the ranch made on her. But no matter how honorable those marks, when John looked at them it was as if he'd stripped her naked and looked at her, as if he'd exposed something private. She didn't want him to know so much about her; she didn't want that intense interest turned on her. She didn't want pity from anyone, but she especially didn't want him to soften toward her.

Then his gaze lifted, those midnight eyes examining every inch of her proud, closed expression, and every instinct in her shrilled an alarm. Too late! Perhaps it had been too late from the moment he'd stepped onto the porch. From the beginning she'd sensed the tension in him, the barely controlled anticipation that she had mistaken for his usual hostility. Rafferty wasn't used to waiting for any woman he wanted, and she'd held him off for ten years. The only time she'd been truly safe from him had been during her brief marriage, when the distance between Philadelphia and central Florida had been more than hundreds of miles; it had been the distance between two totally different life-styles, in both form and substance. But now she was back within reach, and this time she was vulnerable. She was broke, she was alone, and she owed him a hundred thousand dollars. He probably expected it to be easy.

"You didn't have to do it alone," he finally said, his deep voice somehow deeper and quieter. He still held her hands, and his rough thumbs still moved gently, caressingly, over her palms, as he stood and drew her to her feet. She realized that at no time had he hurt her; he'd held her against her will, but he hadn't hurt her. His touch was gentle, but she knew without even trying that she wouldn't be able to pull away from him until he voluntarily let her go.

Her only defense was still the light mockery she'd used against him from the beginning. She gave him a bright, careless smile. "Of course I did. As you so charmingly pointed out, I'm not exactly being trampled by all my friends rushing to my rescue, am I?"

His upper lip curled with contempt for those "friends." He'd never had any patience with the bored and idle rich. "You could've come to me."

Again she gave him that smile, knowing he hated it. "But it would take so *long* to work off a hundred-thousand-dollar debt in that fashion, wouldn't it? You know how I hate being bored. A really good prostitute makes—what?—a hundred dollars a throw? Even if you were up to three times a day, it would still take about a year—"

Swift, dark fury burned in his eyes, and he finally released her hands, but only to move his grip to her shoulders. He held her still while he raked his gaze down her body again. "Three times a day?" he asked with that deceptive softness, looking at her breasts and hips. "Yeah, I'm up to it. But you forgot about interest, honey. I charge a lot of interest."

She quivered in his hands, wanting to close her eyes against that look. She'd taunted him rashly, and he'd turned her words back on her. Yes, he was capable of it. His sexual drive was so fierce that he practically burned with it, attracting women like helpless moths. Desperately she dredged up the control to keep smiling, and managed a little shrug despite his hands on her shoulders. "Thanks anyway, but I prefer shoveling manure."

If he'd lost control of his temper then she would have breathed easier, knowing that she still had the upper hand, by however slim a margin. If she could push him away with insults, she'd be safe. But though his hands tightened a little on her shoulders, he kept a tight rein on his temper.

"Don't push too hard, honey," he advised quietly. "It wouldn't take much for me to show you right now what you really like. You'd be better off telling me just how in hell you think you're going to keep this ranch alive by yourself."

For a moment her eyes were clear and bottomless, filled with a desperation he wasn't quite certain he'd seen. Her skin was tight over her chiseled cheekbones; then the familiar cool mockery and defiance were back, her eyes mossy and opaque, her lips curling a little in the way that made him want to shake her. "The ranch is my problem," she said, dismissing the offer of aid implicit in his words. She knew the price he'd demand for his help. "The only way it concerns you is in how you want the debt repaid."

Finally he released her shoulders and propped himself against the desk again, stretching his long legs and crossing his booted feet at the ankle. "A hundred thousand is a lot of money. It wasn't easy to come up with that much cash."

She didn't need to be told that. John might be a millionaire in assets, but a rancher's money is tied up in land and stock, with the profits constantly being plowed back into the ranch. Cash simply wasn't available for wasting on frivolities. Her jaw tightened. "When do you want your money?" she demanded. "Now or later?"

His dark brows lifted. "Considering the circumstances, you should be trying to sweeten me up instead of snapping at me. Why haven't you just put the ranch and cattle up for sale? You can't run the place anyway, and at least then you'd have money to live on until you find another meal ticket."

"I *can* run it," she flared, turning pale. She had to; it was all she had.

"No way, honey."

"Don't call me honey!" The ragged fury of her own voice startled her. He called every woman "honey." It was a careless endearment that meant nothing, because so many other women had heard it from him. She couldn't stand to think of him lying in the dark with another woman, his voice lazy and dark as they talked and he called her "honey."

He caught her chin in his big, rough hand, turning her face up to his while his thumb rubbed over her lower lip. "I'll call you whatever I want...*honey*, and you'll keep your mouth shut, because you owe me a lot of money that you can't repay. I'm going to think awhile about that debt and what we're going to do about it. Until I decide, why don't you think about this?"

Too late she tried to draw her head back, but he still held her chin, and his warm mouth settled over hers before she could jerk free. Her eyes closed as she tried to ignore the surge of pleasure in her midsection, tried to ignore the way his lips moved over hers and his tongue probed for entrance. If anything, this was worse than before, because now he was kissing her with a slow assurance that beguiled even as he demanded. She tried to turn her head away, but he forestalled the movement, spreading his legs and pulling her inside the cradle of his iron-muscled thighs. Michelle began shaking. Her hands flattened against his chest, but she could feel his heartbeat pulsing strongly against her palm, feel the accelerated rhythm of it, and she wanted to sink herself into him. Slowly he wedged her head back against his shoulder, his fingers woven into her hair as he held her. There was no way she could turn her head away from him now, and slowly she began to give way to his will. Her mouth opened beneath his, accepting the slow thrust of his tongue as he penetrated her in that small way and filled her with his taste.

He kissed her with shattering absorption, as if he couldn't get enough of her. Even the dim thought that he must have practised his technique with hundreds of women didn't lessen its power. She was utterly wrapped around by him, overwhelmed by his touch and scent and taste, her body tingling and aching with both pleasure and the need to have more of him. She wanted him; she'd always wanted him. He'd been an obsession with her from the moment she had seen him, and she'd spent most of the past ten years running from the power of that obsession, only to wind up practically at his mercy anyway—if he had any mercy.

He lifted his head in slow motion, his dark eyes heavy lidded, his mouth moist from kissing her. Blatant satisfaction was written across his hard face as he surveyed her. She was lying limply against him, her face dazed with pure want, her lips red and swollen. Very gently he put her away from him, holding her with his hands on her waist until she was steady on her feet; then he got to his own feet.

As always when he towered over her, Michelle automatically retreated a step. Frantically she searched for control, for something to say to him to deny the response she'd just given him, but what could she say that he'd believe? She couldn't have been more obvious! But then, neither could he. It was useless to try to regain lost ground, and she wasn't going to waste time trying. All she could do was try to put a halt to things now.

Her face was pale as she faced him, her hands twisted together in a tight knot. "I won't sleep with you to pay that debt, no matter what you decide. Did you come here tonight expecting to whisk me straight up to bed, assuming that I'd choose to turn whore for you?"

He eyed her sharply. "The thought crossed my mind. I was willing."

"Well, I'm not!" Breath rushed swiftly in and out of her lungs as she tried to control the outrage that burned in her at the insult. She had to control it; she couldn't afford to fall apart now.

"I'm glad, because I've changed my mind," he said lazily.

"Gosh, that's big of you!" she snapped.

"You'll go to bed with me, all right, but it won't be because of any money you owe me. When the time comes, you'll spread your legs for me because you want me just the way I want you."

The way he was looking at her made her shiver, and the image his rough words provoked shot through her brain like lightning. He would use her up and toss her away, just as he had all those other women, if she let him get too close to her. "Thanks, but no thanks. I've never gone in for group sex, and that's what it would be like with you!"

She wanted to make him angry, but instead he cupped her knotted-up hands in his palm and lightly rubbed his thumb over her knuckles. "Don't worry, I can guarantee there'll just be the two of us between the sheets. Settle down and get used to the idea. I'll be back out tomorrow to look over the ranch and see what needs to be done—"

"No," she interrupted fiercely, jerking her hands from his grip. "The ranch is mine. I can handle it on my own."

"Honey, you've never even handled a checkbook on your own. Don't worry about it; I'll take care of everything."

His amused dismissal set her teeth on edge, more because of her own fear that he was right than anything else. "I don't want you to take care of everything!"

"You don't know what you want," he replied, leaning down to kiss her briefly on the mouth. "I'll see you tomorrow."

Just like that he turned and walked out of the room, and after a moment Michelle realized he was leaving. She ran after him and reached the front door in time to see him sprinting through the downpour to his truck.

He didn't take her seriously. Well, why should he? Michelle thought bitterly. No one else ever had, either. She leaned on the doorframe and watched him drive away; her shaky legs needed the extra support. Why now? For years she'd kept him at a distance with her carefully manufactured hostility, but all of a sudden her protective barrier had shattered. Like a predator, he'd sensed her vulnerability and moved in for the kill.

Quietly she closed the door, shutting out the sound of rain. The silent house enclosed her, an empty reminder of the shambles of her life.

Her jaw clenched as she ground her teeth together, but she didn't cry. Her eyes remained dry. She couldn't afford to waste her time or strength indulging in useless tears. Somehow she had to hold on to the ranch, repay that debt, and hold off John Rafferty....

The last would be the hardest of all, because she'd be fighting against herself. She didn't want to hold him off; she wanted to creep into his iron-muscled arms and feel them close around her. She wanted to feed her hunger for him, touch him as she'd never allowed herself to do, immerse herself in the man. Guilt arose in her throat, almost choking her. She'd married another man wanting John, loving John, *obsessed* with John;

somehow Roger, her ex-husband, had sensed it, and his jealousy had turned their marriage into a nightmare.

Her mind burned with the memories, and to distract herself she walked briskly into the kitchen and prepared dinner for one; in this case, a bowl of cornflakes in milk. It was also what she'd had for breakfast, but her nerves were too raw to permit any serious cooking. She was actually able to eat half of the bowlful of cereal before she suddenly dropped the spoon and buried her face in her hands.

All her life she'd been a princess, the darling, pampered apple of her parents' eyes, born to them when they were both nearing forty and had given up hope of ever having children. Her mother had been a gentle, vague person who had passed straight from her father's keeping into that of her husband, and thought that a woman's role in life was to provide a comfortable, loving home for her husband, who supported her. It wasn't an unusual outlook for her generation, and Michelle didn't fault her mother for it. Langley Cabot had protected and spoiled both his wife and his daughter; that was the way life was supposed to be, and it was a source of pride to him that he supported them very well indeed. When her mother died, Michelle had become the recipient of all that protective devotion. Langley had wanted her to have the best of everything; he had wanted her to be happy, and to his way of thinking he had failed as a father and provider if she weren't.

In those days Michelle had been content to let her father shower her with gifts and luxuries. Her life had been humming along just as she had always expected, until the day Langley had turned her world upside down by selling the Connecticut house where she'd grown up, and moved her down to a cattle ranch in central Florida, not far from the Gulf coast. For the first time in her life, Langley had been unmoved by her pleas. The cattle ranch was his dream come true, the answer to some deeply buried need in him that had been hidden under silk shirts, pin-striped suits and business appointments. Because he'd wanted it so badly, he had ignored Michelle's tears and tantrums and jovially assured her that before long she'd have new friends and would love the ranch as much as he did.

In that, he was partially right. She made new friends, gradually became accustomed to the heat, and even enjoyed life on a working cattle ranch. Langley had completely remodeled the old ranch house when he'd bought it, to ensure that his beloved daughter wasn't deprived in any way of the comfort she was accustomed to. So she'd adjusted, and even gone out of her way to assure him of her contentment. He deserved his dream, and she had felt ashamed that she'd tried to talk him out of it. He did so much to make her happy, the least she could do was return as much of the effort as she could.

Then she'd met John Rafferty. She couldn't believe that she'd spent ten years running from him, but it was true. She'd hated him and feared him and loved him all at once, with a teenager's wildly passionate obsession, but she had always seen one thing very clearly: he was more than she could handle. She had never daydreamed of being the one woman who could tame the rake; she was far too vulnerable to him, and he was too strong. He might take her and use her, but she wasn't woman enough to hold him. She was spoiled and pampered; he didn't even like her. In self-defense, she had devoted herself to making him dislike her even more to make certain he never made a move on her.

She had gone to an exclusive women's college back east, and after graduation had spent a couple of weeks with a friend who lived in Philadelphia. During that visit she'd met Roger Beckman, scion of one of the oldest and richest families in town. He was tall and black haired, and he even had a trim mustache. His resemblance to John was slight, except for those points, and Michelle couldn't say that she had consciously married Roger because he reminded her of John, but she was very much afraid that subconsciously she had done exactly that.

Roger was a lot of fun. He had a lazy manner about him, his eyes wrinkled at the edges from smiling so much, and he loved organized crazy games, like scavenger hunts. In his company Michelle could forget about John and simply have fun. She was genuinely fond of Roger, and came to love him as much as she would ever love any man who wasn't John Rafferty. The best thing she could do was forget about John, put him behind her, and get on with her life. After all, there had never been anything between them except her own fantasies, and Roger absolutely adored her. So she had married him, to the delight of both her father and his parents.

It was a mistake that had almost cost her her life.

At first everything had been fine. Then Roger had begun to show signs of jealousy whenever Michelle was friendly to another man. Had he sensed that she didn't love him as she should? That he owned only the most superficial part of her heart? Guilt ate at her even now, because Roger's jealousy hadn't been groundless. He hadn't been able to find the true target, so he'd lashed out whenever she smiled at any man, danced with any man.

The scenes had gotten worse, and one night he'd actually slapped her during a screaming fight after a party; she'd made the mistake of speaking to the same man twice while they raided the buffet table. Shocked, her face burning, Michelle had stared at her husband's twisted features and realized that his jealousy had driven him out of control. For the first time, she was afraid of him.

His action had shocked Roger, too, and he'd buried his face in her lap, clinging to her as he wept and begged her forgiveness. He'd sworn never to hurt her again; he'd said he would rather cut off his own hands than hurt her. Shaken to the core, Michelle did what thousands of women did when their husbands turned on them: she forgave him.

But it wasn't the last time. Instead, it got worse.

Michelle had been too ashamed and shocked to tell anyone, but finally she couldn't take any more and pressed charges against him. To her horror, his parents quietly bought off everyone involved, and Michelle was left without a legal leg to stand on, all evidence destroyed. Come hell or high water, the Beckmans would protect their son.

Finally she tried to leave him, but she had gotten no further than Baltimore before he caught up with her, his face livid with rage. It was then that Michelle realized he wasn't quite sane; his jealousy had pushed him over the edge. Holding her arm in a grip that left bruises for two weeks, he made the threat that kept her with him for the next two years: if she left him again, he'd have her father killed.

She hadn't doubted him, nor did she doubt that he'd get away with it; he was too well protected by his family's money and prestige, by a network of old family friends in the law business. So she'd stayed, terrified that he might kill her in one of his rages, but not daring to leave. No matter what, she had to protect her father.

But finally she found a way to escape. Roger had beaten her with a belt one night. But his parents had been in Europe on vacation, and by the time they found out about the incident it was too late to use their influence. Michelle had crept out of the house, gone to a hospital where her bruises and lacerations were treated and recorded, and she'd gotten copies of the records. Those records had bought her a divorce.

The princess would carry the scars to her grave.

Chapter Three

The telephone rang as Michelle was nursing her second cup of coffee, watching the sun come up and preparing herself for another day of chores that seemed to take more and more out of her. Dark circles lay under her heavy-lidded eyes, testimony to hours of twisting restlessly in bed while her mind insisted on replaying every word John had said, every sensation his mouth and hands had evoked. His reputation was well earned, she had thought bitterly in the early hours. Lady-killer. His touch was burningly tender, but he was hell on his women anyway.

She didn't want to answer the phone, but she knew John well enough to know he never gave up once he set his mind on something. He'd be back, and she knew it. If that was him on the telephone, he'd come over if she didn't answer. She didn't feel up to dealing with him in person, so she picked up the receiver and muttered a hello.

"Michelle, darling."

She went white, her fingers tightening on the receiver. Had she conjured him up by thinking about him the night before? She tried *not* to think of him, to keep him locked in the past, but sometimes the nightmare memories surfaced, and she felt again the terror of being so alone and helpless, with no one she could trust to come to her aid, not even her father.

"Roger," she said faintly. There was no doubt. No one but her ex-husband said her name in that caressing tone, as if he adored her.

His voice was low, thick. "I need you, darling. Come back to me, please. I'm begging. I promise I'll never hurt you again. I'll treat you like a princess—"

"No," she gasped, groping for a chair to support her shaking legs. Cold horror made her feel sick. How could he even suggest that she come back?

"Don't say that, please," he groaned. "Michelle, Mother and Dad are dead. I need you now more than ever. I thought you'd come for their funeral last week, but you stayed away, and I can't stand it any longer. If you'll just come back I swear everything will be different—"

"We're divorced," she broke in, her voice thin with strain. Cold sweat trickled down her spine.

"We can be remarried. Please, darling—"

"No!" The thought of being remarried to him filled her with so much revulsion that she couldn't even be polite. Fiercely she struggled for control. "I'm sorry about your parents; I didn't know. What happened?"

"Plane crash." Pain still lingered in his hoarse voice. "They were flying up to the lake and got caught in a storm."

"I'm sorry," she said again, but even if she'd known in time to attend the funeral, she never would have gone. She would never willingly be in Roger's presence again.

He was silent a moment, and she could almost see him rub the back of his neck in the unconscious nervous gesture she'd seen so many times. "Michelle, I still love you. Nothing's any good for me without you. I swear, it won't be the same as it was; I'll never hurt you again. I was just so damned jealous, and I know now I didn't have any reason."

But he did! she thought, squeezing her eyes shut as guilt seeped in to mix with the raw terror evoked by simply hearing his voice. Not physically, but had there been any day during the past ten years when she hadn't thought of John Rafferty? When part of her hadn't been locked away from Roger and every other man because they weren't the heartbreaker who'd stolen her heart?

"Roger, don't," she whispered. "It's over. I'll never come back. All I want to do now is work this ranch and make a living for myself."

He made a disgusted sound. "You shouldn't be working that dinky little ranch! You're used to much better than that. I can give you anything you want."

"No," she said softly. "You can't. I'm going to hang up now. Goodbye, and please don't call me again."

Very gently she replaced the receiver, then stood by the phone with her face buried in her hands. She couldn't stop trembling, her mind and body reeling with the ramifications of what he'd told her. His parents were dead, and she had been counting on them to control him. That was the deal she'd made with them; if they would keep Roger away from her, she wouldn't release the photos and medical report to the press, who would have a field day with the scandal. Imagine, a Beckman of Philadelphia nothing but a common wife-beater! That evidence had kept her father safe from Roger's insane threats, too, and now he was forever beyond Roger's reach. She had lived in hell to protect her father, knowing that Roger was capable of doing exactly what he'd threatened, and knowing after the first incident that his parents would make certain Roger was protected, no matter what.

She had honestly liked her in-laws until then, but her affection had died an irrevocable death when they had bought Roger out of trouble the first time he'd really hurt her. She had known their weakness then, and she had forced herself to wait. There was no one to help her; she had only herself. Once she had been desperate enough to mention it to her father, but he'd become so upset that she hadn't pushed it, and in only a moment he'd convinced himself that she'd been exaggerating. Marriage was always an adjustment, and Michelle was spoiled, highly strung. Probably it was just an argument over some minor thing, and the young couple would work things out.

The cold feeling of aloneness had spread through

her, but she hadn't stopped loving him. He loved her, she knew he did, but he saw her as more of a doll than a human being. His perfect, loving darling. He couldn't accept such ugliness in her life. She had to be happy, or it would mean he'd failed her in some basic way as a father, protector and provider. For his own sake, he had to believe she was happy. That was his weakness, so she had to be strong for both of them. She had to protect him, and she had to protect herself.

There was no way she would ever go back to Roger. She had dealt with the nightmares and put them behind her; she had picked up the pieces of her life and gone on, not letting the memories turn her into a frightened shell. But the memories, and the fear, were still there, and all it took was hearing Roger's voice to make her break out in a cold sweat. The old feeling of vulnerability and isolation swept over her, making her feel sick.

She jerked around, wrenching herself from the spell, and dashed what was left of her coffee down the drain. The best thing was to be active, to busy herself with whatever came to hand. That was the way she'd handled it when she had finally managed to get away from Roger, globe-trotting for two years because her father had thought that would take her mind off the divorce, and she had let the constant travel distract her. Now she had real work to do, work that left her exhausted and aching but was somehow healing, because it was the first worthwhile work she'd ever done.

It had been eating at him all morning.

He'd been in a bad mood from the moment he'd

gotten out of bed, his body aching with frustration, as if he were some randy teenager with raging hormones. He was a long way from being a teenager, but his hormones were giving him hell, and he knew exactly why. He hadn't been able to sleep for remembering the way she'd felt against him, the sweetness of her taste and the silky softness of her body. And she wanted him, too; he was too experienced to be mistaken about something like that. But he'd pushed too hard, driven by ten years of having an itch he couldn't scratch, and she'd balked. He'd put her in the position of paying him with her body, and she hadn't liked that. What woman would? Even the ones who were willing usually wanted a pretty face put on it, and Michelle was haughtier than most.

But she hadn't looked haughty the day before. His frown grew darker. She had tried, but the old snooty coldness was missing. She was dead broke and had nowhere to turn. Perhaps she was scared, wondering what she was going to do without the cushion of money that had always protected her. She was practically helpless, having no job skills or talents other than social graces, which weren't worth a hell of a lot on the market. She was all alone on that ranch, without the people to work it.

He made a rough sound and pulled his horse's head around. "I'll be back later," he told Nev, nudging the horse's flanks with his boot heels.

Nev watched him ride away. "Good riddance," he muttered. Whatever was chewing on the boss had put him in the worst mood Nev had ever seen; it would be a relief to work without him.

John's horse covered the distance with long, easy strides; it was big and strong, seventeen hands high, and inclined to be a bit stubborn, but they had fought that battle a long time ago. Now the animal accepted the mastery of the iron-muscled legs and strong, steady hands of his rider. The big horse liked a good run, and he settled into a fast, smooth rhythm as they cut across pastures, his pounding hooves sending clods of dirt flying.

The more John thought about it, the less he liked it. She'd been trying to work that ranch by herself. It didn't fit in with what he knew of Michelle, but her fragile hands bore the marks. He had nothing but contempt for someone who disdained good honest work and expected someone else to do it for them, but something deep and primitive inside him was infuriated at the idea of Michelle even trying to manage the backbreaking chores around the ranch. Damn it, why hadn't she asked for help? Work was one thing, but no one expected her to turn into a cowhand. She wasn't strong enough; he'd held her in his arms, felt the delicacy of her bones, the greyhound slenderness of her build. She didn't need to be working cattle any more than an expensive thoroughbred should be used to plow a field. She could get hurt, and it might be days before anyone found her. He'd always been disgusted with Langley for spoiling and protecting her, and with Michelle for just sitting back and accepting it as her due, but suddenly he knew just how Langley had felt. He gave a disgusted snort at himself, making the horse flick his ears back curiously at the sound, but the hard fact was that he didn't like the idea of Michelle's trying to work that ranch. It was a man's work, and more than one man, at that.

Well, he'd take care of all that for her, whether she liked it or not. He had the feeling she wouldn't, but she'd come around. She was too used to being taken care of, and, as he'd told her, now it was his turn.

Yesterday had changed everything. He'd felt her response to him, felt the way her mouth had softened and shaped itself to his. She wanted him, too, and the knowledge only increased his determination to have her. She had tried to keep him from seeing it; that acid tongue of hers would have made him lose his temper if he hadn't seen the flicker of uncertainty in her eyes. It was so unusual that he'd almost wanted to bring back the haughtiness that aggravated him so much.... Almost, but not quite. She was vulnerable now, vulnerable to him. She might not like it, but she needed him. It was an advantage he intended to use.

There was no answer at the door when he got to the ranch house, and the old truck was missing from its customary parking place in the barn. John put his fists on his hips and looked around, frowning. She had probably driven into town, though it was hard to think that Michelle Cabot was willing to let herself be seen in that kind of vehicle. It was her only means of transportation, though, so she didn't have much choice.

Maybe it was better that she was gone; he could check around the ranch without her spitting and hissing at him like an enraged cat, and he'd look at those cattle in the south pasture. He wanted to know just how many head she was running, and how they looked. She couldn't possibly handle a big herd by herself, but for her sake he hoped they were in good shape, so she could get a fair price for them. He'd handle it himself, make certain she didn't get rooked. The cattle business wasn't a good one for beginners.

He swung into the saddle again. First he checked the east pasture, where she had said the fence was down. Whole sections of it would have to be replaced, and he made mental notes of how much fencing it would take. The entire ranch was run-down, but fencing was critical; it came first. Lush green grass covered the east pasture; the cattle should be in it right now. The south pasture was probably overgrazed, and the cattle would show it, unless the herd was small enough that the south pasture could provide for its needs.

It was a couple of hours before he made it to the south pasture. He reined in the horse as he topped a small rise that gave him a good view. The frown snapped into place again, and he thumbed his hat onto the back of his head. The cattle he could see scattered over the big pasture didn't constitute a big herd, but made for far more than the small one he'd envisioned. The pasture was badly overgrazed, but scattered clumps of hay testified to Michelle's efforts to feed her herd. Slow-rising anger began to churn in him as he thought of her wrestling with heavy bales of hay; some of them probably weighed more than she did.

Then he saw her, and in a flash the anger rose to boiling point. The old truck was parked in a clump of trees, which was why he hadn't noticed it right off, and she was down there struggling to repair a section of fencing by herself. Putting up fencing was a two-man job; one person couldn't hold the barbed wire securely enough, and there was always the danger of the wire backlashing. The little fool! If the wire got wrapped around her, she wouldn't be able to get out of it without help, and those barbs could really rip a person up. The thought of her lying tangled and bleeding in a coil of barbed wire made him both sick and furious.

He kept the horse at an easy walk down the long slope to where she was working, deliberately giving himself time to get control of his temper. She looked up and saw him, and even from the distance that still separated them he could see her stiffen. Then she turned back to the task of hammering a staple into the fence post, her jerky movements betraying her displeasure at his presence.

He dismounted with a fluid, easy motion, never taking his gaze from her as he tied the reins to a low-hanging tree branch. Without a word he pulled the strand of wire to the next post and held it taut while Michelle, equally silent, pounded in another staple to hold it. Like him, she had on short leather work gloves, but her gloves were an old pair of men's gloves that had been left behind and were far too big for her, making it difficult for her to pick up the staples, so she had pulled off the left glove. She could handle the staples then, but the wire had already nicked her unprotected flesh several times. He saw the angry red scratches; some of which were deep enough for blood to well, and he wanted to shake her until her teeth rattled.

"Don't you have any better sense than to try to put up fencing on your own?" he rasped, pulling another strand tight.

She hammered in the staple, her expression closed. "It has to be done. I'm doing it."

"Not anymore, you aren't."

His flat statement made her straighten, her hand closing tightly around the hammer. "You want the payment right away," she said tonelessly, her eyes sliding to the cattle. She was a little pale, and tension pulled the skin tight across her high cheekbones.

"If that's what I have to do." He pried the hammer from her grip, then bent to pick up the sack of staples. He walked over to the truck, then reached in the open window and dropped them onto the floorboard. Then he lifted the roll of barbed wire onto the truck bed. "That'll hold until I can get my men out here to do it right. Let's go."

It was a good thing he'd taken the hammer away from her. Her hands balled into fists. "I don't want your men out here doing it right! This is still my land, and I'm not willing to pay the price you want for your help."

"I'm not giving you a choice." He took her arm, and no matter how she tried she couldn't jerk free of those long, strong fingers as he dragged her over to the truck, opened the door and lifted her onto the seat. He released her then, slamming the door and stepping back.

"Drive carefully, honey. I'll be right behind you."

She had to drive carefully; the pasture was too rough for breakneck speed, even if the old relic had been capable of it. She knew he was easily able to keep up with her on his horse, though she didn't check the rearview mirror even once. She didn't want to see him, didn't want to think about selling the cattle to pay her debt. That would be the end of the ranch, because she'd been relying on that money to keep the ranch going.

She'd hoped he wouldn't come back today, though it had been a fragile hope at best. After talking to Roger that morning, all she wanted was to be left alone. She needed time by herself to regain her control, to push all the ugly memories away again, but John hadn't given her that time. He wanted her, and like any predator he'd sensed her vulnerability and was going to take advantage of it.

She wanted to just keep driving, to turn the old truck down the driveway, hit the road and keep on going. She didn't want to stop and deal with John, not now. The urge to run was so strong that she almost did it, but a glance at the fuel gauge made her mouth twist wryly. If she ran, she'd have to do it on foot, either that or steal John's horse.

She parked the truck in the barn, and as she slid off the high seat John walked the horse inside, ducking his head a little to miss the top of the doorframe. "I'm going to cool the horse and give him some water," he said briefly. "Go on in the house. I'll be there in a minute."

Was postponing the bad news for a few minutes supposed to make her feel better? Instead of going straight to the house, she walked down to the end of the driveway and collected the mail. Once the mailbox had been stuffed almost every day with magazines, catalogs, newspapers, letters from friends, business papers, but now all that came was junk mail and bills. It was odd how the mail reflected a person's solvency, as if no one in the world wanted to communicate with someone who was broke. Except for past-due bills, of course. Then the communications became serious. A familiar envelope took her attention, and a feeling of dread welled in her as she trudged up to the house. The electric bill was past due; she'd already had one late notice, and here was another one. She had to come up with the money fast, or the power would be disconnected. Even knowing what it was, she opened the envelope anyway and scanned the notice. She had ten days to bring her account up to date. She checked the date of the notice; it had taken three days to reach her. She had seven days left.

But why worry about the electricity if she wouldn't have a ranch? Tiredness swept over her as she entered the cool, dim house and simply stood for a moment, luxuriating in the relief of being out of the broiling sun. She shoved the bills and junk mail into the same drawer of the entry table where she had put the original bill and the first late notice; she never forgot about them, but at least she could put them out of sight.

She was in the kitchen, having a drink of water, when she heard the screen door slam, then the sharp sound of boot heels on the oak parquet flooring as he came down the hallway. She kept drinking, though she was acutely aware of his progress through the house. He paused to look into the den, then the study. The slow, deliberate sound of those boots as he came closer made her shiver in reaction. She could see him in her mind's eye; he had a walk that any drugstore cowboy would kill for: that loose, long-legged, slim-hipped saunter, tight buttocks moving up and down. It was a walk that came naturally to hell-raisers and heartbreakers, and Rafferty was both.

She knew the exact moment when he entered the kitchen, though her back was to him. Her skin suddenly tingled, as if the air had become charged, and the house no longer seemed so cool.

"Let me see your hand." He was so close behind her that she couldn't turn without pressing against him, so she remained where she was. He took her left hand in his and lifted it.

"They're just scratches," she muttered.

She was right, but admitting it didn't diminish his anger. She shouldn't have any scratches at all; she shouldn't be trying to repair fencing. Her hand lay in his bigger, harder one like a pale, fragile bird, too tired to take flight, and suddenly he knew that the image was exactly right. She was tired.

He reached around her to turn on the water, then thoroughly soaped and rinsed her hand. Michelle hurriedly set the water glass aside, before it slipped from her trembling fingers, then stood motionless, with her head bowed. He was very warm against her back; she felt completely surrounded by him, with his arms around her while he washed her hand with the gentleness a mother would use to wash an infant. That gentleness staggered her senses, and she kept her head bent precisely to prevent herself from letting it drop back against his shoulder to let him support her.

The soap was rinsed off her hand now, but still he held it under the running water, his fingers lightly stroking. She quivered, trying to deny the sensuality of his touch. He was just washing her hand! The water was warm, but his hand was warmer, the rough calluses rasping against her flesh as he stroked her with a lover's touch. His thumb traced circles on her sensitive palm, and Michelle felt her entire body tighten. Her pulse leaped, flooding her with warmth. "Don't," she said thickly, trying unsuccessfully to pull free.

He turned off the water with his right hand, then moved it to her stomach and spread his fingers wide, pressing her back against his body. His hand was wet; she felt the dampness seeping through her shirt in front, and the searing heat of him at her back. The smell of horse and man rose from that seductive heat. Everything about the man was a come-on, luring women to him.

"Turn around and kiss me," he said, his voice low, daring her to do it.

She shook her head and remained silent, her head bent.

He didn't push it, though they both knew that if he had, she wouldn't have been able to resist him. Instead he dried her hand, then led her to the downstairs bathroom and made her sit on the lid of the toilet while he thoroughly cleaned the scratches with antiseptic. Michelle didn't flinch from the stinging; what did a few scratches matter, when she was going to lose the ranch? She had no other home, no other place she wanted to be. After being virtually imprisoned in that plush penthouse in Philadelphia, she needed the feeling of space around her. The thought of living in a city again made her feel stifled and panicky, and she would have to live in some city somewhere to get a job, since she didn't even have a car to commute. The old truck in the barn wouldn't hold up to a long drive on a daily basis.

John watched her face closely; she was distracted about something, or she would never have let him tend her hand the way he had. After all, it was something she could easily have done herself, and he'd done it merely to have an excuse to touch her. He wanted to know what she was thinking, why she insisted on working this ranch when it had to be obvious even to her that it was more than she could handle. It simply wasn't in character for her.

"When do you want the money?" she asked dully.

His mouth tightened as he straightened and pulled her to her feet. "Money isn't what I want," he replied.

Her eyes flashed with green fire as she looked at him. "I'm not turning myself into a whore, even for you! Did you think I'd jump at the chance to sleep with you? Your reputation must be going to your head...*stud*."

He knew people called him that, but when Michelle said it, the word dripped with disdain. He'd always hated that particular tone, so icy and superior, and it made him see red now. He bent down until his face was level with hers, their noses almost touching, and his black eyes were so fiery that she could see gold sparks in them. "When we're in bed, honey, you can decide for yourself about my reputation."

"I'm not going to bed with you," she said through clenched teeth, spacing the words out like dropping stones into water.

"The hell you're not. But it won't be for this damned ranch." Straightening to his full height again, he caught her arm. "Let's get that business settled right now, so it'll be out of the way and you can't keep throwing it in my face."

"You're the one who put it on that basis," she shot back as they returned to the kitchen. He dropped several ice cubes in a glass and filled it with water, then draped his big frame on one of the chairs. She watched his muscular throat working as he drained the glass, and a weak, shivery feeling swept over her. Swiftly she looked away, cursing her own powerful physical response to the mere sight of him.

"I made a mistake," he said tersely, putting the glass down with a thump. "Money has nothing to do with it. We've been circling each other from the day we met, sniffing and fighting like cats in heat. It's time we did something about it. As for the debt, I've decided what I want. Deed that land you were going to sell over to me instead, and we'll be even."

It was just like him to divide her attention like that, so she didn't know how to react or what to say. Part of her wanted to scream at him for being so smugly certain she would sleep with him, and part of her was flooded with relief that the debt had been settled so easily. He could have ruined her by insisting on cash, but he hadn't. He wasn't getting a bad deal, by any means; it was good, rich pastureland he was obtaining, and he knew it.

It was a reprieve, one she hadn't expected, and she didn't know how to deal with it, so she simply sat and stared at him. He waited, but when she didn't say anything he leaned back in his chair, his hard face becoming even more determined. "There's a catch," he drawled.

The high feeling of relief plummeted, leaving her sick and empty. "Let me guess," she said bitterly, shoving her chair back and standing. So it had all come down to the same thing after all.

His mouth twisted wryly in self-derision. "You're way off, honey. The catch is that you let me help you. My men will do the hard labor from now on, and if I even hear of you trying to put up fencing again, you'll be sitting on a pillow for a month."

"If your men do my work, I'll still be in debt to you."

"I don't consider it a debt; I call it helping a neighbor."

"I call it a move to keep me obligated!"

"Call it what you like, but that's the deal. You're one woman, not ten men; you're not strong enough to take care of the livestock and keep the ranch up, and you don't have the money to afford help. You're mighty short on options, so stop kicking. It's your fault, anyway. If you hadn't liked to ski so much, you wouldn't be in this position."

She drew back, her green eyes locked on him. Her face was pale. "What do you mean?"

John got to his feet, watching her with the old look that said he didn't much like her. "I mean that part of the reason your daddy borrowed the money from me was so he could afford to send you to St. Moritz with your friends last year. He was trying to hold his head above water, but that didn't matter to you as much as living in style, did it?"

She had been pale before, but now she was deathly white. She stared at him as if he'd slapped her, and too late he saw the shattered look in her eyes. Swiftly he rounded the table, reaching for her, but she shrank away from him, folding in on herself like a wounded animal. How ironic that she should now be struggling to repay a debt made to finance a trip she hadn't wanted! All she'd wanted had been time alone in a quiet place, a chance to lick her wounds and finish recovering from a brutal marriage, but her father had thought resuming a life of trips and shopping with her friends would be better, and she'd gone along with him because it had made him happy.

"I didn't even want to go," she said numbly, and to her horror tears began welling in her eyes. She didn't want to cry; she hadn't cried in years, except once when her father died, and she especially didn't want to cry in front of Rafferty. But she was tired and off balance, disturbed by the phone call from Roger that morning, and this just seemed like the last straw. The hot tears slipped silently down her cheeks.

"God, don't," he muttered, wrapping his arms around her and holding her to him, her face pressed against his chest. It was like a knife in him to see those tears on her face, because in all the time he'd known her, he'd never before seen her cry. Michelle Cabot had faced life with either a laugh or a sharp retort, but never with tears. He found he preferred an acid tongue to this soundless weeping.

For just a moment she leaned against him, letting him support her with his hard strength. It was too tempting; when his arms were around her, she wanted to forget everything and shut the world out, as long as he was holding her. That kind of need frightened her, and she stiffened in his arms, then pulled free. She swiped her palms over her cheeks, wiping away the dampness, and stubbornly blinked back the remaining tears.

His voice was quiet. "I thought you knew."

She threw him an incredulous look before turning away. What an opinion he had of her! She didn't mind his thinking she was spoiled; her father had spoiled her, but mostly because he'd enjoyed doing it so much. Evidently John not only considered her a common whore, but a stupid one to boot.

"Well, I didn't. And whether I knew or not doesn't change anything. I still owe you the money."

"We'll see my lawyer tomorrow and have the deed drawn up, and that'll take care of the damned debt. I'll be here at nine sharp, so be ready. A crew of men will be here in the morning to take care of the fencing and get the hay out to the herd."

He wasn't going to give in on that, and he was right; it *was* too much for her, at least right now. She couldn't do it all simply because it was too much for one person to do. After she fattened up the beef cattle and sold them off, she'd have some capital to work with and might be able to hire someone part-time.

"All right. But keep a record of how much I owe you. When I get this place back on its feet, I'll repay every penny." Her chin was high as she turned to face him, her green eyes remote and proud. This didn't solve all her problems, but at least the cattle would be cared for. She still had to get the money to pay the bills, but that problem was hers alone.

"Whatever you say, honey," he drawled, putting his hands on her waist.

She only had time for an indrawn breath before his mouth was on hers, as warm and hard as she remembered, his taste as heady as she remembered. His hands tightened on her waist and drew her to him; then his arms were around her, and the kiss deepened, his tongue sliding into her mouth. Hunger flared, fanned into instant life at his touch. She had always known that once she touched him, she wouldn't be able to get enough of him.

She softened, her body molding itself to him as she instinctively tried to get close enough to him to feed that burning hunger. She was weak where he was concerned, just as all women were. Her arms were clinging around his neck, and in the end it was he who broke the kiss and gently set her away from him.

"I have work to get back to," he growled, but his eyes were hot and held dark promises. "Be ready tomorrow."

"Yes," she whispered.

Chapter Four

Two pickup trucks came up the drive not long after sunrise, loaded with fencing supplies and five of John's men. Michelle offered them all a cup of fresh coffee, which they politely refused, just as they refused her offer to show them around the ranch. John had probably given them orders that she wasn't to do anything, and they were taking it seriously. People didn't disobey Rafferty's orders if they wanted to continue working for him, so she didn't insist, but for the first time in weeks she found herself with nothing to do.

She tried to think what she'd done with herself before, but years of her life were a blank. What *had* she done? How could she fill the hours now, if working on her own ranch was denied her?

John drove up shortly before nine, but she had been

ready for more than an hour and stepped out on the porch to meet him. He stopped on the steps, his dark eyes running over her in heated approval. "Nice," he murmured just loud enough for her to hear. She looked the way she should always look, cool and elegant in a pale yellow silk surplice dress, fastened only by two white buttons at the waist. The shoulders were lightly padded, emphasizing the slimness of her body, and a white enamel peacock was pinned to her lapel. Her sunshine hair was sleeked back into a demure twist; oversized sunglasses shielded her eyes. He caught the tantalizing fragrance of some softly bewitching perfume, and his body began to heat. She was aristocratic and expensive from her head to her daintily shod feet; even her underwear would be silk, and he wanted to strip every stitch of it away from her, then stretch her out naked on his bed. Yes, this was exactly the way she should look.

Michelle tucked her white clutch under her arm and walked with him to the car, immensely grateful for the sunglasses covering her eyes. John was a hard-working rancher, but when the occasion demanded he could dress as well as any Philadelphia lawyer. Any clothing looked good on his broad-shouldered, slim-hipped frame, but the severe gray suit he wore seemed to heighten his masculinity instead of restraining it. All hint of waviness had been brushed from his black hair. Instead of his usual pickup truck he was driving a dark gray two-seater Mercedes, a sleek beauty that made her think of the Porsche she had sold to raise money after her father had died.

"You said your men were going to help me," she said expressionlessly as he turned the car onto the highway several minutes later. "You didn't say they were going to take over."

He'd put on sunglasses, too, because the morning sun was glaring, and the dark lenses hid the probing look he directed at her stiff profile. "They're going to do the heavy work."

"After the fencing is repaired and the cattle are moved to the east pasture, I can handle things from there."

"What about dipping, castrating, branding, all the things that should've been done in the spring? You can't handle that. You don't have any horses, any men, and you sure as hell can't rope and throw a young bull from that old truck you've got."

Her slender hands clenched in her lap. Why did he have to be so right? She couldn't do any of those things, but neither could she be content as a useless ornament. "I know I can't do those things by myself, but I can help."

"I'll think about it," he answered noncommittally, but he knew there was no way in hell he'd let her. What could she do? It was hard, dirty, smelly, bloody work. The only thing she was physically strong enough to do was brand calves, and he didn't think she could stomach the smell or the frantic struggles of the terrified little animals.

"It's my ranch," she reminded him, ice in her tone. "Either I help, or the deal's off."

John didn't say anything. There was no point in

arguing. He simply wasn't going to let her do it, and that was that. He'd handle her when the time came, but he didn't expect much of a fight. When she saw what was involved, she wouldn't want any part of it. Besides, she couldn't possibly like the hard work she'd been doing; he figured she was just too proud to back down now.

It was a long drive to Tampa, and half an hour passed without a word between them. Finally she said, "You used to make fun of my expensive little cars."

He knew she was referring to the sleek Mercedes, and he grunted. Personally, he preferred his pickup. When it came down to it, he was a cattle rancher and not much else, but he was damned good at what he did, and his tastes weren't expensive. "Funny thing about bankers," he said by way of explanation. "If they think you don't need the money all that badly, they're eager to loan it to you. Image counts. This thing is part of the image."

"And the members of your rotating harem prefer it, too, I bet," she gibed. "Going out on the town lacks something when you do it in a pickup."

"I don't know about that. Ever done it in a pickup?" he asked softly, and even through the dark glasses she could feel the impact of his glance.

"I'm sure *you* have."

"Not since I was fifteen." He chuckled, ignoring the biting coldness of her comment. "But a pickup never was your style, was it?"

"No," she murmured, leaning her head back. Some of her dates had driven fancy sports cars, some had driven souped-up Fords and Chevys, but it hadn't made any difference what they'd driven, because she hadn't made out with any of them. They had been nice boys, most of them, but none of them had been John Rafferty, so it hadn't mattered. He was the only man she'd ever wanted. Perhaps if she'd been older when she'd met him, or if she'd been secure enough in her own sexuality, things might have been different. What would have happened if she hadn't initiated those long years of hostility in an effort to protect herself from an attraction too strong for her to handle? What if she'd tried to get him interested in her, instead of warding him off?

Nothing, she thought tiredly. John wouldn't have wasted his time with a naive eighteen-year-old. Maybe later, when she'd graduated from college, the situation might have changed, but instead of coming home after graduation she had gone to Philadelphia...and met Roger.

They were out of the lawyer's office by noon; it hadn't been a long meeting. The land would be surveyed, the deed drawn up, and John's ranch would increase by quite a bit, while hers would shrink, but she' was grateful that he'd come up with that solution. At least now she still had a chance.

His hand curled warmly around her elbow as they walked out to the car. "Let's have lunch. I'm too hungry to wait until we get home."

She was hungry, too, and the searing heat made her feel lethargic. She murmured in agreement as she fumbled for her sunglasses, missing the satisfied smile that briefly curled his mouth. John opened the car door and held it as she got in, his eyes lingering on the length of silken leg exposed by the movement. She promptly restored her skirt to its proper position and crossed her legs as she settled in the seat, giving him a questioning glance when he continued to stand in the open door. "Is something wrong?"

"No." He closed the door and walked around the car. Not unless she counted the way looking at her made him so hot that a deep ache settled in his loins. She couldn't move without making him think of making love to her. When she crossed her legs, he thought of uncrossing them. When she pulled her skirt down, he thought of pulling it up. When she leaned back the movement thrust her breasts against her lapels, and he wanted to tear the dress open. Damn, what a dress! It wrapped her modestly, but the silk kissed every soft curve just the way he wanted to do, and all morning long it had been teasing at him that the damned thing was fastened with only those two buttons. Two buttons! He had to have her, he thought savagely. He couldn't wait much longer. He'd already waited ten years, and his patience had ended. It was time.

The restaurant he took her to was a posh favorite of the city's business community, but he didn't worry about needing a reservation. The maître d' knew him, as did most of the people in the room, by sight and reputation if not personally. They were led across the crowded room to a select table by the window.

Michelle had noted the way so many people had watched them. "Well, this is one," she said dryly.

He looked up from the menu. "One what?"

"I've been seen in public with you once. Gossip has

it that any woman seen with you twice is automatically assumed to be sleeping with you."

His mustache twitched as he frowned in annoyance. "Gossip has a way of being exaggerated."

"Usually, yes."

"And in this case?"

"You tell me."

He put the menu aside, his eyes never leaving her. "No matter what gossip says, you won't have to worry about being just another member of a harem. While we're together, you'll be the only woman in my bed."

Her hands shook, and Michelle quickly put her menu on the table to hide that betraying quiver. "You're assuming a lot," she said lightly in an effort to counter-act the heat she could feel radiating from him.

"I'm not assuming anything. I'm planning on it." His voice was flat, filled with masculine certainty. He had reason to be certain; how many women had ever refused him? He projected a sense of overwhelming virility that was at least as seductive as the most expert technique, and from what she'd heard, he had that, too. Just looking at him made a woman wonder, made her begin dreaming about what it would be like to be in bed with him.

"Michelle, darling!"

Michelle couldn't stop herself from flinching at that particular phrase, even though it was spoken in a lilting female voice rather than a man's deeper tones. Quickly she looked around, grateful for the interruption despite the endearment she hated; when she recognized the speaker, gratefulness turned to mere politeness, but her face was so schooled that the approaching woman didn't catch the faint nuances of expression.

"Hello, Bitsy, how are you?" she asked politely as John got to his feet. "This is John Rafferty, my neighbor. John, this is Bitsy Sumner, from Palm Beach. We went to college together."

Bitsy's eyes gleamed as she looked at John, and she held her hand out to him. "I'm so glad to meet you, Mr. Rafferty."

Michelle knew Bitsy wouldn't pick it up, but she saw the dark amusement in John's eyes as he gently took the woman's faultlessly manicured and bejeweled hand in his. Naturally he'd seen the way Bitsy was looking at *him*. It was a look he'd probably been getting since puberty.

"Mrs. Sumner," he murmured, noting the diamond-studded wedding band on her left hand. "Would you like to join us?"

"Only for a moment," Bitsy sighed, slipping into the chair he held out. "My husband and I are here with some business associates and their wives. He says it's good business to socialize with them occasionally, so we flew in this morning. Michelle, dear, I haven't seen you in so long! What are you doing on this side of the state?"

"I live north of here," Michelle replied.

"You must come visit. Someone mentioned just the other day that it had been forever since we'd seen you! We had the most fantastic party at Howard Cassa's villa last month; you should have come."

"I have too much work to do, but thank you for the invitation." She managed to smile at Bitsy, but she understood that Bitsy hadn't been inviting her to visit them personally; it was just something that people said, and probably her old acquaintances were curious about why she had left their circle.

Bitsy shrugged elegantly. "Oh, work, schmurk. Let someone else take care of it for a month or so. You need to have some fun! Come to town, and bring Mr. Rafferty with you." Bitsy's gaze slid back to John, and that unconsciously hungry look crawled into her eyes again. "You'd enjoy it, Mr. Rafferty, I promise. Everyone needs a break from work occasionally, don't you think?"

His brows lifted. "Occasionally."

"What sort of business are you in?"

"Cattle. My ranch adjoins Michelle's."

"Oh, a *rancher*!"

Michelle could tell by Bitsy's fatuous smile that the other woman was lost in the romantic images of cowboys and horses that so many people associated with ranching, ignoring or simply not imagining the backbreaking hard work that went in to building a successful ranch. Or maybe it was the rancher instead of the ranch that made Bitsy look so enraptured. She was looking at John as if she could eat him alive. Michelle put her hands in her lap to hide them because she had to clench her fists in order to resist slapping Bitsy so hard she'd never even think of looking at John Rafferty again.

Fortunately good manners drove Bitsy back to her own table after a few moments. John watched her sway through the tangle of tables, then looked at Michelle with amusement in his eyes. "Who in hell would call a grown woman *Bitsy*?"

It was hard not to share his amusement. "I think her real name is Elizabeth, so Bitsy is fairly reasonable as a nickname. Of course, she was the ultimate preppy in college, so it fits."

"I thought it might be an indication of her brain power," he said caustically; then the waiter approached to take their orders, and John turned his attention to the menu.

Michelle could only be grateful that Bitsy hadn't been able to remain with them. The woman was one of the worst gossips she'd ever met, and she didn't feel up to hearing the latest dirt on every acquaintance they had in common. Bitsy's particular circle of friends were rootless and a little savage in their pursuit of entertainment, and Michelle had always made an effort to keep her distance from them. It hadn't always been possible, but at least she had never been drawn into the center of the crowd.

After lunch John asked if she would mind waiting while he contacted one of his business associates. She started to protest, then remembered that his men were taking care of the cattle today; she had no reason to hurry back, and, in truth, she could use the day off. The physical strain had been telling on her. Besides, this was the most time she'd ever spent in his company, and she was loathe to see the day end. They weren't arguing, and if she ignored his arrogant certainty that they were going to sleep together, the day had really been rather calm. "I don't have to be back at any certain time," she said, willing to let him decide when they would return.

As it happened, it was after dark before they left Tampa. John's meeting had taken up more time than he'd expected, but Michelle hadn't been bored, because he hadn't left her sitting in the reception area. He'd taken her into the meeting with him, and it had been so interesting that she hadn't been aware of the hours slipping past. It was almost six when they finished, and by then John was hungry again; it was another two hours before they were actually on their way.

Michelle sat beside him, relaxed and a little drowsy. John had stayed with coffee, because he was driving, but she'd had two glasses of wine with her meal, and her bones felt mellow. The car was dark, illuminated only by the dash lights, which gave a satanic cast to his hard-planed face, and the traffic on U.S. 19 was light. She snuggled down into the seat, making a comment only when John said something that required an answer.

Soon they ran into a steady rain, and the rhythmic motion of the windshield wipers added to her drowsiness. The windows began to fog, so John turned the air conditioning higher. Michelle sat up, hugging her arms as the cooler air banished her drowsiness. Her silk dress didn't offer much warmth. He glanced at her, then pulled to the side of the road.

"Why are we stopping?"

"Because you're cold." He shrugged out of his suit jacket and draped it around her, enveloping her in the transferred heat and the smell of his body. "We're almost two hours from home, so why don't you take a nap? That wine's getting to you, isn't it?"

"Mmmm." The sound of agreement was distinctly

drowsy. John touched her cheek gently, watching as her eyelids closed, as if her lashes were too heavy for her to hold them open a moment longer. Let her sleep, he thought. She'd be recovered from the wine by the time they got home. His loins tightened. He wanted her awake and responsive when he took her to bed. There was no way he was going to sleep alone tonight. All day long he'd been fighting the need to touch her, to feel her lying against him. For ten years she'd been in his mind, and he wanted her. As difficult and spoiled as she was, he wanted her. Now he understood what made men want to pamper her, probably from the day she'd been placed in her cradle. He'd just taken his place in line, and for his reward he'd have her in his bed, her slim, silky body open for his pleasure. He knew she wanted him; she was resisting him for some reason he couldn't decipher, perhaps only a woman's instinctive hesitance.

Michelle usually didn't sleep well. Her slumber was frequently disturbed by dreams, and she hadn't been able to nap with even her father anywhere nearby. Her subconscious refused to relax if any man was in the vicinity. Roger had once attacked her in the middle of the night, when she'd been soundly asleep, and the trauma of being jerked from a deep, peaceful sleep into a nightmare of violence had in some ways been worse than the pain. Now, just before she slept, she realized with faint surprise that the old uneasiness wasn't there tonight. Perhaps the time had come to heal that particular hurt, too, or perhaps it was that she felt so unutterably safe with John. His coat warmed her; his nearness surrounded her. He had touched her in passion and in anger, but his touch had never brought pain. He tempered his great strength to handle a woman's softness, and she slept, secure in the instinctive knowledge that she was safe.

His deep, dark-velvet voice woke her. "We're home, honey. Put your arms around my neck."

She opened her eyes to see him leaning in the open door of the car, and she gave him a sleepy smile. "I slept all the way, didn't I?"

"Like a baby." He brushed her mouth with his, a brief, warm caress; then his arms slid behind her neck and under her thighs. She gasped as he lifted her, grabbing him around the neck as he'd instructed. It was still raining, but his coat kept most of the dampness from her as he closed the car door and carried her swiftly through the darkness.

"I'm awake now; I could've walked," she protested, her heart beginning a slow, heavy thumping as she responded to his nearness. He carried her so easily, leaping up the steps to the porch as if she weighed no more than a child.

"I know," he murmured, lifting her a little so he could bury his face in the curve of her neck. Gently he nuzzled her jaw, drinking in the sweet, warm fragrance of her skin. "Mmmm, you smell good. Are you clear from the wine yet?"

The caress was so tender that it completely failed to alarm her. Rather, she felt coddled, and the feeling of utter safety persisted. He shifted her in his arms to open the door, then turned sideways to carry her through.

Had he thought she was drunk? "I was just sleepy, not tipsy," she clarified.

"Good," he whispered, pushing the door closed and blocking out the sound of the light rain, enveloping them in the dark silence of the house. She couldn't see anything, but he was warm and solid against her, and it didn't matter that she couldn't see. Then his mouth was on hers, greedy and demanding, convincing her lips to open and accept the shape of his, accept the inward thrust of his tongue. He kissed her with burning male hunger, as if he wanted to draw all the sweetness and breath out of her to make it his own, as if the need was riding him so hard that he couldn't get close enough. She couldn't help responding to that need, clinging to him and kissing him back with a sudden wildness, because the very rawness of his male hunger called out to everything in her that was female and ignited her own fires.

He hit the light switch with his elbow, throwing on the foyer light and illuminating the stairs to the right. He lifted his mouth briefly, and she stared up at him in the dim light, her senses jolting at the hard, grim expression on his face, the way his skin had tightened across his cheekbones. "I'm staying here tonight," he muttered harshly, starting up the stairs with her still in his arms. "This has been put off long enough."

He wasn't going to stop; she could see it in his face. She didn't want him to stop. Every pore in her body cried out for him, drowning out the small voice of caution that warned against getting involved with a heartbreaker like John Rafferty. Maybe it had been a useless struggle anyway; it had always been between them, this burning hunger that now flared out of control.

His mouth caught hers again as he carried her up the stairs, his muscle-corded arms holding her weight easily. Michelle yielded to the kiss, sinking against him. Her blood was singing through her veins, heating her, making her breasts harden with the need for his touch. An empty ache made her whimper, because it was an ache that only he could fill.

He'd been in the house a lot over the years, so the location of her room was no mystery to him. He carried her inside and laid her on the bed, following her down to press her into the mattress with his full weight. Michelle almost cried out from the intense pleasure of feeling him cover her with his body. His arm stretched over her head, and he snapped on one of the bedside lamps; he looked at her, and his black eyes filled with masculine satisfaction as he saw the glaze of passion in her slumberous eyes, the trembling of her pouty, kiss-stung lips.

Slowly, deliberately, he levered his knee between hers and spread her legs, then settled his hips into the cradle formed by her thighs. She inhaled sharply as she felt his hardness through the layers of their clothing. Their eyes met, and she knew he'd known before the day even began that he would end it in her bed. He was tired of waiting, and he was going to have her. He'd been patient all day, gentling her by letting her get accustomed to his presence, but now his patience was at an end, and he knew she had no resistance left to offer him. All she had was need.

"You're mine." He stated his possession baldly, his voice rough and low. He raised his weight on one elbow, and with his free hand unbuttoned the two buttons at her waist, spreading the dress open with the deliberate air of a man unwrapping a gift he'd wanted for a long time. The silk caught at her hips, pinned by his own weight. He lifted his hips and pushed the edges of the dress open, baring her legs, then resettled himself against her.

He felt as if his entire body would explode as he looked at her. She had worn neither bra nor slip; the silk dress was lined, hiding from him all day the fact that the only things she had on beneath that wisp of fabric were her panty hose and a minute scrap of lace masquerading as panties. If he'd known that her breasts were bare under her dress, there was no way he could have kept himself from pulling those lapels apart and touching, tasting, nor could he stop himself now. Her breasts were high and round, the skin satiny, her coral-colored nipples small and already tightly beaded. With a rough sound he bent his head and sucked strongly at her, drawing her nipple into his mouth and molding his lips to that creamy, satiny flesh. He cupped her other breast in his hand, gently kneading it and rubbing the nipple with his thumb. A high, gasping cry tore from her throat, and she arched against his mouth, her hands digging into his dark hair to press his head into her. Her breasts were so firm they were almost hard, and the firmness excited him even more. He had to taste the other one, surround himself with the sweet headiness of her scent and skin.

Slowly Michelle twisted beneath him, plucking now at the back of his shirt in an effort to get rid of the fabric between them. She needed to feel the heat and power of his bare skin under her hands, against her body, but his mouth on her breasts was driving her mad with pleasure, and she couldn't control herself enough to strip the shirt away. Every stroke of his tongue sent wildfire running along her nerves, from her nipples to her loins, and she was helpless to do anything but feel.

Then he left her, rising up on his knees to tear at his shirt and throw it aside. His shoes, socks, pants and underwear followed, flung blindly away from the bed, and he knelt naked between her spread thighs. He stripped her panty hose and panties away, leaving her open and vulnerable to his penetration.

For the first time, she felt fear. It had been so long for her, and sex hadn't been good in her marriage anyway. John leaned over her, spreading her legs further, and she felt the first shock of his naked flesh as he positioned himself for entry. He was so big, his muscled body dominating her smaller, softer one completely. She knew from harsh experience how helpless a woman was against a man's much greater strength; John was stronger than most, bigger than most, and he was intent on the sexual act as males have been from the beginning of time. He was quintessentially male, the sum and substance of masculine aggression and sexuality. Panic welled in her, and her slim, delicate hand pressed against him, her fingers sliding into the curling dark hair that covered his chest. The black edges of fear were coming closer.

Her voice was thready, begging for reassurance. "John? Don't hurt me, please."

He froze, braced over her on the threshold of entry. Her warm, sweet body beckoned him, moistly ready for him, but her eyes were pleading. Did she expect pain? Good God, who could have hurt her? The seeds of fury formed deep in his mind, shunted aside for now by the screaming urges of his body. For now, he had to have her. "No, baby," he said gently, his dark voice so warm with tenderness that the fear in her eyes faded. "I won't hurt you."

He slid one arm under her, leaning on that elbow and raising her so her nipples were buried in the hair on his chest. Again he heard that small intake of breath from her, an unconscious sound of pleasure. Their eyes locked, hers misty and soft, his like black fire, as he tightened his buttocks and very slowly, very carefully, began to enter her.

Michelle shuddered as great ripples of pleasure washed through her, and her legs climbed his to wrap around his hips. A soft, wild cry tore from her throat, and she shoved her hand against her mouth to stifle the sound. Still his black eyes burned down at her. "No," he whispered. "Take your hand away. I want to hear you, baby. Let me hear how good it feels to you."

Still there was that slow, burning push deep into her, her flesh quivering as she tried to accommodate him. Panic seized her again. "Stop! John, please, no more! You're…I can't…"

"Shh, shh," he soothed, kissing her mouth, her eyes, nibbling at the velvety lobes of her ears. "It's okay, baby, don't worry. I won't hurt you." He continued soothing her with kisses and soft murmurs, and though every instinct in him screamed to bury himself in her to the hilt, he clamped down on those urges with iron control. There was no way he was going to hurt her, not with the fear he'd seen in the misty green depths of her eyes. She was so delicate and silky, and so tight around him that he could feel the gentle pulsations of adjustment. His eyes closed as pure pleasure shuddered through him.

She was aroused, but not enough. He set about exciting her with all the sensual skill he possessed, holding her mouth with deep kisses while his hands gently stroked her, and he began moving slowly inside her. So slow, holding himself back, keeping his strokes shallow even though every movement wrung new degrees of ecstasy from him. He wanted her mindless with need.

Michelle felt her control slipping away by degrees, and she didn't care. Control didn't matter, nothing mattered but the heat that was consuming her body and mind, building until all sense of self was gone and she was nothing but a female body, twisting and surging beneath the overpowering male. A powerful tension had her in its grip, tightening, combining with the heat as it swept her inexorably along. She was burning alive, writhing helplessly, wild little pleading sobs welling up and escaping. John took them into his own mouth, then put his hand between their bodies, stroking her. She trembled for a moment on the crest of a great wave; then she was submerged in exploding sensation. He held her safely, her heaving body locked in his arms while he thrust deeply, giving her all the pleasure he could.

When it was over she was limp and sobbing, drenched with both her sweat and his. "I didn't know," she said brokenly, and tears tracked down her face. He murmured to her, holding her tightly for a moment, but he was deep inside her now, and he couldn't hold back any longer. Sliding his hands beneath her hips, he lifted her up to receive his deep, powerful thrusts.

Now it was she who held him, cradling him in her body and with her arms tight around him; he cried out, a deep, hoarse sound, blind and insensible to everything but the great, flooding force of his pleasure.

It was quiet for a long time afterward. John lay on top of her, so sated and relaxed that he couldn't tolerate the idea of moving, of separating his flesh from hers. It wasn't until she stirred, gasping a little for breath, that he raised himself on his elbows and looked down at her.

Intense satisfaction, mingled with both gentleness and a certain male arrogance, was written on his face as he leaned above her. He smoothed her tangled hair back from her face, stroking her cheeks with his fingers. She looked pale and exhausted, but it was the sensuous exhaustion of a woman who has been thoroughly satisfied by her lover. He traced the shape of her elegant cheekbones with his lips, his tongue dipping out to sneak tastes that sent little ripples of arousal through him again.

Then he lifted his head again, curiosity burning in his eyes. "You've never enjoyed it before, have you?"

A quick flush burned her cheeks, and she turned her

head on the pillow, staring fixedly at the lamp. "I suppose that does wonders for your ego."

She was withdrawing from him, and that was the last thing he wanted. He decided to drop the subject for the time being, but there were still a lot of questions that he intended to have answered. Right now she was in his arms, warm and weak from his lovemaking, just the way he was going to keep her until she became used to his possession and accepted it as fact.

She was his now.

He'd take care of her, even spoil her. Why not? She was made to be pampered and indulged, at least up to a point. She'd been putting up a good fight to work this ranch, and he liked her guts, but she wasn't cut out for that type of life. Once she realized that she didn't have to fight anymore, that he was going to take care of her, she'd settle down and accept it as the natural order of things.

He didn't have money to waste on fancy trips, or to drape her in jewels, but he could keep her in comfort and security. Not only that, he could guarantee that the sheets on their bed would stay hot. Even now, so soon after having her, he felt the hunger and need returning.

Without a word he began again, drawing her down with him into a dark whirlpool of desire and satisfaction. Michelle's eyes drifted shut, her body arching in his arms. She had known instinctively, years ago, that it would be like this, that even her identity would be swamped with the force of his passion. In his arms she lost herself and became only his woman.

Chapter Five

Michelle woke early, just as the first gray light of dawn was creeping into the room. The little sleep she'd gotten had been deep and dreamless for a change, but she was used to sleeping alone; the unaccustomed presence of a man in her bed had finally nudged her awake. A stricken look edged into her eyes as she looked over at him, sprawled on his stomach with one arm curled under the pillow and the other arm draped across her naked body.

How easy she'd been for him. The knowledge ate at her as she gingerly slipped from the bed, taking care not to wake him. He might sleep for hours yet; he certainly hadn't had much sleep during the night.

Her legs trembled as she stood, the soreness in her thighs and deep in her body providing yet another reminder of the past night, as if she needed any further confirmation of her memory. Four times. He'd taken her four times, and each time it had seemed as if the pleasure intensified. Even now she couldn't believe how her body had responded to him, soaring wildly out of her control. But he'd controlled himself, and her, holding her to the rhythm he set in order to prolong their lovemaking. Now she knew that all the talk about him hadn't been exaggerated; both his virility and his skill had been, if anything, underrated.

Somehow she had to come to terms with the unpleasant fact that she had allowed herself to become the latest of his one-night stands. The hardest fact to face wasn't that she'd been so easily seduced, but her own piercing regret that such ecstasy wouldn't last. Oh, he might come back…but he wouldn't stay. In time he'd become bored with her and turn his predatory gaze on some other woman just as he always had before.

And she'd go on loving him, just as she had before.

Quietly she got clean underwear from the dresser and her bathrobe from the adjoining bath, but she went to the bathroom down the hall to take a shower. She didn't want the sound of running water to awaken him. Right now she needed time to herself, time to gather her composure before she faced him again. She didn't know what to say, how to act.

The stinging hot water eased some of the soreness from her muscles, though a remaining ache reminded her of John's strength with every step she took. After showering she went down to the kitchen and started brewing a fresh pot of coffee. She was leaning against the cabinets, watching the dark brew drip into the pot, when the sound of motors caught her attention. Turning to look out the window, she saw the two pickup trucks from John's ranch pull into the yard. The same men who had been there the day before got out; one noticed John's car parked in front of the house and poked his buddy in the ribs, pointing. Even from that distance Michelle could hear the muffled male laughter, and she didn't need any help imagining their comments. The boss had scored again. It would be all over the county within twenty-four hours. In the manner of men everywhere, they were both proud and slightly envious of their boss's sexual escapades, and they'd tell the tale over and over again.

Numbly she turned back to watch the coffee dripping; when it finished, she filled a big mug, then wrapped her cold fingers around the mug to warm them. It had to be nerves making her hands so cold. Quietly she went upstairs to look into her bedroom, wondering if he would still be sleeping.

He wasn't, though evidently he'd awoken only seconds before. He propped himself up on one elbow and ran his hand through his tousled black hair, narrowing his eyes as he returned her steady gaze. Her heart lurched painfully. He looked like a ruffian, with his hair tousled, his jaw darkened by the overnight growth of beard, his bare torso brown and roped with the steely muscles that were never found on a businessman. She didn't know what she'd hoped to see in his expression: desire, possibly, even affection. But whatever she'd wanted to see wasn't there. Instead his face was as hard as always, measuring her with that narrowed gaze that made her feel like squirming. She could feel him waiting for her to move, to say something.

Her legs were jerky, but she managed not to spill the coffee as she walked into the room. Her voice was only slightly strained. "Congratulations. All the gossip doesn't give you due credit. My, my, you're really something when you decide to score; I didn't even think of saying no. Now you can go home and put another notch in your bedpost."

His eyes narrowed even more. He sat up, ignoring the way the sheet fell below his waist, and held out his hand for the coffee mug. When she gave it to him, he turned it and drank from the place where she'd been sipping, then returned it to her, his eyes never leaving hers.

"Sit down."

She flinched a little at his hard, raspy, early-morning voice. He saw the small movement and reached out to take her wrist, making coffee lap alarmingly close to the rim of the mug. Gently but inexorably he drew her down to sit facing him on the edge of the bed.

He kept his hand on her wrist, his callused thumb rubbing over the fine bones and delicate tracery of veins. "Just for the record, I don't notch bedposts. Is that what's got your back up this morning?"

She gave a small defensive shrug, not meeting his eyes.

She'd withdrawn from him again; his face was grim as he watched her, trying to read her expression. He remembered the fear in her last night, and he wondered who'd put it there. White-hot embers of rage began to flicker to life at the thought of some bastard abusing her in bed, hurting her. Women were vulnerable when they made love, and Michelle especially wouldn't have the strength to protect herself. He had to get her to talk, or she'd close up on him completely. "It had been a long time for you, hadn't it?"

Again she gave that little shrug, as if hiding behind the movement. Again he probed, watching her face. "You didn't enjoy sex before." He made it a statement, not a question.

Finally her eyes darted to his, wary and resentful. "What do you want, a recommendation? You know that was the first time I'd...enjoyed it."

"Why didn't you like it before?"

"Maybe I just needed to go to bed with a stud," she said flippantly.

"Hell, don't give me that," he snapped, disgusted. "Who hurt you? Who made you afraid of sex?"

"I'm not afraid," she denied, disturbed by the idea that she might have let Roger warp her to such an extent. "It was just...well, it had been so long, and you're a big man...." Her voice trailed off, and abruptly she flushed, her gaze sliding away from him.

He watched her thoughtfully; considering what he'd learned about her last night and this morning, it was nothing short of a miracle that she hadn't knocked his proposal and half his teeth down his throat when he'd suggested she become his mistress as payment of the debt. It also made him wonder if her part in the breakup of Mike Webster's marriage hadn't been blown out of all proportion; after all, a

woman who didn't enjoy making love wasn't likely
to be fast and easy.

It was pure possessiveness, but he was glad no other
man had pleased her the way he had; it gave him a hold
on her, a means of keeping her by his side. He would
use any weapon he had, because during the night he had
realized that there was no way he could let her go. She
could be haughty, bad-tempered and stubborn; she
could too easily be spoiled and accept it as her due,
though he'd be damned if he hadn't almost decided it
was her due. She was proud and difficult, trying to
build a stone wall around herself to keep him at a
distance, like a princess holding herself aloof from the
peasants, but he couldn't get enough of her. When they
were making love, it wasn't the princess and the peasant
any longer; they were a man and his woman, writhing
and straining together, moaning with ecstasy. He'd
never been so hungry for a woman before, so hot that
he'd felt nothing and no one could have kept him away
from her.

She seemed to think last night had been a casual
thing on his part, that sunrise had somehow ended it.
She was in for a surprise. Now that she'd given herself
to him, he wasn't going to let her go. He'd learned how
to fight for and keep what was his, but his single-
minded striving over the years to build the ranch into
one of the biggest cattle ranches in Florida was nothing
compared to the intense possessiveness he felt for
Michelle.

Finally he released her wrist, and she stood immediately, moving away from him. She sipped at the

coffee she still held, and her eyes went to the window. "Your men got a big kick out of seeing your car still here this morning. I didn't realize they'd be back, since they put up the fencing yesterday."

Indifferent to his nakedness, he threw the sheet back and got out of bed. "They didn't finish. They'll do the rest of the job today, then move the herd to the east pasture tomorrow." He waited, then said evenly, "It bothers you that they know?"

"Being snickered about over a beer bothers me. It polishes up your image a little more, but all I'll be is the most recent in a long line of one-nighters for you."

"Well, everyone will know differently when you move in with me, won't they?" he asked arrogantly, walking into the bathroom. "How long will it take you to pack?"

Stunned, Michelle whirled to stare at him, but he'd already disappeared into the bathroom. The sound of the shower came on. Move in with him? If there was any limit to his gall, she hadn't seen it yet! She sat down on the edge of the bed, watching the bathroom door and waiting for him to emerge as she fought the uneasy feeling of sliding further and further down a precipitous slope. Control of her own life was slipping from her hands, and she didn't know if she could stop it. It wasn't just that John was so domineering, though he was; the problem was that, despite how much she wished it were different, she was weak where he was concerned. She wanted to be able to simply walk into his arms and let them lock around her, to rest against him and let him handle everything. She was so tired, physically and mentally. But if she let him take over completely, what would happen when he became bored with her? She would be right back where she'd started, but with a broken heart added to her problems.

The shower stopped running. An image of him formed in her mind, powerfully muscled, naked, dripping wet. Drying himself with her towels. Filling her bathroom with his male scent and presence. He wouldn't look diminished or foolish in her very feminine rose-and-white bathroom, nor would it bother him that he'd bathed with perfumed soap. He was so intensely masculine that female surroundings merely accentuated that masculinity.

She began to tremble, thinking of the things he'd done during the night, the way he'd made her feel. She hadn't known her body could take over like that, that she could revel in being possessed, and despite the outdated notion that a man could physically "possess" a woman, that was what had happened. She felt it, instinctively and deeply, the sensation sinking into her bones.

He sauntered from the bathroom wearing only a towel hitched low on his hips, the thick velvety fabric contrasting whitely with the bronzed darkness of his abdomen. His hair and mustache still gleamed wetly; a few drops of moisture glistened on his wide shoulders and in the curls that darkened his broad chest. Her mouth went dry. His body hair followed the tree of life pattern, with the tufts under his arms and curls across his chest, then the narrowing line that ran down his abdomen before spreading again at his groin. He was as superbly built as a triathlete, and she actually ached to touch him, to run her palms all over him.

He gave her a hard, level look. "Stop stalling and get packed."

"I'm not going." She tried to sound strong about it; if her voice lacked the volume she'd wanted, at least it was even.

"You'll be embarrassed if you don't have anything on besides that robe when I carry you into my house," he warned quietly.

"John—" She stopped, then made a frustrated motion with her hand. "I don't want to get involved with you."

"It's a little late to worry about that now," he pointed out.

"I know," she whispered. "Last night shouldn't have happened."

"Damn it to hell, woman, it should've happened a long time ago." Irritated, he dropped the towel to the floor and picked up his briefs. "Moving in with me is the only sensible thing to do. I normally work twelve hours a day, sometimes more. Sometimes I'm up all night. Then there's the paperwork to do in the evenings; hell, you know what it takes to run a ranch. When would I get over to see you? Once a week? I'll be damned if I'll settle for an occasional quickie."

"What about *my* ranch? Who'll take care of it while I make myself convenient to you whenever you get the urge?"

He gave a short bark of laughter. "Baby, if you lay down every time I got the urge, you'd spend the next year on your back. I get hard every time I look at you."

Involuntarily her eyes dropped down his body, and a wave of heat washed over her when she saw the proof of his words swelling against the white fabric of his underwear. She jerked her gaze away, swallowing to relieve the dry tightness of her throat. "I have to take care of my ranch," she repeated stubbornly, as if they were magic words that would keep him at bay.

He pulled on his pants, impatience deepening the lines that bracketed his mouth. "I'll take care of both ranches. Face facts, Michelle. You need help. You can't do it on your own."

"Maybe not, but I need to try. Don't you understand?" Desperation edged into her tone. "I've never had a job, never done anything to support myself, but I'm trying to learn. You're stepping right into Dad's shoes and taking over, handling everything yourself, but what happens to me when you get bored and move on to the next woman? I still won't know how to support myself!"

John paused in the act of zipping his pants, glaring at her. Damn it, what did she think he'd do, toss her out the door with a casual, "It's been fun, but I'm tired of you now?" He'd make certain she was on her feet, that the ranch was functioning on a profitable basis, if the day ever came when he looked at her and *didn't* want her. He couldn't imagine it. The desire for her consumed him like white-burning fire, sometimes banked, but never extinguished, heating his body and mind. He'd wanted her when she was eighteen and too young to handle him, and he wanted her now.

He controlled his anger and merely said, "I'll take care of you."

She gave him a tight little smile. "Sure." In her experience, people looked after themselves. Roger's parents had protected him to keep his slipping sanity from casting scandal on *their* family name. Her own father, as loving as he'd been, had ignored her plea for help because he didn't like to think his daughter was unhappy; it was more comfortable for him to decide she'd been exaggerating. The complaint she'd filed had disappeared because some judge had thought it would be advantageous to make friends with the powerful Beckmans. Roger's housekeeper had looked the other way because she liked her cushy well-paid job. Michelle didn't blame them, but she'd learned not to expect help, or to trust her life to others.

John snatched his shirt from the floor, his face dark with fury. "Do you want a written agreement?"

Tiredly she rubbed her forehead. He wasn't used to anyone refusing to obey him whenever he barked out an order. If she said yes, she would be confirming what he'd thought of her in the beginning, that her body could be bought. Maybe he even wanted her to say yes; then she'd be firmly under his control, bought and paid for. But all she said was, "No, that isn't what I want."

"Then what, damn it?"

Just his love. To spend the rest of her life with him. That was all.

She might as well wish for the moon.

"I want to do it on my own."

The harshness faded from his face. "You can't." Knowledge gave the words a finality that lashed at her.

"I can try."

The hell of it was, he had to respect the need to try, even though nature and logic said she wouldn't succeed. She wasn't physically strong enough to do what had to be done, and she didn't have the financial resources; she'd started out in a hole so deep that she'd been doomed to fail from the beginning. She would wear herself to the bone, maybe even get hurt, but in the end it would come full circle and she would need someone to take care of her. All he could do was wait, try to watch out for her, and be there to step in when everything caved in around her. By then she'd be glad to lean on a strong shoulder, to take the place in life she'd been born to occupy.

But he wasn't going to step back and let her pretend nothing had happened between them the night before. She was his now, and she had to understand that before he left. The knowledge had to be burned into her flesh the way it was burned into his, and maybe it would take a lesson in broad daylight for her to believe it. He dropped his shirt and slowly unzipped his pants, watching her. When he left, he'd leave his touch on her body and his taste in her mouth, and she'd feel him, taste him, think of him every time she climbed into this bed without him.

Her green eyes widened, and color bloomed on her cheekbones. Nervously she glanced at the bed, then back at him.

His heart began slamming heavily against his rib cage. He wanted to feel the firmness of her breasts in his hands again, feel her nipples harden in his mouth. She whispered his name as he dropped his pants and came toward her, putting his hands on her waist, which was so slender that he felt he might break her in two if he wasn't careful.

As he bent toward her, Michelle's head fell back as if it were too heavy for her neck to support. He instantly took advantage of her vulnerable throat, his mouth burning a path down its length. She had wanted to deny the force of what had happened, but her body was responding feverishly to him, straining against him in search of the mindless ecstasy he'd given her before. She no longer had the protection of ignorance. He was addictive, and she'd already become hooked. As he took her down to the bed, covering her with his heated nakedness, she didn't even think of denying him, or herself.

Are you on the pill?
No.
Damn. Then, *How long until your next period?*
Soon. Don't worry. The timing isn't right.
Famous last words. You'd better get a prescription.
I can't take the pill. I've tried; it makes me throw up all day long. Just like being pregnant.
Then we'll do something else. Do you want to take care of it, or do you want me to?

The remembered conversation kept replaying in her mind; he couldn't have made it plainer that he considered the relationship to be an ongoing one. He had been so matter-of-fact that it hadn't registered on her until later, but now she realized her acquiescent "I will" had acknowledged and accepted his right to make love to her. It hadn't hit her until he'd kissed her and had driven away that his eyes had been gleaming with satisfaction that had nothing to do with being physically sated.

She had some paperwork to do and forced herself to concentrate on it, but that only brought more problems to mind. The stack of unpaid bills was growing, and she didn't know how much longer she could hold her creditors off. They needed their money, too. She needed to fatten the cattle before selling them, but she didn't have the money for grain. Over and over she tried to estimate how much feed would cost, balanced against how much extra she could expect from the sale of heavier cattle. An experienced rancher would have known, but all she had to go on were the records her father had kept, and she didn't know how accurate they were. Her father had been wildly enthusiastic about his ranch, but he'd relied on his foreman's advice to run it.

She could ask John, but he'd use it as another chance to tell her that she couldn't do it on her own.

The telephone rang, and she answered it absently.

"Michelle, darling."

The hot rush of nausea hit her stomach, and she jabbed the button, disconnecting the call. Her hands were shaking as she replaced the receiver. Why wouldn't he leave her alone? It had been two years! Surely he'd had time to get over his sick obsession; surely his parents had gotten him some sort of treatment!

The telephone rang again, the shrill tone filling her ears over and over. She counted the rings in a kind of frozen agony, wondering when he'd give up, or if her nerves would give out first. What if he just let it keep ringing? She'd have to leave the house or go screaming mad. On the eighteenth ring, she answered.

"Darling, don't hang up on me again, please," Roger whispered. "I love you so much. I have to talk to you or go crazy."

They were the words of a lover, but she was shaking with cold. Roger was already crazy. How many times had he whispered love words to her only moments after a burst of rage, when she was stiff with terror, her body already aching from a blow? But then he'd be sorry that he'd hurt her, and he'd tell her over and over how much he loved her and couldn't live without her.

Her lips were so stiff that she could barely form the words. "Please leave me alone. I don't want to talk to you."

"You don't mean that. You know I love you. No one has ever loved you as much as I do."

"I'm sorry," she managed.

"Why are you sorry?"

"I'm not going to talk to you, Roger. I'm going to hang up."

"Why can't you talk? Is someone there with you?"

Her hand froze, unable to remove the receiver from her ear and drop it onto its cradle. Like a rabbit numbed by a snake's hypnotic stare, she waited without breathing for what she knew was coming.

"Michelle! Is someone there with you?"

"No," she whispered. "I'm alone."

"You're lying! That's why you won't talk to me. Your lover is there with you, listening to every word you're saying."

Helplessly she listened to the rage building in his voice, knowing nothing she said would stop it, but unable to keep herself from trying. "I promise you, I'm alone."

To her surprise he fell silent, though she could hear his quickened breath over the wire as clearly as if he were standing next to her. "All right, I'll believe you. If you'll come back to me, I'll believe you."

"I can't—"

"There's someone else, isn't there? I always knew there was. I couldn't catch you, but I always knew!"

"No. There's no one. I'm here all alone, working in Dad's study." She spoke quickly, closing her eyes at the lie. It was the literal truth, that she was alone, but it was still a lie. There had always been someone else deep in her heart, buried at the back of her mind.

Suddenly his voice was shaking. "I couldn't stand it if you loved someone else, darling. I just couldn't. Swear to me that you're alone."

"I swear it." Desperation cut at her. "I'm completely alone, I swear!"

"I love you," Roger whispered, and hung up.

Wildly she ran for the bathroom, where she retched until she was empty and her stomach muscles ached from heaving. She couldn't take this again; she would have the phone number changed, keep it unlisted. Leaning against the basin, she wiped her face with a wet cloth and stared at her bloodless reflection in the mirror. She didn't have the money to pay for having her number changed and taken off the listing.

A shaky bubble of laughter escaped her trembling

lips. The way things were going, the phone service would be disconnected soon because she couldn't pay her bill. That would certainly take care of the problem; Roger couldn't call if she didn't have a telephone. Maybe being broke had some advantages after all.

She didn't know what she'd do if Roger came down here personally to take her back to Philadelphia where she "belonged." If she'd ever "belonged" any one place, it was here, because John was here. Maybe she couldn't go to the symphony, or go skiing in Switzerland, or shopping in Paris. It didn't matter now and hadn't mattered then. All those things were nice, but unimportant. Paying bills was important. Taking care of the cattle was important.

Roger was capable of anything. Part of him was so civilized that it was truly difficult to believe he could be violent. People who'd known him all his life thought he was one of the nicest men walking the face of the earth. And he could be, but there was another part of him that flew into insanely jealous rages.

If he came down here, if she had to see him again…if he touched her in even the smallest way…she knew she couldn't handle it.

The last time had been the worst.

His parents had been in Europe. Roger had accepted an invitation for them to attend a dinner party with a few of his business associates and clients. Michelle had been extremely careful all during the evening not to say or do anything that could be considered flirtatious, but it hadn't been enough. On the way home, Roger had started the familiar catechism: She'd smiled a lot at

Mr. So-and-So; had he propositioned her? He had, hadn't he? Why didn't she just admit it? He'd seen the looks passing between them.

By the time they'd arrived home, Michelle had been braced to run, if necessary, but Roger had settled down in the den to brood. She'd gone to bed, so worn out from mingled tension and relief that she'd drifted to sleep almost immediately.

Then, suddenly, the light had gone on and he'd been there, his face twisted with rage as he yelled at her. Terrified, screaming, stunned by being jerked from a sound sleep, she'd fought him when he jerked her half off the bed and began tearing at her nightgown, but she'd been helpless against him. He'd stripped the gown away and begun lashing at her with his belt, the buckle biting into her flesh again and again.

By the time he'd quit, she had been covered with raw welts and a multitude of small, bleeding cuts from the buckle, and she'd screamed so much she could no longer make a sound. Her eyes had been almost swollen shut from crying. She could still remember the silence as he'd stood there by the bed, breathing hard as he looked down at her. Then he'd fallen on his knees, burying his face in her tangled hair. "I love you so much," he'd said.

That night, while he'd slept, she had crept out and taken a cab to a hospital emergency room. Two years had passed, but the small white scars were still visible on her back, buttocks and upper thighs. They would fade with time, becoming impossible to see, but the scar left on her mind by the sheer terror of that night hadn't faded at all. The demons she feared all wore Roger's face.

But now she couldn't run from him; she had no other place to go, no other place where she wanted to be. She was legally free of him now, and there was nothing he could do to make her return. Legally she could stop him from calling her. He was harassing her; she could get a court order prohibiting him from contacting her in any way.

But she wouldn't, unless he forced her to it. She opened her eyes and stared at herself again. Oh, it was classic. A counselor at the hospital had even talked with her about it. She didn't want anyone to know her husband had abused her; it would be humiliating, as if it were somehow her fault. She didn't want people to pity her, she didn't want them to talk about her, and she especially didn't want John to know. It was too ugly, and she felt ashamed.

Suddenly she felt the walls closing in on her, stifling her. She had to get out and *do* something, or she might begin crying, and she didn't want that to happen. If she started crying now, she wouldn't be able to stop.

She got in the old truck and drove around the pastures, looking at the new sections of fence John's men had put up. They had finished and returned to their regular chores. Tomorrow they'd ride over on horseback and move the herd to this pasture with its high, thick growth of grass. The cattle could get their fill without walking so much, and they'd gain weight.

As she neared the house again she noticed how high the grass and weeds had gotten in the yard. It was so bad she might need to move the herd to the yard to graze instead of to the pasture. Yard work had come in a poor second to all the other things that had needed doing, but now, thanks to John, she had both the time and energy to do something about it.

She got out the lawnmower and pushed it up and down the yard, struggling to force it through the high grass. Little green mounds piled up in neat rows behind her. When that was finished, she took a knife from the kitchen and hacked down the weeds that had grown up next to the house. The physical activity acted like a sedative, blunting the edge of fear and finally abolishing it altogether. She didn't have any reason to be afraid; Roger wasn't going to do anything.

Subconsciously she dreaded going to bed that night, wondering if she would spend the night dozing, only to jerk awake every few moments, her heart pounding with fear as she waited for her particular demon to leap screaming out of the darkness and drag her out of bed. She didn't want to let Roger have that kind of power over her, but memories of that night still nagged at the edges of her mind. Someday she would be free of him. She swore it; she promised it to herself.

When she finally went reluctantly up the stairs and paused in the doorway to her delicately feminine room, she was overcome by a wave of memories that made her shake. She hadn't expected this reaction; she'd been thinking of Roger, but it was John who dominated this room. Roger had never set foot in here. John had slept sprawled in that bed. John had showered in that bathroom. The room was filled with his presence.

She had lain beneath him on that bed, twisting and straining with a pleasure so intense that she'd been mindless with it. She remembered the taut, savage look on his face, the gentleness of his hands as he restrained his strength which could too easily bruise a woman's soft skin. Her body tingled as she remembered the way he'd touched her, the places he'd touched her.

Then she realized that John had given her more than pleasure. She hadn't been aware of fearing men, but on some deep level of her mind, she had. In the two years since her divorce she hadn't been out on a date, and she'd managed to disguise the truth from herself by being part of a crowd that included men. Because she'd laughed with them, skied and swam with them—as long as it was a group activity, but never *alone* with a man—she'd been able to tell herself that Roger hadn't warped her so badly after all. She was strong; she could put all that behind her and not blame all men for what one man had done.

She hadn't blamed them, but she'd feared their strength. Though she'd never gone into a panic if a man touched her casually, she hadn't liked it and had always retreated.

Perhaps it would have been that way with John, too, if her long obsession with him hadn't predisposed her to accept his touch. But she'd yearned for him for so long, like a child crying for the moon, that her hunger had overcome her instinctive reluctance.

And he'd been tender, careful, generous in the giving of pleasure. In the future his passion might become rougher, but a bond of physical trust had been forged during the night that would never be broken.

Not once was her sleep disturbed by nightmares of Roger. Even in sleep, she felt John's arms around her.

Chapter Six

She had half expected John to be among the men who rode over the next morning to move the cattle to the east pasture, and a sharp pang of disappointment went through her as she realized he hadn't come. Then enthusiasm overrode her disappointment as she ran out to meet them. She'd never been in on an actual "cattle drive," short as it was, and was as excited as a child, her face glowing when she skidded to a stop in front of the mounted men.

"I want to help," she announced, green eyes sparkling in the early morning sun. The respite from the hard physical work she'd been doing made her feel like doing cartwheels on the lawn. She hadn't realized how tired she'd been until she'd had the opportunity to rest, but now she was bubbling over with energy.

Nev Luther, John's lanky and laconic foreman, looked down at her with consternation written across his weathered face. The boss had been explicit in his instructions that Michelle was not to be allowed to work in any way, which was a damned odd position for him to take. Nev couldn't remember the boss ever wanting anyone *not* to work. But orders were orders, and folks who valued their hides didn't ignore the boss's orders.

Not that he'd expected any trouble doing what he'd been told. Somehow he just hadn't pictured fancy Michelle Cabot doing any ranch work, let alone jumping up and down with joy at the prospect. Now what was he going to do? He cleared his throat, reluctant to do anything that would wipe the glowing smile off her face, but even more reluctant to get in trouble with Rafferty.

Inspiration struck, and he looked around. "You got a horse?" He knew she didn't, so he figured that was a detail she couldn't get around.

Her bright face dimmed, then lit again. "I'll drive the truck," she said, and raced toward the barn. Thunderstruck, Nev watched her go, and the men with him muttered warning comments.

Now what? He couldn't haul her out of the truck and order her to stay here. He didn't think she would take orders too well, and he also had the distinct idea the boss was feeling kinda possessive about her. Nev worked with animals, so he tended to put his thoughts in animal terms. One stallion didn't allow another near his mare, and the possessive mating instinct was still alive and well in humans. Nope, he wasn't going to manhandle that woman and have Rafferty take his head off for touching her. Given the choice, he'd rather have the boss mad about his orders not being followed than in a rage because someone had touched his woman, maybe upset her and made her cry.

The stray thought that she might cry decided him in a hurry. Like most men who didn't have a lot of contact with women, he went into a panic at the thought of tears. Rafferty could just go to hell. As far as Nev was concerned, Michelle could do whatever she wanted.

Having the burden of doing everything lifted off her shoulders made all the difference in the world. Michelle enjoyed the sunshine, the lowing of the cattle as they protested the movement, the tight-knit way the cowboys and their horses worked together. She bumped along the pasture in the old truck, which wasn't much good for rounding up strays but could keep the herd nudging forward. The only problem was, riding—or driving—drag was the dustiest place to be.

It wasn't long before one of the cowboys gallantly offered to drive the truck and give her a break from the dust. She took his horse without a qualm. She loved riding; at first it had been the only thing about ranch life that she'd enjoyed. She quickly found that riding a horse for pleasure was a lot different from riding a trained cutting horse. The horse didn't wait for her to tell it what to do. When a cow broke for freedom, the horse broke with it, and Michelle had to learn to go with the movement. She soon got the hang of it though, and before long she was almost hoping a stray would bolt, just for the joy of riding the quick-moving animal.

Nev swore long and eloquently under his breath when he saw the big gray coming across the pasture. Damn, the fat was in the fire now.

John was eyeing the truck with muted anger as he rode up, but there was no way the broad-shouldered figure in it was Michelle. Disbelieving, his black gaze swept the riders and lighted unerringly on the wand-slim rider with sunny hair tumbling below a hat. He reined in when he reached Nev, his jaw set as he looked at his foreman. "Well?" he asked in a dead-level voice.

Nev scratched his jaw, turning his head to watch Michelle snatch her hat off her head and wave it at a rambunctious calf. "I tried," he mumbled. He glanced back to meet John's narrowed gaze. Damned if eyes as black as hell couldn't look cold. "Hell, boss, it's her truck and her land. What was I supposed to do? Tie her down?"

"She's not in the truck," John pointed out.

"Well, it was so dusty back there that…ah, *hell!*"

Nev gave up trying to explain himself in disgust and spurred to head off a stray. John let him go, picking his way over to Michelle. He would take it up with Nev later, though already his anger was fading. She wasn't doing anything dangerous, even if he didn't like seeing her covered with dust.

She smiled at him when he rode up, a smile of such pure pleasure that his brows pulled together in a little frown. It was the first time he'd seen that smile since she'd been back, but until now he hadn't realized it had been missing. She looked happy. Faced with a smile like that, no wonder Nev had caved in and let her do what she wanted.

"Having fun?" he asked wryly.

"Yes, I am." Her look dared him to make something of it.

"I had a call from the lawyer this morning. He'll have everything ready for us to sign the day after tomorrow."

"That's good." Her ranch would shrink by a sizable hunk of acreage, but at least it would be clear of any large debt.

He watched her for a minute, leaning his forearms on the saddle horn. "Want to ride back to the house with me?"

"For a quickie?" she asked tartly, her green eyes beginning to spit fire at him.

His gaze drifted to her breasts. "I was thinking more of a slowie."

"So your men would have even more to gossip about?"

He drew a deep, irritated breath. "I suppose you want me to sneak over in the dead of night. We're not teenagers, damn it."

"No, we're not," she agreed. Then she said abruptly, "I'm not pregnant."

He didn't know if he should feel relieved, or irritated that this news meant it would be several days before she'd let him make love to her again. He wanted to curse, already feeling frustrated. Instead he said, "At least we didn't have to wait a couple of weeks, wondering."

"No, we didn't." She had known that the timing made it unlikely she'd conceive, but she'd still felt a small pang of regret that morning. Common sense aside, there was a deeply primitive part of her that wondered what woman wouldn't want to have his baby. He was so intensely masculine that he made other men pale in comparison, like a blooded stallion matched against scrub stock.

The gray shifted restively beneath him, and John controlled the big animal with his legs. "Actually, I don't have time, even for a quickie. I came to give Nev some instructions, then stop by the house to let you know where I'll be. I have to fly to Miami this afternoon, and I may not be back for a couple of days. If I'm not, drive to Tampa by yourself and sign those papers, and I'll detour on my way back to sign them."

Michelle twisted in the saddle to look at the battered, rusting old truck bouncing along behind the cattle. There was no way she would trust that relic to take her any place she couldn't get back from on foot. "I think I'll wait until you're back."

"Use the Mercedes. Just call the ranch and Nev will have a couple of men bring it over. I wouldn't trust that piece of junk you've been driving to get you to the grocery store and back."

It could have been a gesture between friends, a neighborly loan of a car, even something a lover might do, but Michelle sensed that John intended it to mean more than that. He was maneuvering her into his home as his mistress, and if she accepted the loan of the car, she would be just that much more dependent on him.

Yet she was almost cornered into accepting because she had no other way of getting to Tampa, and her own sense of duty insisted that she sign those papers as soon as possible, to clear the debt.

He was waiting for her answer, and finally she couldn't hesitate any longer. "All right." Her surrender was quiet, almost inaudible.

He hadn't realized how tense he'd been until his muscles relaxed. The thought that she might try driving to Tampa in that old wreck had been worrying him since he'd gotten the call from Miami. His mother had gotten herself into financial hot water again, and, distasteful as it was to him, he wouldn't let her starve. No matter what, she was his mother. Loyalty went bone deep with him, a lot deeper than aggravation.

He'd even thought of taking Michelle with him, just to have her near. But Miami was too close to Palm Beach; too many of her old friends were there, bored, and just looking for some lark to spice up their lives. It was possible that some jerk with more money than brains would make an offer she couldn't refuse. He had to credit her with trying to make a go of the place, but she wasn't cut out for the life and must be getting tired of working so hard and getting nowhere. If someone offered to pay her fare, she might turn her back and walk away, back to the jet-set life-style she knew so well. No matter how slim the chance of it happening, any chance at all was too much for him. No way would he risk losing her now.

For the first time in his life he felt insecure about a woman. She wanted him, but was it enough to keep her with him? For the first time in his life, it was important. The hunger he felt for her was so deep that he wouldn't be satisfied until she was living under his roof and sleeping in his bed, where he could take care of her and pamper her as much as he wanted.

Yes, she wanted him. He could please her in bed; he could take care of her. But she didn't want him as much as he wanted her. She kept resisting him, trying to keep a distance between them even now, after they'd shared a night and a bed, and a joining that still shook him with its power. It seemed as if every time he tried to bring her closer, she backed away a little more.

He reached out and touched her cheek, stroking his fingertips across her skin and feeling the patrician bone structure that gave her face such an angular, haughty look. "Miss me while I'm gone," he said, his tone making it a command.

A small wry smile tugged at the corners of her wide mouth. "Okay."

"Damn it," he said mildly. "You're not going to boost my ego, are you?"

"Does it need it?"

"Where you're concerned, yeah."

"That's a little hard to believe. Is missing someone a two-way street, or will you be too busy in Miami to bother?"

"I'll be busy, but I'll bother anyway."

"Be careful." She couldn't stop the words. They were the caring words that always went before a trip, a magic incantation to keep a loved one safe. The thought of not seeing him made her feel cold and empty. Miss him?

He had no idea how much, that the missing was a razor, already slashing at her insides.

He wanted to kiss her, but not with his men watching. Instead he nodded an acknowledgment and turned his horse away to rejoin Nev. The two men rode together for a time, and Michelle could see Nev give an occasional nod as he listened to John's instructions. Then John was gone, kicking the gray into a long ground-eating stride that quickly took horse and rider out of sight.

Despite the small, lost feeling she couldn't shake, Michelle didn't allow herself to brood over the next several days. There was too much going on, and even though John's men had taken over the ranching chores, there were still other chores that, being cowboys, they didn't see. If it didn't concern cattle or horses, then it didn't concern them. Now Michelle found other chores to occupy her time. She painted the porch, put up a new post for the mailbox and spent as much time as she could with the men.

The ranch seemed like a ranch again, with all the activity, dust, smells and curses filling the air. The cattle were dipped, the calves branded, the young bulls clipped. Once Michelle would have wrinkled her nose in distaste, but now she saw the activity as new signs of life, both in the ranch and in herself.

On the second day Nev drove the Mercedes over while one of the other men brought an extra horse for Nev to ride. Michelle couldn't quite look the man in the eye as she took the keys from him, but he didn't seem to see anything unusual about her driving John's car.

After driving the pickup truck for so long, the power and responsiveness of the Mercedes felt odd. She was painfully cautious on the long drive to Tampa. It was hard to imagine that she'd ever been blasé about the expensive, sporty cars she'd driven over the years, but she could remember her carelessness with the white Porsche her father had given her on her eighteenth birthday. The amount of money represented by the small white machine hadn't made any impression on her.

Everything was relative. Then, the money spent for the Porsche hadn't been much. If she had that much now, she would feel rich.

She signed the papers at the lawyer's office, then immediately made the drive back, not wanting to have the Mercedes out longer than necessary.

The rest of the week was calm, though she wished John would call to let her know when he would be back. The two days had stretched into five, and she couldn't stop the tormenting doubts that popped up in unguarded moments. Was he with another woman? Even though he was down there on business, she knew all too well how women flocked to him, and he wouldn't be working twenty-four hours a day. He hadn't made any commitments to her; he was free to take other women out if he wanted. No matter how often she repeated those words to herself, they still hurt.

But if John didn't call, at least Roger didn't, either. For a while she'd been afraid he would begin calling regularly, but the reassuring silence continued. Maybe something or someone else had taken his attention. Maybe his business concerns were taking all his time. Whatever it was, Michelle was profoundly grateful.

The men didn't come over on Friday morning. The cattle were grazing peacefully in the east pasture; all the fencing had been repaired; everything had been taken care of. Michelle put a load of clothing in the washer, then spent the morning cutting the grass again. She was soaked with sweat when she went inside at noon to make a sandwich for lunch.

It was oddly silent in the house, or maybe it was just silent in comparison to the roar of the lawnmower. She needed water. Breathing hard, she turned on the faucet to let the water get cold while she got a glass from the cabinet, but only a trickle of water ran out, then stopped altogether. Frowning, Michelle turned the faucet off, then on again. Nothing happened. She tried the hot water. Nothing.

Groaning, she leaned against the sink. That was just what she needed, for the water pump to break down.

It took only a few seconds for the silence of the house to connect with the lack of water, and she slowly straightened. Reluctantly she reached for the light switch and flicked it on. Nothing.

The electricity had been cut off.

That was why it was so quiet. The refrigerator wasn't humming; the clocks weren't ticking; the ceiling fan was still.

Breathing raggedly, she sank into a chair. She had forgotten the last notice. She had put it in a drawer and forgotten it, distracted by John and the sudden activity around the ranch. Not that any excuse was worth a hill of beans, she reminded herself. Not that she'd had the money to pay the bill even if she had remembered it.

She had to be practical. People had lived for thousands of years without electricity, so she could, too. Cooking was out; the range top, built-in oven and microwave were all electric, but she wasn't the world's best cook anyway, so that wasn't critical. She could eat without cooking. The refrigerator was empty except for milk and some odds and ends. Thinking about the milk reminded her how thirsty she was, so she poured a glass of the cold milk and swiftly returned the carton to the refrigerator.

There was a kerosene lamp and a supply of candles in the pantry, so she would have light. The most critical item was water. She had to have water to drink and bathe. At least the cattle could drink from the shallow creek that snaked across the east pasture, so she wouldn't have to worry about them.

There was an old well about a hundred yards behind the house, but she didn't know if it had gone dry or simply been covered when the other well had been drilled. Even if the well was still good, how would she get the water up? There was a rope in the barn, but she didn't have a bucket.

She did have seventeen dollars, though, the last of her cash. If the well had water in it, she'd coax the old truck down to the hardware store and buy a water bucket.

She got a rope from the barn, a pan from the kitchen and trudged the hundred yards to the old well.

It was almost overgrown with weeds and vines that she had to clear away while keeping an uneasy eye out for snakes. Then she tugged the heavy wooden cover to the side and dropped the pan into the well, letting the rope slip lightly through her hands. It wasn't a deep well; in only a second or two there was a distinct splash, and she began hauling the pan back up. When she got it to the top, a half cup of clear water was still in the pan despite the banging it had received, and Michelle sighed with relief. Now all she had to do was get the bucket.

By the time dusk fell, she was convinced that the pioneers had all been as muscular as the Incredible Hulk; every muscle in her body ached. She had drawn a bucket of water and walked the distance back to the house so many times she didn't want to think about it. The electricity had been cut off while the washer had been in the middle of its cycle, so she had to rinse the clothes out by hand and hang them to dry. She had to have water to drink. She had to have water to bathe. She had to have water to flush the toilet. Modern conveniences were damned *in*convenient without electricity.

But at least she was too tired to stay up long and waste the candles. She set a candle in a saucer on the bedside table, with matches alongside in case she woke up during the night. She was asleep almost as soon as she stretched out between the sheets.

The next morning she ate a peanut butter and jelly sandwich for breakfast, then cleaned out the refrigerator, so she wouldn't have to smell spoiled food. The house was oddly oppressive, as if the life had gone out of it, so she spent most of the day outdoors, watching the cattle graze, and thinking.

She would have to sell the beef cattle now, rather than wait to fatten them on grain. She wouldn't get as much for them, but she had to have money *now*. It had been foolish of her to let things go this far. Pride had kept her from asking for John's advice and help in arranging the sale; now she had to ask him. He would know who to contact and how to transport the cattle. The money would keep her going, allow her to care for the remainder of the herd until spring, when she would have more beef ready to sell. Pride was one thing, but she had carried it to the point of stupidity.

Still, if this had happened ten days earlier she wouldn't even have considered asking John's advice. She had been so completely isolated from human trust that any overture would have made her back away, rather than entice her closer. But John hadn't let her back away; he'd come after her, taken care of things over her protests, and very gently, thoroughly seduced her. A seed of trust had been sown that was timidly growing, though it frightened her to think of relying on someone else, even for good advice.

It was sultry that night, the air thick with humidity. The heat added by the candles and kerosene lamp made it unbearable inside, and though she bathed in the cool water she had hauled from the well, she immediately felt sticky again. It was too early and too hot to sleep, so finally she went out on the porch in search of a breeze.

She curled up in a wicker chair padded with overstuffed cushions, sighing in relief as a breath of wind fanned her face. The night sounds of crickets and frogs surrounded her with a hypnotic lullaby, and before long her eyelids were drooping. She never quite dozed, but sank into a peaceful lethargy where time passed unnoticed. It might have been two hours or half an hour later when she was disturbed by the sound of a motor and the crunching of tires on gravel; headlights flashed into her eyes just as she opened them, making her flinch and turn her face from the blinding light. Then the lights were killed and the motor silenced. She sat up straighter, her heart beginning to pound as a tall, broad-shouldered man got out of the truck and slammed the door. The starlight wasn't bright, but she didn't need light to identify him when every cell in her body tingled with awareness.

Despite his boots, he didn't make a lot of noise as he came up the steps. "John," she murmured, her voice only a low whisper of sound, but he felt the vibration and turned toward her chair.

She was completely awake now, and becoming indignant. "Why didn't you call? I waited to hear from you—"

"I don't like telephones," he muttered as he walked toward her. That was only part of the reason. Talking to her on the telephone would only have made him want her more, and his nights had been pure hell as it was.

"That isn't much of an excuse."

"It'll do," he drawled. "What are you doing out here? The house is so dark I thought you must have gone to bed early."

Which wouldn't have stopped him from waking her, she thought wryly. "It's too hot to sleep."

He grunted in agreement, bending down to slide his arms under her legs and shoulders. Startled, Michelle grabbed his neck with both arms as he lifted her, then took her place in the chair and settled her on his lap. An almost painful sense of relief filled her as his nearness eased tension she hadn't even been aware of feeling. She was surrounded by his strength and warmth, and the subtle male scent of his skin reaffirmed the sense of homecoming, of rightness. Bonelessly she melted against him, lifting her mouth to his.

The kiss was long and hot, his lips almost bruising hers in his need, but she didn't mind, because her own need was just as urgent. His hands slipped under the light nightgown that was all she wore, finding her soft and naked, and a shudder wracked his body.

He muttered a soft curse. "Sweet hell, woman, you were sitting out here practically naked."

"No one else is around to see." She said the words against his throat, her lips moving over his hard flesh and finding the vibrant hollow where his pulse throbbed.

Heat and desire wrapped around them, sugar-sweet and mindless. From the moment he touched her, she'd wanted only to lie down with him and sink into the textures and sensations of lovemaking. She twisted in his arms, trying to press her breasts fully against him and whimpering a protest as he prevented her from moving.

"This won't work," he said, securing his hold on her

and getting to his feet with her still in his arms. "We'd better find a bed, because this chair won't hold up to what I have in mind."

He carried her inside, and as he had done before, he flipped the switch for the light in the entry, so he would be able to see while going up the stairs. He paused when the light didn't come on. "You've got a blown bulb."

Tension invaded her body again. "The power's off."

He gave a low laugh. "Well, hell. Do you have a flashlight? The last thing I want to do right now is trip on the stairs and break our necks."

"There's a kerosene lamp on the table." She wriggled in his arms, and he slowly let her slide to the floor, reluctant to let her go even for a moment. She fumbled for the matches and struck one, the bright glow guiding her hands as she removed the glass chimney and held the flame to the wick. It caught, and the light grew when she put the chimney back in place.

John took the lamp in his left hand, folding her close to his side with his other arm as they started up the stairs. "Have you called the power company to report it?"

She had to laugh. "They know."

"How long will it take them to get it back on?"

Well, he might as well know now. Sighing, she admitted, "The electricity's been cut off. I couldn't pay the bill."

He stopped, his brows drawing together in increasing temper as he turned. "Damn it to hell! How long has it been off?"

"Since yesterday morning."

He exhaled through his clenched teeth, making a hissing sound. "You've been here without water and lights for a day and a half? Of all the damned stubborn stunts… Why in hell didn't you give the bill to me?" He yelled the last few words at her, his eyes snapping black fury in the yellow light from the lamp.

"I don't want you paying my bills!" she snapped, pulling away from him.

"Well, that's just tough!" Swearing under his breath, he caught her hand and pulled her up the stairs, then into her bedroom. He set the lamp on the bedside table and crossed to the closet, opened the doors and began pulling her suitcases from the top shelf.

"What are you doing?" she cried, wrenching the suitcase from him.

He lifted another case down. "Packing your things," he replied shortly. "If you don't want to help, just sit on the bed and stay out of the way."

"Stop it!" She tried to prevent him from taking an armful of clothes from the closet, but he merely side-stepped her and tossed the clothes onto the bed, then returned to the closet for another armful.

"You're going with me," he said, his voice steely. "This is Saturday; it'll be Monday before I can take care of the bill. There's no way in hell I'm going to leave you here. God Almighty, you don't even have water!"

Michelle pushed her hair from her eyes. "I have water. I've been drawing it from the old well."

He began swearing again and turned from the closet to the dresser. Before she could say anything her underwear was added to the growing pile on the bed. "I can't stay with you," she said desperately, knowing events were already far out of her control. "You know how it'll look! I can manage another couple of days—"

"I don't give a damn how it looks!" he snapped. "And just so you understand me, I'm going to give it to you in plain English. You're going with me now, and you won't be coming back. This isn't a two-day visit. I'm tired of worrying about you out here all by yourself; this is the last straw. You're too damned proud to tell me when you need help, so I'm going to take over and handle everything, the way I should have in the beginning."

Michelle shivered, staring at him. It was true that she shrank from the gossip she knew would run through the county like wildfire, but that wasn't the main reason for her reluctance. Living with him would destroy the last fragile buffers she had retained against being overwhelmed by him in every respect. She wouldn't be able to keep any emotional distance as a safety precaution, just as physical distance would be impossible. She would be in his home, in his bed, eating his food, totally dependent on him.

It frightened her so much that she found herself backing away from him, as if by increasing the distance between them she could weaken his force and fury. "I've been getting by without you," she whispered.

"Is this what you call `getting by'?" he shouted, slinging the contents of another drawer onto the bed. "You were working yourself half to death, and you're damned lucky you weren't hurt trying to do a two-man job! You don't have any money. You don't have a safe

car to drive. You probably don't have enough to eat—
and now you don't have electricity."

"I know what I don't have!"

"Well, I'll tell you something else you don't have: a
choice. You're going. Now get dressed."

She stood against the wall on the other side of the
room, very still and straight. When she didn't move his
head jerked up, but something about her made his
mouth soften. She looked defiant and stubborn, but her
eyes were frightened, and she looked so frail it was like
a punch in the gut, staggering him.

He crossed the room with quick strides and hauled
her into his arms, folding her against him as if he
couldn't tolerate another minute of not touching her. He
buried his face in her hair, wanting to sweep her up and
keep her from ever being frightened again. "I won't let
you do it," he muttered in a raspy voice. "You're trying
to keep me at a distance, and I'll be damned if I'll let
you do it. Does it matter so much if people know about
us? Are you ashamed because I'm not a member of your
jet set?"

She gave a shaky laugh, her fingers digging into his
back. "Of course not. *I'm* not one of the jet set." How
could any woman ever be ashamed of him?

His lips brushed her forehead, leaving warmth
behind. "Then what is it?"

She bit her lip, her mind whirling with images of the
past and fears of the future. "The summer I was
nineteen…you called me a parasite." She had never forgotten the words or the deep hurt they'd caused, and an
echo of it was in her low, drifting voice. "You were right."

"Wrong," he whispered, winding his fingers through the strands of her bright hair. "A parasite doesn't give anything, it only takes. I didn't understand, or maybe I was jealous because I wanted it all. I have it all now, and I won't give it up. I've waited ten years for you, baby; I'm not going to settle for half measures now."

He tilted her head back, and his mouth closed warmly, hungrily, over hers, overwhelming any further protests. With a little sigh Michelle gave in, going up on her tiptoes to press herself against him. Regrets could wait; if this were all she would have of heaven, she was going to grab it with both hands. He would probably decide that she'd given in so she could have an easier life, but maybe that was safer than for him to know she was head over heels in love with him.

She slipped out of his arms and quietly changed into jeans and a silk tunic, then set about restoring order out of the chaos he'd made of her clothes. Traveling had taught her to be a fast, efficient packer. As she finished each case, he carried it out to the truck. Finally only her makeup and toiletries were left.

"We'll come back tomorrow for anything else you want," he promised, holding the lamp for the last trip down the stairs. When she stepped outside he extinguished the lamp and placed it on the table, then followed her and locked the door behind him.

"What will your housekeeper think?" she blurted nervously as she got in the truck. It hurt to be leaving her home. She had hidden herself away here, sinking deep roots into the ranch. She had found peace and healing in the hard work.

"That I should have called to let her know when I'd be home," he said, laughing as relief and anticipation filled him. "I came here straight from the airport. My bag is in back with yours." He couldn't wait to get home, to see Michelle's clothing hanging next to his in the closet, to have her toiletries in his bathroom, to sleep with her every night in his bed. He'd never before wanted to live with a woman, but with Michelle it felt necessary. There was no way he would ever feel content with less than everything she had to give.

Chapter Seven

It was midmorning when Michelle woke, and she lay there for a moment alone in the big bed, trying to adjust to the change. She was in John's house, in his bed. He had gotten up hours ago, before dawn, and left her with a kiss on the forehead and an order to catch up on her sleep. She stretched, becoming aware of both her nakedness and the ache in her muscles. She didn't want to move, didn't want to leave the comforting cocoon of sheets and pillows that carried John's scent. The memory of shattering pleasure made her body tingle, and she moved restlessly. He hadn't slept much, hadn't let her sleep until he'd finally left the bed to go about his normal day's work.

If only he had taken her with him. She felt awkward with Edie, the housekeeper. What must she be thinking?

They had met only briefly, because John had ushered Michelle upstairs with blatantly indecent haste, but her impression had been of height, dignity and cool control. The housekeeper wouldn't say anything if she disapproved, but then, she wouldn't have to; Michelle would know.

Finally she got out of bed and showered, smiling wryly to herself as she realized she wouldn't have to skimp on hot water. Central air-conditioning kept the house comfortably cool, which was another comfort she had given up in an effort to reduce the bills. No matter what her mental state, she would be physically comfortable here. It struck her as odd that she'd never been to John's house before; she'd had no idea what to expect. Perhaps another old ranch house like hers, though her father had remodeled and modernized it completely on the inside before they had moved in, and it was in fact as luxurious as the home she had been used to. But John's house was Spanish in style, and was only eight years old. The cool adobe-colored brick and high ceilings kept the heat at bay, and a colorful array of houseplants brought freshness to the air. She'd been surprised at the greenery, then decided that the plants were Edie's doing. The U-shaped house wrapped around a pool landscaped to the point that it resembled a jungle lagoon more than a pool, and every room had a view of the pool and patio.

She had been surprised at the luxury. John was a long way from poor, but the house had cost a lot of money that he would normally have plowed back into the ranch. She had expected something more utilitarian, but at the same time it was very much his *home*. His presence permeated it, and everything was arranged for his comfort.

Finally she forced herself to stop hesitating and go downstairs; if Edie intended to be hostile, she might as well know now.

The layout of the house was simple, and she found the kitchen without any problem. All she had to do was follow her nose to the coffee. As she entered, Edie looked around, her face expressionless, and Michelle's heart sank. Then the housekeeper planted her hands on her hips and said calmly, "I told John it was about damned time he got a woman in this house."

Relief flooded through Michelle, because something in her would have shriveled if Edie had looked at her with contempt. She was much more sensitive to what other people thought now than she had been when she was younger and had the natural arrogance of youth. Life had defeated that arrogance and taught her not to expect roses.

Faint color rushed to her cheeks. "John didn't make much of an effort to introduce us last night. I'm Michelle Cabot."

"Edie Ward. Are you ready for breakfast? I'm the cook, too."

"I'll wait until lunch, thank you. Does John come back for lunch?" It embarrassed her to have to ask.

"If he's working close by. How about coffee?"

"I can get it," Michelle said quickly. "Where are the cups?"

Edie opened the cabinet to the left of the sink and

got down a cup, handing it to Michelle. "It'll be nice to have company here during the day," she said. "These damn cowhands aren't much for talking."

Whatever Michelle had expected, Edie didn't conform. She had to be fifty; though her hair was still dark, there was something about her that made her look her age. She was tall and broad shouldered, with the erect carriage of a Mother Superior and the same sort of unflappable dignity, but she also had the wise, slightly weary eyes of someone who has been around the block a few times too many. Her quiet acceptance made Michelle relax; Edie didn't pass judgments.

But for all the easing of tension, Edie quietly and firmly discouraged Michelle from helping with any of the household chores. "Rafferty would have both our heads," she said. "Housework is what he pays me to do, and around here we try not to rile him."

So Michelle wandered around the house, poking her head into every room and wondering how long she would be able to stand the boredom and emptiness. Working the ranch by herself had been so hard that she had sometimes wanted nothing more than to collapse where she stood, but there had always been a purpose to the hours. She liked ranching. It wasn't easy, but it suited her far better than the dual roles of ornament and mistress. This lack of purpose made her uneasy. She had hoped living with John would mean doing things with him, sharing the work and the worries with him… just as married couples did.

She sucked in her breath at the thought; she was in his—still *his*—bedroom at the time, standing in front of the open closet staring at his clothes, as if the sight of his personal possessions would bring him closer. Slowly she reached out and fingered a shirt sleeve. Her clothes were in the closet beside his, but she didn't belong. This was his house, his bedroom, his closet, and she was merely another possession, to be enjoyed in bed but forgotten at sunrise. Wryly she admitted that it was better than nothing; no matter what the cost to her pride, she would stay here as long as he wanted her, because she was so sick with love for him that she'd take anything she could get. But what she wanted, what she really wanted more than anything in her life, was to have his love as well as his desire. She wanted to marry him, to be his partner, his friend as well as his lover, to belong here as much as he did.

Part of her was startled that she could think of marriage again, even with John. Roger had destroyed her trust, her optimism about life; at least, she'd thought he had. Trust had already bloomed again, a fragile phoenix poking its head up from the ashes. For the first time she recognized her own resilience; she had been altered by the terror and shame of her marriage, but not destroyed. She was healing, and most of it was because of John. She had loved him for so long that her love seemed like the only continuous thread of her life, always there, somehow giving her something to hold on to even when she'd thought it didn't matter.

At last restlessness drove her from the house. She was reluctant to even ask questions, not wanting to interfere with anyone's work, but she decided to walk around and look at everything. There was a world of difference between John's ranch and hers. Here everything was neat and well-maintained, with fresh paint on the barns and fences, the machinery humming. Healthy, spirited horses pranced in the corral or grazed in the pasture. The supply shed was in better shape than her barn. Her ranch had once looked like this, and determination filled her that it would again.

Who was looking after her cattle? She hadn't asked John, not that she'd been given a chance to ask him anything. He'd had her in bed so fast that she hadn't had time to think; then he'd left while she was still dozing.

By the time John came home at dusk, Michelle was so on edge that she could feel her muscles twitching with tension. As soon as he came in from the kitchen his eyes swept the room, and hard satisfaction crossed his face when he saw her. All day long he'd been fighting the urge to come back to the house, picturing her here, under his roof at last. Even when he'd built the house, eight years before, he'd wondered what *she* would think of it, if she'd like it, how she would look in these rooms. It wasn't a grand mansion like those in Palm Beach, but it had been custom built to his specifications for comfort, beauty and a certain level of luxury.

She looked as fresh and perfect as early-morning sunshine, while he was covered with sweat and dust, his jaw dark with a day's growth of beard. If he touched her now, he'd leave dirty prints on her creamy white dress, and he had to touch her soon or go crazy. "Come on up with me," he growled, his boots ringing on the flagstone floor as he went to the stairs.

Michelle followed him at a slower pace, wondering

if he already regretted bringing her here. He hadn't kissed her, or even smiled.

He was stripping off his shirt by the time she entered the bedroom, and he carelessly dropped the dirty, sweat-stained garment on the carpet. She shivered in response at the sight of his broad, hair-covered chest and powerful shoulders, her pulse throbbing as she remembered how it felt when he moved over her and slowly let her take his weight, nestling her breasts into that curly hair.

"What've you been doing today?" he asked as he went into the bathroom.

"Nothing," Michelle answered with rueful truthfulness, shaking away the sensual lethargy that had been stealing over her.

Splashing sounds came from the bathroom, and when he reappeared a few minutes later his face was clean of the dust that had covered it before. Damp strands of black hair curled at his temples. He looked at her, and an impatient scowl darkened his face. Bending down, he pried his boots off, then began unbuckling his belt.

Her heart began pounding again. He was going to take her to bed right now, and she wouldn't have a chance to talk to him if she didn't do it before he reached for her. Nervously she picked up his dirty boots to put them in the closet, wondering how to start. "Wait," she blurted. "I need to talk to you."

He didn't see any reason to wait. "So talk," he said, unzipping his jeans and pushing them down his thighs.

She inhaled deeply. "I've been bored with nothing to do all day—"

John straightened, his eyes hardening as she broke off. Hell, he should have expected it. When you acquired something expensive, you had to pay for its upkeep. "All right," he said in an even tone. "I'll give you the keys to the Mercedes, and tomorrow I'll open a checking account for you."

She froze as the meaning of his words seared through her, and all the color washed out of her face. No. There was no way she'd let him turn her into a pet, a chirpy sexual toy, content with a fancy car and charge accounts. Fury rose in her like an inexorable wave, rushing up and bursting out of control. Fiercely she hurled the boots at him; startled, he dodged the first one, but the second one hit him in the chest. "What the hell—"

"No!" she shouted, her eyes like green fire in a face gone curiously pale. She was standing rigidly, her fists clenched at her sides. "I don't want your money or your damned car! I want to take care of my cattle and my ranch, not be left here every day like some fancy...*sex doll*, waiting for you to get home and play with me!"

He kicked his jeans away, leaving him clad only in his briefs. His own temper was rising, but he clamped it under control. That control was evident in his quiet, level voice. "I don't think of you as a sex doll. What brought that on?"

She was white and shaking. "You brought me straight up here and started undressing."

His brows rose. "Because I was dirty from head to foot. I couldn't even kiss you without getting you dirty, and I didn't want to ruin your dress."

Her lips trembled as she looked down at the dress. "It's just a dress," she said, turning away. "It'll wash. And I'd rather be dirty myself than just left here every day with nothing to do."

"We've been over this before, and it's settled." He walked up behind her and put his hands on her shoulders, gently squeezing. "You can't handle the work; you'd only hurt yourself. Some women can do it, but you're not strong enough. Look at your wrist," he said, sliding his hand down her arm and grasping her wrist to lift it. "Your bones are too little."

Somehow she found herself leaning against him, her head resting in the hollow of his shoulder. "Stop trying to make me feel so useless!" she cried desperately. "At least let me go with you. I can chase strays—"

He turned her in his arms, crushing her against him and cutting off her words. "God, baby," he muttered. "I'm trying to protect you, not make you feel useless. It made me sick when I saw you putting up that fence, knowing what could happen if the wire lashed back on you. You could be thrown, or gored—"

"So could you."

"Not as easily. Admit it; strength counts out there. I want you safe."

It was a battle they'd already fought more times than she could remember, and nothing budged him. But she couldn't give up, because she couldn't stand many more days like today had been. "Could you stand it if you had nothing to do? If you had to just stand around and watch everybody else? Edie won't even let me help!"

"She'd damned well better not."

"See what I mean? Am I supposed to just sit all day?"

"All right, you've made your point," he said in a low voice. He'd thought she'd enjoy living a life of leisure again, but instead she'd been wound to the breaking point. He rubbed her back soothingly, and gradually she relaxed against him, her arms sliding up to hook around his neck. He'd have to find something to keep her occupied, but right now he was at a loss. It was hard to think when she was lying against him like warm silk, her firm breasts pushing into him and the sweet scent of woman rising to his nostrils. She hadn't been far from his mind all day, the thought of her pulling at him like a magnet. No matter how often he took her, the need came back even stronger than before.

Reluctantly he moved her a few inches away from him. "Dinner will be ready in about ten minutes, and I need a shower. I smell like a horse."

The hot, earthy scents of sweat, sun, leather and man didn't offend her. She found herself drawn back to him; she pressed her face into his chest, her tongue flicking out to lick daintily at his hot skin. He shuddered, all thoughts of a shower gone from his mind. Sliding his fingers into the shiny, pale gold curtain of her hair, he turned her face up and took the kiss he'd been wanting for hours.

She couldn't limit her response to him; whenever he reached for her, she was instantly his, melting into him, opening her mouth for him, ready to give as little or as much as he wanted to take. Loving him went beyond the boundaries she had known before, taking her into emotional and physical territory that was new to her. It was his control, not hers, that prevented him from tumbling her onto the bed right then. "Shower," he muttered, lifting his head. His voice was strained. "Then dinner. Then I have to do some paperwork, damn it, and it can't wait."

Michelle sensed that he expected her to object and demand his company, but more than anyone she understood about chores that couldn't be postponed. She drew back from his arms, giving him a smile. "I'm starving, so hurry up with your shower." An idea was forming in the back of her mind, one she needed to explore.

She was oddly relaxed during dinner; it somehow seemed natural to be here with him, as if the world had suddenly settled into the natural order of things. The awkwardness of the morning was gone, perhaps because of John's presence. Edie ate with them, an informality that Michelle liked. It also gave her a chance to think, because Edie's comments filled the silence and made it less apparent.

After dinner, John gave Michelle a quick kiss and a pat on the bottom. "I'll finish as fast as I can. Can you entertain yourself for a while?"

Swift irritation made up her mind for her. "I'm coming with you."

He sighed, looking down at her. "Baby, I won't get any work done at all if you're in there with me."

She gave him a withering look. "You're the biggest chauvinist walking, John Rafferty. You're going to work, all right, because you're going to show me what you're doing, and then I'm taking over your bookwork."

He looked suddenly wary. "I'm not a chauvinist."

He didn't want her touching his books, either. He might as well have said it out loud, because she read his thoughts in his expression. "You can either give me something to do, or I'm going back to my house right now," she said flatly, facing him with her hands on her hips.

"Just what do you know about keeping books?"

"I minored in business administration." Let him chew on that for a while. Since he obviously wasn't going to willingly let her in his office, she stepped around him and walked down the hall without him.

"Michelle, damn it," he muttered irritably, following her.

"Just what's wrong with my doing the books?" she demanded, taking a seat at the big desk.

"I didn't bring you here to work. I want to take care of you."

"Am I going to get hurt in here? Is a pencil too heavy for me to lift?"

He scowled down at her, itching to lift her out of her chair. But her green eyes were glittering at him, and her chin had that stubborn tilt to it, showing she was ready to fight. If he pushed her, she really might go back to that dark, empty house. He could keep her here by force, but he didn't want it that way. He wanted her sweet and willing, not clawing at him like a wildcat. Hell, at least this was safer than riding herd. He'd double-check the books at night.

"All right," he growled.

Her green eyes mocked him. "You're so gracious."

"You're full of sass tonight," he mused, sitting down.

"Maybe I should have made love to you before dinner after all, worked some of that out."

"Like I said, the world's biggest chauvinist." She gave him her haughty look, the one that had always made him see red before. She was beginning to enjoy baiting him.

His face darkened but he controlled himself, reaching for the pile of invoices, receipts and notes. "Pay attention, and don't screw this up," he snapped. "Taxes are bad enough without an amateur bookkeeper fouling up the records."

"I've been doing the books since Dad died," she snapped in return.

"From the looks of the place, honey, that's not much of a recommendation."

Her face froze, and she looked away from him, making him swear under his breath. Without another word she jerked the papers from him and began sorting them, then put them in order by dates. He settled back in his big chair, his face brooding as he watched her enter the figures swiftly and neatly in the ledger, then run the columns through the adding machine twice to make certain they were correct.

When she was finished, she pushed the ledger across the desk. "Check it so you'll be satisfied I didn't make any mistakes."

He did, thoroughly. Finally he closed the ledger and said, "All right."

Her eyes narrowed. "Is that all you have to say? No wonder you've never been married, if you think women don't have the brains to add two and two!"

"I've been married," he said sharply.

The information stunned her, because she'd never heard anyone mention his being married, nor was marriage something she readily associated with John Rafferty. Then hot jealousy seared her at the thought of some other woman living with him, sharing his name and his bed, having the right to touch him. "Who... when?" she stammered.

"A long time ago. I'd just turned nineteen, and I had more hormones than sense. God only knows why she married me. It only took her four months to decide ranch life wasn't for her, that she wanted money to spend and a husband who didn't work twenty hours a day."

His voice was flat, his eyes filled with contempt. Michelle felt cold. "Why didn't anyone ever mention it?" she whispered. "I've known you for ten years, but I didn't know you'd been married."

He shrugged. "We got divorced seven years before you moved down here, so it wasn't exactly the hottest news in the county. It didn't last long enough for folks to get to know her, anyway. I worked too much to do any socializing. If she married me thinking a rancher's wife would live in the lap of luxury, she changed her mind in a hurry."

"Where is she now?" Michelle fervently hoped the woman didn't still live in the area.

"I don't know, and I don't care. I heard she married some old rich guy as soon as our divorce was final. It didn't matter to me then, and it doesn't matter now."

It was beyond her how any woman could choose

another man, no matter how rich, over John. She would live in a hut and eat rattlesnake meat if it meant staying with him. But she was beginning to understand why he was so contemptuous of the jet-setters, the idle rich, why he'd made so many caustic remarks to her in the past about letting others support her instead of working to support herself. Considering that, it was even more confusing that now he didn't want her doing anything at all, as if he wanted to make her totally dependent on him.

He was watching her from beneath hooded lids, wondering what she was thinking. She'd been shocked to learn he'd been married before. It had been so long ago that he never thought about it, and he wouldn't even have mentioned it if her crack about marriage hadn't reminded him. It had happened in another lifetime, to a nineteen-year-old boy busting his guts to make a go of the rundown little ranch he'd inherited. Sometimes he couldn't even remember her name, and it had been years since he'd been able to remember what she looked like. He wouldn't recognize her if they met face to face.

It was odd, because even though he hadn't seen Michelle during the years of her marriage, he'd never forgotten her face, the way she moved, the way sunlight looked in her hair. He knew every line of her striking, but too angular face, all high cheekbones, stubborn chin and wide, soft mouth. She had put her mouth to his chest and tasted his salty, sweaty skin, her tongue licking at him. She looked so cool and untouchable now in that spotless white dress, but when he made love to her she turned into liquid heat. He thought of the way her legs wrapped around his waist, and he began to harden as desire heated his body. He leaned back in his chair, shifting restlessly.

Michelle had turned back to the stack of papers on his desk, not wanting to pry any further. She didn't want to know any more about his ex-wife, and she especially didn't want him to take the opportunity to ask about her failed marriage. It would be safer to get back to business; she needed to talk to him about selling her beef cattle, anyway.

"I need your advice on something. I wanted to fatten the cattle up for sale this year, but I need operating capital, so I think I should sell them now. Who do I contact, and how is transportation arranged?"

Right at that moment he didn't give a damn about any cattle. She had crossed her legs, and her skirt had slid up a little, drawing his eyes. He wanted to slide it up more, crumple it around her waist and completely bare her legs. His jeans were under considerable strain, and he had to force himself to answer. "Let the cattle fatten; you'll get a lot more money for them. I'll keep the ranch going until then."

She turned her head with a quick, impatient movement, sending her hair swirling, but whatever she had been about to say died when their eyes met and she read his expression. "Let's go upstairs," he murmured.

It was almost frightening to have that intense sexuality focused on her, but she was helpless to resist him. She found herself standing, shivering as he put his hand on her back and ushered her upstairs. Walking beside

him made her feel vulnerable; sometimes his size overwhelmed her, and this was one of those times. He was
so tall and powerful, his shoulders so broad, that when
she lay beneath him in bed he blocked out the light.
Only his own control and tenderness protected her.

He locked the bedroom door behind them, then stood
behind her and slowly began unzipping her dress. He felt
her shivering. "Don't be afraid, baby. Or is it excitement?"

"Yes," she whispered as he slid his hands inside the
open dress and around to cup her bare breasts, molding
his fingers over her. She could feel her nipples throb
against his palms, and with a little whimper she leaned
back against him, trying to sink herself into his hardness
and warmth. It felt so good when he touched her.

"Both?" he murmured. "Why are you afraid?"

Her eyes were closed, her breath coming in shallow
gulps as he rubbed her nipples to hard little points of
fire. "The way you make me feel," she gasped, her head
rolling on his shoulder.

"You make me feel the same." His voice was slow and
guttural as the hot pressure built in him. "Hot, like I'll
explode if I don't get inside you. Then you're so soft and
tight around me that I know I'm going to explode
anyway."

The words made love to her, turning her shivers into
shudders. Her legs were liquid, unable to support her;
if it hadn't been for John's muscular body behind her,
she would have fallen. She whispered his name, the
single word vibrant with longing.

His warm breath puffed around her ear as he nuzzled

the lobe. "You're so sexy, baby. This dress has been driving me crazy. I wanted to pull up your skirt…like this…." His hands had left her breasts and gone down to her hips, and now her skirt rose along her thighs as he gathered the material in his fists. Then it was at her waist, and his hands were beneath it, his fingers spread over her bare stomach. "I thought about sliding my hands under your panties…like this. Pulling them down…like this."

She moaned as he slipped her panties down her hips and over her buttocks, overcome by a sense of voluptuous helplessness and exposure. Somehow being only partially undressed made her feel even more naked and vulnerable. His long fingers went between her legs, and she quivered like a wild thing as he stroked and probed, slowly building her tension and pleasure to the breaking point.

"You're so sweet and soft," he whispered. "Are you ready for me?"

She tried to answer, but all she could do was gasp. She was on fire, her entire body throbbing, and still he held her against him, his fingers slowly thrusting into her, when he knew she wanted him and was ready for him. He *knew* it. He was too experienced not to know, but he persisted in that sweet torment as he savored the feel of her.

She felt as sexy as he told her she was; her own sensuality was unfolding like a tender flower under his hands and his low, rough voice. Each time he made love to her, she found a little more self-assurance in her own capacity for giving and receiving pleasure. He was

strongly, frankly sexual, so experienced that she wanted
to slap him every time she thought about it, but she had
discovered that she could satisfy him. Sometimes he
trembled with hunger when he touched her; this man,
whose raw virility gave him sensual power over any
woman he wanted, trembled with the need for *her*. She
was twenty-eight years old, and only now, in John's
hands, was she discovering her power and pleasure as a
woman.

Finally she couldn't take any more and whirled away
from his hands, her eyes fierce as she stripped off her
dress and reached for him, tearing at his clothes. He
laughed deeply, but the sound was of excitement rather
than humor, and helped her. Naked, already entwined,
they fell together to the bed. He took her with a slow,
strong thrust, for the first time not having to enter her
by careful degrees, and the inferno roared out of
control.

Michelle bounced out of bed before he did the next
morning, her face glowing. "You don't have to get up,"
he rumbled in his hoarse, early-morning voice. "Why
don't you sleep late?" Actually he liked the thought of
her dozing in his bed, rosily naked and exhausted after
a night of making love.

She pushed her pale, tousled hair out of her eyes,
momentarily riveted by his nudity as he got out of bed.
"I'm going with you today," she said, and dashed to beat
him to the bathroom.

He joined her in the shower a few minutes later, his
black eyes narrowed after her announcement. She

waited for him to tell her that she couldn't go, but instead he muttered, "I guess it's okay, if it'll make you happy."

It did. She had decided that John was such an over-protective chauvinist that he would cheerfully keep her wrapped in cotton, so reasoning with him was out of the question. She knew what she could do; she would do it. It was that simple.

Over the next three weeks a deep happiness began forming inside her. She had taken over the paperwork completely, working on it three days out of the week, which gave John more free time at night than he'd ever had before. He gave up checking her work, because he never found an error. On the other days she rode with him, content with his company, and he discovered that he liked having her nearby. There were times when he was so hot, dirty and aggravated that he'd be turning the air blue with savage curses, then he'd look up and catch her smiling at him, and his aggravation would fade away. What did a contrary steer matter when she looked at him that way? She never seemed to mind the dust and heat, or the smells. It wasn't what he'd expected, and sometimes it bothered him. It was as if she were hiding here, burying herself in this self-contained world. The Michelle he'd known before had been a laughing, teasing, social creature, enjoying parties and dancing. This Michelle seldom laughed, though she was so generous with her smiles that it took him a while to notice. One of those smiles made him and all his men a little giddy, but he could remember her sparkling laughter, and he wondered where it had gone.

But it was still so new, having her to himself, that he wasn't anxious to share her with others. They spent the nights tangled together in heated passion, and instead of abating, the hunger only intensified. He spent the days in constant, low-level arousal, and sometimes all he had to do was look at her and he'd be so hard he'd have to find some way of disguising it.

One morning Michelle remained at the house to work in the office; she was alone because Edie had gone grocery shopping. The telephone rang off the hook that morning, interrupting her time and again. She was already irritated with it when it jangled yet again and made her stop what she was doing to answer it. "Rafferty residence."

No one answered, though she could hear slow, deep breathing, as though whoever was on the other end was deliberately controlling his breath. It wasn't a "breather," though; the sound wasn't obscenely exaggerated.

"Hello," she said. "Can you hear me?"

A quiet click sounded in her ear, as if whoever had been calling had put down the receiver with slow, controlled caution, much as he'd been breathing.

He. For some reason she had no doubt it was a man. Common sense said it could be some bored teenager playing a prank, or simply a wrong number, but a sudden chill swept over her.

A sense of menace had filled the silence on the line. For the first time in three weeks she felt isolated and somehow threatened, though there was no tangible reason for it. The chills wouldn't stop running up and down her spine, and suddenly she had to get out of the house, into the hot sunshine. She had to see John, just be able to look at him and hear his deep voice roaring curses, or crooning gently to a horse or a frightened calf. She needed his heat to dispel the coldness of a menace she couldn't define.

Two days later there was another phone call and again, by chance, she answered the phone. "Hello," she said. "Rafferty residence."

Silence.

Her hand began shaking. She strained her ears and heard that quiet, even breathing, then the click as the phone was hung up, and a moment later the dial tone began buzzing in her ear. She felt sick and cold, without knowing why. What was going on? Who was doing this to her?

Chapter Eight

Michelle paced the bedroom like a nervous cat, her silky hair swirling around her head as she moved. "I don't feel like going," she blurted. "Why didn't you ask me before you told Addie we'd be there?"

"Because you'd have come up with one excuse after another why you couldn't go, just like you're doing now," he answered calmly. He'd been watching her pace back and forth, her eyes glittering, her usually sinuous movements jerky with agitation. It had been almost a month since he'd moved her to the ranch, and she had yet to stir beyond the boundaries of his property, except to visit her own. He'd given her the keys to the Mercedes and free use of it, but to his knowledge she'd never taken it out. She hadn't been shopping, though he'd made certain she had money. He had received the usual invitations to the neighborhood Saturday night barbecues that had become a county tradition, but she'd always found some excuse not to attend.

He'd wondered fleetingly if she were ashamed of having come down in the world, embarrassed because he didn't measure up financially or in terms of sophistication with the men she'd known before, but he'd dismissed the notion almost before it formed. It wasn't that. He'd come to know her better than that. She came into his arms at night too eagerly, too hungrily, to harbor any feelings that he was socially inferior. A lot of his ideas about her had been wrong. She didn't look down on work, never had. She had simply been sheltered from it her entire life. She was willing to work. Damn it, she insisted on it! He had to watch her to keep her from trying her hand at bulldogging. He was as bad as her father had ever been, willing to do just about anything to keep her happy.

Maybe she was embarrassed because they were living together. This was a rural section, where mores and morality changed slowly. Their arrangement wouldn't so much as raise an eyebrow in Miami or any other large city, but they weren't in a large city. John was too self-assured and arrogant to worry about gossip; he thought of Michelle simply as his woman, with all the fierce possessiveness implied by the term. She was his. He'd held her beneath him and made her his, and the bond was reinforced every time he took her.

Whatever her reason for hiding on the ranch, it was time for it to end. If she were trying to hide their relationship, he wasn't going to let her get away with it any longer. She had to become accustomed to being his woman. He sensed that she was still hiding something of herself from him, carefully preserving a certain distance between them, and it enraged him. It wasn't a physical distance. Sweet Lord, no. She was liquid fire in his arms. The distance was mental; there were times when she was silent and withdrawn, the sparkle gone from her eyes, but whenever he asked her what was wrong she would stonewall, and no amount of probing would induce her to tell him what she'd been thinking.

He was determined to destroy whatever it was that pulled her away from him; he wanted all of her, mind and body. He wanted to hear her laugh, to make her lose her temper as he'd used to do, to hear the haughtiness and petulance in her voice. It was all a part of her, the part she wasn't giving him now, and he wanted it. Damn it, was she tiptoeing around him because she thought she *owed* him?

She hadn't stopped pacing. Now she sat down on the bed and stared at him, her lips set. "I don't want to go."

"I thought you liked Addie." He pulled off his boots and stood to shrug out of his shirt.

"I do," Michelle said.

"Then why don't you want to go to her party? Have you even seen her since you've been back?"

"No, but Dad had just died, and I wasn't in the mood to socialize! Then there was so much work to be done...."

"You don't have that excuse now."

She glared at him. "I decided you were a bully when

I was eighteen years old, and nothing you've done over the years has changed my opinion!"

He couldn't stop the grin that spread over his face as he stripped off his jeans. She was something when she got on her high horse. Going over to the bed, he sat beside her and rubbed her back. "Just relax," he soothed. "You know everyone who'll be there, and it's as informal as it always was. You used to have fun at these things, didn't you? They haven't changed."

Michelle let him coax her into lying against his shoulder. She would sound crazy if she told him that she didn't feel safe away from the ranch. He'd want to know why, and what could she tell him? That she'd had two phone calls and the other person wouldn't say anything, just quietly hung up? That happened to people all the time when someone had dialed a wrong number. But she couldn't shake the feeling that something menacing was waiting out there for her if she left the sanctuary of the ranch, where John Rafferty ruled supreme. She sighed, turning her face into his throat. She was overreacting to a simple wrong number; she'd felt safe enough all the time she'd been alone at her house. This was just another little emotional legacy from her marriage.

She gave in. "All right, I'll go. What time does it start?"

"In about two hours." He kissed her slowly, feeling the tension drain out of her, but he could still sense a certain distance in her, as if her mind were on something else, and frustration rose in him. He couldn't pinpoint it, but he knew it was there.

Michelle slipped from his arms, shaking her head as she stood. "You gave me just enough time to get ready, didn't you?"

"We could share a shower," he invited, dropping his last garment at his feet. He stretched, his powerful torso rippling with muscle, and Michelle couldn't take her eyes off him. "I don't mind being late if you don't."

She swallowed. "Thanks, but you go ahead." She was nervous about this party. Even aside from the spooky feeling those phone calls had given her, she wasn't certain how she felt about going. She didn't know how much the ranching crowd knew of her circumstances, but she certainly didn't want anyone pitying her, or making knowing remarks about her position in John's house. On the other hand, she didn't remember anyone as being malicious, and she had always liked Addie Layfield and her husband, Steve. This would be a family oriented group, ranging in age from Frank and Yetta Campbell, in their seventies, to the young children of several families. People would sit around and talk, eat barbecue and drink beer, the children and some of the adults would swim, and the thing would break up of its own accord at about ten o'clock.

John was waiting for her when she came out of the bathroom after showering and dressing. She had opted for cool and comfortable, sleeking her wet hair straight back and twisting it into a knot, which she'd pinned at her nape, and she wore a minimum of makeup. She had on an oversize white cotton T-shirt, with the tail tied in a knot on one hip, and loose white cotton drawstring pants. Her sandals consisted of soles and two straps each. On someone else the same ensemble might have looked sloppy, but on Michelle it looked chic. He decided she could wear a feed sack and make it look good.

"Don't forget your swimsuit," he said, remembering that she had always gone swimming at these parties. She'd loved the water.

Michelle looked away, pretending to check her purse for something. "I'm not swimming tonight."

"Why not?"

"I just don't feel like it."

Her voice had that flat, expressionless sound he'd come to hate, the same tone she used whenever he tried to probe into the reason she sometimes became so quiet and distant. He looked at her sharply, and his brows drew together. He couldn't remember Michelle ever "not feeling" like swimming. Her father had put in a pool for her the first year they'd been in Florida, and she had often spent the entire day lolling in the water. After she'd married, the pool had gone unused and had finally been emptied. He didn't think it had ever been filled again, and now it was badly in need of repairs before it would be usable.

But she'd been with him almost a month, and he didn't think she'd been in his pool even once. He glanced out at the balcony; he could just see a corner of the pool, blue and glittering in the late afternoon sun. He didn't have much time for swimming, but he'd insisted, eight years ago, on having the big pool and its luxurious landscaping. For her. Damn it, this whole place was for her: the big house, the comforts, that pool, even the damn Mercedes. He'd built it for her, not admitting it to himself then because he couldn't. Why wasn't she using the pool?

Michelle could feel his sharpened gaze on her as they left the room, but he didn't say anything and, relieved, she realized he was going to let it go. Maybe he just accepted that she didn't feel like swimming. If he only knew how much she wanted to swim, how she'd longed for the feel of cool water on her over-heated skin, but she just couldn't bring herself to put on a bathing suit, even in the privacy of his house.

She knew that the little white scars were hardly visible now, but she still shrank from the possibility that someone might notice them. She still felt that they were glaringly obvious, even though the mirror told her differently. It had become such a habit to hide them that she couldn't stop. She didn't dress or undress in front of John if she could help it, and if she couldn't, she always remained facing him, so he wouldn't see her back. It was such a reversal of modesty that he hadn't even noticed her reluctance to be nude in front of him. At night, in bed, it didn't matter. If the lights were on, they were dim, and John had other things on his mind. Still she insisted on wearing a nightgown to bed. It might be off most of the night, but it would be on when she got out of bed in the mornings. Everything in her shrank from having to explain those scars.

The party was just as she had expected, with a lot of food, a lot of talk, a lot of laughter. Addie had once been one of Michelle's best friends, and she was still the warm, talkative person she'd been before. She'd put on a little weight, courtesy of two children, but her pretty face still glowed with good humor. Steve, her husband, sometimes managed to put his own two cents into a conversation by the simple means of putting his hand over her mouth. Addie laughed more than anyone whenever he resorted to that tactic.

"It's an old joke between us," she told Michelle as they put together tacos for the children. "When we were dating, he'd do that so he could kiss me. Holy cow, you look good! Something must be agreeing with you, and I'd say that `something' is about six-foot-three of pure hunk. God, I used to swoon whenever he spoke to me! Remember? You'd sniff and say he didn't do anything for you. Liar, liar, pants on fire." Addie chanted the childish verse, her eyes sparkling with mirth, and Michelle couldn't help laughing with her.

On the other side of the pool, John's head swiveled at the sound, and he froze, stunned by the way her face lit as she joked with Addie. He felt the hardening in his loins and swore silently to himself, jerking his attention back to the talk of cattle and shifting his position to make his arousal less obvious. Why didn't she laugh like that more often?

Despite Michelle's reservations, she enjoyed the party. She'd missed the relaxed gatherings, so different from the sophisticated dinner parties, yacht parties, divorce parties, fund-raising dinners, et cetera, that had made up the social life John thought she'd enjoyed so much, but had only tolerated. She liked the shrieks of the children as they cannonballed into the pool, splashing any unwary adult in the vicinity, and she liked it that no one got angry over being wet. Probably it felt good in the sweltering heat, which had abated only a little.

True to most of the parties she'd attended, the men tended to group together and the women did the same, with the men talking cattle and weather, and the women talking about people. But the groups were fluid, flowing together and intermingling, and by the time the children had worn down, all the adults were sitting together. John had touched her arm briefly when he sat down beside her, a small, possessive gesture that made her tingle. She tried not to stare at him like an infatuated idiot, but she felt as if everyone there could tell how warm she was getting. Her cheeks flushed, and she darted a glance at him to find him watching her with blatant need.

"Let's go home," he said in a low voice.

"So soon?" Addie protested, but at that moment they all heard the distant rumble of thunder.

As ranchers, they all searched the night sky for signs of a storm that would break the heat, if only for a little while, and fill the slow-moving rivers and streams. Out to the west, over the Gulf, lightning shimmered in a bank of black clouds.

Frank Campbell said, "We sure could use a good rain. Haven't had one in about a month now."

It had stormed the day John had come over to her ranch for the first time, Michelle remembered, and again the night they'd driven back from Tampa...the first time he'd made love to her. His eyes glittered, and she knew he was thinking the same thing.

Wind suddenly kicked up from the west, bringing with it the cool smell of rain and salt, the excitement of a storm. Everyone began gathering up children and food, cleaning up the patio before the rain hit. Soon people were calling out goodbyes and piling into pickup trucks and cars.

"Glad you went?" John asked as he turned onto the highway.

Michelle was watching the lacy patterns the lightning made as it forked across the sky. "Yes, I had fun." She moved closer against him, seeking his warmth.

He held the truck steady against the gusts of wind buffeting it, feeling her breast brush his arm every time he moved. He inhaled sharply at his inevitable response.

"What's wrong?" she asked sleepily.

For answer he took her hand and pressed it to the straining fabric of his jeans. She made a soft sound, and her slender fingers outlined the hard ridge beneath the fabric as her body automatically curled toward him. He felt his jeans open; then her hand slid inside the parted fabric and closed over him, her palm soft and warm. He groaned aloud, his body jerking as he tried to keep his attention on the road. It was the sweetest torture he could imagine, and he ground his teeth as her hand moved further down to gently cup him for a moment before returning to stroke him to the edge of madness.

He wanted her, and he wanted her now. Jerking the steering wheel, he pulled the truck onto the side of the road just as fat raindrops began splattering the windshield. "Why are we stopping?" Michelle murmured.

He killed the lights and reached for her, muttering a graphic explanation.

"John! We're on the highway! Anyone could pass by and see us!"

"It's dark and raining," he said roughly, untying the drawstring at her waist and pulling her pants down. "No one can see in."

She'd been enjoying teasing him, exciting him, exciting herself with the feel of his hardness in her hand, but she'd thought he would wait until they got home. She should have known better. He didn't care if they were in a bedroom or not; his appetites were strong and immediate. She went weak under the onslaught of his mouth and hands, no longer caring about anything else. The rain was a thunderous din, streaming over the windows of the truck as if they were sitting under a waterfall. She could barely hear the rawly sexual things he was saying to her as he slid to the middle of the seat and lifted her over him. She cried out at his penetration, her body arching in his hands, and the world spun away in a whirlwind of sensations.

Later, after the rain had let up, she was limp in his arms as he carried her inside the house. Her hands slid around his neck as he bent to place her gently on the bed, and obeying that light pressure he stretched out on the bed with her. She was exhausted, sated, her body still throbbing with the remnants of pleasure. He kissed her deeply, rubbing his hand over her breasts and stomach. "Do you want me to undress you?" he murmured.

She nuzzled his throat. "No, I'll do it...in a minute. I don't feel like moving right now."

His big hand paused on her stomach, then slipped lower. "We didn't use anything."

"It's okay," she assured him softly. The timing was wrong. She had just finished her cycle, which was one reason he'd exploded out of control.

He rubbed his lips over hers in warm, quick kisses. "I'm sorry, baby. I was so damned ready for you, I thought I was going to go off like a teenager."

"It's okay," she said again. She loved him so much she trembled with it. Sometimes it was all she could do to keep from telling him, from crying the words aloud, but she was terrified that if she did he'd start putting distance between them, wary of too many entanglements. It had to end sometime, but she wanted it to last every possible second.

Nothing terrible had happened to her because she'd gone to the party; in fact, the trip home had been wonderful. For days afterward, she shivered with delight whenever she thought about it. There hadn't been any other out of the ordinary phone calls, and gradually she relaxed, convinced that there had been nothing to them. She was still far more content remaining on the ranch than she was either socializing or shopping, but at John's urging she began using the Mercedes to run small errands and occasionally visit her friends on those days when she wasn't riding with him or working on the books. She drove over to her house several times to check on things, but the silence depressed her. John had had the electricity turned back on, though he hadn't mentioned it to her, but she didn't say anything about moving back in. She couldn't leave him, not now; she was so helplessly, hopelessly in love with him that she knew she'd stay with him until he told her to leave.

One Monday afternoon she'd been on an errand for John, and on the return trip she detoured by her house to check things again. She walked through the huge rooms, making certain no pipes had sprung a leak or anything else needed repair. It was odd; she hadn't been away that long, but the house felt less and less like her home. It was hard to remember how it had been before John Rafferty had come storming into her life again; his presence was so intense it blocked out lesser details. Her troubled dreams had almost disappeared, and even when she had one, she would wake to find him beside her in the night, strong and warm. It was becoming easier to trust, to accept that she wasn't alone to face whatever happened.

It was growing late, and the shadows lengthened in the house; she carefully locked the door behind her and walked out to the car. Abruptly she shivered, as if something cold had touched her. She looked around, but everything was normal. Birds sang in the trees; insects hummed. But for a moment she'd felt it again, that sense of menace. It was odd.

Logic told her there was nothing to it, but when she was in the car she locked the doors. She laughed a little at herself. First a couple of phone calls had seemed spooky, and now she was "feeling" things in the air.

Because there was so little traffic on the secondary roads between her ranch and John's, she didn't use the rearview mirrors very much. The car was on her rear bumper before she noticed it, and even then she got only a glimpse before it swung to the left to pass. The road was narrow, and she edged to the right to give the other car more room. It pulled even with her, and she gave it a cursory glance just as it suddenly swerved toward her.

"Watch it!" she yelled, jerking the steering wheel to the right, but there was a loud grinding sound as metal rubbed against metal. The Mercedes, smaller than the other car, was pushed violently to the right. Michelle slammed on the brakes as she felt the two right wheels catch in the sandy soil of the shoulder, pulling the car even harder to that side.

She wrestled with the steering wheel, too scared even to swear at the other driver. The other car shot past, and somehow she managed to jerk the Mercedes back onto the road. Shaking, she braked to a stop and leaned her head on the steering wheel, then sat upright as she heard tires squealing. The other car had gone down the road, but now had made a violent U-turn and was coming back. She only hoped whoever it was had insurance.

The car was a big, blue full-size Chevrolet. She could tell that a man was driving, because the silhouette was so large. It was only a silhouette, because he had something black pulled over his head, like a ski mask.

The coldness was back. She acted instinctively, jamming her foot onto the gas pedal, and the sporty little Mercedes leaped forward. The Chevrolet swerved toward her again, and she swung wildly to the side. She almost missed it…almost. The Chevrolet clipped her rear bumper, and the smaller, lighter car spun in a nauseating circle before sliding off the road, across the wide sandy shoulder, and scraping against an enormous pine before it bogged down in the soft dirt and weeds.

She heard herself screaming, but the hard jolt that stopped the car stopped her screams, too. Dazed, her head lolled against the broken side window for a moment before terror drove the fogginess away. She groped for the handle, but couldn't budge the door. The pine tree blocked it. She tried to scramble across the seat to the other door, and only then realized she was still buckled into her seat. Fumbling, looking around wildly for the Chevrolet, she released the buckle and threw herself to the other side of the car. She pushed the door open and tumbled out in the same motion, her breath wheezing in and out of her lungs.

Numbly she crouched by the fender and tried to listen, but she could hear nothing over her tortuous breathing and the thunder of her heart. Old habits took over, and she used a trick she'd often used before to calm herself after one of Roger's insane rages, taking a deep breath and holding it. The maneuver slowed her heartbeat almost immediately, and the roar faded out of her ears.

She couldn't hear anything. Oh, God, had he stopped? Cautiously she peered over the car, but she couldn't see the blue Chevrolet.

Slowly she realized it had gone. He hadn't stopped. She stumbled to the road and looked in both directions, but the road was empty.

She couldn't believe it had happened. He had deliberately run her off the road, not once, but twice. If the small Mercedes had hit one of the huge pines that thickly lined the road head-on, she could easily have been killed. Whoever the man was, he must have figured the heavier Chevrolet could muscle her off the road without any great risk to himself.

He'd tried to kill her.

It was five minutes before another car came down the road; it was blue, and for a horrible moment she panicked, thinking the Chevrolet was returning, but as it came closer she could tell this car was much older and wasn't even a Chevrolet. She stumbled to the middle of the road, waving her arms to flag it down.

All she could think of was John. She wanted John. She wanted him to hold her close and shut the terror away with his strength and possessiveness. Her voice shook as she leaned in the window and told the young boy, "Please—call John Rafferty. Tell him I've been… I've had an accident. Tell him I'm all right."

"Sure, lady," the boy said. "What's your name?"

"Michelle," she said. "My name's Michelle."

The boy looked at the car lodged against the pine. "You need a wrecker, too. Are you sure you're all right?"

"Yes, I'm not hurt. Just hurry, please."

"Sure thing."

Either John called the sheriff's department or the boy had, because John and a county sheriff's car arrived from opposite directions almost simultaneously. It hadn't been much more than ten minutes since the boy had stopped, but in that short length of time it had grown considerably darker. John threw his door open as the truck ground to a stop and was out of the vehicle before it had settled back on its wheels, striding toward her. She couldn't move toward him; she was shaking too violently. Beneath his mustache his lips were a thin, grim line.

He walked all the way around her, checking her from head to foot. Only when he didn't see any blood on her did he haul her against his chest, his arms so tight they almost crushed her. He buried his hand in her hair and bent his head down until his jaw rested on her temple. "Are you really all right?" he muttered hoarsely.

Her arms locked around his waist in a death grip. "I was wearing my seat belt," she whispered. A single tear slid unnoticed down her cheek.

"God, when I got that phone call—" He broke off, because there was no way he could describe the stark terror he'd felt despite the kid's assurance that she was okay. He'd had to see her for himself, hold her, before he could really let himself believe she wasn't harmed. If he'd seen blood on her, he would have gone berserk. Only now was his heartbeat settling down, and he looked over her head at the car.

The deputy approached them, clipboard in hand. "Can you answer a few questions, ma'am?"

John's arms dropped from around her, but he remained right beside her as she answered the usual questions about name, age and driver's license number. When the deputy asked her how it had happened, she began shaking again.

"A…a car ran me off the road," she stammered. "A blue Chevrolet."

The deputy looked up, his eyes abruptly interested as a routine accident investigation became something more. "Ran you off the road? How?"

"He sideswiped me." Fiercely she clenched her fingers together in an effort to still their trembling. "He pushed me off the road."

"He didn't just come too close, and you panicked and ran off the road?" John asked, his brows drawing together.

"No! He pushed me off the road. I slammed on my brakes and he went on past, then turned around and came back."

"He came back? Did you get his name?" The deputy made a notation on his pad. Leaving the scene of an accident was a crime.

"No, he didn't stop. He…he tried to ram me. He hit my bumper, and I spun off the road, then into that pine tree."

John jerked his head at the deputy and they walked over to the car, bending down to inspect the damage. They talked together in low voices; Michelle couldn't make out what they were saying, but she didn't move closer. She stood by the road, listening to the peaceful sounds of the deepening Florida twilight. It was all so out of place. How could the crickets be chirping so happily when someone had just tried to commit murder? She felt dazed, as if none of this were real. But the damaged car was real. The blue Chevrolet had been real, as had the man wearing the black ski mask.

The two men walked back toward her. John looked at her sharply; her face was deathly white, even in the growing gloom, and she was shaking. She looked terrified. The Mercedes *was* an expensive car; did she expect him to tear a strip off her hide because she'd wrecked it? She'd never had to worry about things like that before, never had to be accountable for anything. If she'd banged a fender, it hadn't been important; her father had simply had the car repaired, or bought her a new one. Hell, he wasn't happy that she'd wrecked the damn car, but he wasn't a fanatic about cars, no matter how much they cost. It would have been different if she'd ruined a good horse. He was just thankful she wasn't hurt.

"It's all right," he said, trying to soothe her as he took her arm and walked her to the truck. "I have insurance on it. You're okay, and that's what matters. Just calm down. I'll take you home as soon as the deputy's finished with his report and the wrecker gets here."

Frantically she clutched his arm. "But what about—"

He kissed her and rubbed her shoulder. "I said it's all right, baby. I'm not mad. You don't have to make excuses."

Frozen, Michelle sat in the truck and watched as he walked back to the deputy. He didn't believe her; neither of them believed her. It was just like before, when no one would believe handsome, charming Roger Beckman was capable of hitting his wife, because it was obvious he adored her. It was just too unbelievable. Even her father had thought she was exaggerating.

She was so cold, even though the temperature was still in the nineties. She had begun to trust, to accept that John stood behind her, as unmoving as a block of granite, his strength available whenever she needed him. For the first time she hadn't felt alone. He'd been there, ready to shoulder her burdens. But suddenly it was just like before, and she was cold and alone again. Her father had given her everything materially, but had been too weak to face an ugly truth. Roger had showered her with gifts, pampering her extravagantly to make up for the bruises and terror. John had given her a place to live, food to eat, mind-shattering physical pleasure…but now he, too, was turning away from a horribly real threat. It was too much effort to believe such a tale. Why would anyone try to kill her?

She didn't know, but someone had. The phone calls… the phone calls were somehow connected. They'd given her the same feeling she'd had just before she got in the car, the same sense of menace. God, had he been watching her at her house? Had he been waiting for her? He could be anywhere. He knew her, but she didn't know him, and she was alone again. She'd always been alone, but she hadn't known it. For a while she'd trusted, hoped, and the contrast with that warm feeling of security made cold reality just that much more piercing.

The wrecker arrived with its yellow lights flashing and backed up to the Mercedes. Michelle watched with detached interest as the car was hauled away from the pine. She didn't even wince at the amount of damage that had been done to the left side. John thought she'd made up a wild tale to keep from having to accept blame for wrecking the car. He didn't believe her. The deputy didn't believe her. There should be blue paint on the car, but evidently the scrapes left by the big pine had obscured it. Maybe dirt covered it. Maybe it was too dark for them to see. For whatever reason, they didn't believe her.

She was utterly silent as John drove home. Edie came to the door, watching anxiously, then hurried forward as Michelle slid out of the truck.

"Are you all right? John left here like a bat out of

hell, didn't stop to tell us anything except you'd had an accident."

"I'm fine," Michelle murmured. "I just need a bath. I'm freezing."

Frowning, John touched her arm. It was icy, despite the heat. She wasn't hurt, but she'd had a shock.

"Make some coffee," he instructed Edie as he turned Michelle toward the stairs. "I'll give her a bath."

Slowly Michelle pulled away from him. Her face was calm. "No, I'll do it. I'm all right. Just give me a few minutes by myself."

After a hot but brief shower, she went downstairs and drank coffee, and even managed to eat a few bites of the meal Edie had put back when John tore out of the house.

In bed that night, for the first time she couldn't respond to him. He needed her almost desperately, to reassure himself once again that she was truly all right. He needed to strengthen the bond between them, to draw her even closer with ties as old as time. But though he was gentle and stroked her for a long time, she remained tense under his hands. She was still too quiet, somehow distant from him.

Finally he just held her, stroking her hair until she slept and her soft body relaxed against him. But he lay awake for hours, his body burning, his eyes open. God, how close he'd come to losing her!

Chapter Nine

John listened impatiently, his hard, dark face angry, his black eyes narrowed. Finally he said, "It hasn't been three months since I straightened all that out. How the hell did you manage to get everything in a mess this fast?"

Michelle looked up from the figures she was posting in, curious to learn the identity of his caller. He hadn't said much more than hello before he'd begun getting angry. Finally he said, "All right. I'll be down tomorrow. And if you're out partying when I get there, the way you were last time, I'll turn around and come home. I don't have time to cool my heels while you're playing." He hung up the phone and muttered a graphic expletive.

"Who was it?" Michelle asked.

"Mother." A wealth of irritation was in the single word.

She was stunned. "*Your* mother?"

He looked at her for a moment; then his mustache twitched a little as he almost smiled. "You don't have to sound so shocked. I got here by the normal method."

"But you've never mentioned… I guess I assumed she was dead, like your father."

"She cut out a long time ago. Ranching wasn't good enough for her; she liked the bright lights of Miami and the money of Palm Beach, so she walked out one fine day and never came back."

"How old were you?"

"Six or seven, something like that. Funny, I don't remember being too upset when she left, or missing her very much. Mostly I remember how she used to complain because the house was small and old, and because there was never much money. I was with Dad every minute I wasn't in school, but I was never close to Mother."

She felt as she had when she'd discovered he had been married. He kept throwing out little tidbits about himself, then dismissing these vital points of his life as if they hadn't affected him much at all. Maybe they hadn't. John was a hard man, made so by a lifetime of backbreaking work and the combination of arrogance and steely determination in his personality. But how could a child not be affected when his mother walked away? How could a young man, little more than a boy, not be affected when his new wife walked out rather than work by his side? To this day John would do anything to help someone who was *trying*, but he wouldn't lift a finger to aid anyone who sat around waiting for help. All his employees were loyal to him down to their last drop of blood. If they hadn't been, they wouldn't still be on his ranch.

"When you went to Miami before, it was to see your mother?"

"Yeah. She makes a mess of her finances at least twice a year and expects me to drop everything, fly down there and straighten it out."

"Which you do."

He shrugged. "We may not be close, but she's still my mother."

"Call me this time," she said distinctly, giving him a hard look that underlined her words.

He grunted, looking irritated, then gave her a wink as he turned to call the airlines. Michelle listened as he booked a flight to Miami for the next morning. Then he glanced at her and said "Wait a minute" into the receiver before putting his hand over the mouthpiece. "Want to come with me?" he asked her.

Panic flared in her eyes before she controlled it and shook her head. "No thanks. I need to catch up on the paperwork."

It was a flimsy excuse, as the accumulated work wouldn't take more than a day, but though John gave her a long, level look, he didn't argue with her. Instead he moved his fingers from the mouthpiece and said, "Just one. That's right. No, not round trip. I don't know what day I'll be coming back. Yeah, thanks."

He scribbled his flight number and time on a notepad

as he took the phone from his ear and hung up. Since the accident, Michelle hadn't left the ranch at all, for any reason. He'd picked up the newly repaired Mercedes three days ago, but it hadn't been moved from the garage since. Accidents sometimes made people nervous about driving again, but he sensed that something more was bothering her.

She'd begun totalling the figures she had posted in the ledger. His eyes drifted over her, drinking in her serious, absorbed expression and the way she chewed her bottom lip when she was working. She'd taken over his office so completely that he sometimes had to ask *her* questions about what was going on. He wasn't certain he liked having part of the ranch out of his direct control, but he was damn certain he liked the extra time he had at night.

That thought made him realize he'd be spending the next few nights alone, and he scowled. Once he would have found female companionship in Miami, but now he was distinctly uninterested in any other woman. He wanted Michelle and no one else. No other woman had ever fit in his arms as well as she did, or given him the pleasure she gave just by being there. He liked to tease her until she lost her temper and lashed back at him, just for the joy of watching her get snooty. An even greater joy was taking her to bed and loving her out of her snooty moods. Thanks to his mother, it was a joy he'd have to do without for a few days. He didn't like it worth a damn.

Suddenly he realized it wasn't just the sex. He didn't want to leave her, because she was upset about some-

thing. He wanted to hold her and make everything right
for her, but she wouldn't tell him about it. He felt uneasy.
She insisted nothing was wrong, but he knew better. He
just didn't know what it was. A couple of times he'd
caught her staring out the window with an expression
that was almost…terrified. He had to be wrong, because
she had no reason to be scared. And of what?

It had all started with the accident. He'd been
trying to reassure her that he wasn't angry about the
car, but instead she'd drawn away from him as if he'd
slapped her, and he couldn't bridge the distance
between them. For just an instant she'd looked
shocked, even hurt, then she'd withdrawn in some
subtle way he couldn't describe, but felt. The withdrawal wasn't physical; except for the night of the
accident, she was as sweet and wild in his arms as
she'd ever been. But he wanted all of her, mind and
body, and the accident had only made his wanting
more intense by taunting him with the knowledge of
how quickly she could be taken away.

He reached out and touched his fingertips to her
cheekbone, needing to touch her even in so small a way.
Her eyes cut up to him with a flash of green, their gazes
catching, locking. Without a word she closed the ledger
and stood. She didn't look back as she walked out of
the room with the fluid grace he'd always admired and
sometimes hated because he couldn't have the body
that produced it. But now he could, and as he followed
her from the room he was already unbuttoning his shirt.
His booted feet were deliberately placed on the stairs,
his attention on the bedroom at the top and the woman
inside it.

* * *

Sometimes, when the days were hot and slow and the sun was a disc of blinding white, Michelle would feel that it had all been a vivid nightmare and hadn't really happened at all. The phone calls had meant nothing. The danger she'd sensed was merely the product of an overactive imagination. The man in the ski mask hadn't tried to kill her. The accident hadn't been a murder attempt disguised to look like an accident. None of that had happened at all. It was only a dream, while reality was Edie humming as she did housework, the stamping and snorting of the horses, the placid cattle grazing in the pastures, John's daily phone calls from Miami that charted his impatience to be back home.

But it hadn't been a dream. John didn't believe her, but his nearness had nevertheless kept the terror at bay and given her a small pocket of safety. She felt secure here on the ranch, ringed by the wall of his authority, surrounded by his people. Without him beside her in the night, her feeling of safety weakened. She was sleeping badly, and during the days she pushed herself as relentlessly as she had when she'd been working her own ranch alone, trying to exhaust her body so she could sleep.

Nev Luther had received his instructions, as usual, but again he was faced with the dilemma of how to carry them out. If Michelle wanted to do something, how was he supposed to stop her? Call the boss in Miami and tattle? Nev didn't doubt for a minute the boss would spit nails and strip hide if he saw Michelle doing the work she was doing, but she didn't *ask* if she could do it, she simply did it. Not much he could do about that. Besides, she seemed to need the work to occupy her mind. She was quieter than usual, probably missing the boss. The thought made Nev smile. He approved of the current arrangement, and would approve even more if it turned out to be permanent.

After four days of doing as much as she could, Michelle was finally exhausted enough that she thought she could sleep, but she put off going to bed. If she were wrong, she'd spend more hours lying tense and sleepless, or shaking in the aftermath of a dream. She forced herself to stay awake and catch up on the paperwork, the endless stream of orders and invoices that chronicled the prosperity of the ranch. It could have waited, but she wanted everything to be in order when John came home. The thought brought a smile to her strained face; he'd be home tomorrow. His afternoon call had done more to ease her mind than anything. Just one more night to get through without him, then he'd be beside her again in the darkness.

She finished at ten, then climbed the stairs and changed into one of the light cotton shifts she slept in. The night was hot and muggy, too hot for her to tolerate even a sheet over her, but she was tired enough that the heat didn't keep her awake. She turned on her side, almost groaning aloud as her muscles relaxed, and was instantly asleep.

It was almost two in the morning when John silently let himself into the house. He'd planned to take an 8:00 a.m. flight, but after talking to Michelle he'd paced restlessly, impatient with the hours between them. He had to hold her close, feel her slender, too fragile body in his arms before he could be certain she was all right. The worry was even more maddening because he didn't know its cause.

Finally he couldn't stand it. He'd called the airport and gotten a seat on the last flight out that night, then thrown his few clothes into his bag and kissed his mother's forehead. "Take it easy on that damned checkbook," he'd growled, looking down at the elegant, shallow and still pretty woman who had given birth to him.

The black eyes he'd inherited looked back at him, and one corner of her crimson lips lifted in the same one-sided smile that often quirked his mouth. "You haven't told me anything, but I've heard rumors even down here," she'd said smoothly. "Is it true you've got Langley Cabot's daughter living with you? Really, John, he lost everything he owned."

He'd been too intent on getting back to Michelle to feel more than a spark of anger. "Not everything."

"Then it's true? She's living with you?"

"Yes."

She had given him a long, steady look. Since he'd been nineteen he'd had a lot of women, but none of them had lived with him, even briefly, and despite the distance between them, or perhaps because of it, she knew her son well. No one took advantage of him. If Michelle Cabot was in his house, it was because he wanted her there, not due to any seductive maneuvers on her part.

As John climbed the stairs in the dark, silent house, his heart began the slow, heavy rhythm of anticipation. He wouldn't wake her, but he couldn't wait to lie beside her again, just to feel the soft warmth of her body and smell the sweetness of her skin. He was tired; he could use a few hours' sleep. But in the morning… Her skin would be rosy from sleep, and she'd stretch drowsily with that feline grace of hers. He would take her then.

Noiselessly he entered the bedroom, shutting the door behind him. She was small and still in the bed, not stirring at his presence. He set his bag down and went into the bathroom. When he came out a few minutes later he left the bathroom light on so he could see while he undressed.

He looked at the bed again, and every muscle in his body tightened. Sweat beaded on his forehead. He couldn't have torn his eyes away even if a tornado had hit the house at that moment.

She was lying half on her stomach, with all the covers shoved down to the foot of the bed. Her right leg was stretched out straight, her left one drawn up toward the middle of the mattress. She was wearing one of those flimsy cotton shifts she liked, and during the night it had worked its way up to her buttocks. She was exposed to him. His burning gaze slowly, agonizingly moved over the bare curves of her buttocks from beneath the thin cotton garment, to the soft, silky female cleft and folds he loved to touch.

He shuddered convulsively, grinding his teeth to hold back the deep, primal sound rumbling in his chest. He'd gotten so hard, so fast, that his entire body ached and throbbed. She was sound asleep, her breath coming in a deep, slow rhythm. His own breath was billowing in and out of his lungs; sweat was pouring out of him, his muscles shaking like a stallion scenting a mare ready for mounting. Without taking his eyes from her he began unbuttoning his shirt. He had to have her; he couldn't wait. She was moist and vulnerable, warm and female, and...his. He was coming apart just looking at her, his control shredded, his loins surging wildly.

He left his clothes on the bedroom floor and bent over her, forcing his hands to gentleness as he turned her onto her back. She made a small sound that wasn't quite a sigh and adjusted her position, but didn't awaken. His need was so urgent that he didn't take the time to wake her; he pulled the shift to her waist, spread her thighs and positioned himself between them. With his last remnant of control he eased into her, a low, rough groan bursting from his throat as her hot, moist flesh tightly sheathed him.

She whimpered a little, her body arching in his hands, and her arms lifted to twine around his neck. "I love you," she moaned, still more asleep than awake. Her words went through him like lightning, his body jerking in response. Oh God, he didn't even know if she said it to him or to some dream, but everything in him shattered. He wanted to hear the words again, and he wanted her awake, her eyes looking into his when she said them, so he'd know who was in her mind. Desperately he sank deeper into her, trying to absorb her body into his so irrevocably that nothing could separate them.

"Michelle," he whispered in taut agony, burying his open mouth against her warm throat.

Michelle lifted, arching toward him again as her mind swam upward out of a sleep so deep it had bordered on unconsciousness. But even asleep she had known his touch, her body reacting immediately to him, opening for him, welcoming him. She didn't question his presence; he was there, and that was all that mattered. A great burst of love so intense that she almost cried out reduced everything else to insignificance. She was on fire, her senses reeling, her flesh shivering under the slamming thrusts of his loins. She felt him deep inside her, touching her, and she screamed into his mouth like a wild creature as sharp ecstasy detonated her nerves. He locked her to him with iron-muscled thighs and arms, holding her as she strained madly beneath him, and the feel of her soft internal shudders milking him sent him blasting into his own hot, sweet insanity.

He couldn't let her go. Even when it was over, he couldn't let her go. He began thrusting again, needing even more of her to satisfy the hunger that went so deep he didn't think it would ever be satisfied.

She was crying a little, her luminous green eyes wet as she clung to him. She said his name in a raw, shaking voice. He hadn't let her slide down to a calm plateau but kept her body tense with desire. He was slow and tender now, gentling her into ecstasy instead of hurling her into it, but the culmination was no less shattering.

It was almost dawn before she curled up in his arms, both of them exhausted. Just before she went to sleep she said in mild surprise, "You came home early."

His arms tightened around her. "I couldn't stand another night away from you." It was the bald, frightening truth. He would have made it back even if he'd had to walk.

No one bothered them the next morning, and they slept until long after the sun began pouring brightly into the room. Nev Luther, seeing John's truck parked in its normal location, came to the house to ask him a question, but Edie dared the foreman to disturb them with such a fierce expression on her face that he decided the question wasn't important after all.

John woke shortly after one, disturbed by the heat of the sunlight streaming directly onto the bed. His temples and mustache were already damp with sweat, and he badly needed a cool shower to drive away the sluggishness of heat and exhaustion. He left the bed quietly, taking care not to wake Michelle, though a purely male smile touched his hard lips as he saw her shift lying in the middle of the floor. He didn't even remember pulling it off her, much less throwing it. Nothing had mattered but loving her.

He stood under the shower, feeling utterly sated but somehow uneasy. He kept remembering the sound of her voice when she said "I love you" and it was driving him crazy. Had she been dreaming, or had she known it was him? She'd never said it before, and she hadn't said it again. The uncertainty knifed at him. It had felt so right, but then, they had always fitted together in bed so perfectly that his memories of other women were destroyed. Out of bed... There was always that small distance he couldn't bridge, that part of herself that she wouldn't let him know. Did she love someone else? Was it one of her old crowd? A tanned, sophisticated jet-setter who was out of her reach now that she didn't have money? The thought tormented him, because he knew it was possible to love someone even when they were far away and years passed between meetings. He knew, because he'd loved Michelle that way.

His face was drawn as he cut the water off with a savage movement. *Love*. God, he'd loved her for years, and lied to himself about it by burying it under hostility, then labeling it as lust, want, need, anything to keep from admitting he was as vulnerable as a naked baby when it came to her. He was hard as nails, a sexual outlaw who casually used and left women, but he'd only prowled from woman to woman so restlessly because none of them had been able to satisfy his hunger. None of them had been the one woman he wanted, the one woman he loved. Now he had her physically, but not mentally, not emotionally, and he was scared spitless. His hands were trembling as he rubbed a towel over his body. Somehow he had to make her love him. He'd use any means necessary to keep her with him, loving her and taking care of her until no one existed in her mind except him, and every part of her became his to cherish.

Would she run if he told her he loved her? If he said the words, would she be uncomfortable around him? He remembered how he'd felt whenever some woman had tried to cling to him, whimpering that she loved him, begging him to stay. He'd felt embarrassment, impatience, pity. Pity! He couldn't take it if Michelle pitied him.

He'd never felt uncertain before. He was arrogant, impatient, determined, and he was used to men jumping when he barked out an order. It was unsettling to discover that he couldn't control either his emotions or Michelle's. He'd read before that love made strong men weak, but he hadn't understood it until now. Weak? Hell, he was terrified!

Naked, he returned to the bedroom and pulled on underwear and jeans. She was a magnet, drawing his eyes to her time and again. Lord, she was something to look at, with that pale gold hair gleaming in the bright sunlight, her bare flesh glowing. She lay on her stomach with her arms under the pillow, giving him a view of her supple back, firmly rounded buttocks and long, sleek legs. He admired her graceful lines and feminine curves, the need growing in him to touch her. Was she going to sleep all day?

He crossed to the bed and sat down on the side, stroking his hand over her bare shoulder. "Wake up, lazybones. It's almost two o'clock."

She yawned, snuggling deeper into the pillow. "So?" Her mouth curved into a smile as she refused to open her eyes.

He chuckled. "So get up. I can't even get dressed when you're lying here like this. My attention keeps wander—" He broke off, frowning at the small white scar marring the satiny shoulder under his fingers. She was lying naked under the bright rays of the afternoon sun, or he might not have noticed. Then he saw another one, and he touched it, too. His gaze moved, finding more of them marring the perfection of her skin. They were all down her back, even on her bottom and the backs of her upper thighs. His fingers touched all of them, moving slowly from scar to scar. She was rigid under his hands, not moving or looking at him, not even breathing.

Stunned, he tried to think of what could have made those small, crescent-shaped marks. Accidental cuts, by broken glass for instance, wouldn't all have been the same size and shape. The cuts hadn't been deep; the scarring was too faint, with no raised ridges. That was why he hadn't felt them, though he'd touched every inch of her body. But if they weren't accidental, that meant they had to be deliberate.

His indrawn breath hissed roughly through his teeth. He swore, his voice so quiet and controlled that the explicitly obscene words shattered the air more effectively than if he'd roared. Then he rolled her over, his hands hard on her shoulders, and said only three words. "Who did it?"

Michelle was white, frozen by the look on his face. He looked deadly, his eyes cold and ferocious. He lifted her by the shoulders until she was almost nose to nose with him, and he repeated his question, the words evenly spaced, almost soundless. "Who did it?"

Her lips trembled as she looked helplessly at him. She couldn't talk about it; she just couldn't. "I don't… It's noth—"

"Who did it?" he yelled, his neck corded with rage.

She closed her eyes, burning tears seeping from beneath her lids. Despair and shame ate at her, but she knew he wouldn't let her go until she answered. Her lips were trembling so hard she could barely talk. "John, please!"

"Who?"

Crumpling, she gave in, turning her face away. "Roger Beckman. My ex-husband." It was hard to say the words; she thought they would choke her.

John was swearing again, softly, endlessly. Michelle struggled briefly as he swept her up and sat down in a chair, holding her cradled on his lap, but it was a futile effort, so she abandoned it. Just saying Roger's name had made her feel unclean. She wanted to hide, to scrub herself over and over to be rid of the taint, but John wouldn't let her go. He held her naked on his lap, not saying a word after he'd stopped cursing until he noticed her shivering. The sun was hot, but her skin was cold. He stretched until he could reach the corner of the sheet, then jerked until it came free of the bed, and wrapped it around her.

He held her tight and rocked her, his hands stroking up and down her back. She'd been beaten. The knowledge kept ricocheting inside his skull, and he shook with a black rage he'd never known before. If he'd been able to get his hands on that slimy bastard right then, he'd have killed him with his bare hands and enjoyed every minute of it. He thought of Michelle cowering in fear and pain, her delicate body shuddering under the blows, and red mist colored his vision. No wonder she'd asked him not to hurt her the first time he'd made love to her! After her experience with men, it was something of a miracle that she'd responded at all.

He crooned to her, his rough cheek pressed against her sunny hair, his hard arms locked around her. He didn't know what he said, and neither did she, but the sound of his voice was enough. The gentleness came through, washing over her and warming her on the inside just as the heat of his body warmed her cold skin. Even after her shivering stopped he simply held her, waiting, letting her feel his closeness.

Finally she shifted a little, silently asking him to let her go. He did, reluctantly, his eyes never leaving her white face as she walked into the bathroom and shut the door. He started to go into the bathroom after her, alarmed by her silence and lack of color; his hand was on the doorknob when he reined himself under control. She needed to be alone right now. He heard the sound of the shower, and waited with unprecedented patience until she came out. She was still pale, but not as completely colorless as she'd been. The shower had taken the remaining chill from her skin, and she was wrapped in the terry-cloth robe she kept hanging on the back of the bathroom door.

"Are you all right?" he asked quietly.

"Yes." Her voice was muted.

"We have to talk about it."

"Not now." The look she gave him was shattered. "I can't. Not now."

"All right, baby. Later."

Later was that night, lying in his arms again, with the darkness like a shield around them. He'd made love to her, very gently and for a long time, easing her into rapture. In the lengthening silence afterward she felt his determination to know all the answers, and though she dreaded it, in the darkness she felt able to give them to him. When it came down to it, he didn't even have to ask. She simply started talking.

"He was jealous," she whispered. "Insane with it. I couldn't talk to a man at a party, no matter how ugly or happily married; I couldn't smile at a waiter. The smallest things triggered his rages. At first he'd just scream, accusing me of cheating on him, of loving someone else, and he'd ask me over and over who it was until I couldn't stand it anymore. Then he began slapping me. He was always sorry afterward. He'd tell me how much he loved me, swear he'd never do it again. But of course he did."

John had gone rigid, his muscles shaking with the rage she felt building in him again. In the darkness she stroked his face, giving him what comfort she could and never wondering at the illogic of it.

"I filed charges against him once; his parents bought him out of it and made it plain I wasn't to do such a thing again. Then I tried leaving him, but he found me and carried me back. He…he said he'd have Dad killed if I ever tried to leave him again."

"You believed him?" John asked harshly, the first words he'd spoken. She didn't flinch from the harshness, knowing it wasn't for her.

"Oh, yes, I believed him." She managed a sad little laugh. "I still do. His family has enough money that he could have it done and it would never be traced back to him."

"But you left him anyway."

"Not until I found a way to control him."

"How?"

She began trembling a little, and her voice wavered out of control. "The...the scars on my back. When he did that, his parents were in Europe; they weren't there to have files destroyed and witnesses bribed until it was too late. I already had a copy of everything, enough to press charges against him. I bought my divorce with it, and I made his parents promise to keep him away from me or I'd use what I had. They were very conscious of their position and family prestige."

"Screw their prestige," he said flatly, trying very hard to keep his rage under control.

"It's academic now; they're dead."

He didn't think it was much of a loss. People who cared more about their family prestige than about a young woman being brutally beaten and terrorized didn't amount to much in his opinion.

Silence stretched, and he realized she wasn't going to add anything else. If he let her, she'd leave it at that highly condensed and edited version, but he needed to know more. It hurt him in ways he'd never thought he could be hurt, but it was vital to him that he know all he could about her, or he would never be able to close the distance between them. He wanted to know where she went in her mind and why she wouldn't let him follow, what she was thinking, what had happened in the two years since her divorce.

He touched her back, caressing her with his fingertips. "Is this why you wouldn't go swimming?"

She stirred against his shoulder, her voice like gossamer wings in the darkness. "Yes. I know the scars aren't bad; they've faded a lot. But in my mind they're still like they were…. I was so scared someone would see them and ask how I got them."

"That's why you always put your nightgown back on after we'd made love."

She was silent, but he felt her nod.

"Why didn't you want *me* to know? I'm not exactly some stranger walking down the street."

No, he was her heart and her heartbreaker, the only man she'd ever loved, and therefore more important to her than anyone else in the world. She hadn't wanted him to know the ugliness that had been in her life.

"I felt dirty," she whispered. "Ashamed."

"Good God!" he exploded, raising up on his elbow to lean over her. "Why? It wasn't your fault. You were the victim, not the villain."

"I know, but sometimes knowledge doesn't help. The feelings were still there."

He kissed her, long and slow and hot, loving her with his tongue and letting her know how much he desired her. He kissed her until she responded, lifting her arms up to his neck and giving him her tongue in return. Then he settled onto the pillow again, cradling her head on his shoulder. She was nude; he had gently but firmly refused to let her put on a gown. That secret wasn't between them any longer, and she was glad. She loved the feel of his warm, hard-muscled body against her bare skin.

He was still brooding, unable to leave it alone. She felt his tension and slowly ran her hand over his chest, feeling the curly hair and small round nipples with their tiny center points. "Relax," she murmured, kissing his shoulder. "It's over."

"You said his parents controlled him, but they're dead. Has he bothered you since?"

She shivered, remembering the phone calls she'd had from Roger. "He called me a couple of times, at the house. I haven't seen him. I hope I never have to see him again." The last sentence was full of desperate sincerity.

"At the house? Your house? How long ago?"

"Before you brought me here."

"I'd like to meet him," John said quietly, menacingly.

"I hope you never do. He's...not sane."

They lay together, the warm, humid night wrapped around them, and she began to feel sleepy. Then he touched her again, and she felt the raw anger in him, the savage need to know. "What did he use?"

She flinched away from him. Swearing softly, he caught her close. "Tell me."

"There's no point in it."

"I want to know."

"You already know." Tears stung her eyes. "It isn't original."

"A belt."

Her breath caught in her throat. "He...he wrapped the leather end around his hand."

John actually snarled, his big body jerking. He thought of a belt buckle cutting into her soft skin, and it made him sick. It made him murderous. More than ever, he wanted to get his hands on Roger Beckman.

He felt her hands on him, clinging. "Please," she whispered. "Let's go to sleep."

He wanted to know one more thing, something that struck him as odd. "Why didn't you tell your dad? He had a lot of contacts; he could have done something. You didn't have to try to protect him."

Her laugh was soft and faintly bitter, not really a laugh at all. "I did tell him. He didn't believe me. It was easier for him to think I'd made it all up than to admit my life had gone so wrong."

She didn't tell him that she'd never loved Roger, that her life had gone wrong because she'd married one man while loving another.

Chapter Ten

"Telephone, Michelle!" Edie called from the kitchen.

Michelle had just come in, and she was on her way upstairs to shower; she detoured into the office to take the call there. Her mind was on her cattle; they were in prime condition, and John had arranged the sale. She would soon be leaving the ranks of the officially broke and entering those of the merely needy. John had scowled when she'd told him that.

"Hello," she said absently.

Silence.

The familiar chill went down her spine. "Hello!" she almost yelled, her fingers turning white from pressure.

"Michelle."

Her name was almost whispered, but she heard it,

recognized it. "No," she said, swallowing convulsively. "Don't call me again."

"How could you do this to me?"

"Leave me alone!" she screamed, and slammed the phone down. Her legs were shaking, and she leaned on the desk, gulping in air. She was frightened. How had Roger found her here? Dear God, what would John do if he found out Roger was bothering her? He'd be furious.... More than furious. He'd be murderous. But what if Roger called again and John answered? Would Roger ask for her, or would he remain silent?

The initial silence haunted her, reminding her of the other phone calls she had received. She'd had the same horrible feeling from all of them. Then she knew: Roger had made those other phone calls. She couldn't begin to guess why he hadn't spoken, but suddenly she had no doubt about who her caller had been. Why hadn't she realized it before? He had the resources to track her down, and he was sick and obsessive enough to do so. He knew where she was, knew she was intimately involved with another man. She felt nauseated, thinking of his jealous rages. He was entirely capable of coming down here to snatch her away from the man he would consider his rival and take her back "where she belonged."

More than two years, and she still wasn't free of him.

She thought about getting an injunction against him for harassment, but John would have to know, because the telephone was his. She didn't want him to know; his reaction could be too violent, and she didn't want him to get in any trouble.

She wasn't given the option of keeping it from him.

He opened the door to the office, a questioning look on his face as he stepped inside; Edie must have told him Michelle had a call, and that was unusual enough to make him curious. Michelle didn't have time to compose her face. He stopped, eyeing her sharply. She knew she looked pale and distraught. She watched as his eyes went slowly, inevitably, to the telephone. He never missed a detail, damn him; it was almost impossible to hide anything from him. She could have done it if she'd had time to deal with the shock, but now all she could do was stand frozen in her tracks. Why couldn't he have remained in the stable five minutes longer? She would have been in the shower; she would have had time to think of something.

"That was him, wasn't it?" he asked flatly.

Her hand crept toward her throat as she stared at him like a rabbit in a snare. John crossed the room with swift strides, catching her shoulders in his big warm hands.

"What did he say? Did he threaten you?"

Numbly she shook her head. "No. He didn't threaten me. It wasn't what he said; it's just that I can't stand hearing—" Her voice broke, and she tried to turn away, afraid to push her self-control any further.

John caught her more firmly to him, tucking her in the crook of one arm as he picked up the receiver. "What's his number?" he snapped.

Frantically Michelle tried to take the phone from him. "No, don't! That won't solve anything!"

His face grim, he evaded her efforts and pinned her arms to her sides. "He's good at terrorizing a woman, but it's time he knows there's someone else he'll have to deal with if he ever calls you again. Do you still remember his number or not? I can get it, but it'll be easier if you give it to me."

"It's unlisted," she said, stalling.

He gave her a long, level look. "I can get it," he repeated.

She didn't doubt that he could. When he decided to do something, he did it, and lesser people had better get out of his way. Defeated, she gave him the number and watched as he punched the buttons.

As close to him as she was, she could hear the ringing on the other end of the line, then a faint voice as someone answered. "Get Roger Beckman on the line," he ordered in the hard voice that no one disobeyed.

His brows snapped together in a scowl as he listened, then he said "Thanks" and hung up. Still frowning, he held her to him for a minute before telling her, "The housekeeper said he's on vacation in the south of France, and she doesn't know when he'll be back."

"But I just talked to him!" she said, startled. "He wasn't in France!"

John let her go and walked around to sit behind the desk, the frown turning abstracted. "Go on and take a shower," he said quietly. "I'll be up in a few minutes."

Michelle drew back, feeling cold all over again. Didn't he believe her? She knew Roger wasn't in the south of France; that call certainly hadn't been an overseas call. The connection had been too good, as clear as a local call. No, of course he didn't believe her, just as he hadn't believed her about the blue Chevrolet.

She walked away, her back rigid and her eyes burning. Roger wasn't in France, even if the housekeeper had said he was, but why was he trying to keep his location a secret?

After Michelle left, John sat in the study, pictures running through his mind, and he didn't like any of them. He saw Michelle's face, so white and pinched, her eyes terrified; he saw the small white scars on her back, remembered the sick look she got when she talked about her ex-husband. She'd worn the same look just now. Something wasn't right. He'd see Roger Beckman in hell before he let the man anywhere near Michelle again.

He needed information, and he was willing to use any means available to him to get it. Michelle meant more to him than anything else in the world.

Something had happened the summer before at his neighbor's house over on Diamond Bay, and his neighbor, Rachel Jones, had been shot. John had seen pure hell then, in the black eyes of the man who had held Rachel's wounded body in his arms. The man had looked as if the pain Rachel had been enduring had been ripping his soul out. At the time John hadn't truly understood the depths of the man's agony; at the time he'd still been hiding the truth of his own vulnerability from himself. Rachel had married her black-eyed warrior this past winter. Now John understood the man's anguish, because now he had Michelle, and his own life would be worthless without her.

He'd like to have Rachel's husband, Sabin, with him

now, as well as the big blond man who had been helping them. Those two men had something wild about them, the look of predators, but they would understand his need to protect Michelle. They would gladly have helped him hunt Beckman down like the animal he was.

He frowned. They weren't here, but Andy Phelps was, and Phelps had been involved with that mess at Diamond Bay last summer. He looked up a number and punched the buttons, feeling the anger build in him as he thought of Michelle's terrified face. "Andy Phelps, please."

When the sheriff's deputy answered, John said, "Andy, this is Rafferty. Can you do some quiet investigating?"

Andy was a former D.E.A. agent, and, besides that, he had a few contacts it wasn't safe to know too much about. He said quietly, "What's up?"

John outlined the situation, then waited while Andy thought of the possibilities.

"Okay, Michelle says the guy calling her is her ex-husband, but his housekeeper says he's out of the country, right?"

"Yeah."

"Is she sure it's her ex?"

"Yes. And she said he wasn't in France."

"You don't have a lot to go on. You'd have to prove he was the one doing the calling before you could get an injunction, and it sounds as if he's got a good alibi."

"Can you find out if he's really out of the country? I don't think he is, but why would he pretend, unless he's trying to cover his tracks for some reason?"

"You're a suspicious man, Rafferty."

"I have reason to be," John said in a cold, even tone. "I've seen the marks he left on Michelle. I don't want him anywhere near her."

Andy's voice changed as he digested that information, anger and disgust entering his tone. "Like that, huh? Do you think he's in the area?"

"He's certainly not at his home, and we know he isn't in France. He's calling Michelle, scaring her to death. I'd say it's a possibility."

"I'll start checking. There are a few favors I can call in. You might put a tape on your phone, so if he calls back you'll have proof."

"There's something else," John said, rubbing his forehead. "Michelle had an accident a few weeks ago. She said someone ran her off the road, a guy in a blue Chevrolet. I didn't believe her, damn it, and neither did the deputy. No one saw anything, and we didn't find any paint on the car, so I thought someone might have gotten a little close to her and she panicked. But she said he turned around, came back and tried to hit her again."

"That's not your usual someone-ran-me-off-the-road tale," Andy said sharply. "Has she said anything else?"

"No. She hasn't talked about it at all."

"You're thinking it could be her ex-husband."

"I don't know. It might not have anything at all to do with the phone calls, but I don't want to take the chance."

"Okay, I'll check around. Keep an eye on her, and hook a tape recorder up to the phone."

John hung up and sat there for a long time, silently

using every curse word he knew. Keeping an eye on her would be easy; she hadn't been off the ranch since the accident, hadn't even gone to check her own house. Now he knew why, and he damned himself and Roger Beckman with equal ferocity. If he'd only paid attention the night of the accident, they might have been able to track down the Chevrolet, but so much time had passed now that he doubted it would ever be found. At least Michelle hadn't connected Beckman with the accident, and John didn't intend to mention the possibility to her. She was scared enough as it was.

It infuriated him that he couldn't do anything except wait for Andy to get back to him. Even then, it might be a dead end. But if Beckman was anywhere in the area, John intended to pay him a visit and make damned certain he never contacted Michelle again.

Michelle bolted upright in bed, her eyes wide and her face chalky. Beside her, John stirred restlessly and reached for her, but didn't awaken. She lay back down, taking comfort in his nearness, but both her mind and her heart were racing.

It was Roger.

Roger had been driving the blue Chevrolet. Roger had tried to kill her. He wasn't in France at all, but here in Florida, biding his time and waiting to catch her out alone. She remembered the feeling she had had before the accident, as if someone were watching her with vile malice, the same feeling the phone calls had given her. She should have tied it all together before.

He'd found out about John. Michelle even knew how

he'd found out. Bitsy Sumner, the woman she and John had met in Tampa when they'd gone down to have the deed drawn up, was the worst gossip in Palm Beach. It wouldn't have taken long for the news to work its way up to Philadelphia that Michelle Cabot was very snuggly with an absolute *hunk*, a gorgeous, macho rancher with bedroom eyes that made Bitsy feel so *warm*. Michelle could almost hear Bitsy on the telephone, embroidering her tale and laughing wickedly as she speculated about the sexy rancher.

Roger had probably convinced himself that Michelle would come back to him; she could still hear him whispering how much he loved her, that he'd make it up to her and show her how good it could be between them. He would have gone into a jealous rage when he found out about John. At last he had known who the other man was, confirming the suspicions he'd had all along.

His mind must have snapped completely. She remembered what he'd said the last time he had called: "How could you do this to me?"

She felt trapped, panicked by the thought that he was out there somewhere, patiently waiting to catch her alone. She couldn't go to the police; she had no evidence, only her intuition, and people weren't arrested on intuition. Besides, she didn't put a lot of faith in the police. Roger's parents had bought them off in Philadelphia, and now Roger controlled all those enormous assets. He had unlimited funds at his disposal; who knew what he could buy? He might even have hired someone, in which case she had no idea who to be on guard against.

Finally she managed to go to sleep, but the knowledge that Roger was nearby ate at her during the next few days, disturbing her rest and stealing her appetite away. Despite the people around her, she felt horribly alone.

She wanted to talk to John about it, but bitter experience made her remain silent. How could she talk to him when he didn't believe her about the phone calls or the accident? He had hooked a tape recorder up to the telephone, but he hadn't discussed it with her, and she hadn't asked any questions. She didn't want to know about it if he were only humoring her. Things had become stilted between them since the last time Roger had called, and she felt even less able to approach him than she had before. Only in bed were things the same; she had begun to fear that he was tiring of her, but he didn't seem tired of her in bed. His lovemaking was still as hungry and frequent as before.

Abruptly, on a hot, sunny morning, she couldn't stand it any longer. She had been pushed so far that she had reached her limit. Even a rabbit will turn and fight when it's cornered. She was tired of it all, so tired that she sometimes felt she was dragging herself through water. Damn Roger! What did she have to do to get him out of her life? There had to be something. She couldn't spend the rest of her days peering around every corner, too terrified to even go to a grocery store. It made her angry when she thought how she had let him confine her as surely as if he'd locked her in a prison, and beginning today she was going to do something about it.

She still had the file that had won her a divorce; now that his parents were dead the file didn't mean as much, but it still meant something. It was documented proof that Roger had attacked her once before. If he would only call again, she would have his call on tape, and perhaps she could get him to say something damaging. This was Florida, not Philadelphia; that much money would always be influential, but down here he wouldn't have the network of old family friends to protect him.

But the file was in the safe at her house, and she wanted it in her possession, at John's. She didn't feel secure leaving it in an empty house, even though she kept the door locked. The house could easily be broken into, and the safe was a normal household one; she doubted whether it would prove to be all that secure if anyone truly wanted to open it. If Roger somehow got the file, she'd have no proof at all. Those photographs and records couldn't be replaced.

Making up her mind, she told Edie she was going riding and ran out to the stables. It was a pleasant ride across the pastures to her ranch, but she didn't enjoy it as she normally would have, because of the knot of tension forming in her stomach. Roger had seen her the last time she'd been there, and she couldn't forget the terror she'd felt when she'd seen the blue Chevrolet bearing down on her.

She approached the house from the rear, looking around uneasily as she slid off the horse, but everything was normal. The birds in the trees were singing. Quickly she checked all the doors and windows, but they all seemed tight, with no signs of forced entry. Only then did she enter the house and hurry to the office to open the safe. She removed the manila envelope and checked the contents, breathing a sigh of relief that everything was undisturbed, then slid the envelope inside her shirt and re-locked the safe.

The house had been closed up for a long time; the air was hot and stuffy. She felt dizzy as she stood up, and her stomach moved queasily. She hurried outside to the back porch, leaning against the wall and gulping fresh air into her lungs until her head cleared and her stomach settled. Her nerves were shot. She didn't know how much longer she could stand it, but she had to wait. He would call again; she knew it. Until then, there was precious little she could do.

Everything was still calm, quiet. The horse nickered a welcome at her as she mounted and turned toward home.

The stableman came out to meet her as she rode up, relief plain on his face. "Thank God you're back," he said feelingly. "The boss is raising pure hell—excuse me, ma'am. Anyway, he's been tearing the place up looking for you. I'll get word to him that you're back."

"Why is he looking for me?" she asked, bewildered. She had told Edie that she was going riding.

"I don't know, ma'am." He took the horse's reins from her hands as she slid to the ground.

Michelle went into the house and sought out Edie. "What has John in such an uproar?" she asked.

Edie lifted her eyebrows. "I didn't get close enough to ask."

"Didn't you tell him I'd gone riding?"

"Yep. That's when he really blew up."

She thought something might have come up and he

couldn't find the paperwork he needed on it, but when she checked the office everything looked just as it had when she'd left that morning. Taking the manila envelope from inside her shirt, she locked it inside John's safe, and only then did she feel better. She *was* safe here, surrounded by John's people.

A few minutes later she heard his truck come up the drive, and judging from its speed, his temper hadn't settled any. More curious than alarmed, she walked out to meet him as the truck skidded to a stop, the tires throwing up a spray of sand and gravel. John thrust the door open and got out, his rifle clutched in his hand. His face was tight, and black fire burned in his eyes as he strode toward her. "Where in hell have you been?" he roared.

Michelle looked at the rifle. "I was out riding."

He didn't stop when he reached her, but caught her arm and hauled her inside the house. "Out riding where, damn it? I've had everyone combing the place for you."

"I went over to the house." She was beginning to get a little angry herself at his manner, though she still didn't know what had set him off. She lifted her nose and gave him a cool look. "I didn't realize I had to ask permission to go to my own house."

"Well, honey bunch, you have to do exactly that," he snapped, replacing the rifle in the gun cabinet. "I don't want you going anywhere without asking me first."

"I don't believe I'm your prisoner," she said icily.

"Prisoner, hell!" He whirled on her, unable to forget the raw panic that had filled him when he hadn't been able to find her. Until he knew what was going on and where Roger Beckman was, he'd like to have her locked up in the bedroom for safekeeping. One look at her outraged face, however, told him that he'd gone about it all wrong, and she was digging her heels in.

"I thought something had happened to you," he said more quietly.

"So you went tearing around the ranch looking for something to shoot?" she asked incredulously.

"No. I went tearing around the ranch looking for you, and I carried the rifle in case you were in any danger."

She balled her hands into fists, wanting to slap him. He wouldn't believe her about a real danger, but he was worried that she might sprain an ankle or take a tumble off a horse. "What danger could I possibly be in?" she snapped. "I'm sure there's not a snake on the ranch that would dare bite anything without your permission!"

His expression became rueful as he stared down at her. He lifted his hand and tucked a loose strand of sun-streaked hair behind her ear, but she still glared at him like some outraged queen. He liked her temper a lot better than the distant manner he'd been getting from her lately. "You're pretty when you're mad," he teased, knowing how that would get her.

For a moment she looked ready to spit. Then suddenly she sputtered, "You jackass," and began laughing.

He chuckled. No one could say "jackass" quite like Michelle, all hoity-toity and precise. He loved it. She could call him a jackass any time she wanted. Before she could stop laughing, he put his arms around her and hauled her against him, covering her mouth with his and slowly sliding his tongue between her lips. Her laughter stopped abruptly, her hands coming up to clutch his bulging biceps, and her tongue met his.

"You worried the hell out of me," he murmured when he lifted his mouth.

"Not all of it, I noticed," she purred, making him grin.

"But I wasn't kidding. I want to know whenever you go somewhere, and I don't want you going over to your place alone. It's been empty for quite a while, and a bum could start hanging around."

"What would a bum be doing this far out?" she asked.

"What would a bum be doing anywhere? Crime isn't restricted to cities. Please. For my peace of mind?"

It was so unusual for John Rafferty to plead for anything that she could only stare at him. It struck her that even though he'd said please, he still expected that she would do exactly as he'd said. In fact, she was only being perverse because he'd been his usual autocratic, arrogant self and made her angry. It suited her perfectly to be cautious, for the time being.

The dizziness and nausea she'd felt at the house must have been the beginning symptoms of some sort of bug, because she felt terrible the next day. She spent most of the day in bed, too tired and sick to worry about anything else. Every time she raised her head, the awful dizziness brought on another attack of nausea. She just wanted to be left alone.

She felt marginally better the next morning, and managed to keep something in her stomach. John held her in his arms, worried about her listlessness. "If you aren't a lot better tomorrow, I'm taking you to a doctor," he said firmly.

"It's just a virus," she sighed. "A doctor can't do anything."

"You could get something to settle your stomach."

"I feel better today. What if you catch it?"

"Then you can wait on me hand and foot until I'm better," he said, chuckling at her expression of horror. He wasn't worried about catching it. He couldn't remember the last time he'd even had a cold.

She was much better the next day, and though she still didn't feel like riding around the ranch, she did spend the morning in the office, feeding information into the computer and catching up on the books. It would be easier if they had a bookkeeping program for the computer; she made a note to ask John about it.

Roger still hadn't called.

She balled her fist. She knew he was somewhere close by! How could she get him to come out of hiding? She could never live a normal life as long as she was afraid to leave the ranch by herself.

But perhaps that was what she would have to do. Obviously Roger had some way of watching the ranch; she simply couldn't believe the blue Chevrolet had been a coincidence, unconnected to Roger. He'd caught her off guard that time, but now she'd be looking for him. She had to draw him out.

When John came to the house for lunch, she had twisted her hair up and put on a bit of makeup, and she knew she looked a lot better. "I thought I'd go to town for a few things," she said casually. "Is there anything you need?"

His head jerked up. She hadn't driven at all since the

accident, and now here she was acting as nonchalant about driving as if the accident had never happened at all. Before he had worried that she was so reluctant to go anywhere, but now he wanted her to stay close. "What things?" he asked sharply. "Where exactly are you going?"

Her brows lifted at his tone. "Shampoo, hair conditioner, things like that."

"All right." He made an impatient gesture. "Where are you going? What time will you be back?"

"Really, you missed your calling. You should have been a prison guard."

"Just tell me."

Because she didn't want him to deny her the use of the car, she said in a bored voice, "The drugstore, probably. I'll be back by three."

He looked hard at her, then sighed and thrust his fingers through his thick black hair. "Just be careful."

She got up from the table. "Don't worry. If I wreck the car again, I'll pay for the damages with the money from the cattle sale."

He swore as he watched her stalk away. Damn, what could he do now? Follow her? He slammed into the office and called Andy Phelps to find out if he had any information on Roger Beckman yet. All Andy had come up with was that no one by the name of Roger Beckman had been on a flight to France in the last month, but he might not have gone there directly. It took time to check everything.

"I'll keep trying, buddy. That's all I can do."

"Thanks. Maybe I'm worried over nothing, but maybe I'm not."

"Yeah, I know. Why take chances? I'll call when I get something."

John hung up, torn by the need to do something, anything. Maybe he should tell Michelle of his suspicions, explain why he didn't want her wandering around by herself. But as Andy had pointed out, he really had nothing to go on, and he didn't want to upset her needlessly. She'd had enough worry in her life. If he had his way, nothing would ever worry her again.

Michelle drove to town and made her purchases, steeling herself every time a car drew near. But nothing happened; she didn't see anything suspicious, not even at the spot where the Chevrolet had forced her off the road. Fiercely she told herself that she wasn't paranoid, she hadn't imagined it all. Roger was there, somewhere. She simply had to find him. But she wasn't brave at all, and she was shaking with nerves by the time she got back to the ranch. She barely made it upstairs to the bathroom before her stomach rebelled and she retched miserably.

She tried it again the next day. And the next. Nothing happened, except that John was in the foulest mood she could imagine. He never came right out and forbade her to go anywhere, but he made it plain he didn't like it. If she hadn't been desperate, she would have thrown the car keys in his face and told him what he could do with them.

Roger had been watching her at her house that day. Could it be that he was watching that road instead of the one leading to town? He wouldn't have seen her when she'd gone over to get the file from the safe because she had ridden in from the back rather than using the road. John had told her not to go to her house alone, but she wouldn't have to go to the house. All she had to do was drive by on the road…and if Roger was there, he would follow her.

Chapter Eleven

She had to be crazy; she knew that. The last thing she wanted was to see Roger, yet here she was trying to find him, even though she suspected he was trying to kill her. No, she wanted to find him *because* of that. She certainly didn't want to die, but she wanted this to be over. Only then could she lead a normal life.

She wanted that life to be with John, but she had never fooled herself that their relationship was permanent, and the mood he was in these days could herald the end of it. Nothing she did seemed to please him, except when they were in bed, but perhaps that was just a reflection of his intense sex drive and any woman would have done.

Her nerves were so raw that she couldn't even think of eating the morning she planned to go to the house, and she paced restlessly, waiting until she saw John get in his pickup and drive across the pastures. She hadn't wanted him to know she was going anywhere; he asked too many questions, and it was hard to hide anything from him. She would only be gone half an hour, anyway, because when it came down to it, she didn't have the courage to leave herself hanging out as bait. All she could manage was one quick drive by; then she would come home.

She listened to the radio in an effort to calm her nerves as she drove slowly down the narrow gravel road. It came as a shock that the third hurricane of the season, Hurricane Carl, had formed in the Atlantic and was meandering toward Cuba. She had completely missed the first two storms. She hadn't even noticed that summer had slid into early autumn, because the weather was still so hot and humid, perfect hurricane weather.

Though she carefully searched both sides of the road for any sign of a car tucked away under the trees, she didn't see anything. The morning was calm and lazy. No one else was on the road. Frustrated, she turned around to drive back to the house.

A sudden wave of nausea hit her, and she had to halt the car. She opened the door and leaned out, her stomach heaving even though it was empty and nothing came out. When the spasm stopped she leaned against the steering wheel, weak and perspiring. This had hung on far too long to be a virus.

She lay there against the steering wheel for a long time, too weak to drive and too sick to care. A faint breeze wafted into the open door, cooling her hot face, and just as lightly the truth eased into her mind.

If this was a virus, it was the nine-month variety.

She let her head fall back against the seat, and a smile played around her pale lips. Pregnant. Of course. She even knew when it had happened: the night John had come home from Miami. He had been making love to her when she woke up, and neither of them had thought of taking precautions. She had been so on edge she hadn't noticed that she was late.

John's baby. It had been growing inside her for almost five weeks. Her hand drifted down to her stomach, a sense of utter contentment filling her despite the miserable way she felt. She knew the problems this would cause, but for the moment those problems were distant, unimportant compared to the blinding joy she felt.

She began to laugh, thinking of how sick she'd been. She remembered reading in some magazine that women who had morning sickness were less likely to miscarry than women who didn't; if that were true, this baby was as secure as Fort Knox. She still felt like death warmed over, but now she was happy to feel that way.

"A baby," she whispered, thinking of a tiny, sweet-smelling bundle with a mop of thick black hair and melting black eyes, though she realized any child of John Rafferty's would likely be a hellion.

But she couldn't continue sitting in the car, which was parked more on the road than off. Shakily, hoping the nausea would hold off until she could get home, she put the car in gear and drove back to the ranch with painstaking caution. Now that she knew what was wrong, she knew what to do to settle her stomach. And she needed to make an appointment with a doctor.

Sure enough, her stomach quieted after she ate a meal of dry toast and weak tea. Then she began to think about the problems.

Telling John was the first problem and, to Michelle, the biggest. She had no idea how he would react, but she had to face the probability that he would not be as thrilled as she was. She feared he was getting tired of her anyway; if so, he'd see the baby as a burden, tying him to a woman he no longer wanted.

She lay on the bed, trying to sort out her tangled thoughts and emotions. John had a right to know about his child, and, like it or not, he had a responsibility to it. On the other hand, she couldn't use the baby to hold him if he wanted to be free. Bleak despair filled her whenever she tried to think of a future without John, but she loved him enough to let him go. Since their first day together she had been subconsciously preparing for the time when he would tell her that he didn't want her any longer. That much was clear in her mind.

But what if he decided that they should marry because of the baby? John took his responsibilities seriously, even to the point of taking a wife he didn't want for the sake of his child. She could be a coward and grab for anything he offered, on the basis that the crumbs of affection that came her way would be better than nothing, or she could somehow find the courage to deny herself the very thing she wanted most. Tears filled her eyes, the tears that came so easily these days. She sniffled and wiped them away.

She couldn't decide anything; her emotions were see-sawing wildly between elation and depression. She didn't know how John would react, so any plans she made were a waste of time. This was something they would have to work out together.

She heard someone ride up, followed by raised, excited voices outside, but cowboys were always coming and going at the ranch, and she didn't think anything of it until Edie called upstairs, "Michelle? Someone's hurt. The boys are bringing him in— My God, it's the boss!" She yelled the last few words and Michelle shot off the bed. Afterward she never remembered running down the stairs; all she could remember was Edie catching her at the front door as Nev and another man helped John down from a horse. John was holding a towel to his face, and blood covered his hands and arms, and soaked his shirt.

Michelle's face twisted, and a thin cry burst from her throat. Edie was a big, strong woman, but somehow Michelle tore free of her clutching arms and got to John. He shrugged away from Nev and caught Michelle with his free arm, hugging her to him. "I'm all right," he said gruffly. "It looks worse than it is."

"You'd better get to a doc, boss," Nev warned. "Some of those cuts need stitches."

"I will. Get on back to the men and take care of things." John gave Nev a warning look over Michelle's head, and though one eye was covered with the bloody towel, Nev got the message. He glanced quickly at Michelle, then nodded.

"What happened?" Michelle cried frantically as she helped John into the kitchen. His arm was heavy around her shoulders, which told her more than anything that he was hurt worse than he wanted her to know. He sank onto one of the kitchen chairs.

"I lost control of the truck and ran into a tree," he muttered. "My face hit the steering wheel."

She put her hand on the towel to keep it in place, feeling him wince even under her light touch, and lifted his hand away. She could see thin shards of glass shining in the black depths of his hair.

"Let me see," she coaxed, and eased the towel away from his face.

She had to bite her lip to keep from moaning. His left eye was already swollen shut, and the skin on his cheekbone was broken open in a jagged wound. His cheekbone and brow ridge were already purple and turning darker as they swelled almost visibly, huge knots distorting his face. A long cut slanted across his forehead, and he was bleeding from a dozen other smaller cuts. She took a deep breath and schooled her voice to evenness. "Edie, crush some ice to go on his eye. Maybe we can keep the swelling from getting any worse. I'll get my purse and the car keys."

"Wait a minute," John ordered. "I want to clean up a little; I've got blood and glass all over me."

"That isn't important—"

"I'm not hurt that badly," he interrupted. "Help me out of this shirt."

When he used that tone of voice, he couldn't be budged. Michelle unbuttoned the shirt and helped him out of it, noticing that he moved with extreme caution. When the shirt was off, she saw the big red welt across his ribs and knew why he was moving so carefully. In a few hours he would be too sore to move at all. Easing out of the chair, he went to the sink and washed off the blood that stained his hands and arms, then stood patiently while Michelle took a wet cloth and gently cleaned his chest and throat, even his back. His hair was matted with blood on the left side, but she didn't want to try washing his head until he'd seen a doctor.

She ran upstairs to get a clean shirt for him and helped him put it on. Edie had crushed a good amount of ice and folded it into a clean towel to make a cold pad. John winced as Michelle carefully placed the ice over his eye, but he didn't argue about holding it in place.

Her face was tense as she drove him to the local emergency care clinic. He was hurt. It staggered her, because somehow she had never imagined John as being vulnerable to anything. He was as unyielding as granite, somehow seeming impervious to fatigue, illness or injury. His battered, bloody face was testimony that he was all too human, though, being John, he wasn't giving in to his injuries. He was still in control.

He was whisked into a treatment room at the clinic, where a doctor carefully cleaned the wounds and stitched the cut on his forehead. The other cuts weren't severe enough to need stitches, though they were all cleaned and bandaged. Then the doctor spent a long time examining the swelling around John's left eye.

"I'm going to have you admitted to a hospital in Tampa so an eye specialist can take a look at this," he told John.

"I don't have time for a lot of poking," John snapped, sitting up on the table.

"It's your sight," the doctor said evenly. "You took a hell of a blow, hard enough to fracture your cheekbone. Of course, if you're too busy to save your eyesight—"

"He'll go," Michelle interrupted.

John looked at her with one furious black eye, but she glared back at him just as ferociously. There was something oddly magnificent about her, a difference he couldn't describe because it was so subtle. But even as pale and strained as she was, she looked good. She always looked good to him, and he'd be able to see her a lot better with two eyes than just one.

He thought fast, then growled, "All right." Let her think what she wanted about why he was giving in; the hard truth was that he didn't want her anywhere near the ranch right now. If he went to Tampa, he could insist that she stay with him, which would keep her out of harm's way while Andy Phelps tracked down whoever had shot out his windshield. What had been a suspicion was now a certainty as far as John was concerned; Beckman's threat went far beyond harassing telephone calls. Beckman had tried to make it look like an accident when he had run Michelle off the road, but now he had gone beyond that; a bullet wasn't accidental.

Thank God Michelle hadn't been with him as she usually was. At first he'd thought the bullet was intended for him, but now he wasn't so certain. The bullet had been too far to the right. Damn it, if only he hadn't lost control of the truck when the windshield shattered! He'd jerked the wheel instinctively, and the truck had started sliding on the dewy grass, hitting a big oak head-on. The impact had thrown him forward, and his cheekbone had hit the steering wheel with such force that he'd been unconscious for a few minutes. By the time he'd recovered consciousness and his head had cleared, there had been no point in sending any of his men to investigate where the shot had come from. Beckman would have been long gone, and they would only have destroyed any signs he might have left. Andy Phelps could take over now.

"I'll arrange for an ambulance," the doctor said, turning to leave the room.

"No ambulance. Michelle can take me down there."

The doctor sighed. "Mr. Rafferty, you have a concussion; you should be lying down. And in case of damage to your eye, you shouldn't strain, bend over, or be jostled. An ambulance is the safest way to get you to Tampa."

John scowled as much as he could, but the left side of his face was so swollen that he couldn't make the muscles obey. No way was he going to let Michelle drive around by herself in the Mercedes; the car would instantly identify her to Beckman. If he had to go to Tampa, she was going to be beside him every second. "Only if Michelle rides in the ambulance with me."

"I'll be right behind," she said. "No, wait. I need to go back home first, to pick up some clothes for both of us."

"No. Doc, give me an hour. I'll have clothes brought

out to us and arrange for the car to be driven back to the house." To Michelle he said, "You either ride with me, or I don't go at all."

Michelle stared at him in frustration, but she sensed he wasn't going to back down on this. He'd given in surprisingly easy about going to the hospital, only to turn oddly stubborn about keeping her beside him. If someone drove the car back to the ranch, they would be stranded in Tampa, so it didn't make sense. This entire episode seemed strange, but she didn't know just why and didn't have time to figure it out. If she had to ride in an ambulance to get John to Tampa, she'd do it. She was still so scared and shocked by his accident that she would do anything to have him well again.

He took her acquiescence for granted, telling her what he wanted and instructing her to have Nev bring the clothes, along with another man to drive the car home. Mentally she threw her hands up and left the room to make the phone call. John waited a few seconds after the door had closed behind her, then said, "Doc, is there another phone I can use?"

"Not in here, and you shouldn't be walking around. You shouldn't even be sitting up. If the call is so urgent it won't wait, let your wife make it for you."

"I don't want her to know about it." He didn't bother to correct the doctor's assumption that Michelle was his wife. The good doctor was a little premature, that was all. "Do me a favor. Call the sheriff's department, tell Andy Phelps where I am and that I need to talk to him. Don't speak to anyone except Phelps."

The doctor's eyes sharpened, and he looked at the

big man for a moment. Anyone else would have been flat on his back. Rafferty should have been, but his system must be like iron. He was still steady, and giving orders with a steely authority that made it almost impossible not to do as he said.

"All right, I'll make the call if you'll lie down. You're risking your eyesight, Mr. Rafferty. Think about being blind in that eye for the rest of your life."

John's lips drew back in a feral grin that lifted the corners of his mustache. "Then the damage has probably already been done, doctor." Losing the sight in his left eye didn't matter much when stacked against Michelle's life. Nothing was more important than keeping her safe.

"Not necessarily. You may not even have any damage to your eye, but with a blow that forceful it's better to have it checked. You may have what's called a blowout fracture, where the shock is transmitted to the wall of the orbital bone, the eye socket. The bone is thin, and it gives under the pressure, taking it away from the eyeball itself. A blowout fracture can save your eyesight, but if you have one you'll need surgery to repair it. Or you can have nerve damage, a dislocated lens, or a detached retina. I'm not an eye specialist, so I can't say. All I can tell you is to stay as quiet as possible or you can do even greater damage."

Impatiently John lay down, putting his hands behind his head, which was throbbing. He ignored the pain, just as he ignored the numbness of his face. Whatever damage had been done, was done. So he'd broken his cheekbone and maybe shattered his eye socket; he could live with a battered face or with just one good eye, but he couldn't live without Michelle.

He went over the incident again and again in his mind, trying to pull details out of his subconscious. In that split second before the bullet had shattered the windshield, had he seen a flash that might pinpoint Beckman's location? Had Beckman been walking? Not likely. The ranch was too big for a man to cover on foot. Nor was it likely he would have been on horseback; riding horses were harder to come by than cars, which could easily be rented. Going on the assumption that Beckman had been driving, what route could he have taken that would have kept him out of sight?

Andy Phelps arrived just moments before Nev. For Michelle's benefit, the deputy joked about John messing up his pretty face, then waited while John gave Nev detailed instructions. Nev nodded, asking few questions. Then John glanced at Michelle. "Why don't you check the things Nev brought; if you need anything else, he can bring it to Tampa."

Michelle hesitated for a fraction of a second, feeling both vaguely alarmed and in the way. John wanted her out of the room for some reason. She looked at the tall, quiet deputy, then back at John, before quietly leaving the room with Nev. Something was wrong; she knew it.

Even Nev was acting strangely, not quite looking her in the eye. Something had happened that no one wanted her to know, and it involved John.

He had given in too easily about going to the hospital, though the threat of losing his eyesight was certainly enough to give even John pause; then he had been so illogical about the car. John was never illogical. Nev was uneasy about something, and now John wanted to talk privately to a deputy. She was suddenly certain the deputy wasn't there just because he'd heard a friend was hurt.

Too many things didn't fit. Even the fact that John had had an accident at all didn't fit. He'd been driving across rough pastures since boyhood, long before he'd been old enough to have a driver's license. He was also one of the surest drivers she had ever seen, with quick reflexes and eagle-eyed attention to every other driver on the road. It just didn't make sense that he would lose control of his truck and hit a tree. It was too unlikely, too pat, too identical to her own accident.

Roger.

What a fool she had been! She had considered him as a danger only to herself, not to John. She should have expected his insane jealousy to spill over onto the man he thought had taken her away from him. While she had been trying to draw him out, he had been stalking John. Fiercely her hands knotted into fists. Roger wouldn't stand a chance against John in an open fight, but he would sneak around like the coward he was, never taking the chance of a face-to-face confrontation.

She looked down at the two carryons Edie had packed for them and put her hand to her head. "I feel a little sick, Nev," she whispered. "Excuse me, I have to get to the restroom."

Nev looked around, worry etched on his face. "Do you want me to get a nurse? You do look kinda green."

"No, I'll be all right." She managed a weak smile as

she lied, "I never have been able to stand the sight of blood, and it just caught up with me."

She patted his arm and went around the partition to the public restrooms, but didn't enter. Instead she waited a moment, sneaking peeks around the edge of the partition; as soon as Nev turned to sit down while waiting for her, she darted across the open space to the corridor where the examining rooms were. The door to John's room was closed, but not far enough for the latch to catch. When she cautiously nudged it, the door opened a crack. It was on the left side of the room, so John wouldn't be able to see it. Phelps should be on John's right side, facing him; with luck, he wouldn't notice the slight movement of the door, either.

Their voices filtered through the crack.

"—think the bullet came from a little rise just to the left of me," John said. "Nev can show you."

"Is there any chance the bullet could be in the up-holstery?"

"Probably not. The trajectory wasn't angled enough."

"Maybe I can find the cartridge. I'm coming up with a big zero from the airlines, but I have another angle I can check. If he flew in, he'd have come in at Tampa, which means he'd have gotten his rental car at the airport. If I can get a match on his description, we'll have his license plate number."

"A blue Chevrolet. That should narrow it down," John said grimly.

"I don't even want to think about how many blue Chevrolets there are in this state. It was a good idea to keep Michelle with you in Tampa; it'll give me a few days to get a lead on this guy. I can get a buddy in Tampa to put surveillance on the hospital, if you think you'll need it."

"He won't be able to find her if the doctor here keeps quiet and if my file is a little hard to find."

"I can arrange that." Andy chuckled.

Michelle didn't wait to hear more. Quietly she walked back down the corridor and rejoined Nev. He was reading a magazine and didn't look up until she sat down beside him. "Feeling better?" he asked sympathetically.

She gave some answer, and it must have made sense, because it satisfied him. She sat rigidly in the chair, more than a little stunned. What she had overheard had verified her suspicion that Roger was behind John's "accident," but it was hard for her to take in the rest of it. John not only believed her about the phone calls, he had tied them in to the blue Chevrolet and had been quietly trying to track Roger down. That explained why he had suddenly become so insistent that she tell him exactly where she was going and how long she would be there, why he didn't want her going anywhere at all. He had been trying to protect her, while she had been trying to bait Roger into the open.

She hadn't told him what she was doing because she hadn't thought he would believe her; she had learned well the bitter lesson that she could depend only on herself, perhaps learned it too well. Right from the beginning John had helped her, sometimes against her will. He had stepped in and taken over the ranch chores that were too much for her; he was literally carrying her ranch until she could rebuild it into a profitable enterprise. He had given her love, comfort, care and concern, and now a child, but still she hadn't trusted him. He hadn't been tiring of her; he'd been under considerable strain to protect her.

Being John, he hadn't told her of his suspicions or what he was doing because he hadn't wanted to "worry" her. It was just like him. That protective, possessive streak of his was bone deep and body wide, defying logical argument. There were few things or people in his life that he cared about, but when he did care, he went full measure. He had claimed her as his, and what was his, he kept.

Deputy Phelps stopped by to chat; Michelle decided to give him an opportunity to talk to Nev, and she walked back to John's room. The ambulance had just arrived, so she knew they would be leaving soon.

When the door opened, he rolled his head until he could see her with his right eye. "Is everything okay?"

She had to grit her teeth against the rage that filled her when she saw his battered, discolored face. It made her want to destroy Roger in any way she could. The primitive, protective anger filled her, pumping into every cell in her body. It took every bit of control she had to calmly walk over to him as if she weren't in a killing rage and take his hand. "If you're all right, then I don't care what Edie packed or didn't pack."

"I'll be all right." His deep voice was confident. He might or might not lose the sight in his eye, but he'd be all right. John Rafferty was made of the purest, hardest steel.

She sat beside him in the ambulance and held his hand all the way to Tampa, her eyes seldom leaving his face. Perhaps he dozed; perhaps it was simply less painful if he kept his right eye closed, too. For whatever reason, little was said during the long ride.

It wasn't until they reached the hospital that he opened his eye and looked at her, frowning when he saw how drawn she looked. She needed the bed rest more than he did; if it hadn't been for his damned eye, and the opportunity to keep Michelle away from the ranch, he would already have been back at work.

He should have gotten her away when he'd first suspected Beckman was behind her accident, but he'd been too reluctant to let her out of his sight. He wasn't certain about her or how much she needed him, so he'd kept her close at hand. But the way she had looked when she saw he was hurt…a woman didn't look like that unless she cared. He didn't know how much she cared, but for now he was content with the fact that she did. He had her now, and he wasn't inclined to let go. As soon as this business with Beckman was settled, he'd marry her so fast she wouldn't know what was happening.

Michelle went through the process of having him admitted to the hospital while he was whisked off, with three—*three!*—nurses right beside him. Even as battered as he was, he exuded a masculinity that drew women like a magnet.

She didn't see him again for three hours. Fretting, she wandered the halls until a bout of nausea drove her to find the cafeteria, where she slowly munched on stale crackers. Her stomach gradually settled. John

would probably be here for at least two days, maybe
longer; how could she hide her condition from him
when she would be with him practically every hour of
the day? Nothing escaped his attention for long,
whether he had one good eye or two. Breeding wasn't
anything new to him; it was his business. Cows calved;
mares foaled. On the ranch, everything mated and re-
produced. It wouldn't take long for him to discard the
virus tale she'd told him and come up with the real
reason for her upset stomach.

What would he say if she told him? She closed her
eyes, her heart pounding wildly at the thought. He
deserved to know. She wanted him to know; she wanted
to share every moment of this pregnancy with him. But
what if it drove him to do something foolish, knowing
that Roger not only threatened her but their child as
well?

She forced herself to think clearly. They were safe
here in the hospital; this was bought time. He wouldn't
leave the hospital when staying here meant that she
was also protected. She suspected that was the only
reason he'd agreed to come at all. He was giving
Deputy Phelps time to find Roger, if he could.

But what if Phelps hadn't found Roger by the time
John left the hospital? What evidence did they have
against him, anyway? He had had time to have any
damage to the Chevrolet repaired, and no one had seen
him shoot at John. He hadn't threatened her during any
of those phone calls. He hadn't had to; she knew him,
and that was enough.

She couldn't run, not any longer. She had run for two

years, fleeing emotionally long after she had stopped physically running. John had brought her alive with his fierce, white-hot passion, forcing her out of her protective reserve. She couldn't leave him, especially now that she carried his child. She had to face Roger, face all the old nightmares and conquer them, or she would never be rid of this crippling fear. She could fight him, something she had always been too terrified to do before. She could fight him for John, for their baby, and she could damn well fight him for herself.

Finally she went back to the room that had been assigned to John to wait. It was thirty minutes more before he was wheeled into the room and transferred very carefully to the bed. When the door closed behind the orderlies he said, from between clenched teeth, "If anyone else comes through that door to do anything to me, I'm going to throw them out the window." Gingerly he eased into a more upright position against the pillow, then punched the button that raised the head of the bed.

She ignored his bad temper. "Have you seen the eye specialist yet?"

"Three of them. Come here."

There was no misreading that low demanding voice or the glint in his right eye as he looked at her. He held his hand out to her and said again, "Come here."

"John Patrick Rafferty, you aren't in any shape to begin carrying on like that."

"Aren't I?"

She refused to look at his lap. "You shouldn't be jostled."

"I don't want to be jostled. I just want a kiss." He

gave her a slow, wicked grin despite the swelling in his face. "The spirit's willing, but the body's tired as hell."

She bent to kiss him, loving his lips gently with her own. When she tried to lift her head he thrust his fingers into her hair and held her down while his mouth molded to hers, his tongue making teasing little forays to touch hers. He gave a sigh of pleasure and let her up, but shifted his hand to her bottom to hold her beside him. "What've you been doing while I've been lying in cold halls in between bouts of being stuck, prodded, x-rayed and prodded some more?"

"Oh, I've been really entertained. You don't realize what an art mopping is until you've seen a master do it. There's also a four-star cafeteria here, specializing in the best stale crackers I've ever eaten." She grinned, thinking he'd never realize the truth of that last statement.

He returned the grin, thinking that once he would have accused her of being spoiled. He knew better now, because he'd been trying his damnedest to spoil her, and she persisted in being satisfied with far less than he would gladly have given her any day of the week. Her tastes didn't run to caviar or mink, and she'd been content to drive that old truck of hers instead of a Porsche. She liked silk and had beautiful clothes, but she was equally content wearing a cotton shirt and jeans. It wasn't easy to spoil a woman who was happy with whatever she had.

"Arrange to have a bed moved in here for you," he ordered. "Unless you want to sleep up here with me?"

"I don't think the nurses would allow that."

"Is there a lock on the door?"

She laughed. "No. You're out of luck."

His hand moved over her bottom, the slow, intimate touch of a lover. "We need to talk. Will it bother you if I lose this eye?"

Until then she hadn't realized that he might lose the eye as well as his sight. She sucked in a shocked breath, reaching blindly for his hand. He continued to watch her steadily, and slowly she relaxed, knowing what was important.

"It would bother me for your sake, but as for me… You can be one-eyed, totally blind, crippled, whatever, and I'll still love you."

There. She'd said it. She hadn't meant to, but the words had come so naturally that even if she could take them back, she wouldn't.

His right eye was blazing black fire at her. She had never seen anyone else with eyes as dark as his, night-black eyes that had haunted her from the first time she'd met him. She looked down at him and managed a tiny smile that was only a little hesitant as she waited for him to speak.

"Say that again."

She didn't pretend not to know what he meant, but she had to take another deep breath. Her heart was pounding. "I love you. I'm not saying that to try to trap you into anything. It's just the way I feel, and I don't expect you to—"

He put his fingers over her mouth. "It's about damn time," he said.

Chapter Twelve

"**Y**ou're very lucky, Mr. Rafferty," Dr. Norris said, looking over his glasses. "Your cheekbone seems to have absorbed most of the impact. It's fractured, of course, but the orbital bone is intact. Nor does there seem to be any damage to the eye itself, or any loss of sight. In other words, you have a hell of a shiner."

Michelle drew a deep breath of relief, squeezing John's hand. He winked at her with his right eye, then drawled, "So I've spent four days in a hospital because I have a black eye?"

Dr. Norris grinned. "Call it a vacation."

"Well, vacation's over, and I'm checking out of the resort."

"Just take it easy for the next few days. Remember

that you have stitches in your head, your cheekbone is fractured, and you had a mild concussion."

"I'll keep an eye on him," Michelle said with a note of warning in her voice, looking at John very hard. He was probably planning to get on a horse as soon as he got home.

When they were alone again John put his hands behind his head, watching her with a distinct glitter in his eyes. After four days the swelling around his eye had subsided enough that he could open it a tiny slit, enough for him to see with it again. His face was still a mess, discolored in varying shades of black and purple, with a hint of green creeping in, but none of that mattered beside the fact that his eye was all right. "This has been a long four days," he murmured. "When we get home, I'm taking you straight to bed."

Her blood started running wild through her veins again, and she wondered briefly if she would always have this uncontrolled response to him. She'd been completely vulnerable to him from the start, and her reaction now was even stronger. Her body was changing as his baby grew within her, invisible changes as yet, but her skin seemed to be more sensitive, more responsive to his lightest touch. Her breasts throbbed slightly, aching for the feel of his hands and mouth.

She had decided not to tell him about the baby just yet, especially not while his eyesight was still in doubt, and had been at pains during the past four days to keep her uneasy stomach under control. She munched on crackers almost constantly, and had stopped drinking coffee because it made the nausea worse.

She could still see the hard satisfaction that had filled his face when she'd told him she loved him, but he hadn't returned the words. For a horrible moment she'd wondered if he was gloating, but he'd kissed her so hard and hungrily that she had dismissed the notion even though she'd felt a lingering pain. That night, after the lights were out and she was lying on the cot that had been brought in, he had said, "Michelle."

His voice was low, and he hadn't moved. She'd lifted her head to stare through the darkness at him. "Yes?"

"I love you," he had said quietly.

Tremors shook her, and tears leaped to her eyes, but they were happy tears. "I'm glad," she had managed to say.

He'd laughed in the darkness. "You little tease, just wait until I get my hands on you again."

"I can't wait."

Now he was all right, and they were going home. She called Nev to come pick them up, then hung up the phone with hands that had become damp. She wiped them on her slacks and lifted her chin. "Have you heard if Deputy Phelps has found a lead on Roger yet?"

John had been dressing, but at her words his head snapped around and his good eye narrowed on her. Slowly he zipped his jeans and fastened them, then walked around the bed to tower over her threateningly. Michelle's gaze didn't waver, nor did she lower her chin, even though she abruptly felt very small and helpless.

He didn't say anything, but simply waited, his mouth a hard line beneath his mustache. "I eavesdropped," she said calmly. "I had already made the connection between the phone calls and the guy who forced me off the road, but how did you tie everything together?"

"Just an uneasy feeling and a lot of suspicions," he said. "After that last call, I wanted to make certain I knew where he was. There were too many loose ends, and Andy couldn't find him on any airline's overseas passenger list. The harder Beckman was to find, the more suspicious it looked."

"You didn't believe me at first, about the blue Chevrolet."

He sighed. "No, I didn't. Not at first. I'm sorry. It was hard for me to face the fact that anyone would want to hurt you. But something was bothering you. You didn't want to drive, you didn't want to leave the ranch at all, but you wouldn't talk about it. That's when I began to realize you were scared."

Her green eyes went dark. "Terrified is a better word," she whispered, looking out the window. "Have you heard from Phelps?"

"No. He wouldn't call here unless he'd found Beckman."

She shivered, the strained look coming back into her face. "He tried to kill you. I should have known, I should have done something."

"What could you have done?" he asked roughly. "If you'd been with me that day, the bullet would have hit you, instead of just shattering the windshield."

"He's so jealous he's insane." Thinking of Roger made her feel sick, and she pressed her hand to her stomach. "He's truly insane. He probably went wild when I moved in with you. The first couple of phone calls, he didn't say anything at all. Maybe he had just been calling to see if I answered the phone at your house. He couldn't stand for me to even talk to any other man, and when he found out that you and I—" She broke off, a fine sheen of perspiration on her face.

Gently John pulled her to him, pressing her head against his shoulder while he soothingly stroked her hair. "I wonder how he found out."

"Bitsy Sumner," Michelle said shakily.

"The airhead we met in the restaurant?"

"That airhead is the biggest gossip I know."

"If he's that far off his rocker, he probably thinks he's finally found the `other man' after all these years."

She jumped, then gave a tight little laugh. "He has."

"What?" His voice was startled.

She eased away from him and pushed her hair back from her face with a nervous gesture. "It's always been you," she said in a low voice, looking anywhere except at him. "I couldn't love him the way I should have, and somehow he…seemed to know it."

He put his hand on her chin and forced her head around. "You acted like you hated me, damn it."

"I had to have some protection from you." Her green eyes regarded him with a little bitterness. "You had women falling all over you, women with a lot more experience, and who were a lot prettier. I was only eighteen, and you scared me to death. People called you 'Stud!' I knew I couldn't handle a man like you, even if you'd ever looked at me twice."

"I looked," he said harshly. "More than twice. But

you turned your nose up at me as if you didn't like my smell, so I left you alone, even though I wanted you so much my guts were tied in knots. I built that house for you, because you were used to a lot better than the old house I was living in. I built the swimming pool because you liked to swim. Then you married some fancy-pants rich guy, damn you, and I felt like tearing the place down stone by stone."

Her lips trembled. "If I couldn't have you, it didn't matter who I married."

"You could have had me."

"As a temporary bed partner? I was so young I thought I had to have it all or nothing. I wanted forever after, for better or worse, and your track record isn't that of a marrying man. Now…" She shrugged, then managed a faint smile. "Now all that doesn't matter."

Hard anger crossed his face, then he said, "That's what you think," and covered her mouth with his. She opened her lips to him, letting him take all he wanted. The time was long past when she could deny him anything, any part of herself. Even their kisses had been restrained for the past four days, and the hunger was so strong in him that it overwhelmed his anger; he kissed her as if he wanted to devour her, his strong hands kneading her flesh with barely controlled ferocity, and she reveled in it. She didn't fear his strength or his roughness, because they sprang from passion and aroused an answering need inside her.

Her nails dug into his bare shoulders as her head fell back, baring her throat for his mouth. His hips moved rhythmically, rubbing the hard ridge of his manhood against her as his self-control slipped. Only the knowledge that a nurse could interrupt them at any moment gave him the strength to finally ease away from her, his breath coming hard and fast. The way he felt now was too private, too intense, for him to allow even the chance of anyone walking in on them.

"Nev had better hurry," he said roughly, unable to resist one more kiss. Her lips were pouty and swollen from his kisses, her eyes half-closed and drugged with desire; that look aroused him even more, because he had put it there.

Michelle slipped out of the bedroom, her clothes in her hand. She didn't want to take a chance on waking John by dressing in the bedroom; he had been sleeping heavily since the accident, but she didn't want to push her luck. She had to find Roger. He had missed killing John once; he might not miss the second time. And she knew John; if he made even a pretense of following the doctor's order to take it easy, she'd be surprised. No, he would be working as normal, out in the open and vulnerable.

He had talked to Deputy Phelps the night before, but all Andy had come up with was that a blue Chevrolet had been rented to a man generally matching Roger's physical description, and calling himself Edward Walsh. The familiar cold chill had gone down Michelle's spine. "Edward is Roger's middle name," she had whispered. "Walsh was his mother's maiden name." John had stared at her for a long moment before relaying the information to Andy.

She wouldn't allow Roger another opportunity to

hurt John. Oddly, she wasn't afraid for herself. She had already been through so much at Roger's hands that she simply couldn't be afraid any longer, but she was deathly afraid for John, and for this new life she carried. She couldn't let this go on.

Lying awake in the darkness, she had suddenly known how to find him. She didn't know exactly where he was, but she knew the general vicinity; all she had to do was bait the trap, and he would walk into it. The only problem was that she was the bait, and she would be in the trap with him.

She left a note for John on the kitchen table and ate a cracker to settle her stomach. To be on the safe side, she carried a pack of crackers with her as she slipped silently out the back door. If her hunch was right, she should be fairly safe until someone could get there. Her hand strayed to her stomach. She had to be right.

The Mercedes started with one turn of the ignition key, its engine smooth and quiet. She put it in gear and eased it down the driveway without putting on the lights, hoping she wouldn't wake Edie or any of the men.

Her ranch was quiet, the old house sitting silent and abandoned under the canopy of big oak trees. She unlocked the door and let herself in, her ears straining to hear every noise in the darkness. It would be dawn within half an hour; she didn't have much time to bait the trap and lure Roger in before Edie would find the note on the table and wake John.

Her hand shook as she flipped on the light in the foyer. The interior of the house jumped into focus, light and shadow rearranging themselves into things she knew as well as she knew her own face. Methodically she walked around, turning on the lights in the living room, then moving into her father's office, then the dining room, then the kitchen. She pulled the curtains back from the windows to let the lights shine through like beacons, which she meant them to be.

She turned on the lights in the laundry room, and in the small downstairs apartment used by the housekeeper a long time ago, when there had been a housekeeper. She went upstairs and turned on the lights in her bedroom, where John had taken her for the first time and made it impossible for her to ever be anything but his. Every light went on, both upstairs and downstairs, piercing the predawn darkness. Then she sat down on the bottom step of the stairs and waited. Soon someone would come. It might be John, in which case he would be furious, but she suspected it would be Roger.

The seconds slipped past, becoming minutes. Just as the sky began to take on the first gray tinge of daylight, the door opened and he walked in.

She hadn't heard a car, which meant she had been right in thinking he was close by. Nor had she heard his steps as he crossed the porch. She had no warning until he walked through the door, but, oddly, she wasn't startled. She had known he would be there.

"Hello, Roger," she said calmly. She had to remain calm.

He had put on a little weight in the two years since she had seen him, and his hair was a tad thinner, but other than that he looked the same. Even his eyes still looked the same, too sincere and slightly mad. The sincerity masked the fact that his mind had slipped, not far enough that he couldn't still function in society, but enough that he could conceive of murder and be perfectly logical about it, as if it were the only thing to do.

He carried a pistol in his right hand, but he held it loosely by the side of his leg. "Michelle," he said, a little confused by her manner, as if she were greeting a guest. "You're looking well." It was a comment dictated by a lifetime of having the importance of good manners drilled into him.

She nodded gravely. "Thank you. Would you like a cup of coffee?" She didn't know if there was any coffee in the house, and even if there were, it would be horribly stale, but the longer she could keep him off balance, the better. If Edie wasn't in the kitchen now, she would be in a few minutes, and she would wake John. Michelle hoped John would call Andy, but he might not take the time. She figured he would be here in fifteen minutes. Surely she could handle Roger for fifteen minutes. She thought the brightly lit house would alert John that something was wrong, so he wouldn't come bursting in, startling Roger into shooting. It was a chance, but so far the chances she had taken had paid off.

Roger was staring at her with a feverish glitter in his eyes, as if he couldn't look at her enough. Her question startled him again. "Coffee?"

"Yes. I think I'd like a cup, wouldn't you?" The very thought of coffee made her stomach roll, but making it would take time. And Roger was very civilized; he would see nothing wrong with sharing a cup of coffee with her.

"Why, yes. That would be nice, thank you."

She smiled at him as she got up from the stairs. "Why don't you chat with me while the coffee's brewing? I'm certain we have a lot of gossip to catch up on. I only hope I have coffee; I may have forgotten to buy any. It's been so hot this summer, hasn't it? I've become an iced-tea fanatic."

"Yes, it's been very hot," he agreed, following her into the kitchen. "I thought I might spend some time at the chalet in Colorado. It should be pleasant this time of year."

She found a half-empty pack of coffee in the cabinet; it was probably so stale it would be undrinkable, but she carefully filled the pot with water and poured it into the coffeemaker, then measured out the coffee into the paper filter. Her coffeemaker was slow; it took almost ten minutes to make a pot. The perking, hissing sounds it made were very soothing.

"Please sit down," she invited, indicating the chairs at the kitchen table.

Slowly he took a chair, then placed the pistol on the table. Michelle didn't let herself look at it as she turned to take two mugs from the cabinet. Then she sat down and took another cracker from the pack she had brought with her; she had left it on the table earlier, when she was going around the house turning on all the lights. Her stomach was rolling again, perhaps from tension as much as the effects of pregnancy.

"Would you like a cracker?" she asked politely.

He was watching her again, his eyes both sad and wild. "I love you," he whispered. "How could you leave me when I need you so much? I wanted you to come back to me. Everything would have been all right. I promised you it would be all right. Why did you move in with that brute rancher? *Why did you have to cheat on me like that?*"

Michelle jumped at the sudden lash of fury in his voice. His remarkably pleasant face was twisting in the hideous way she remembered in her nightmares. Her heart began thudding against her ribs so painfully that she thought she might be sick after all, but somehow she managed to say with creditable surprise, "But, Roger, the electricity had been disconnected. You didn't expect me to live here without lights or water, did you?"

Again he looked confused by the unexpected change of subject, but only momentarily. He shook his head. "You can't lie to me anymore, darling. You're still living with him. I just don't understand. I offered you so much more: all the luxury you could want, jewelry, shopping trips in Paris, but instead you ran away from me to live with a sweaty rancher who smells of cows."

She couldn't stop the coldness that spread over her when he called her "darling." She swallowed, trying to force back the panic welling in her. If she panicked, she wouldn't be able to control him. How many minutes did she have left? Seven? Eight?

"I wasn't certain you wanted me back," she managed to say, though her mouth was so dry she could barely form the words.

Slowly he shook his head. "You had to know. You just didn't want to come back. You *like* what that sweaty rancher can give you, when you could have lived like a queen. Michelle, darling, it's so sick for you to let someone like him touch you, but you enjoy it, don't you? It's *unnatural!*"

She knew all the signs. He was working himself into a frenzy, the rage and jealousy building in him until he lashed out violently. How could even Roger miss seeing why she would prefer John's strong, clean masculinity and earthy passions to his own twisted parody of love? How much longer would it be? Six minutes?

"I called your house," she lied, desperately trying to defuse his temper. "Your housekeeper said you were in France. I wanted you to come get me. I wanted to come back to you."

He looked startled, the rage draining abruptly from his face as if it had never been. He didn't even look like the same man. "You...you wanted..."

She nodded, noting that he seemed to have forgotten about the pistol. "I missed you. We had so much fun together, didn't we?" It was sad, but in the beginning they *had* had fun. Roger had been full of laughter and gentle teasing, and she had hoped he could make her forget about John.

Some of that fun was suddenly echoed in his eyes, in the smile that touched his mouth. "I thought you were the most wonderful thing I'd ever seen," he said softly. "Your hair is so bright and soft, and when you smiled at me, I felt ten feet tall. I would have given you the world. I would have killed for you." Still smiling, his hand moved toward the pistol.

Five minutes?

The ghost of the man he had been faded, and suddenly pity moved her. It wasn't until that moment that she understood Roger was truly ill; something in his mind had gone very wrong, and she didn't think all the psychiatrists or drugs in the world would be able to help him.

"We were so young," she murmured, wishing things could have been different for the laughing young man she had known. Little of him remained now, only moments of remembered fun to lighten his eyes. "Do you remember June Bailey, the little redhead who fell out of Wes Conlan's boat? We were all trying to help her back in, and somehow we all wound up in the water except for Toni. She didn't know a thing about sailing, so there she was on the boat, screaming, and we were swimming like mad, trying to catch up to her."

Four minutes.

He laughed, his mind sliding back to those sunny, goofy days.

"I think the coffee's about finished," she murmured, getting up. Carefully she poured two cups and carried them back to the table. "I hope you can drink it. I'm not much of a coffee-maker." That was better than telling him the coffee was stale because she had been living with John.

He was still smiling, but his eyes were sad. As she watched, a sheen of tears began to brighten his eyes, and he picked up the pistol. "I do love you so much," he said. "You never should have let that man touch you." Slowly the barrel came around toward her.

A lot of things happened simultaneously. The back door exploded inward, propelled by a kick that took it off the hinges. Roger jerked toward the sound and the pistol fired, the shot deafening in the confines of the house. She screamed and ducked as two other men leaped from the inside doorway, the biggest one taking Roger down with a tackle that sent him crashing into the table. Curses and shouts filled the air, along with the sound of wood splintering; then another shot assaulted her ears and strengthened the stench of cordite. She was screaming John's name over and over, knowing he was the one rolling across the floor with Roger as they both struggled for the gun. Then suddenly the pistol skidded across the floor and John was straddling Roger as he drove his fist into the other man's face.

The sickening thudding made her scream again, and she kicked a shattered chair out of her way, scrambling for the two men. Andy Phelps and another deputy reached them at the same time, grabbing John and trying to wrestle him away, but his face was a mask of killing fury at the man who had tried to murder his woman. He slung their hands away with a roar. Sobbing, Michelle threw her arms around his neck from behind, her shaking body against his back. "John, don't, please," she begged, weeping so hard that the words were almost unintelligible. "He's very sick."

He froze, her words reaching him as no one else's could. Slowly he let his fists drop and got to his feet, hauling her against him and holding her so tightly that she could barely breathe. But breathing wasn't important right then; nothing was as important as holding him and having him hold her, his head bent down to hers as he whispered a choked mixture of curses and love words.

The deputies had pulled Roger to his feet and cuffed his hands behind his back, while the pistol was put in a plastic bag and sealed. Roger's nose and mouth were bloody, and he was dazed, looking at them as if he didn't know who they were, or where he was. Perhaps he didn't.

John held Michelle's head pressed to his chest as he watched the deputies take Beckman out. God, how could she have been so cool, sitting across the kitchen table from that maniac and calmly serving him coffee? The man made John's blood run cold.

But she was safe in his arms now, the most precious part of his world. She had said a lot about his tomcatting reputation and the women in his checkered past; she had even called him a heartbreaker. But she was the true heartbreaker, with her sunlight hair and summergreen eyes, a golden woman who he never would have forgotten, even if she'd never come back into his life. Beckman had been obsessed with her, had gone mad when he lost her, and for the first time John thought he might understand. He wouldn't have a life, either, if he lost Michelle.

"I lost twenty years off my life when I found that note," he growled into her hair.

She clung to him, not loosening her grip. "You got here faster than I'd expected," she gasped, still crying a little. "Edie must've gotten up early."

"No, I got up early. You weren't in bed with me, so I started hunting you. As it was, we barely got here in time. Edie would have been too late."

Andy Phelps sighed, looking around the wrecked

kitchen. Then he found another cup in the cabinet and poured himself some coffee. He made a face as he sipped it. "This stuff is rank. It tastes just like what we get at work. Anyway, I think I have my pajama bottoms on under my pants. When John called I took the time to dress, but I don't think I took the time to undress first."

They both looked at him. He still looked a little sleepy, and he certainly wasn't in uniform. He had on jeans, a T-shirt, and running shoes with no socks. He could have worn an ape suit for all she cared.

"I need both of you to make statements," he said. "But I don't think this will ever come to trial. From what I saw, he won't be judged mentally competent."

"No," Michelle agreed huskily. "He isn't."

"Do we have to make the statements right now?" John asked. "I want to take Michelle home for a while."

Andy looked at both of them. Michelle was utterly white, and John looked the worse for wear, too. He had to still be feeling the effects of hitting a steering wheel with his face. "No, go on. Come in sometime this afternoon."

John nodded and walked Michelle out of the house. He'd commandeered Nev's truck, and now he led her to it. Someone else could get the car later.

It was a short, silent drive back to the ranch. She climbed numbly out of the truck, unable to believe it was all over. John swung her up in his arms and carried her into the house, his hard arms tight around her. Without a word to anyone, even Edie, who watched them with lifted brows, he took her straight upstairs to their bedroom and kicked the door shut behind him.

He placed her on the bed as if she might shatter, then suddenly snatched her up against him again. "I could kill you for scaring me like that," he muttered, even though he knew he'd never be able to hurt her. She must have known it, too, because she cuddled closer against him.

"We're getting married right away," he ordered in a voice made harsh with need. "I heard part of what he said, and maybe he's right that I can't give you all the luxuries you deserve, but I swear to God I'll try to make you happy. I love you too much to let you go."

"I've never said anything about going," Michelle protested. Married? He wanted to get married? Abruptly she lifted her head and gave him a glowing smile, one that almost stopped his breathing.

"You never said anything about staying, either."

"How could I? This is your house. It was up to you."

"Good manners be damned," he snapped. "I was going crazy, wondering if you were happy."

"Happy? I've been sick with it. You've given me something that doesn't have a price on it." She lifted her nose at him. "I've heard that mingling red blood with blue makes very healthy babies."

He looked down at her with hungry fire in his eyes. "Well, I hope you like babies, honey, because I plan on about four."

"I like them very much," she said as she touched her stomach. "Even though this is making me feel really ghastly."

For a moment he looked puzzled, then his gaze drifted downward. His expression changed to one of stunned surprise, and he actually paled a little. "You're pregnant?"

"Yes. Since the night you came back from your last trip to Miami."

His right brow lifted as he remembered that night; the left side of his face was still too swollen for him to be able to move it much. Then a slow grin began to widen his mouth, lifting the corners of his mustache. "I was careless one time too many," he said with visible satisfaction.

She laughed. "Yes, you were. Were you trying to be?"

"Who knows?" he asked, shrugging. "Maybe. God knows I like the idea. How about you?"

She reached for him, and he pulled her onto his lap, holding her in his arms and loving the feel of her. She rubbed her face against his chest. "All I've ever wanted is for you to love me. I don't need all that expensive stuff; I like working on the ranch, and I want to build my own ranch up again, even after we're married. Having your baby is…just more of heaven."

He laid his cheek on her golden hair, thinking of the terror he'd felt when he'd read her note. But now she was safe, she was his, and he would never let her go. She'd never seen any man as married as he planned to be. He'd spend the rest of his life trying to pamper her, and she'd continue to calmly ignore his orders whenever the mood took her, just as she did now. It would be a long, peaceful life, anchored in hard work and happily shrieking kids.

It would be good.

Their wedding day dawned clear and sunny, though the day before Michelle had resigned herself to having the wedding inside. But Hurricane Carl, after days of meandering around like a lost bee, had finally decided to head west and the clouds had vanished, leaving behind a pure, deep blue sky unmarred by even a wisp of cloud.

Michelle couldn't stop smiling as she dressed. If there were any truth in the superstition that it was bad luck for the groom to see the bride on their wedding day, she and John were in for a miserable life, but somehow she just couldn't believe it. He had not only refused to let her sleep in another room the night before, he'd lost his temper over the subject. She was damn well going to sleep with him where she belonged, and that was that. Tradition could just go to hell as far as he was concerned, if it meant they had to sleep apart. She had noticed that he hadn't willingly let her out of his sight since the morning they had caught Roger, so she understood.

His rather calm acceptance of his impending fatherhood had been a false calm, one shock too many after a nerve-wracking morning. The reality of it had hit him during the night, and Michelle had awakened to find herself clutched tightly to his chest, his face buried in her hair and his muscled body shaking, while he muttered over and over, "A baby. My God, a baby." His hand had been stroking her stomach as if he couldn't quite imagine his child growing inside her slim body. It had become even more real to him the next morning when even crackers couldn't keep her stomach settled, and he had held her while she was sick.

Some mornings weren't bad at all, while some were wretched. This morning John had put a cracker in her mouth before she was awake enough to even open her eyes, so she had lain in his arms with her eyes closed, chewing on her "breakfast." When it became evident that this was going to be a good morning, the bride-groom had made love to the bride, tenderly, thoroughly, and at length.

They were even dressing together for their wedding. She watched as he fastened his cuff links, his hard mouth curved in a very male, very satisfied way. He had found her lace teddy and garter belt extremely erotic, so much so that now they risked being late to their own wedding.

"I need help with my zipper when you've finished with that," she said.

He looked up, and a slow smile touched his lips, then lit his black eyes. "You look good enough to eat."

She couldn't help laughing. "Does this mean we'll have to reschedule the wedding for tomorrow?"

The smile became a grin. "No, we'll make this one." He finished his cuff links. "Turn around."

She turned, and his warm fingers touched her bare back, making her catch her breath and shiver in an echo of delight. He kissed her exposed nape, holding her as the shiver became a sensuous undulation. He wouldn't have traded being with her on this particular morning for all the tradition in the world.

Her dress was a pale, icy yellow, as was the garden hat she had chosen to wear. The color brought out the bright sunniness of her hair and made her glow, though maybe it wasn't responsible for the color in her cheeks or the sparkle in her eyes. That could be due to early pregnancy, or to heated lovemaking. Or maybe it was sheer happiness.

He worked the zipper up without snagging any of the delicate fabric, then bent to straighten and smooth her skirt. He shrugged into his jacket as she applied lipstick and carefully set the hat on her head. The yellow streamers flowed gracefully down her back. "Are we ready?" she asked, and for the first time he heard a hint of nervousness in her voice.

"We're ready," he said firmly, taking her hand. Their friends were all waiting on the patio; even his mother had flown up from Miami, a gesture that had surprised him but, on reflection, was appreciated.

Without the shadow of Roger Beckman hanging over her, Michelle had flowered in just these few days. Until she had made the effort to confront Roger, to do something about him once and for all, she hadn't realized the burden she'd been carrying around with her. Those black memories had stifled her spirit, made her wary and defensive, unwilling to give too much of herself. But she had faced him, and in doing so she had faced the past. She wasn't helpless any longer, a victim of threats and violence.

Poor Roger. She couldn't help feeling pity for him, even though he had made her life hell. At her insistence, John and Andy had arranged for Roger to have medical tests immediately, and it hadn't taken the doctors long to make a diagnosis. Roger had a slow but relentlessly degenerative brain disease. He would never be any better, and would slowly become worse until he finally died an early death, no longer knowing anyone or anything. She couldn't help feeling grief for him, because at one time he'd been a good, kind young man.

She wished there were some help for him, but the doctors didn't hold out any hope.

John put his arm around her, seeing the shadows that had come into her eyes. He didn't share her sympathy for Beckman, though perhaps in time he would be able to forget the moment when that pistol had swung toward her. Maybe in a few centuries.

He tilted her head up and kissed her, taking care not to smear her lipstick. "I love you," he murmured.

The sun came back out in her eyes. "I love you, too."

He tucked her hand into the crook of his arm. "Let's go get married."

Together they walked down the stairs and out to the patio, where their friends waited and the sun shone down brightly, as if to apologize for the threat of a storm the day before. Michelle looked at the tall man by her side; she wasn't naive enough to think there wouldn't be storms in their future, because John's arrogance would always make her dig in her heels, but she found herself looking forward to the battles they would have. The worst was behind them, and if the future held rough weather and sudden squalls…well, what future didn't? If she could handle John, she could handle anything.

* * * * *

Overload

LINDA HOWARD

Chapter One

It was hot, even for Dallas.

The scorching heat of the pavement seared through the thin leather of Elizabeth Major's shoes, forcing her to hurry even though it was an effort to move at all in the suffocating heat. The sleek office building where she worked didn't have its own underground parking garage, the builders having thought it unnecessary, since a parking deck was situated right across the street. Every time Elizabeth crossed the street in the rain, and every time she had risked being broiled by crossing it since this heat wave had begun, she swore that she would start looking for other office space. She always changed her mind as soon as she got inside, but it made her feel better to know she had the option of relocating.

Except for the parking situation, the building was perfect. It was only two years old, and managed to be both charming and convenient. The color scheme in the lobby was a soothing mixture of gray, dark mauve and white, striking the precise balance between masculine and feminine, so both genders felt comfortable. The lush greenery so carefully tended by a professional service added to the sense of freshness and spaciousness. The elevators were both numerous and fast and, so far, reliable. Her office having previously been in an older building where the elevator service had been cramped and erratic, Elizabeth doubly appreciated that last quality.

A private guard service handled the security, with a man stationed at a desk in the lobby for two shifts, from six in the morning until ten at night, as none of the businesses located in the building currently worked a third shift. Anyone wanting to come in earlier than six or stay later than ten had to let the guard service know. There was a rumor that the data processing firm on the tenth floor was considering going to three full shifts, and if that happened there would be a guard on duty around the clock. Until then, the building was locked down tight at 10:00 p.m. on weekdays and at 6:00 p.m. on weekends.

She pushed open the first set of doors and sighed with relief as the cool air rushed to greet her, washing over her hot face, evaporating the uncomfortable sweat that had formed in the time it had taken her to park her car and cross the street. When she entered the lobby itself through the second set of heavy glass doors, the full benefit of air conditioning swirled around her, making her shiver uncontrollably for just a second. Her panty hose had been clinging uncomfortably to her damp legs, and now the clammy feel made her grimace. For all that, however, she was jubilant as she crossed the lobby to the bank of elevators.

A big, unkempt man, a biker from the looks of him, entered the elevator just ahead of her. Immediately alert and wary, Elizabeth shifted her shoulder bag to her left shoulder, leaving her right hand unencumbered, as she stepped in and immediately turned to punch the button for the fifth floor, only to see a big, callused hand already pressing it. She aimed a vague smile, the kind people give each other in elevators, at the big man, then resolutely kept her gaze on the doors in front of her as they were whisked silently and rapidly to the fifth floor. But she relaxed somewhat, for if he was going to the fifth floor, he was undoubtedly involved, in some way, with Quinlan Securities.

She stepped out, and he was right on her heels as she marched down the hallway. Her offices were on the left, the chic interior revealed by the huge windows, and she saw that her secretary, Chickie, was back from lunch on time. Not only that, Chickie looked up and watched her coming down the hall. Or rather, she watched the man behind her. Elizabeth could see Chickie's big dark eyes fasten on the big man and widen with fascination.

Elizabeth opened her office door. The biker, without pausing, opened the door to Quinlan Securities, directly across the hall from her. Quinlan Securities didn't have any windows into the hallway, only a discreet sign on a solid-looking door. She had been glad, on more than one occasion, that there were no windows for more than one reason. The people who went through that door were ...*interesting,* to say the least.

"Wow," Chickie said, her gaze now fastened on the closed door across the hall. "Did you see that?"

"I saw it," Elizabeth said dryly.

Chickie's taste in men, regrettably, tended toward the unpolished variety. "He wore an earring," she said dreamily. "And did you see his hair?"

"Yes. It was long and uncombed."

"What a *mane!* I wonder why he's going into Quinlan's." Chickie's eyes brightened. "Maybe he's a new staffer!"

Elizabeth shuddered at the thought, but it was possible. Unfortunately the "Securities" in Quinlan Securities didn't refer to the financial kind but the physical sort. Chickie, who didn't have a shy bone in her body, had investigated when they had first moved into the building and cheerfully reported that Quinlan handled security of all types, from security systems to bodyguards. To Elizabeth's way of thinking, that didn't explain the type of people they saw coming and going from the Quinlan offices. The clientele, or maybe it was the *staff,* had a decidedly rough edge. If they were the former, she couldn't imagine them having enough money to afford security services. If they were the latter, she likewise couldn't imagine a client feeling comfortable around bodyguards who looked like mass murderers.

She had dated Tom Quinlan, the owner, for a while last winter, but he had been very closemouthed about his business, and she had been wary about asking. In fact, everything about Tom had made her wary. He was a big, macho, take-charge type of man, effortlessly overwhelming in both personality and body. When she had realized how he was taking over her life, she had swiftly ended the relationship and since then gone out of her way to avoid him. She would *not* lose control of her life again, and Tom Quinlan had overstepped the bounds in a big way.

Chickie dragged her attention away from the closed door across the hall and looked expectantly at Elizabeth. "Well?"

Elizabeth couldn't hold back the grin that slowly widened as her triumph glowed through. "She loved it."

"She did? You *got* it?" Chickie shrieked, jumping up and sending her chair spinning.

"I got it. We'll start next month." Her lunch meeting had been with Sandra Eiland, possessor of one of the oldest fortunes in Dallas. Sandra had decided to renovate her lavish hacienda-style house, and Elizabeth had just landed the interior-design account. She had owned her own firm for five years now, and this was the biggest job she had gotten, as well as being the most visible one. Sandra Eiland loved parties and entertained often; Elizabeth couldn't have paid for better advertising. This one account lifted her onto a completely different level of success.

Chickie's enthusiasm was immediate and obvious; she danced around the reception area, her long black hair flying. "Look out, Dallas, we are cooking now!" she crowed. "Today the Eiland account, tomorrow— tomorrow you'll do something else. We are going to be *busy.*"

"I hope," Elizabeth said as she passed through into her office.

"No hoping to it." Chickie followed, still dancing. "It's guaranteed. The phone will be ringing so much I'll have to have an assistant. Yeah, I like the idea of that. Someone else can answer the phone, and I'll chase around town finding the stuff you'll need for all the jobs that will be pouring in."

"If you're chasing around town, you won't be able to watch the comings and goings across the hall," Elizabeth pointed out in a casual tone, hiding her amusement.

Chickie stopped dancing and looked thoughtful. She considered Quinlan's to be her own secret treasure trove of interesting, potential men, far more productive than a singles' bar.

"So maybe I'll have *two* assistants," she finally said. "One to answer the phone, and one to chase around town while I stay here and keep things organized."

Elizabeth laughed aloud. Chickie was such an exuberant person that it was a joy to be around her. Their styles complemented each other, Elizabeth's dry, sometimes acerbic wit balanced by Chickie's unwavering good nature. Where Elizabeth was tall and slim, Chickie was short and voluptuous. Chickie tended toward the dramatic in clothing, so Elizabeth toned down her own choices. Clients didn't like to be overwhelmed or restrained. It was subtle, but the contrast between Elizabeth and Chickie in some way relaxed her clients, reassured them that they wouldn't be pressured into a style they weren't comfortable with. Of course, sometimes Elizabeth wasn't comfortable with her own style of dress, such as today, when the heat was so miserable and she would have been much happier in shorts and a cotton T-shirt, but she had mentally, and perhaps literally, girded her loins with panty hose. If it hadn't been for the invention of air conditioning, she never would have made it; just crossing the street in this incredible heat was a feat of endurance.

Chickie's bangle bracelets made a tinkling noise as she seated herself across from Elizabeth's desk. "What time are you leaving?"

"Leaving?" Sometimes Chickie's conversational jumps were a little hard to follow. "I just got back."

"Don't you ever listen to the radio? The heat is *hazardous*. The health department, or maybe it's the weather bureau, is warning everyone to stay inside during the hottest part of the day, drink plenty of water, stuff like that. Most businesses are opening only in the mornings, then letting their people go home early so they won't get caught in traffic. I checked around. Just about everyone in the building is closing up by two this afternoon."

Elizabeth looked at the Eiland folder she had just placed on her desk. She could barely wait to get started. "You can go home anytime you want," she said. "I had some ideas about the Eiland house that I want to work on while they're still fresh in my mind."

"I don't have any plans," Chickie said immediately. "I'll stay."

Elizabeth settled down to work and, as usual, soon became lost in the job. She loved interior design, loved the challenge of making a home both beautiful and functional, as well as suited to the owner's character. For Sandra Eiland, she wanted something that kept the flavor of the old Southwest, with an air of light and spaciousness, but also conveyed Sandra's sleek sophistication.

The ringing of the telephone finally disrupted her concentration, and she glanced at the clock, surprised to find that it was already after three o'clock. Chickie answered the call, listened for a moment, then said, "I'll find out. Hold on." She swiveled in her chair to look through the open door into Elizabeth's office. "It's the guard downstairs. He's a substitute, not our regular guard, and he's checking the offices, since he doesn't know anyone's routine. He says that almost everyone else has already gone, and he wants to know how late we'll be here."

"Why don't you go on home now," Elizabeth suggested. "There's no point in your staying later. And tell the guard I'll leave within the hour. I want to finish this sketch, but it won't take long."

"I'll stay with you," Chickie said yet again.

"No, there's no need. Just switch on the answering machine. I promise I won't be here much longer."

"Well, all right." Chickie relayed the message to the guard, then hung up and retrieved her purse from the bottom desk drawer. "I dread going out there," she said.

"It might be worth it to wait until after sundown, when it cools down to the nineties."

"It's over five hours until sundown. This is July, remember."

"On the other hand, I could spend those five hours beguiling the cute guy who moved in across the hall last week."

"Sounds more productive."

"And more fun." Chickie flashed her quick grin. "He won't have a chance. See you tomorrow."

"Yes. Good luck." By the time Chickie sashayed out of the office, scarlet skirt swinging, Elizabeth had already become engrossed in the sketch taking shape beneath her talented fingers. She always did the best she could with any design, but she particularly wanted this one to be perfect, not just for the benefit to her career, but because that wonderful old house deserved it.

Her fingers finally cramped, and she stopped for a moment, noticing at the same time how tight her shoulders were, though they usually got that way only when she had been sitting hunched over a sketch pad for several hours. Absently she flexed them and was reaching for the pencil again when she realized what that tightness meant. She made a sound of annoyance when a glance at the clock said that it was 5:20, far later than she had meant to stay. Now she would have to deal with the traffic she had wanted to avoid, with this murderous heat wave making everyone ill-tempered and aggressive.

She stood and stretched, then got her bag and turned off the lights. The searing afternoon sun was blocked by the tall building next door, but there was still plenty of light coming through the tinted windows, and the office was far from dark. As she stepped out into the hall and turned to lock her door, Tom Quinlan exited his office and did the same. Elizabeth carefully didn't look at him, but she felt his gaze on her and automatically tensed. Quinlan had that effect on her, always had. It was one of the reasons she had stopped dating him, though not the biggie.

She had the uncomfortable feeling that he'd been waiting for her, somehow, and she glanced around uneasily, but no one else was around. Usually the building was full of people at this hour, as the workday wound down, but she was acutely aware of the silence around them. Surely they weren't the only two people left! But common sense told her that they were, that everyone else had sensibly gone home early; she wouldn't have any buffer between herself and Quinlan.

He fell into step beside her as she strode down the hall to the elevators. "Don't I even rate a hello these days?"

"Hello," she said.

"You're working late. Everyone else left hours ago."

"You didn't."

"No." He changed the subject abruptly. "Have dinner with me." His tone made it more of an order than an invitation.

"No, thank you," she replied as they reached the elevators. She punched the Down button and silently prayed for the elevator to hurry. The sooner she was away from this man, the safer she would feel.

"Why not?"

"Because I don't want to."

A soft chime signaled the arrival of a car; the elevator doors slid open, and she stepped inside. Quinlan followed, and the doors closed, sealing her inside with him. She reached out to punch the ground-floor button, but he caught her hand, moving so that his big body was between her and the control panel.

"You do want to, you're just afraid."

Elizabeth considered that statement, then squared her shoulders and looked up at his grim face. "You're right. I'm afraid. And I don't go out with men who scare me."

He didn't like that at all, even though he had brought up the subject. "Are you afraid I'll hurt you?" he demanded in a disbelieving tone.

"Of course not!" she scoffed, and his expression relaxed. She knew she hadn't quite told the truth, but that was her business, not his, a concept he had trouble grasping. Deftly she tugged her hand free. "It's just that you'd be a big complication, and I don't have time for that. I'm afraid you'd really mess up my schedule."

His eyes widened incredulously, then he exploded. "Hellfire, woman!" he roared, the sound deafening in the small enclosure. "You've been giving me the cold shoulder for over six months because you don't want me to interfere with your *schedule?*"

She lifted one shoulder in a shrug. "What can I say? We all have our priorities." Deftly she leaned past him and punched the button, and the elevator began sliding smoothly downward.

Three seconds later it lurched to a violent stop. Hurled off balance, Elizabeth crashed into Quinlan; his hard arms wrapped around her as they fell, and he twisted his muscular body to cushion the impact for her. Simultaneously the lights went off, plunging them into complete darkness.

Chapter Two

The red emergency lights blinked on almost immediately, bathing them in a dim, unearthly glow. She didn't, couldn't move, not just yet; she was paralyzed by a strange mixture of alarm and pleasure. She lay sprawled on top of Quinlan, her arms instinctively latched around his neck while his own arms cradled her to him. She could feel the heat of his body even through the layers of their clothing, and the musky man-scent of his skin called up potent memories of a night when there had been no clothing to shield her from his heat. Her flesh quickened, but her spirit rebelled, and she pushed subtly against him in an effort to free herself. For a second his arms tightened, forcing her closer, flattening her breasts against the hard muscularity of his chest. The red half-light darkened his blue eyes to black, but even so, she could read the determination and desire revealed in them.

The desire tempted her to relax, to sink bonelessly into his embrace, but the determination had her pulling back. Almost immediately he released her, though she sensed his reluctance, and rolled to his feet with a lithe, powerful movement. He caught her arms and lifted her with ridiculous ease. "Are you all right? Any bruises?"

She smoothed down her skirt. "No, I'm fine. You?"

He grunted in reply, already opening the panel that hid the emergency phone. He lifted the receiver and punched the button that would alert Maintenance. Elizabeth waited, but he didn't say anything. His dark brows drew together, and finally he slammed the receiver down. "No answer. The maintenance crew must have gone home early, like everyone else."

She looked at the telephone. There was no dial on it, no buttons other than that one. It was connected only to Maintenance, meaning they couldn't call out on it.

Then she noticed something else, and her head lifted. "The air has stopped." She lifted her hand to check, but there was no cool air blowing from the vents. The lack of noise had alerted her.

"The power must be off," he said, turning his attention to the door.

The still air in the small enclosure was already becoming stuffy. She didn't like the feeling, but she refused to let herself get panicky. "It probably won't be long before it comes back on."

"Normally I'd agree with you, if we weren't having a heat wave, but the odds are too strong that it's a system overload, and if that's the case, it can take hours to repair. We have to get out. These lights are battery operated and won't stay on long. Not only that, the heat will build up, and we don't have water or enough oxygen in here." Even as he spoke, he was attacking the elevator doors with his strong fingers, forcing them open inch by inch. Elizabeth added her strength to his, though she was aware that he could handle it perfectly well by himself. It was just that she couldn't tolerate the way he had of taking over and making her feel so useless.

They were stuck between floors, with about three feet of the outer doors visible at the bottom of the elevator car. She helped him force open those doors, too. Before she could say anything, he had lowered himself through the opening and swung lithely to the floor below.

He turned around and reached up for her. "Just slide out. I'll catch you."

She sniffed, though she was a little apprehensive about what she was going to try. It had been a long time since she had done anything that athletic. "Thanks, but I don't need any help. I took gymnastics in college." She took a deep, preparatory breath, then swung out of the elevator every bit as gracefully as he had, even encumbered as she was with her shoulder bag and handicapped by her high heels. His dark brows arched, and he silently applauded. She bowed. One of the things that she had found most irresistible about Quinlan was the way she had been able to joke with him. Actually there was a lot about him that she'd found irresistible, so much so that she had ignored his forcefulness and penchant for control, at least until she had found that report in his apartment. She hadn't been able to ignore that.

"I'm impressed," he said.

Wryly she said, "So am I. It's been years."

"You were on the college gymnastics team, huh? You never told me that before."

"Nothing to tell, because I *wasn't* on the college team. I'm too tall to be really good. But I took classes, for conditioning and relaxation."

"From what I remember," he said lazily, "you're still in great shape."

Elizabeth wheeled away and began walking briskly to the stairs, turning her back on the intimacy of that remark. She could feel him right behind her, like a great beast stalking its prey. She pushed open the door and stopped in her tracks. "Uh-oh."

The stairwell was completely dark. It wasn't on an outside wall, but it would have been windowless in any case. The hallway was dim, with only one office on that floor having interior windows, but the stairwell was stygian. Stepping into it would be like stepping into a well, and she felt a sudden primal instinct against it.

"No problem," Quinlan said, so close that his breath stirred her hair and she could feel his chest brush against her back with each inhalation. "Unless you have claustrophobia?"

"No, but I might develop a case any minute now."

He chuckled. "It won't take that long to get down. We're on the third floor, so it's four short flights and out. I'll hold the door until you get your hand on the rail."

Since the only alternative was waiting there until the power came back on, Elizabeth shrugged, took a deep breath as if she were diving and stepped into the dark hole. Quinlan was so big that he blocked most of the light, but she grasped the rail and went down the first step. "Okay, stay right there until I'm with you," he said, and let the door close behind him as he stepped forward.

She had the immediate impression of being enclosed in a tomb, but in about one second he was beside her, his arm stretched behind her back with that hand holding the rail, while he held her other arm with his free hand. In the warm, airless darkness she felt utterly surrounded by his strength. "I'm not going to fall," she said, unable to keep the bite from her voice.

"You're sure as hell not," he replied calmly. He didn't release her.

"Quinlan—"

"Walk."

Because it was the fastest way to get out of his grasp, she walked. The complete darkness was disorienting at first, but she pictured the stairs in her mind, found the rhythm of their placement, and managed to go down at almost normal speed. Four short flights, as he had said. Two flights separated by a landing constituted one floor. At the end of the fourth flight he released her, stepped forward a few steps and found the door that opened onto the first floor. Gratefully Elizabeth hurried into the sunlit lobby. She knew it was all in her imagination, but she felt as if she could breathe easier with space around her.

Quinlan crossed rapidly to the guard's desk, which was unoccupied. Elizabeth frowned. The guard was always there—or rather, he had always been there before, because he certainly wasn't *now*.

When he reached the desk, Quinlan immediately began trying to open the drawers. They were all locked. He straightened and yelled, "Hello?" His deep voice echoed in the eerily silent lobby.

Elizabeth groaned as she realized what had happened. "The guard must have gone home early, too."

"He's supposed to stay until everyone is out."

"He was a substitute. When he called the office, Chickie told him that I would leave before four. If there were other stragglers, he must have assumed that I was among them. What about you?"

"Me?" Quinlan shrugged, his eyes hooded. "Same thing."

She didn't quite believe him, but she didn't pursue it. Instead she walked over to the inner set of doors that led to the outside and tugged at them. They didn't budge. Well, great. They were locked in. "There has to be some way out of here," she muttered.

"There isn't," he said flatly.

She stopped and stared at him. "What do you mean, 'there isn't'?"

"I mean the building is sealed. Security. Keeps looters out during a power outage. The glass is reinforced, shatterproof. Even if we called the guard service and they sent someone over, they couldn't unlock the doors until the electricity was restored. It's like the vault mechanisms in banks."

"Well, you're the security expert. Get us out. Override the system somehow."

"Can't be done."

"Of course it can. Or are you admitting there's something you can't do?"

He crossed his arms over his chest and smiled benignly. "I mean that I designed the security system in this building, and it can't be breached. At least, not until the power comes back on. Until then, I can't get into the system. No one can."

Elizabeth caught her breath on a surge of fury, more at his attitude than the circumstances. He just looked so damn *smug.*

"So we call 911," she said.

"Why?"

"What do you mean, why? We're stuck in this building!"

"Is either of us ill? Hurt? Are we in any danger? This isn't an emergency, it's an inconvenience, and believe me, they have their hands full with real emergencies right now. And they can't get into the building, either. The only possible way out is to climb to the roof and be lifted off by helicopter, but that's an awful lot of expense and trouble for someone who isn't in any danger. We have food and water in the building. The sensible thing is to stay right here."

Put that way, she grudgingly accepted that she had no choice. "I know," she said with a sigh. "It's just that I feel so…trapped." In more ways than one.

"It'll be fun. We'll get to raid the snack machines—"

"They operate on electricity, too."

"I didn't say we'd use money," he replied, and winked at her. "Under the circumstances, no one will mind."

She would mind. She dreaded every minute of this, and it could last for *hours*. The last thing she wanted to do was spend any time alone with Quinlan, but it looked as if she had no choice. If only she could relax in his company, she wouldn't mind, but that was beyond her ability. She felt acutely uncomfortable with him, her tension compounded of several different things: uppermost was anger that he had dared to pry into her life the way he had; a fair amount of guilt, for she knew she owed him at least an explanation, and the truth was still both painful and embarrassing; a sort of wistfulness, because she had enjoyed so much about him; and desire—God, yes, a frustrated desire that had been feeding for months on the memory of that one night they had spent together.

"We don't have to worry about the air," he said, looking around at the two-story lobby. "It'll get considerably warmer in here, but the insulation and thermal-glazed windows will keep it from getting critically hot. We'll be okay."

She forced herself to stop fretting and think sensibly. There was no way out of this situation, so she might as well make the best of it, and that meant staying as comfortable as they could. In this case, comfortable meant cool. She began looking around; as he'd said, they had food and water, though they would have to scrounge for it, and there was enough furniture here in the lobby to furnish several living rooms, so they had plenty of cushions to fashion beds. Her mind skittered away from that last thought. Her gaze fell on the stairway doors, and the old saying "hot air rises" came to mind. "If we open the bottom stairway doors, that'll create a chimney effect to carry the heat upward," she said.

"Good idea. I'm going to go back up to my office to get a flashlight and raid the snack machine. Is there anything you want from your office while I'm up there?"

Mentally she ransacked her office, coming up with several items that might prove handy. "Quite a bit, actually. I'll go with you."

"No point in both of us climbing the stairs in the dark," he said casually. "Just tell me what you want."

That was just like him, she thought irritably, wanting to do everything himself and not involve her. "It makes more sense if we both go. You can pilfer your office for survival stuff, and I'll pilfer mine. I think I have a flashlight, too, but I'm not certain where it is."

"It's eight flights, climbing, this time, instead of going down," he warned her, looking down at her high heels.

In answer, she stepped out of her shoes and lifted her eyebrows expectantly. He gave her a thoughtful look, then gave in without more argument, gesturing her ahead of him. He relocated a large potted tree to hold the stairway door propped open, handling it as casually as if the big pot didn't weigh over a hundred pounds. Elizabeth had a good idea how heavy it was, however, for she loved potted plants and her condo was always

full of greenery. She wondered how it would feel to
have such strength, to possess Quinlan's basic self-confidence that he could handle any situation or difficulty.
With him, it was even more than mere confidence; there
was a certain arrogance, subtle but unmistakably there,
the quiet arrogance of a man who knew his own
strengths and skills. Though he had adroitly sidestepped
giving out any personal information about his past, she
sensed that some of those skills were deadly.

She entered the stairwell with less uneasiness this
time, for there was enough light coming in through the
open door to make the first two flights perfectly visible.
Above that, however, they proceeded in thick, all-en-
compassing darkness. As he had before, Quinlan passed
an arm behind her back to grip the rail, and his free hand
held her elbow. His hand had always been there
whenever they had gone up or down steps, she remembered. At first it had been pleasurable, but soon she had
felt a little smothered, and then downright alarmed.
Quinlan's possessiveness had made her uneasy, rather
than secure. She knew too well how such an attitude
could get out of hand.

Just to break the silence she quipped, "If either of us
smoked, we'd have a cigarette lighter to light our path."

"If either of us smoked," he came back dryly, "we
wouldn't have the breath to climb the stairs."

She chuckled, then saved her energy to concentrate
on the steps. Climbing five floors wasn't beyond her ca-
pabilities, but it was still an effort. She was breathing
hard by the time they reached the fifth floor, and the
darkness was becoming unnerving. Quinlan stepped

forward and opened the door, letting in a sweet spill of light.

They parted ways at their respective offices, Quinlan disappearing into his while Elizabeth unlocked hers. The late-afternoon light was still spilling brightly through the windows, reminding her that, in actuality, very little time had passed since the elevator had lurched to a halt. A disbelieving glance at her wrist-watch said that it had been less than half an hour.

The flashlight was the most important item, and she searched the file cabinets until she found it. Praying that the batteries weren't dead, she thumbed the switch and was rewarded by a beam of light. She switched it off and placed it on Chickie's desk. She and Chickie made their own coffee, as it was both more convenient and better tasting than the vending machine kind, so she got their cups and put them on the desk next to the flashlight. Drinking from them would be easier than splashing water into their mouths with their hands, and she knew Chickie wouldn't mind if Quinlan used her cup. Quite the contrary.

Knowing that her secretary had an active sweet tooth, Elizabeth began rifling the desk drawers, smiling in appreciation when she found a six-pack of chocolate bars with only one missing, a new pack of fig bars, chewing gum, a honey bun and a huge blueberry muffin. Granted, it was junk food, but at least they wouldn't be hungry. Finally she got two of the soft pillows that decorated the chairs in her office, thinking that they would be more comfortable for sleeping than the upholstered cushions downstairs.

Quinlan opened the door, and she glanced at him. He

had removed his suit jacket and was carrying a small black leather bag. He looked at her loot and laughed softly. "Were you a scout, by any chance?"

"I can't take the credit for most of it. Chickie's the one with a sweet tooth."

"Remind me to give her a big hug the next time I see her."

"She'd rather have you set her up on a date with that biker who came in after lunch."

He laughed again. "Feeling adventurous, is she?"

"Chickie's *always* adventurous. Was he a client?"

"No."

She sensed that that was all the information he was going to give out about the "biker." As always, Quinlan was extremely closemouthed about his business, both clients and staff. On their dates, he had always wanted to talk about *her,* showing interest in every little detail of her life, while at the same time gently stonewalling her tentative efforts to find out more about him. It hadn't been long before that focused interest, coupled with his refusal to talk about himself, had begun making her extremely uncomfortable. She could understand not wanting to talk about certain things; there was a certain period that she couldn't bring herself to talk about, either, but Quinlan's secretiveness had been so absolute that she didn't even know if he had any family. On the other hand, he had noticed the gap in her own life and had already started asking probing little questions when she had broken off the relationship.

There was a silk paisley shawl draped across a chair, and Elizabeth spread it across the desk to use as an upscale version of a hobo's pouch. As she began piling her collection in the middle of the shawl, Quinlan casually flicked at the fringe with one finger. "Do people actually buy shawls just because they look good draped across chairs?"

"Of course. Why not?"

"It's kind of silly, isn't it?"

"I guess it depends on your viewpoint. Do you think it's silly when people spend hundreds of dollars on mag wheels for their cars or trucks, just because they look good?"

"Cars and trucks are useful."

"So are chairs," she said dryly. She gathered the four corners of the shawl together and tied them in a knot. "Ready."

"While we're up here, we need to raid the snack machines, rather than rely on what you have there. There's no point in making extra trips upstairs to get more food when we can get it now."

She gave him a dubious look. "Do you think we'll be here so long that we'll need that much food?"

"Probably not, but I'd rather have too much than too little. We can always return what we don't eat."

"Logical," she admitted.

He turned to open the door for her, and Elizabeth stared in shock at the lethal black pistol tucked into his waistband at the small of his back. "Good God," she blurted. "What are you going to do with that?"

Chapter Three

He raised his eyebrows. "Whatever needs doing," he said mildly.

"Thank you so much for the reassurance! Are you expecting any kind of trouble? I thought you said the building was sealed."

"The building *is* sealed, and no, I'm not expecting any trouble. That doesn't mean I'm going to be caught unprepared if I'm wrong. Don't worry about it. I'm always armed, in one way or another. It's just that this is the first time you've noticed."

She stared at him. "You don't usually carry a pistol."

"Yes, I do. You wouldn't have noticed it now if I hadn't taken my coat off."

"You didn't have one the night we—" She cut off the rest of the sentence.

"Made love?" He finished it for her. His blue eyes were steady, watchful. "Not that night, no. I knew I was going to make love to you, and I didn't want to scare you in any way, so I locked the pistol in the glove compartment before I picked you up. But I had a knife in my boot. Just like I do now."

It was difficult to breathe. She fought to suck in a deep breath as she bypassed the issue of the pistol and latched on to the most shocking part of what he'd just said. "You *knew* we were going to make love?"

He gave her another of those thoughtful looks. "You don't want to talk about that right now. Let's get finished here and get settled in the lobby before dark so we can save the batteries in the flashlights."

It was another logical suggestion, except for the fact that night wouldn't arrive until about nine o'clock, giving them plenty of time. She leaned back against the desk and crossed her arms. "Why don't I want to talk about it now?"

"Just an assumption I made. You've spent over half a year avoiding me, so I didn't think you would suddenly want to start an in-depth discussion. If I'm wrong, by all means let's talk." A sudden dangerous glitter lit his eyes. "Was I too rough? Was five times too many? I don't think so, because I could feel your climaxes squeezing me," he said bluntly. "Not to mention the way you had your legs locked around me so tight I could barely move. And I know damn good and well I don't snore or talk in my sleep, so just what in hell happened to send you running?"

His voice was low and hard, and he had moved closer

so that he loomed over her. She had never seen him lose control, but as she saw the rage in his eyes she knew that he was closer to doing so now than she had ever imagined. It shook her a little. Not because she was afraid of him—at least, not in that way—but because she hadn't imagined it would have mattered so much to him.

Then she squared her shoulders, determined not to let him take charge of the conversation and turn it back on her the way he had so many times. "What do you mean, you *knew* we would make love that night?" she demanded, getting back to the original subject.

"Just what I said."

"How could you have been so sure? *I* certainly hadn't planned on it happening."

"No. But I knew you wouldn't turn me down."

"You know a damn lot, don't you?" she snapped, incensed by that unshakable self-confidence of his.

"Yeah. But I don't know why you ran afterward. So why don't you tell me? Then we can get the problem straightened out and pick up where we left off."

She glared at him, not budging. He ran his hand through his dark hair, which he kept in a short, almost military cut. He was so controlled, it was one of the few gestures of irritation she could ever remember him making. "All right," he muttered. "I knew you were hiding things from me, maybe because you didn't trust what was between us. I thought that once we'd made love, once you knew you belonged to me, you'd trust me and stop holding back."

She forgot to glare. Her arms dropped to her sides,

and she gaped at him. "I *belong* to you? I beg your pardon! Do you have a bill of sale that I don't know about?"

"Yes, belong!" he barked. "I had planned on marriage, kids, the whole bit, but you kept edging away from me. And I didn't know why. I still don't."

"Marriage? Kids?" She could barely speak, she was so astounded. The words came out in a squeak. "I don't suppose it ever occurred to you to let me in on all of this planning you were doing, did it? No, don't bother to answer. You made up your mind, and that was it, regardless of how *I* felt."

"I knew how you felt. You were in love with me. You still are. That's why it doesn't make sense that you ran."

"Maybe not to you, but it's crystal clear to me." She looked away, her face burning. She hadn't realized her feelings had been so obvious to him, though she had known fairly early in their relationship that she loved him. The more uneasy she had become, however, the more she had tried to hide the intensity of her feelings.

"Then why don't you let me in on the secret? I'm tired of this. Whatever it is I did, I apologize for it. We've wasted enough time."

His arrogance was astonishing, even though she had recognized that part of his character from the beginning. Quinlan was generally a quiet man, but it was the quietness of someone who had nothing to prove, to himself or anyone else. He had decided to put an end to the situation, and that was that, at least from his viewpoint.

But not from hers.

"You listen to me, Tom Quinlan," she said furiously. "I don't care what plans you've made, you can just write me out of them. I don't want—"

"I can't do that," he interrupted.

"Why not?"

"Because of this."

She saw the glitter in his eyes and immediately bolted away from the desk, intent on escape. She was quick, but he was quicker. He seized her wrists and folded her arms behind her back, effectively wrapping her in his embrace at the same time. The pressure of his iron-muscled arms forced her against the hard planes of his body. Having seen him naked, she knew that his clothing disguised his true strength and muscularity, knew that she didn't have a prayer of escaping until he decided to release her. She declined to struggle, contenting herself with a furious glare.

"Cat eyes," he murmured. "The first time I saw you, I knew you were no lady. Your eyes give you away. And I was right, thank God. The night we spent together proved that you don't give a damn about what's proper or ladylike. You're wild and hot, and we wrecked my bed. You should have known there's no way in hell I'd let you go."

He was aroused. She could feel his hardness thrusting against her, his hips moving ever so slightly in a nestling motion, wordlessly trying to tempt her into opening her thighs to cradle him. It *was* tempting. Damn tempting. She couldn't deny wanting him, had never tried to, but he was right: she didn't trust him.

"It won't work," she said hoarsely.

"It already has." The words were soft, almost crooning, and his warm breath washed over her mouth a second before his lips were there, firm and hot, his head slanting to deepen the kiss and open her mouth to him. She hadn't meant to do so, but she found herself helpless to prevent it. Right from the beginning, his kisses had made her dizzy with delight. His self-confidence was manifested even in this; there was no hesitancy, no awkwardness. He simply took her mouth as if it were his right, his tongue probing deep, and a deep shudder of pleasure made her quake.

Held against him as she was, she could feel the tension in his body, feel his sex throbbing with arousal. He had never made any effort to disguise his response to her. Though it had been obvious even on their first date, he hadn't pressured her in any way. Maybe she had started falling in love with him then, because he had been both amused and matter-of-fact about his frequent arousal, his attitude being that it was a natural result of being in her company. She hadn't felt threatened in any way; in fact, looking back, she realized that Quinlan had gone out of his way to keep from alarming her. He had been remarkably unaggressive, sexually speaking, despite the persistent evidence of his attraction. She had never felt that she might have to face a wrestling match at the end of an evening. Even the night they had made love, she hadn't fully realized the seriousness of his kisses until she had somehow found herself naked in bed with him, her body on fire with need. Then she had discovered that he was very serious, indeed.

The memory made her panic, and she tore her mouth

away from his. She had no doubt that if she didn't stop him now, within five minutes he would be making love to her. The hot sensuality of his kisses was deceptive, arousing her more and faster than she'd expected. It had been the same way that one night. He had just been kissing her; then, before she knew it, she had been wild for him. She hadn't known such intense heat and pleasure had existed, until then.

"What's wrong?" he murmured, reclaiming her mouth with a series of swift, light kisses that nevertheless burned. "Don't you like it? Or do you like it too much?"

His perceptiveness alarmed her even more, and despite herself she began to struggle. To her surprise, he released her immediately, though he didn't step back.

"Tell me what went wrong, babe." His tone was dark and gentle. "I can't make it right if I don't know what it is."

She put her hands on his chest to force him away and was instantly, achingly aware of his hard, warm flesh covered only by a thin layer of cotton. She could even feel the roughness of his hair, the strong, heavy beat of his heart pulsing beneath her fingers. "Quinlan—"

"Tell me," he cajoled, kissing her again.

Desperately she slipped sideways, away from him. Her body felt overheated and slightly achy. If she didn't tell him, he would persist in his seductive cajoling, and she didn't know how long she could resist him. "All right." She owed him that much. She didn't intend to change her mind about dating him, but at least he deserved an explanation. She should have told him before, but at the time all she had wanted was to stay as far away from him as possible. "But…later. Not right now. We need to get everything gathered up and get settled in the lobby."

He straightened, amusement in his eyes. "Where have I heard that before?"

"It isn't polite to gloat."

"Maybe not, but it's sure as hell satisfying."

She was nervous. Quinlan was surprised at the depth of her uneasiness, because that wasn't a trait he associated with Elizabeth. He wondered at the cause of it, just as he had wondered for the past six months why she had run from him so abruptly after spending the night in his arms. She wasn't afraid of him; that was one of the things he liked best about her. For him to find women attractive, they had to be intelligent, but unfortunately that intelligence tended to go hand in glove with a perceptiveness that made them shy away from him.

He couldn't do anything about his aura of dangerousness, because he couldn't lose the characteristics, the habits or the instincts that made him dangerous. He didn't even want to. It was as much a part of him as his bones, and went as deep. He had made do with shallow relationships for the sake of physical gratification, but inside he had been waiting and watching. Though the life he had led sometimes made him feel as if only a few people in this world really *saw* what went on around them, that most people went through life wearing blinders, now that he was mostly out of the action he wanted the normalcy that the average person took for granted. He wanted a wife and family, a secure, settled life; as soon as he had met Elizabeth, he had known that she was the one he wanted.

It wasn't just her looks, though God knew he broke out in a sweat at the sight of her. She was a little over average height, as slim as a reed, with sleek dark hair usually pulled back in a classic chignon. She had the fast lines of a thoroughbred, and until he had met her, he hadn't known how sexy that was. But it was her eyes that had gotten him. Cat eyes, he'd told her, and it was true, but though they were green, it was more the expression in them than the color that made them look so feline. Elizabeth's nature shone in her eyes. She had given him a warning look that had said she wasn't intimidated by him at all, underlaid by a cool disdain that was certainly catlike.

Excitement and arousal had raced through him. The more he'd learned about her, the more determined he had been to have her. She was sharply intelligent, witty, sarcastic at times and had a robust sense of humor that sometimes caught him off guard, though it always delighted him. And she burned with an inner intensity that drew him as inexorably as a magnet draws steel.

The intensity of his attraction had caught him off guard. He wanted to know everything there was to know about her, even her childhood memories, because that was a time in her life that would be forever closed to him. He wanted to have children with her and was fascinated by the possibility of a daughter in Elizabeth's image, a small, strong-willed, sharp-tongued, dimpled cherub. Talking about Elizabeth's own childhood made that possibility seem tantalizingly real.

At first Elizabeth had talked openly, with that faint arrogance of hers that said she had nothing to hide and he could like it or lump it. But then he had begun to sense that she *was* hiding something. It wasn't anything he could put his finger on; it was more of a withdrawal from him, as if she had built an inner wall and had no intention of letting him progress past that point.

Both his training and his nature made it impossible for him just to let it pass. Her withdrawal didn't make sense, because he *knew,* knew with every animal instinct in him that she felt the same way he did. She wanted him. She loved him. If she were truly hiding something, he wanted to know about it, and he had both the skill and the resources to find out just about anything in a person's life. His inquiries had turned up the fact that she had been married before, but the marriage had seemed to be fairly typical, and fairly brief, the sort of thing a lot of college graduates drifted into, quickly finding out they didn't suit. He'd had his own short fling with marriage at that age, so he knew how it happened. But the more he'd thought about it, the more he'd noticed that the period of her marriage was the one period she didn't talk about, not even mentioning that she'd ever been married at all. He was too good at what he did not to realize the significance of that, and he had begun to probe for answers about those two missing years. At the same time, feeling her slipping away from him, he had made a bold move to cement their relationship and taken her to bed, trusting in the bonds of the flesh to both break down the barriers and hold her to him until she learned to trust him completely.

It hadn't worked.

She had fled the next morning while he was still in the shower, and this was the first time he'd gotten her alone since then.

Over half a year wasted. Almost seven long damn months, endless nights spent in burning frustration, both physical and mental.

But he had her now, all alone, and before they left this building he intended to know just what the hell happened and have her back where she belonged, with him.

Chapter Four

"Let's get those snack machines raided," she muttered, grabbing up her ditty bag of goodies and heading for the door. Quinlan had been standing there, staring at her for what seemed like several minutes but had probably been less than thirty seconds. There was a hooded, predatory expression in his gleaming blue eyes, and she just couldn't stand there, like a tethered goat, for another second.

He sauntered out in her wake, and she relocked the office door, then looked up and down the dim hallway. "Just where *are* these snack machines?" she finally asked. "I'm not a junk food junkie, so I've never used them."

"There's a soft drink machine at this end of the hallway," he said, pointing, "but there are snack machines in the insurance offices. They have a break room for their employees, but they let us use them." He set off down the long hallway, away from the bank of elevators, and Elizabeth trailed after him.

"How are we going to get in?" she asked caustically. "Shoot the lock off?"

"If I have to," he replied, lazy good humor in his voice. "But I don't think it will come to that."

She hoped not. From what she could tell, insurance companies tended to be rather humorless about such things. She could well imagine receiving a bill for damages, which she could certainly do without.

Quinlan knelt in front of the insurance company's locked door and unzipped the leather bag, taking from it a small case resembling the one in which she kept her makeup brushes. He flipped it open, though, and the resemblance ended. Instead of plush brushes, there was an assortment of oddly shaped metal tools. He took two of them out, inserted the long, thin, bent one into the keyhole, then slid the other instrument in beside it and jiggled it with small, delicate movements.

Elizabeth sidled closer, bending down to get a better look. "Can you teach me how to do that?" she asked in an absent tone, fascinated with the process.

The corners of his mouth twitched as he continued to gingerly work at the lock. "Why? Have you just discovered a larcenous streak?"

"Do *you* have one?" she shot back. "It just seems like a handy skill to have, since you never know when you'll accidentally lock yourself out."

"And you're going to start carrying a set of locksmith's tools in your purse?"

"Why not?" She nudged the black leather bag with her toe. "Evidently you carry one in yours."

"That isn't a purse. Ah," he said with satisfaction, as he felt the lock open. He withdrew the slender tools, stored them in their proper places in the case and replaced the case in the bag. Then he calmly opened the door.

"Explain the difference between my purse and yours," she said as she entered the dim, silent insurance office.

"It isn't a purse. The difference is the things that are in them."

"I see. So if I emptied the contents of my purse into your leather bag, it would then become a purse?"

"I give up," he said mildly. "Okay, it's a purse. Only men don't call them purses. We call them satchels or just plain leather bags."

"A rose by any other name," she murmured with gentle triumph.

He chuckled. "That's one of the things I like best about you. You're such a gracious winner. You never hesitate at all to gloat."

"Some people just ask for it more than others." She looked around, seeing nothing but empty desks and blank computer screens. "Where's the break room?"

"This way." He led her down a dark interior hallway and opened the last door on the right.

The room had two windows, so it wasn't dark. A variety of vending machines lined one wall, offering soft drinks, coffee, juice and snacks. A microwave oven sat on a counter, and a silent refrigerator stood at another wall. There was a vinyl sofa with splits in the cushions that allowed the stuffing to show, and a number of folding chairs shoved haphazardly around two cafeteria tables.

"Check the refrigerator while I open the machines," Quinlan said. "See if there's any ice. We don't need it now, but it would be nice to know that it's there just in case. Do it as fast as you can, to keep the cold air in."

"I do know about refrigerators and power failures," she said pointedly. Swiftly she opened the freezer compartment, and vapor poured out as cold air met warm. There were six ice trays there, all of them full. She shut the door just as fast as she had opened it. "We have ice."

"Good." He had the snack machine open and was removing packs of crackers.

Elizabeth opened the main refrigerator door but was disappointed with the contents. A brown paper bag sat in lone splendor, with several translucent greasy spots decorating it. She had no interest in investigating its contents. There was an apple, though, and she took it. The shelves in the door were lined with various condiments, nothing that tempted her. The thought of putting ketchup on the honey bun was revolting.

"Just an apple here," she said.

He finished loading his booty into the leather bag. "Okay, we have cakes, crackers and candy bars, plus the stuff you got from Chickie's desk. My best guess is we'll get out of here sometime tomorrow morning, so this should be more than enough. Do you want a soft drink, or juice? There's water downstairs, so we don't need to raid the drink machines. It's strictly a matter of preference."

She thought about it, then shook her head. "Water will be enough."

He zipped the bag. "That's it, then. Let's make ourselves comfy downstairs."

"Should we leave a note?" she asked.

"No need. I'll take care of things when the power comes on and everything gets back to normal."

The trip downstairs was considerably easier with the aid of one of the flashlights, and soon they reentered the lobby, which was noticeably cooler because of the two-story ceiling. She looked out through the dark glass of the double entrance; the street was oddly deserted, with only the occasional car passing by. A patrol car crawled past as she watched. "It looks weird," she murmured. "As if everyone has been evacuated."

"If the power doesn't come back on," Quinlan said in a grim tone, "it will probably get a lot busier once the sun goes down and things cool off a little. By the way, I tried to call out from my office, just to see what was going on and let someone know where we were, but I couldn't get a call to go through. If there's a city-wide blackout, which I suspect, the circuits will be jammed with calls. But I did find a battery-operated radio, so we'll be able to listen to the news."

"Turn it on now," she suggested, walking over to a sofa to dump her load on it. "Let's find out what's going on."

He opened the leather bag and took out a small radio, not even as big as her hand. After switching it on and getting only static, he began running through the frequencies, looking for a station. Abruptly a voice jumped out at them, astonishingly clear for such a small radio. "—the National Guard has been called out in several states to help prevent looting—"

"Damn," Quinlan muttered. "This sounds bad."

"Information is sketchy," the announcer continued, "but more reports are coming in, and it looks as if there has been a massive loss of electrical power across the Southeast and most of Texas."

"I'm not an expert," a second voice said, "but the southern tier of the country has been suffering under this heat wave for two weeks, and I imagine the demands for electricity overloaded the system. Have we had any word yet from the governor?"

"Nothing yet, but the phone lines are tied up. Please, people, don't use the telephones unless it's an emergency. Folks can't get through to 911 if you're on the phone to your friends telling them that your power's out, too. Believe me, they *know*."

The second announcer chimed in, "Remember the safety precautions the Health Department has been telling us for two weeks. It's especially critical without electricity for air conditioning and fans. Stay out of the sun if possible. With the power off, open your windows for ventilation, and drink plenty of liquids. Don't move around any more than you have to. Conserve your energy."

"We'll be on the air all night long," said the first announcer, "operating on emergency power. If anything happens you'll hear it first here on—"

Quinlan switched off the radio. "Well, now we know what happened," he said calmly. "We'll save the batteries as much as we can."

She gave him a mock incredulous look. "What? You mean you don't have replacement batteries?"

"It isn't my radio."

It wasn't necessary for him to add that if it had been, of course he would have had extra batteries. She wished it *were* his radio. And while she was wishing, she wished she had left the building on time, though she wasn't certain she wouldn't be in a worse situation at her condo. Certainly she was safer here, inside a sealed building.

The magnitude of the problem was stunning. This wasn't something that was going to be corrected in a couple of hours. It was possible they would still be locked in at this time tomorrow.

She looked at Quinlan. "Are you *sure* it won't get dangerously hot in here?"

"Not absolutely positive, but reasonably sure. We'll be okay. We have water, and that's the most important thing. Actually, we're probably as comfortable as anyone in this city is, except for those places that have emergency generators. If we start getting too warm, we'll just take off some clothes."

Her heart literally jumped, sending her pulse rate soaring, and immediately she began to feel uncomfortably warm. Her stomach muscles clenched at the thought of lying naked in the darkness with him, but it was the tightness of desire. While her mind was wary, her body remembered the intense pleasure of his lovemaking. She turned back to the windows to keep him from reading her expression. Staring at the glass made her think of something else, and gratefully she seized on it.

"When it gets dark, will anyone on the outside be able to see us in here when we turn on a flashlight? Does the privacy glazing work at night?"

"Anyone who looked closely would be able to tell that there's a light in here, I suppose," he said thoughtfully. "But no one will be able to actually *see* us."

Just the possibility was enough. She had been about to arrange their supplies in the seating area closest to the entrance, but now she moved farther away. The lobby had several comfortable seating areas, and she chose one that was close to the middle. It was at least semiprivate, with a long, waist-high planter that created the sense of a small alcove. It was also closer to the bathrooms, making it a better choice all the way around.

She arranged their food supplies on a low table, while Quinlan shoved the chairs around to make more room. Then he collected cushions from the other chairs and stacked them close to hand, ready to make into beds when they decided to sleep. Elizabeth gave the cushions a sidelong glance. She wasn't sure she would be able to close her eyes with Quinlan so close by, or that it would be smart to sleep, even if she could.

She looked at him and started when she found him watching her. He didn't look away as he unknotted his tie and stripped it off, then unbuttoned his shirt down to his waist and rolled up his sleeves. His actions were practical, but the sight of his muscled, hairy chest and hard belly aroused a reaction in her that had nothing to do with common sense.

"Why don't you take off those panty hose?" he suggested in a low, silky voice. "They have to be damn hot."

They were. She hesitated, then decided wryly that it wasn't the thin nylon that would protect her from him. Only *she* could do that. Quinlan wasn't a rapist; if she said no, he wouldn't force himself on her. She had never been afraid of that; her only fear was that she wouldn't be able to say no. That was one reason why she had avoided him for the past six months. So leaving her panty hose on wouldn't keep him from making love to her if she couldn't say no, and taking them off wouldn't put her at risk if she did keep herself under control. It was, simply, a matter of comfort.

She got a flashlight and carried it into the public rest room, where she propped it on one of the basins. The small room felt stuffy and airless, so she hurriedly removed her panty hose and immediately felt much cooler. She turned on the cold water and held her wrists under the stream, using the time-proven method of cooling down, then dampened one of the paper towels and blotted her face. There. That was much better.

A few deep breaths, a silent pep talk and she felt ready to hold Tom Quinlan at arm's length for the duration. With her panty hose in one hand and the flashlight in the other, she returned to the lobby.

He was waiting for her, sprawled negligently in one of the chairs, but those blue eyes watched her as intently as a tiger watches its chosen prey. "Now," he said, "let's have our little talk."

Chapter Five

Her heart lurched in her chest. It strained her composure to walk over to the chairs and sit down, but she did it, even crossed her legs and leaned back as negligently as he. "All right," she said calmly.

He gave her that considering look again, as if he were trying to decide how to handle her. Mentally she bristled at the idea of being "handled," but she forced down her irritation. She knew how relentless Quinlan could be when crossed; she would need to keep her thoughts ordered, not let him trip her up with anger.

He remained silent, watching her, and she knew what he wanted. He had already asked the question; he was simply waiting for the answer.

Despite herself, Elizabeth felt a spurt of anger, even after all these months. She faced him and went straight to the heart of the matter. "I found the file you had on me," she said, every word clipped short. "You had me investigated."

"Ah." He steepled his fingers and studied her over them. "So that's it." He paused a few seconds, then said mildly, "Of course I did."

"There's no 'of course' to it. You invaded my privacy—"

"As you invaded mine," he interrupted smoothly. "That file wasn't lying out in the open."

"No, it wasn't. I looked in your desk," she admitted without hesitation.

"Why?"

"I felt uneasy about you. I was looking for some answers."

"So why didn't you ask *me?*" The words were as sharp as a stiletto.

She gave him a wry, humorless smile. "I did. Many times. You're a master at evasion, though. I've been to bed with you, but I don't know much more about you right now than I did the day we met."

He neatly sidestepped the charge by asking, "What made you feel uneasy? I never threatened you, never pushed you. You know I own and run my company, that I'm solvent and not on the run."

"You just did it again," she pointed out. "Your ability to evade is very good. It took me a while to catch on, but then I noticed that you didn't answer my questions. You always responded, so it wasn't obvious, but you'd just ask your own question and ignore mine."

He surveyed her silently for a moment before saying,

"I'm not interested in talking about myself. I already know all the details."

"I'd say that the same holds true for me, wouldn't you?" she asked sweetly. "I wanted to know about *you,* and got nowhere. But I didn't have you investigated."

"I wouldn't have minded if you had." Not that she would have been able to find out much, he thought. Great chunks of his life after high school graduation weren't to be found in public records.

"Bully for you. *I* minded."

"And that's it? You walked out on me and broke off our relationship because you were angry that I had you investigated? Why didn't you just yell at me? Throw things at me? For God's sake, Elizabeth, don't you think you took it a little far?"

His tone was both angry and incredulous, making it plain that he considered her reaction to be nothing short of hysteric, far out of proportion to the cause.

She froze inside, momentarily paralyzed by the familiar ploy of being made to feel that she was in the wrong, that no matter what happened it was her fault for not being good enough. But then she fought the memories back; she would never let anyone make her feel that way again. She had gotten herself back, and she knew her own worth. She knew she hadn't handled the matter well, but only in the way she had done it; the outcome itself had never been in question.

Her voice was cool when she replied. "No, I don't think I took it too far. I'd been feeling uneasy about you for quite a while. Finding that you had investigated me was the final factor, but certainly not all of it."

"Because I hadn't answered a few questions?" That incredulous note was still there.

"Among other things."

"Such as?"

In for a penny, in for a pound. "Such as your habit of taking over, of ignoring my objections or suggestions as if I hadn't even said anything."

"Objections to what?" Now the words were as sharp as a lash. His blue eyes were narrowed and vivid. A bit surprised, she realized that he was angry again.

She waved her hand in a vague gesture. "Any little thing. I didn't catalog them—"

"Surprises the hell out of me," he muttered.

"But you were constantly overriding me. If I told you I was going shopping, you insisted that I wait until you could go with me. If I wanted to wear a sweater when we were going out, you insisted that I wear a coat. Damn it, Quinlan, you even tried to make me change where I bank!"

His eyebrows rose. "The bank you use now is too far away. The one I suggested is much more convenient."

"For whom? If I'm perfectly happy with my bank, then it isn't inconvenient for me, is it?"

"So don't change your bank. What's the big deal?"

"The big deal," she said slowly, choosing her words, "is that you want to make all the decisions, handle everything yourself. You don't want a relationship, you want a dictatorship."

One moment he was lounging comfortably, long legs sprawled out in front of him; the next he was in front of her, bending over to plant his hands on the arms of her chair and trap her in place. Elizabeth stared up at him, blinking at the barely controlled rage in his face, but she refused to let herself shrink from him. Instead she lifted her chin and met him glare for glare.

"I don't believe it!" he half shouted. "You walked out on me because I wanted you to change banks? God in heaven." He shoved himself away from the chair and stalked several paces away, running his hand through his hair.

"No," she shouted back, "I walked out because I refuse to let you take over my life!" She was unable to sit still, either, and surged out of the chair. Instantly Quinlan whirled with those lightning-quick reactions of his, catching her arms and hauling her close to him, so close that she could see the white flecks in the deep blue of his irises and smell the hot, male scent of his body. Her nostrils flared delicately as she instinctively drank in the primal signal, even though she stiffened against his touch.

"Why didn't you tell me you were married before?"

The question was soft, and not even unexpected, but still she flinched. Of course he knew; it had been in that damn investigative report.

"It isn't on my list of conversational topics," she snapped. "But neither is it a state secret. *If* our relationship had ever progressed far enough, I would have told you then. What was I supposed to do, trot out my past life the minute we met?"

Quinlan watched her attentively. As close as they were, he could see every flicker of expression on her face, and he had noticed the telltale flinch even though she had replied readily enough. Ah, so there *was* something there.

"Just how far did our relationship have to go?" he asked, still keeping his voice soft. "We weren't seeing anyone else. We didn't actually have sex until that last night together, but things got pretty hot between us several times before that."

"And I was having doubts about you even then," she replied just as softly.

"Maybe so, but that didn't stop you from wanting me, just like now." He bent his head and settled his mouth on hers, the pressure light and persuasive. She tried to pull away and found herself powerless against his strength, even though he was taking care not to hurt her. "Be still," he said against her lips.

Desperately she wrenched her head away. He forced it back, but instead of kissing her again, he paused with his mouth only a fraction of an inch above hers. "Why didn't you tell me about it?" he murmured, his warm breath caressing her lips and making them tingle. With his typical relentlessness, he had fastened on an idea and wouldn't let it go until he was satisfied with the answer. The old blind fear rose in her, black wings beating, and in panic she started to struggle. He subdued her without effort, wrapping her in a warm, solid embrace from which there was no escape.

"What happened?" he asked, brushing light kisses across her mouth between words. "What made you flinch when I mentioned it? Tell me about it now. I need to know. Did he run around on you?"

"No." She hadn't meant to answer him, but somehow, caught in those steely arms and cradled against his enticing heat, the word slipped out in a whisper. She heard it and shuddered. "No!" she said more forcefully, fighting for control. "He didn't cheat." If only he had, if only his destructive attention had been diluted in that way, it wouldn't have been so bad. "Stop it, Quinlan. Let me go."

"Why did you start calling me Quinlan?" His voice remained low and soothing, and his warm mouth kept pressing against hers with quick, gentle touches. "You called me Tom before, and when we made love."

She had started calling him Quinlan in an effort to distance herself from him. She didn't want to think of him as Tom, because the name was forever linked in her mind with that night when she had clung to his naked shoulders, her body lifting feverishly to his forceful thrusts as she cried out his name over and over, in ecstasy, in need, in completion. Tom was the name of her lover; Quinlan was the man she had fled.

And Quinlan was the one she had to deal with now, the man who never gave up. He held her helpless in his grasp, taking kiss after kiss from her until she stopped trying to evade his mouth and opened her lips to him with a tiny, greedy sound. Instantly he took her with his tongue, and the sheer pleasure of it made them both shudder.

His warm hand closed over her breast, gently kneading. She groaned, the sound captured by his mouth, and desperately tried to marshal her resistance. He was seducing her just as effortlessly as he had the first time, but even though she realized what was happening she couldn't find the willpower to push him away. She loved him too much, savored his kisses too much, desired him too strongly, found too much pleasure in the stroke of those hard hands.

The pressure of his fingers had hardened her nipple into a tight nub that stabbed his palm even through the layers of fabric protecting her. He deepened the kiss as he roughly opened the buttons of her blouse and shoved a hand inside the opening, then under the lacy cup of her bra to find the bare flesh he craved. She whimpered as his fingers found her sensitive nipple and lightly pinched at it, sending sharp waves of sensation down to her tightening loins. The sound she made was soft, more of a vibration than an actual noise, but he was so attuned to her that he felt it as sharply as an electrical shock.

She was limp as he bent her back over his arm and freed her breast from the lace that confined it, cupping the warm mound and lifting it up to his hungry mouth. He bent over her, sucking fiercely at her tender flesh, wild with the taste and scent and feel of her. He stabbed at her nipple with his tongue, excited and triumphant at the way she arched responsively at every lash of sensation. She wanted him. He had told himself that there had been no mistaking her fiery response that night, but the six months since then had weakened his assurance. Now he knew he hadn't been wrong. He barely had to touch her and she trembled with excitement, already needing him, ready for him.

He left her breast for more deeply voracious kisses taken from her sweetly swollen lips. God, he wanted her! No other woman had ever made him feel as Elizabeth did, so completely attuned with and lost within her.

He wanted to make love to her, *now,* but there were still too many unanswered questions. If he didn't get things settled while he had her marooned here, unable to get away from him, it might be another six months before he could corner her again. No, by God, it wouldn't be; he couldn't stand it again.

Reluctantly he left her mouth, every instinct in him wanting to take this to completion, knowing that he could if only he didn't give her a chance to surface from the drugging physical delight, but he still wanted answers and couldn't wait, didn't dare wait, to get them. "Tell me," he cajoled as he trailed his mouth down the side of her neck, nibbling on the taut tendon and feeling the response ripple through her. Finally—*finally*—he was on the right track. "Tell me what *he* did that made you run from *me.*"

Chapter Six

Frantically Elizabeth tried to jerk away, but he controlled her so easily that her efforts were laughable. Nevertheless, she lodged her hands against his heavy shoulders and pushed as hard as she could. "Let me go!"

"No." His refusal was flat and calm. "Stop fighting and answer me."

She couldn't do either one, and she began to panic, not because she feared Quinlan, but because she didn't want to talk about her marriage to Eric Landers, didn't want to think about it, didn't want to revive that hell even in memory. But Quinlan, damn his stubborn temperament, had fastened on the subject and wouldn't drop it until he got what he wanted. She knew him, knew that he intended to drag every detail out of her, and she simply couldn't face it.

Sheer survival instinct made her suddenly relax in his arms, sinking against him, clutching his shoulders instead of pushing against them. She felt his entire body tighten convulsively at her abrupt capitulation; her own muscles quivered with acute relief, as if she had been forcing them to an unnatural action. Her breath caught jerkily as her hips settled against his and she felt the thick ridge of his sex. His arousal was so familiar, and unbearably seductive. The lure of his sexuality pulled her even closer, her loins growing heavy and taut with desire.

He felt the change in her, saw it mirrored almost instantly in her face. One moment she had been struggling against him, and the next she was shivering in carnal excitement, her body tense as she moved against him in a subtle demand. He cursed, his voice thick, as he tried to fight his own response. It was a losing battle; he had wanted her too intensely, for too long. Talking would have to wait; for now, she had won. All he could think about was that she was finally in his arms again, every small movement signaling eager compliance. He didn't know what had changed her mind, and at this moment he didn't particularly care. It was enough that she was once again clinging to him, as she had the one night they had spent together, the night that was burned into his memory. He had tossed restlessly through a lot of dark, sleepless hours since then, remembering how it had been and aching for the same release, needing her beneath him, bewildered by and angry at her sudden coldness.

There was nothing cold about her now. He could feel her heat, feel her vibrating under his hands. Her hips moved in an ancient search, and a low moan hummed in her throat as she found what she had sought, her legs parting slightly to nestle his hard sex between them.

Fiercely he thrust his hand into her hair and pulled her head back. "Do you want this?" he asked hoarsely, hanging on to his control with grim concentration. It had happened so abruptly that he wanted to make sure before another second had passed, before she moved again and launched him past the point of no return. He hadn't felt like this since he'd been a teenager, the tide of desire rising like floodwaters in his veins, drowning thought. God, he didn't care what had caused her to change; right now, all he wanted was to thrust into her.

For a second she didn't answer, and his teeth were already clenching against a curse when she dug her nails into his shoulder and said, "Yes."

Her senses whirled dizzily as he lowered her to the floor, right where they stood. "The sofa…" she murmured, but then his weight came down on top of her and she didn't care anymore. Her initial tactic had been a panicked effort to distract him, but her own desire had blindsided her, welling up and overwhelming her senses so swiftly that she had no defense against it. She had hungered for him for so long, lying awake during the long, dark nights with silent tears seeping from beneath her lids because she missed him so much, almost as much as she feared him—and herself. The relief of being in his arms again was almost painful, and she pushed away all the reasons why this shouldn't happen. She would face the inevitable later; for now, all she wanted was Tom Quinlan.

He was rough, his own hunger too intense, too long denied, for him to control it. He shoved her skirt up to her waist and dragged her panties down, and Elizabeth willingly opened her thighs to receive him. He dealt just as swiftly with his pants, then brought his loins to hers. His penetration was hard and stabbing, and she cried out at the force of it. Her hips arched, accepting, taking him deeper. A guttural sound vibrated in his wide chest; then he caught the backs of her thighs, pulling her legs higher, and he began thrusting hard and fast.

She loved it. She reveled in it. She sobbed aloud at the strong release that pulsed through her almost immediately, the staggering physical response that she had known only with this man and had thought she would never experience again. She had been willing to give up this physical ecstasy in order to protect her inner self from his dominance, but oh, how she had longed for it, and bitterly wondered why the most dangerous traps had the sweetest bait.

Blinded by the ferocity of his own need, he anchored her writhing hips with his big hands and pounded into her. Dazedly she became aware of the hard floor beneath her, bruising her shoulders, but even as her senses were recovering from their sensual battering and allowing her to take stock of her surroundings, he gripped her even harder and convulsed. Instinctively she held him, cradling him with arms and legs, and the gentle clasp of her inner warmth. His harsh, strained cries subsided to low, rhythmic moans, then finally to fast and uneven breathing as he relaxed on top of her, his heavy weight pressing her to the floor.

The silence in the huge, dim lobby was broken only by the erratic intake and release of their breathing. His slowing heartbeat thudded heavily against her breasts, and their heated bodies melded together everywhere that bare flesh touched bare flesh. She felt the moisture of sweat, and the inner wetness that forcibly awakened her to the realization that their frantic mating had been done without any means of protection.

Her own heart lurched in panic; then logic reasserted itself and she calmed down. She had just finished her monthly cycle; it was highly unlikely that she could conceive. Perversely, no sooner had she had that reassuring thought than she was seized by a sense of loss, even of mourning, as if that panicked moment had been truth rather than very remote possibility.

"Elizabeth?"

She didn't open her eyes. She didn't want to face reality just yet, didn't want to have to let him go, and that was something reality would force her to do.

He lifted himself on his elbows, and she could feel the penetrating blue gaze on her face, but still she clung to the safety of her closed eyes.

She felt his muscles gathering, and briefly she tried to hold him, but he lifted himself away from her, and she caught her breath at the slow withdrawal that separated his body from hers. Despite herself, the friction set off a lingering thrill of sensation, and her hips lifted in a small, uncontrollable, telltale movement. Because there was no sanctuary any longer, she opened her eyes and silently met his gaze. That curious, sleepy blankness of sexual satisfaction was on his face, as she knew it must also be on hers, but in his eyes was a predatory watchfulness, as if he knew his prey had been caught but not vanquished.

His astuteness was disturbing, as it had always been. Her own gaze dared him to try to make anything more of what had just happened than an unadorned act of sex, without cause or future.

His mouth twisted wryly as he knelt away from her and pulled his pants up, zipping them with a faint, raspy sound. Then he got to his feet and effortlessly lifted her to hers. Her skirt, which had been bunched around her waist, dropped to the correct position. Elizabeth instinctively clenched her thighs to hold the wetness between them.

Quinlan shrugged out of his shirt and handed it to her, then leaned down and retrieved her panties from the floor. Thrusting them into her hands, too, he said, "Take off those clothes and put on my shirt. It's getting warmer in here, and you'll be more comfortable in something loose."

Silently she turned, picked up the flashlight and went into the ladies' rest room. Her knees were shaking slightly in reaction, and her loins throbbed from the violence of his possession. He hadn't hurt her, but it was as if she could still feel him inside.

She stared at her reflection in the mirror, the image ghostly with only the flashlight for illumination, making her eyes look huge and dark. Her hair had come loose and tumbled around her shoulders; she pushed it back distractedly, still staring at herself, then buried her face in her hands.

How could she go back out there? God, how could

she have been so *stupid?* Alone with him for little more than an hour, and she had had sex with him on the floor like an uncontrolled animal. She couldn't even blame it on him; no, *she* had made the big move, grabbing at him, pushing her hips at him, because she had panicked when he had tried to pull back and begin asking questions again. She had gotten exactly what she had asked for.

She felt confused, both ashamed and elated. She was ashamed that she had used sex as an evasion tactic…or maybe she was ashamed that she had used it as an *excuse* to do what she had been longing to do anyway. The physical desire she felt for him was sharp and strong, so urgently demanding that stopping felt unnatural, all of her instincts pushing her toward him.

Her body felt warm and weak with satiation, faintly trembling in the aftermath. But now that he was no longer touching her, the old wariness was creeping back, pulling her in two directions. She had thought the decision simple, though it had never been easy, but now she was finding that nothing about it, either Quinlan or her own emotions, was simple.

Dazedly she stripped off her disheveled clothing and used some wet paper towels to wash; the cool moisture was momentarily refreshing, but then the close heat of the rest room made sweat form almost as fast as she could wash it off. Ironically she admitted that, no matter how reluctant she was, she had no real choice but to face him again. If she remained in here, she would have heat stroke. It was a sad day when a woman couldn't even count on a rest room for sanctuary. Ah, well, she hadn't yet found any place that was truly safe from him, for her own memories worked against her.

Just as she pulled on her panties, the door was thrust open and Quinlan loomed in the opening, his big body blotting out most of the light from the lobby but allowing the welcome entrance of relatively cooler air. The subtle breeze washed around her body, making her nipples pucker slightly. Or was that an instinctive female reaction to the closeness of her mate? She didn't want to think of him in such primitive, possessive terms, but her body had different priorities.

He noticed, of course. His gaze became smoky with both desire and possessiveness as he openly admired her breasts. But he didn't move toward her, holding himself very still as if he sensed her confusion. "Hiding?" he asked mildly.

"Delaying," she admitted, her tone soft. She didn't try to shield her body from him; such an action would seem silly, after what they had just done. It wasn't as if he hadn't seen her completely naked before, as if they hadn't made love before. Moreover, he had decided to remove his pants and stood before her wearing only a pair of short, dark boxers. Barefoot and mostly naked, his dark hair tousled and wet with both sweat and the water he had splashed on his face, he was stripped of most of the trappings of civilization. Despite the heat, a shiver ran up her spine in yet another feminine response to the primitiveness of his masculinity, and she looked away to keep him from seeing it in her face.

He came to her and took up his shirt, holding it for her to slip into; then, when she had done so, he turned her and began buttoning the garment as if she were a child being dressed. "You can't stay in here," he said. "Too damn hot."

"I know. I was coming out."

He shepherded her toward the door, his hand on her back. She wondered if the action was just his usual take-charge attitude, or if he was acting on some primitive instinct of his own, to keep the female from bolting. Probably a mixture of the two, she thought, and sighed.

He had been busy while she had been in the rest room, and she realized she had delayed in there much longer than she had intended. He had arranged the extra cushions on the floor—in the shape of a double bed, she noticed—and gotten some cool water from the fountain, the cups ready for them to drink. The water was welcome, but if he thought she was going to docilely stretch out on those cushions, he would shortly be disillusioned. She sat down in a chair and reached for a cup, sipping it without enthusiasm at first, then more eagerly as she rediscovered how good plain water was for quenching thirst. It was a delight of childhood that tended to be forgotten in the adult world of coffee, tea and wine spritzers.

"Are you hungry?" he asked.

"No." How could she be hungry? Her nerves were so tightly drawn that she didn't think she would be able to eat until they got out of here.

"Well, I am." He tore open the wrapping on the big blueberry muffin and began eating. "Tell me about your marriage."

She stiffened and glared at him. "It wasn't a good

marriage," she said tightly. "It also isn't any of your business."

He glanced pointedly at the floor where they had so recently made love. "That's debatable. Okay, let's try it this way. I'll tell you about my marriage if you'll tell me about yours. No evasion tactics. I'll answer any question you ask."

She stared at him in shock. "*Your* marriage?"

He shrugged. "Sure. Hell, I'm thirty-seven years old. I haven't lived my entire life in a vacuum."

"You have your nerve!" she flared. "You jumped down my throat for not talking about my past marriage when you've only now mentioned your own?"

He rubbed the side of his nose and gave her a faintly sheepish look. "That occurred to me," he admitted.

"Well, let me put another thought in your dim Neanderthal brain! The time for heart-to-heart confidences was over a long time ago. We aren't involved any longer, so there's no point in 'sharing.'"

He took another bite of the muffin. "Don't kid yourself. What we just did felt pretty damn involved to me."

"That was just sex," she said dismissively. "It had been a while, and I needed it."

"I know exactly how long it had been." His blue gaze sharpened, and she knew he hadn't liked her comment. "You haven't gone out with anyone else since you walked out on me."

She was enraged all over again. "Have you had me followed?"

He had, but he wasn't about to tell her that now.

Instead he said, "Chickie worries because your social life, in her words, resembles Death Valley—nothing of interest moving around."

Elizabeth snorted, but she was mollified, because she had heard Chickie make that exact comment on a couple of occasions. Still, she would have to have a word with her about discretion.

"I've been busy," she said, not caring if he believed her or not, though it happened to be the truth. She had deliberately been as busy as she could manage in order to give herself less free time to think about him.

"I know. You've found a lot of lilies to gild."

Her teeth closed with a snap. "That's so people will have a reason to install your fancy security systems. I gild the lilies, and you protect them."

"I protect *people*," he clarified.

"Uh-huh. That's why you set up so many security systems for people who live in rough neighborhoods, where their lives are really in danger."

"I can see we aren't going to agree on this."

"You brought it up."

"My mistake. Let's get back to the original subject, namely our respective failed marriages. Go ahead, ask me anything you want."

The perfect response, of course, was that she wasn't interested. It would also be a lie, because she was not only interested, she was suddenly, violently jealous of that unknown, hitherto unsuspected woman who had been his wife, who had shared his name and his bed for a time, and who had been, in the eyes of the world, his mate. Elizabeth firmly kept her mouth closed, but she couldn't stop herself from glaring at him.

Quinlan sighed. "All right, I'll tell you the boring facts without making you ask. Her name was Amy. We dated during college. Then, when college was finished, it seemed like we should do adult things, so we got married. But I was away on my job a lot, and Amy found someone in the office where she worked who she liked a lot better. Within six months of getting married we knew it had been a mistake, but we held out for another year, trying to make it 'work,' before we both realized we were just wasting time. The divorce was a relief for both of us. End of story."

She was still glaring at him. "I don't even know where you went to college."

He sighed again. She was getting damn tired of that sigh, as if he were being so noble in his dealings with an irrational woman. "Cal Tech."

"Ah." Well, that explained his expertise with electronics and computers and things.

"No children," he added.

"I should hope not!" It was bad enough that he had, for some reason, concealed all the rest of the details of his life. "If you'd kept *children* hidden, I would never have forgiven you."

His eyes gleamed. "Does this mean you *have?*"

"No."

He gave a startled shout of laughter. "God, I've missed you. You don't dissemble at all. If you're grouchy, you don't feel any need at all to make nice and pretend to be sweetness and light, do you?"

She gave him a haughty look. "I'm not sweetness and light."

"Thank God," he said fervently. He leaned back and spread his hands, then stretched his long, muscular legs out before him in a posture of complete relaxation. "Okay, it's your turn. Tell me all the deep, dark secrets about *your* marriage."

Chapter Seven

"Show-and-tell was your idea, not mine." Her throat tightened at the idea of rehashing the details, reliving the nightmare even in thought. She just couldn't do it.

"You asked questions."

"I asked where you went to college, hardly the same as prying into your private life." Agitated, she stood up and longingly looked through the huge windows to the world outside. Only two thin sheets of transparent material kept her prisoner here with him, but it would take a car ramming into the glass at respectable speed to break it. The glass looked fragile but wasn't, whereas she was the opposite. She looked calm and capable, but inside she hid a weakness that terrified her.

"Don't run away," Quinlan warned softly.

She barely glanced at him as she edged out of the

semicircle of sofa and chairs. "I'm not running," she denied, knowing that it wasn't the truth. "It's cooler moving around."

Silently Quinlan got to his feet and paced after her, big and virtually naked, the dark boxer shorts nothing more than the modern version of the loincloth. His muscled chest was hairy, the thick curls almost hiding his small nipples, and a silky line of hair ran down the center of his abdomen to his groin. His long legs were also covered with hair, finer and straighter, but he was undoubtedly a dominating male animal in his prime. Elizabeth gave him a distracted, vaguely alarmed look that suddenly focused on his loins, and her eyes widened.

He looked down at himself and shrugged, not pausing in his slow, relentless pursuit. "I know, at my age I shouldn't have recovered this fast. I usually don't," he said thoughtfully. "It's just my reaction to you. Come here, sweetheart." His voice had turned soft and cajoling.

Wildly Elizabeth wondered if this was going to degenerate into the stereotypical chase around the furniture. On the heels of that thought came the certain knowledge that if she ran, Quinlan would definitely chase her, instinctively, the marauding male subduing the reluctant female. She could prevent that farce by not running, thereby giving him nothing to chase. On the other hand, if she stood still things would only reach the same conclusion at a faster pace. Evidently the only real choice she had was whether or not to hold on to her dignity. If she had felt differently about him she could have said "no," but she had already faced that weakness in herself. For right now, in these circumstances, she couldn't resist him—and they both knew it.

He drew closer, his eyes gleaming. "For tonight, you're mine," he murmured. "Let me at least have that. You can't get away from me here. You don't even want to get away, not really. The circumstances aren't normal. When we get out of here you'll have options, but right now you're forced to be with me. Whatever happens won't be your fault. Just let go and forget about it."

She drew a deep, shuddering breath. "Pretty good psychologist, aren't you? But I'm not a coward. I'm responsible for whatever decisions I make, period."

He had reached her now, one arm sliding around her back. Elizabeth looked up at him, at the tousled dark hair and intense blue eyes, and her heart squeezed. "All right," she whispered. "For tonight. For as long as we're locked in here." She closed her eyes, shivering with sensual anticipation. She would let herself have this, just for now; she would feast on him, drown herself in sensation, let the darkness of the night wrap protectively around them and hold off thought. The time would come all too soon when she would have to push him away again; why waste even one precious minute by fighting both him and herself?

"Anything," she heard herself say as he lifted her. Her voice sounded strange to her, thick, drugged with desire. "For tonight."

His low, rough laugh wasn't quite steady as he lowered her to the cushions. "Anything?" he asked.

"You could be letting yourself in for an interesting night."

She put out her hand and touched his bare chest. "Yes," she purred. "I could be."

"Cat." His breathing was fast and unsteady as he swiftly stripped her panties down her legs and tossed them to the side. "You won't be needing those again tonight."

She pulled at the waistband of his shorts. "And you won't be needing these."

"Hell, I only kept them on because I figured you'd fight like a wildcat if I came after you stark naked." He dealt with his shorts as rapidly as he had her underwear.

She was already excited by the anticipation of his slow, thorough loveplay. Quinlan was a man who enjoyed the preliminaries and prolonged them, as she had learned during the one night she had spent with him. It didn't happen this time, though. He pushed her legs open, knelt between them and entered her with a heavy thrust that jarred her. The shock of it reverberated through her body; then her inner muscles clamped down in an effort to slow that inexorable invasion.

He pushed deeper, groaning at the tightness of her, until he was in her to the hilt. She writhed, reaching down to grasp his thighs and hold him there, but he slowly withdrew, then just as slowly pushed back into her.

"Did your husband make you feel like this?" he whispered.

Her head rolled on the cushions at the speed and intensity of the sensations. It was an effort to concentrate on his words. "N-no," she finally sighed.

"Good." He couldn't keep the savage satisfaction

out of his voice. He didn't like the thought of anyone else pleasing her. This was something she had known only with him; he had realized it immediately when they had first made love, but he had needed to hear her say it, admit that she had given her response to no one else.

He teased her with another slow withdrawal and thrust. "What did he do to you?" he murmured, and pulled completely away from her.

Her eyes opened in protest and she reached for him, moaning low in her throat as she tried to reestablish that delicious contact. Then comprehension made her eyes flare wider, and she jerked backward, away from him, trying to sit up. "You bastard!" she said in a strangled tone.

Quinlan caught her hips and dragged her back, slipping into her once again. "Tell me," he said relentlessly. "Did he mistreat you? Hurt you in any way? What in hell did he do that you're making me pay for?"

Elizabeth wrenched away from him again. She felt ill, all desire gone. How could he have done that to her? She fought to cover herself with his shirt, all the while calling herself several harsh names for her stupidity in thinking they could have this night, that she could give herself a block of time unattached to either past or present. She should have remembered that Quinlan never gave up.

No, he never gave up. So why didn't she tell him? It wouldn't be easy for her to relive it, but at least then he would know why she refused to allow him any authority in her life, why she had denied herself the love she so desperately wanted to give him.

She curled away from him, letting her head fall forward onto her knees so her hair hid her face. He tried to pull her back into his arms, into his lovemaking, but she resisted him, her body stiff in reaction to the memories already swamping her.

"Don't touch me!" she said hoarsely. "You wanted to know, so sit there and listen, but don't—don't touch me."

Quinlan frowned, feeling vaguely uneasy. He had deliberately pushed her, though he hadn't intended to push so hard that she withdrew from him, but that was what had happened. His body was still tight with desire, demanding release. He ground his teeth together, grimly reaching for control; if Elizabeth was ready to talk, after all these months, then he was damn well going to listen.

She didn't lift her head from her knees, but in the silent, darkening lobby, he could plainly hear every soft word.

"I met him when I was a senior in college. Eric. Eric Landers. But you already know his name, don't you? It was in your damn report. He owned an upscale decorating firm, and getting a part-time job there was a real plum."

She sighed. The little sound was sad, and a bit tired. "He was thirty-five. I was twenty-one. And he was handsome, sophisticated, self-assured, worldly, with quite a reputation as both a ladies' man and a well-known professional. I was more than flattered when he asked me out, I was absolutely giddy. Chickie would seem grim compared to the way I felt.

"We dated for about three months before he asked

me to marry him, and for three months I felt like a princess. He took me everywhere, wined and dined me at the best places. He was interested in every minute of my day, in everything I did. A real princess couldn't have been more coddled. I was a virgin—a bit unusual, to stay that way through college, but I'd been studying hard and working part-time jobs, too, and I hadn't had time for much socializing. Eric didn't push me for sex. He said he could wait until our wedding night, that since I had remained a virgin that long, he wanted to give me all the traditional trappings."

"Let me guess," Quinlan said grimly. "He was gay."

She shook her head. "No. His ladies' man reputation was for real. Eric was very gentle with me on our wedding night. I'll give him that. He never mistreated me that way."

"If you don't mind," Quinlan interrupted, his teeth coming together with an audible snap, "I'd rather not hear about your sex life with him, if that wasn't the problem."

Elizabeth was surprised into lifting her head. "Are you jealous?" she asked warily.

He rubbed his hand over his jaw; as late in the day as it was, his five-o'clock shadow had become more substantial and made a rasping sound as his hand passed over it. "Not jealous, exactly," he muttered. "I just don't want to hear it, if you enjoyed making love with him. Hell, *yes,* I'm jealous!"

She gave a spurt of laughter, startling herself. She had never expected to be able to laugh while discussing Eric Landers, but Quinlan's frustration was so obvious that she couldn't help it.

"I don't mind giving the devil his due," she said in a generous tone. "You can pat yourself on the back, because you know you were the first to—umm—"

"Satisfy you," he supplied. A sheepish expression crossed his face.

"I'm not very experienced. You're the only man I've gone to bed with since my divorce. After Eric, I just didn't want to let anyone close to me."

She didn't continue, and the silence stretched between them. It was growing darker by the minute as the sun set completely, and she was comforted by the shield of night. "Why?" Quinlan finally asked.

It was easier to talk now, after that little bit of laughter and with the growing darkness concealing both their expressions. She felt herself relaxing, uncurling from her protective knot.

"It was odd," she said, "but I don't think he wanted me to be sensual. He wanted me to be his perfect princess, his living, breathing Barbie doll. I had gotten used to his protectiveness while we were dating, so at first I didn't think anything of it when he wanted to be with me every time I set foot outside the door. Somehow he always came up with a reason why I shouldn't put in for this job, or that one, and why I couldn't continue working with him. He went shopping with me, picked out my clothes…at first, it all seemed so flattering. My friends were so impressed by the way he treated me.

"Then he began to find reasons why I shouldn't see my friends, why first this one and then that one wasn't 'good' for me. I couldn't invite them over, and he didn't want me visiting them, or meeting them anywhere for lunch. He began vetting my phone calls. It was all so gradual," she said in a faintly bewildered tone. "And he was so gentle. He seemed to have a good reason for everything he did, and he was always focused on me, giving me the kind of attention all women think they want. He only wanted what was best for me, he said."

Quinlan was beginning to feel uneasy. He shifted position, leaning his back against one of the chairs and stretching out in a relaxed position that belied his inner tension. "A control freak," he growled.

"I think we'd been married about six months before I really noticed how completely he'd cut me off from everyone and everything except him," she continued. "I began trying to shift the balance of power, to make a few decisions for myself, if only in minor things, such as where I got my hair cut."

"Let me make another guess. All of a sudden he wasn't so gentle, right?"

"He was furious that I'd gone to a different place. He took the car keys away from me. That was when I really became angry, for the first time. Until then, I'd made excuses, because he'd been so gentle and loving with me. I'd never defied him until then, but when he took the keys out of my purse I lost my temper and yelled at him. He knocked me down," she said briefly.

Quinlan surged to his feet, raw fury running through him so powerfully that he couldn't sit there any longer. To hell with trying to look relaxed. He paced the lobby like a tiger, naked and primitive, the powerful muscles in his body flexing with every movement.

Elizabeth kept on talking. Now that she had started, she wanted to tell it all. Funny, but reliving it wasn't as traumatic as she had expected, not as bad as it had been in her memories and nightmares. Maybe it was having someone else with her that blunted the pain, because always before she had been alone with it.

"I literally became his prisoner. Whenever I tried to assert myself in any way, he'd punish me. There was no pattern to it. Most of the time he would slap me, or even whip me, but sometimes he would just yell, and I never knew what to expect. It was as if he knew that yelling instead of hitting me made it even worse, because then the next time I *knew* he'd hit me, and I'd try, oh, I'd try so hard, not to do anything that would cause the next time. But I always did. I was so nervous that I always did something. Or he'd make up a reason.

"Looking back," she said slowly, "it's hard to believe I was so stupid. By the time I realized what he had done and started trying to fight back, he had me so isolated, so brainwashed, that I literally felt powerless. I had no money, no friends, no car. I was ashamed for anyone to know what was happening. That was what was so sick, that he could convince me it was my fault. I did try to run away once, but he'd paid the doorman to call him if I left, and he found me within half an hour. He didn't hit me that time. He just tied me to the bed and left me. The terror of waiting, helpless, for him to come back and punish me was so bad that hitting me would have been a relief, because that would have meant it was over. Instead he kept me tied for two days, and I nearly became hysterical every time he came into the room."

Quinlan had stopped pacing. He was standing motionless, but she could feel the tension radiating from
him.

"He put locks on the phone so I couldn't call out, or
even answer it," she said. "But one day he blacked my
eye. I don't even remember why. It didn't take much to
set him off. When I looked in the mirror the next
morning, all of a sudden something clicked in my brain
and I knew I had to either get away from him or kill
him. I couldn't live like that another day, another hour."

"I'd have opted for killing him," Quinlan said tonelessly. "I may yet."

"After that, it was all so easy," she murmured,
ignoring him. "I just packed my suitcases and walked
out. The doorman saw me and reached for the phone…
and then stopped. He looked at my eye and let the
phone drop back into the cradle, and then he opened the
door for me and asked if he could call a cab for me.
When I told him I didn't have any money, he pulled out
his wallet and gave me forty dollars.

"I went to a shelter for abused women. It was the
hardest, most humiliating thing I've ever done. It's strange
how the women are the ones who are so embarrassed," she
said reflectively. "Never the men who have beaten them,
terrorized them. *They* seem to think it was their right, or
that the women deserved it. But I understand how the
women feel, because I was one of them. Its like standing
up in public and letting everyone see how utterly stupid
you are, what bad judgment you have, what horrible
mistakes you've made. The women I met there could
barely look anyone in the eye, and they were the victims!

"I got a divorce. It was that simple. With the photographs taken at the shelter, I had evidence of abuse, and Eric would have done anything to preserve his reputation. Oh, he tried to talk me into coming back, he made all sorts of promises, he swore things would be different. I was even tempted," she admitted. "But I couldn't trust my own judgment any longer, so the safest thing, the only thing to do was stay away from romantic relationships in general and Eric Landers in particular."

God, it was so plain now. Quinlan could barely breathe with the realization of the mistakes he'd made in dealing with her. No wonder she had pulled away from him. Because he'd wanted her so much, he had tried to take over, tried to coddle and protect her. It was a normal male instinct, but nothing else could have been more calculated to set off her inner alarms. When she had needed space, he had crowded her, so determined to have her that he hadn't let anything stand in his way. Instead of binding her to him, he had made her run.

"I'm not like Landers," he said hoarsely. "I'll never abuse you, Elizabeth, I swear."

She was silent, and he could sense the sadness in her. "How can I trust you?" she finally asked. "How can I trust *myself*? What if I make the wrong decision about you, too? You're a much stronger man than Eric could ever hope to be, both physically and mentally. What if you *did* try to hurt me? How could I protect myself? You want to be in charge. You admit it. You're dominating and secretive. God, Quinlan, I love you, but you scare me to death."

His heart surged wildly in his chest at her words. He had known it, but this was the first time she had actually said so. She loved him! At the same time he was suddenly terrified, because he didn't see any way he could convince her to trust him. And that was what it was: a matter of trust. She had lost confidence in her own ability to read character.

He didn't know what to do; for the first time in his life he had no plan of action, no viable option. All he had were his instincts, and he was afraid they were all wrong, at least as far as Elizabeth was concerned. He had certainly bungled it so far. He tried to think what his life would be like without her, if he never again could hold her, and the bleakness of the prospect shook him. Even during these past hellish months, when she had avoided him so totally, even refusing to speak to him on the phone, he hadn't felt this way, because he had still thought he would eventually be able to get her back.

He had to have her. No other woman would do. And he wanted her just as she was: elegant, acerbic, independent, wildly passionate in bed. That, at last, he had done right. She had burned bright and hot in his arms.

He suspected that if he asked for an affair, and only that, she would agree. It was the thought of a legal, binding relationship that had sent her running. She had acted outraged when he had mentioned marriage and kids, getting all huffy because he hadn't included her in the decision-making, but in truth it was that very thing that had so terrified her. Had she sensed he had been about to propose? Finding the file had made her furious, but what had sent her fleeing out the door had been the prospect that he wanted more than just a sexual relationship with her. She could handle being intimate with him; it was the thought of giving him legal rights that gave her nightmares.

He cleared his throat. He felt as if he were walking blindfolded through a mine field, but he couldn't just give up. "I have a reason for not talking about myself," he said hesitantly.

Her reply was an ironic, "I'm sure you do."

He stopped, shrugging helplessly. There was nothing he could tell her that wouldn't sound like an outrageous lie. Okay, that had been a dead end.

"I love you."

The words shook him. He'd admitted the truth of it to himself months ago, not long after meeting her, in fact, but it had been so long since he'd said them aloud that he was startled. Oh, he'd said them during his marriage, at first. It had been so easy, and so expected. Now he realized that the words had been easy because he hadn't meant them. When something really mattered, it was a lot harder to get out.

Elizabeth nodded her head. It had gotten so dark that all he could see was the movement, not her expression. "I believe you do," she replied.

"But you still can't trust me with your life."

"If I needed someone to protect me from true danger, I can't think of anyone I would trust more. But for the other times, the day-to-day normal times that make up a true lifetime, I'm terrified of letting someone close enough to ever have that kind of influence on me again."

Quinlan took another mental sidestep. "We could still see each other," he suggested cautiously. "I know I came on too strong. I'll hold it down. I won't pressure you to make any kind of commitment."

"That wouldn't be fair to you. Marriage is what you want."

"I want *you*," he said bluntly. "With or without the legal trappings. We're great in bed together, and we enjoy each other's company. We have fun together. We can do that without being married, if that's all that's making you shy away from me."

"You want to have an affair?" she asked, needing to pin him down on his exact meaning.

"Hell, no. I want everything. The ring, the kids, all of it. But if an affair is all I can have, I'll take it. What do you say?"

She was silent a long time, thinking it over. At last she sighed and said, "I think I'd be a fool to make any decision right now. These aren't normal circumstances. When the power is back on and our lives are back to normal, then I'll decide."

Quinlan had always had the knack of cutting his losses. He took a step toward her. "But I still have tonight," he said in a low tone. "And I don't intend to waste a minute of it."

Chapter Eight

It was much as it had been that other night, and yet it was much more intense. Quinlan made love to her until she literally screamed with pleasure, and then loved her past her embarrassment. The darkness wrapped around them like a heated cocoon, suspending time and restrictions, allowing anything to be possible. The hours seemed endless, unmarked as they were by any clock or other means that civilized man had developed. The streets outside remained dark and mostly empty; he didn't turn on the radio again, because he didn't want the outside world to intrude, and neither did she.

It was too hot to sleep, despite the high ceiling in the lobby that carried the heat upward. They lay on the cushions and talked, their voices not much more than slow murmurs in the sultry heat. Quinlan's big hands never left her bare body, and Elizabeth suspended her thoughts for this one magic night. She became drowsy, but all inclination to sleep fled when he turned to her in the thick, heated darkness, pressing down on her, his callused hands stroking and probing until she writhed on the cushions. His lovemaking was as steamy as the night, as enveloping. In the darkness she had no inhibitions. She not only let him do as he wanted with her, she reveled in it. There wasn't an inch of her body that he didn't explore.

Daylight brought sunlight and steadily increasing temperatures, but the power remained off. Even though she knew it was impossible to see inside through the glazed windows, she was glad that they could remain snugly hidden in their own little lair. They drank water and ate, and Elizabeth insisted on washing off again in the smothering heat of the rest room, though she knew it wouldn't do any good to clean up with Quinlan waiting impatiently for her outside. Did the man never get tired?

She heard other voices and froze, panicking at the thought of being caught naked in the rest room. Had the power come back on? Impossible, because it was dark in the bathroom. Or had the guard cut off the lights in here before he'd left the day before? She hadn't even thought to check the switch.

Then she heard a familiar call sign and relaxed. The radio, of course. A bit irritated, with herself for being scared and with him because he'd caused it, she strode out of the rest room. "I nearly had a heart attack," she snapped. "I thought someone had come in and I was caught in the rest room."

Quinlan grinned. "What about me? I'm as naked as you are."

He was still sprawled on the cushions, but somehow he looked absolutely at home in his natural state. She looked down at herself and laughed. "I can't believe this is happening."

He stared to say, *It'll be something to tell our grand-kids,* but bit the words back. She wouldn't want to hear it, and he'd promised he wouldn't push her. He held out his hand to her, and she crawled onto the cushions with him, sinking into his arms.

"What was on the news?"

"A relatively quiet night in Dallas, though there was some sporadic looting. The same elsewhere. It was just too damn hot to do anything very strenuous."

"Oh, yeah?" she asked, giving him a sidelong glance.

He laughed and deftly rolled her onto her back, mounting her with a total lack of haste that demon-strated how many times during the night he'd done the same thing. "The news?" she prompted.

He nuzzled her neck, breathing in the sweet woman scent. "Oh, that. The national guard has been mobilized from Texas to the East Coast. There were riots in Miami, but they're under control now."

"I thought you said things were relatively quiet?"

"That *is* quiet. With electricity off in almost a quarter of the country, that's amazingly quiet." He didn't want to talk about the blackout. Having Elizabeth naked under him went to his head faster than the most potent whiskey. He kissed her, acutely savoring her instant response, even as he positioned her for his penetration and smoothly slid within. He felt the delicious tightening of her inner muscles as she adjusted to him, the way her fingers dug into his shoulders as she tried to arch even closer to him. His feelings for her swamped him, and he found himself wishing the electricity would never come back on.

Afterward, she yawned and nestled down on his shoulder. "Did the radio announcers say when the power company officials thought the power would be back on?"

"Maybe by this afternoon," he said.

So soon? She felt a bit indignant, as if she had been promised a vacation and now it had been cut short. But this wasn't a vacation; for a lot of people, it was a crisis. Electricity could mean the difference between life and death for someone who was ill. If all they had was a few more hours, she meant to make the best of them.

It seemed that he did, too. Except for insisting that they regularly drink water, he kept her in his arms. Even when he finally tired and had to take a break from lovemaking, he remained nestled within her body. Elizabeth was too tired to think; all she could do was feel. Quinlan had so completely dominated her senses that she would have been alarmed, if she hadn't seen the same drugged expression in his eyes that she knew was in hers. This wasn't something he was doing to her; it was something they were sharing.

They dozed, their sweaty bodies pressed tightly together despite the heat.

It was the wash of cool air over her skin that woke her, shivering.

Quinlan sat up. "The power's back on," he said, squinting up at the overhead lights that seemed to be glaring after the long hours without them. He looked at his watch. "It's eleven o'clock."

"That's too soon," Elizabeth said grumpily. "They said it would be this afternoon."

"They probably gave themselves some extra time in case something went wrong."

Feeling incredibly exposed in the artificial light, Elizabeth scrambled into her clothing. She looked at her discarded panty hose in distaste and crumpled them up, then threw them into the trash.

"What do we do now?" she asked, pushing her hair back.

Quinlan zipped his pants. "Now we go home."

"How? Do we call the guard service?"

"Oh, I'll call them all right. Later. I have a few things to say. But now that the power's on, I can get us out of here."

While he tapped into the security system, Elizabeth hastily straightened the furniture, shoving it back into place and restoring all the cushions to their original sites. A blush was already heating her face at the possibility of anyone finding out about their love nest, literally in the middle of the lobby. She didn't know if she would ever be able to walk into this building again without blushing.

Quinlan grunted with satisfaction as he entered a manual override into the system that would allow him to open the side door. "Come on," he said, grabbing Elizabeth's hand.

She barely had time to snatch up her purse before he was hustling her out of there. She blinked in the blinding sunshine. The heat rising off the sidewalk was punishing. "We can't just leave the building unlocked," she protested.

"I didn't. It locked again as soon as the door closed." Taking her arm, he steered her around the corner and across the street to the parking deck.

Before she could react, he was practically stuffing her into his car. "I have my own car!" she said indignantly.

"I know. Don't worry, it isn't going anywhere. But we don't know that the electricity is on all over the city, and we don't know what kind of situation you'll find at your place. Until I know you're safe, I'm keeping you with me."

It was the sort of high-handed action that had always made her uneasy in the past, but now it didn't bother her. Maybe it was because she was so sleepy. Maybe it was because he was right. For whatever reason, she relaxed in the seat and let her eyes close.

He had to detour a couple of times to reach her apartment, but the traffic was surprisingly light, and it didn't take long, not even as long as normal. She didn't protest when he went inside with her. The electricity was on there, too, the central air conditioning humming as it tried to overcome the built-up heat.

"Into the shower," Quinlan commanded.

She blinked at him. "What?"

He put his arm around her, turning her toward her bedroom. "The shower. We're both going to take a nice, cool shower. We're in good shape, but this will make us feel better. Believe me, we're a little dehydrated."

Their bargain had been only for the night, but since it had already extended into the day, she supposed it wouldn't hurt to carry it a little further. She allowed him to strip her and wasn't at all surprised when he undressed and climbed in with her. The shower spray was cool enough to raise a chill, and it felt wonderful. She turned around to let it wash over her spine and tilted her head back so the water soaked through her sweat-matted hair.

"Feel good?" he murmured, running his hands over her. She would have thought that he was washing her, except that he wasn't using soap.

"Mmm." He bent his head and Elizabeth lifted hers. If only she could stay this way, she thought. Kissing him, being kissed by him. His hard arms locked around her. Feeling him so close, all worries pushed aside…

The cool shower was revitalizing in more ways than one. Abruptly he lifted her and braced her against the wall, and she gasped as he drove deep into her. There was nothing slow about it this time; he took her fiercely, as wild as he had been the day before on the floor of the lobby, as if all those times in between had never been.

Later they went to bed. She could barely hold her eyes open while he dried her hair, then carried her to the bed and placed her between the cool, smooth sheets. She sighed, every muscle relaxing, and immediately went to sleep, not knowing that he slipped into bed beside her.

Still, she wasn't surprised when she woke during the afternoon and he was there. Lazily she let her gaze drift over his strong-boned features. He needed to shave; the black beard lay on his skin like a dark shadow. His hair was tousled, and his closed eyelids looked as delicate as a child's. Odd, for she had never thought of Quinlan as delicate in any way, never associated any sort of softness with him. Yet he had been tender with her, even in his passion. It wasn't the same type of gentleness Eric had displayed; Eric had been gentle, she realized now, because he hadn't *wanted* any responding passion from her. He had wanted her to be nothing more than a doll, to be dressed and positioned and shown off for his own ego. Quinlan, on the other hand, had been as helpless in his passion as she had been in hers.

Her body quivered at his nearness. Still half asleep, she pushed at him. His eyes opened immediately, and he rolled onto his back. "What's wrong?"

"Plenty," she said, slithering on top of him and feeling the immediate response between his legs. "It's been at least—" She paused to look at the clock, but it was blinking stupidly at her, not having been reset since the power had come back on. "It's been too damn long since I've had this." She reached between his legs, and he sucked in his breath, his back arching as she guided him into place.

"God, I'm sorry," he apologized fervently, and bit back a moan as she moved on him. This was the way he had always known his Elizabeth could be, hot with uncomplicated passion, a little bawdy, intriguingly earthy. She made him dizzy with delight.

Her eyes were sultry, her lips swollen and pouty

from his kisses, her dark hair tumbling over her shoulders. He watched her expression tighten with desire as she moved slowly up and down on him, her eyes closing even more. "Just for that," she murmured, "I get to be on top."

He reached overhead and caught the headboard, his powerful biceps flexing as his fists locked around the brass bars. "No matter how I beg and plead?"

"No matter what you say," she assured him, and gasped herself as her movements wrenched another spasm of pleasure from her nerve endings.

"Good." Quinlan arched, almost lifting her off the bed. "Then I won't accidentally say something that will make you quit."

He didn't. When she collapsed, exhausted, on his chest, they were both numb with pleasure. He thrust his hand into her tangled hair and held her almost desperately close. She inhaled the hot, musky scent of his skin, and with the slightest of motions rubbed her cheek against the curly hair on his chest. She could feel his heart thudding under her ear, and the strong rhythm was reassuring. They slept again, and woke in the afternoon with the sun going down in a blaze of red and gold, to drowsily make love again.

He got up to turn on the television sitting on her dresser, then returned to bed to hold her while they watched the news, which was, predictably, all about the blackout. Elizabeth felt a little bemused, as if a national crisis had passed without her knowing about it, even though she had been intimately embroiled in this one. Intimately, she thought, in more ways than one. Perhaps that was why she felt so out of touch with reality. She hadn't spent the past twenty-four hours concentrating on the lack of electricity, she had been concentrating on Quinlan.

The Great Blackout, as the Dallas newscasters were calling it, had disrupted electrical services all over the Sun Belt. The heat wave, peak usage and solar flares had all combined to overload and blow circuits, wiping out entire power grids. Elizabeth felt as if her own circuits had been seriously damaged by Quinlan's high-voltage lovemaking.

He spent the night with her. He didn't ask if he could, and she didn't tell him that he couldn't. She knew that she was only postponing the inevitable, but she wanted this time with him. Telling him about Eric hadn't changed her mind, any more than knowing about Eric had changed Quinlan's basic character.

When morning came, they both knew that the time-out had ended. Reality couldn't be held at bay any longer.

"So what happens now?" he asked quietly.

She looked out the window as she sipped her coffee. It was Saturday; neither of them had to work, though Quinlan had already talked to a couple of his staffers, placing the calls almost as soon as he'd gotten out of bed. She knew that all she had to say was one word, "Stay," and they would spend the weekend in bed, too. It would be wonderful, but come Monday, it would make it just that much more difficult to handle.

"I don't see that the situation has changed," she finally said.

"Damn it, Elizabeth!" He got up, his big body coiled with tension. "Can you honestly say that I'm anything like Landers?"

"You're very dominating," she pointed out.

"You love me."

"At the time, I thought I loved him, too. What if I'm wrong again?" Her eyes were huge and stark as she stared at him. "There's no way you can know how bad it was without having lived through it yourself. I would rather die than go through anything like that again. I don't know how I can afford to take the chance on you. I still don't know *you*, not the way you know me. You're so secretive that I can't tell who you really are. How can I trust you when I don't know you?"

"And if you did?" he asked in a harsh tone. "If you knew all there is to know about me?"

"I don't know," she said; then they looked at each other and broke into snickering laughter. "There's a lot of knowing and not knowing in a few short sentences."

"At least we know what we mean," he said, and she groaned; then they started laughing again. When he sobered, he reached out and slid his hand underneath her heavy curtain of hair, clasping the back of her neck. "Let me give something a try," he urged. "Let me have another shot at changing your mind."

"Does this mean that if it doesn't work, you'll stop trying?" she asked wryly, and had to laugh at the expression on his face. "Oh, Tom, you don't even have a clue about how to give up, do you?"

He shrugged. "I've never wanted anyone the way I want you," he said, smiling back just as wryly. "But at least I've made some progress. You've started calling me Tom again."

He dressed and roughly kissed her as he started out the door. "I'll be back as soon as I can. It may not be today. But there's something I want to show you before you make a final decision."

Elizabeth leaned against the door after she had closed it behind him. Final decision? She didn't know whether to laugh or cry. To her, the decision had been final for the past six months. So why did she feel that, unless she gave him the answer he wanted, she would still be explaining her reasons to him five years from now?

Chapter Nine

The doorbell rang just before five on Sunday morning. Elizabeth stumbled groggily out of bed, staring at the clock in bewilderment. She had finally set the thing, but surely she had gotten it wrong. Who would be leaning on her doorbell at 4:54 in the morning?

"Quinlan," she muttered, moving unsteadily down the hall.

She looked through the peephole to make certain, though she really hadn't doubted it. Yawning, she released the chain and locks and opened the door. "Couldn't it have waited another few hours?" she asked grouchily, heading toward the kitchen to put on a pot of coffee. If she had to deal with him at this hour, she needed to be more alert than she was right now.

"No," he said. "I haven't slept, and I want to get this over with."

She hadn't slept all that much herself; after he'd left the morning before, she had wandered around the apartment, feeling restless and unable to settle on anything to do. It had taken her a while to identify it, but at last she had realized that she was lonely. He had been with her for thirty-six hours straight, holding her while they slept, making love, talking, arguing, laughing. The blackout had forced them into a hothouse intimacy, leading her to explore old nightmares and maybe even come to terms with them.

The bed had seemed too big, too cold, too empty. For the first time she began to question whether or not she had been right in breaking off with him. Quinlan definitely was *not* Eric Landers. Physically, she felt infinitely safe and cherished with him; on that level, at least, she didn't think he would ever hurt her.

It was the other facet of his personality that worried her the most, his secrecy and insistence on being in control. She had some sympathy with the control thing; after all, she was a bit fanatic on the subject herself. The problem was that she had had to fight so hard to get herself back, how could she risk her identity again? Quinlan was as relentless as the tides; lesser personalities crumbled before him. She didn't know anything about huge chunks of his life, what had made him the man he was. What if he were hiding something from her that she absolutely couldn't live with? What if there was a darkness to his soul that he could keep under control until it was too late for her to protect herself?

She was under no illusions about marriage. Even in this day and age, it gave a man a certain autonomy over his wife. People weren't inclined to get involved in domestic "disputes," even when the dispute involved a man beating the hell out of his smaller, weaker wife. Some police departments were starting to view it more seriously, but they were so inundated with street crime, drug and highway carnage that, objectively, she could see how a woman's swollen face or broken arm didn't seem as critical when weighed in that balance.

And marriage was what Quinlan wanted. If she resumed a relationship with him, he might not mention it for a while—she gave him a week, at the outside—but he would be as relentless in his pursuit of that goal as he was in everything else. She loved him so much that she knew he would eventually wear her down, which was why she had to make a final decision now. And she *could* do it now—if the answer was no. She still had enough strength to walk away from him, in her own best interests. If she waited, every day would weaken that resolve a little more.

He had been silent while she moved around the kitchen, preparing the coffeemaker and turning it on. Hisses and gurgles filled the air as the water heated; then came the soft tinkle of water into the pot and the delicious aroma of fresh coffee filled the room.

"Let's sit down," he said, and placed his briefcase on the table. It was the first time she had noticed it.

She shook her head. "If this requires thinking, at least wait until I've had a cup of coffee."

His mouth quirked. "I don't know. Somehow I think

I'd stand a better chance if your brain stayed in neutral and you just went with your instincts."

"Hormones, you mean."

"I have nothing against those, either." He rubbed his beard and sighed wearily. "But I guess I could use a cup of coffee, too."

He had taken the time to change clothes, she saw; he was wearing jeans that looked to be at least ten years old, and a soft, white, cotton shirt. But his eyes were circled with dark rings and were bloodshot from lack of sleep, and he obviously hadn't shaved since the morning before the blackout. The blackness of his heavy beard made him look like a ruffian; actually, he looked exactly like the type of people he hired.

When the coffee stopped dripping, she filled two mugs and slid one in front of him as she took a seat at the table. Cautiously sipping the hot brew, she wondered how long it would take to hit the blood-stream.

He opened the briefcase and took out two files, one very thin and the other over an inch thick. He slid the thin one toward her. "Okay, read this one first."

She opened it and lifted her eyebrows when she saw that it was basically the same type of file that he'd had on her, though this one was on himself. Only it seemed to be rather sketchy. *Bare bones* was more like it, and even then, part of the skeleton was missing. It gave his name, birthdate, birthplace, social security number, physical description, education and present employment, as well as the sketchy facts of his brief marriage, so many years ago. Other than that, he seemed not to have existed between the years of his divorce and when he had started his security business.

"Were you in cold storage for about fifteen years?" she finally asked, shoving the file back toward him. "I appreciate the gesture, but if this was supposed to tell me about you, it lacks a little something."

He eyed her warily, then grinned. "Not many people can manage to be sarcastic at five o'clock in the morning."

"At five o'clock, that's about all I *can* manage."

"I'll remember that," he murmured, and slid the second file, the thick one, toward her. "This is the information you wouldn't have gotten if you investigated me."

Her interest level immediately soared, and she flipped the manila folder open. The documents before her weren't originals, but were a mixture of photostats and faxes. She looked at the top of one and then gave him a startled look. "Government, huh?"

"I had to get a buddy to pull up my file and send it to me. Nothing in there is going to reveal state secrets, but the information is protected, for my sake. I could have hacked into the computer, but I'd just as soon not face a jail term, so it took some time to get it all put together."

"Just exactly what did you do?" she asked, not at all certain that she wanted to know. After being so frustrated by his lack of openness, now that his life lay open before her, she wasn't all that eager to know the details. If he had been shot at, if he had been in danger in any way…that could give her a different set of nightmares.

"No Hollywood stuff," he assured her, grinning.

"I'm disappointed. You mean you weren't a secret agent?" Relieved was more like it.

"That's a Hollywood term. In the business, it's called a field operative. And no, that isn't what I did. I gathered information, set up surveillance and security systems, worked with antiterrorist squads. It wasn't the kind of job that you talk over with your buddies in the bar after work."

"I can understand that. You got in the habit of not talking about yourself or what you did."

"It was more than just a habit, it could have meant people's lives. I still don't talk about it, because I still know people in the business. Information is the greatest asset a government can have, and the most dangerous."

She tapped the file. "So why are you showing me this?"

"Because I trust you," he said simply; then another grin spread across his face. "And because I didn't think you'd believe me if I just said, 'I can't talk about myself, government stuff, very hush-hush.' You would have laughed in my face. It's the kind of crap you hear in singles bars, hot-shot studs trying to impress the airheads. You aren't an airhead."

After flipping a few pages and scanning them, she said, "You're right. I wouldn't have believed this. Most people don't do this type of work."

He shrugged. "Like I said, I went to Cal Tech, and I was very good at what I did."

"Did?" she asked incredulously. "It's what you still do. It's just that now you do it for yourself instead of the government." An idea struck her. "The people you hire. Are they—?"

"Some of them," he admitted.

"Like the biker?"

He laughed. "Like the biker. Hell, do you think I'd hire anyone who looked like that if I didn't personally know him? He really was an operative, one mean son of a bitch."

"They come to you for jobs when they retire?"

"No, nothing like that. I'm not a halfway house for burned-out government employees. I keep track of people, contact them to see if they're interested in working for me. Most of them are very normal, and it's just a matter of moving from one computer job to another."

She closed the file and pushed it away from her. Quinlan eyed her with alarm. "Aren't you going to read it?"

"No. I don't need to know every detail of everything you've done. A brief overview is enough."

He drew a deep breath and sat back. "Okay. That's it, then. I've done all I can. I can't convince you, prove it to you in any way, that I'll never treat you the way Landers did. *I* know I won't, but you're the one who has to believe it. Elizabeth, sweetheart, will you marry me?"

She couldn't help it. She knew it wasn't the way a woman was supposed to respond to a marriage proposal, but the relentlessness of it was so typical of Tom Quinlan that she couldn't stop the sharp crack of laughter from exploding into sound. She would probably hear that question every day until she either gave him the answer he wanted or went mad under the pressure. Instead of making her feel pressured, as it would have before, there was a certain amount of comfort in knowing she could depend on him to that extent. Seeing that file had meant more to her than he could know. It wasn't just that it filled in the gaps of his life, but that he trusted her to know about him.

She managed to regain her composure and stared seriously at him. Somehow, what had happened during the blackout had lessened the grip that Eric Landers had still had on her, even after so many years. During the long hours of that hot night she had been forced to truly look at what had happened, to deal with it, and for the first time she'd realized that Eric had still held her captive. Because of him, she had been afraid to truly let herself live. She was still afraid, but all of a sudden she was more afraid of losing what she had. If it were possible to lose Quinlan, she thought, looking at him with wry fondness. But, yes, she could lose him, if she didn't start appreciating the value of what he was offering her. It was sink or swim time.

He had begun to fidget under her silent regard. She inhaled deeply. "Marriage, huh? No living together, seeing how it works?"

"Nope. Marriage. The love and honor vows. Until death."

She scowled a little at him. He was as yielding as rock when he made up his mind about something. "Yours could come sooner than you think," she muttered.

"That's okay, if you're the one who does me in. I have an idea of the method you'd use," he replied, and a look of startlingly intense carnal hunger crossed his face. He shivered a little, then gathered himself and raised his right hand. "I swear I'll be an absolute pussycat of a husband. A woman like you needs room."

She had taken a sip of coffee, and at his words she swallowed wrong, choking on the liquid. She coughed and wheezed, then stared at him incredulously. "Then why haven't you been giving me any?" she yelled.

"Because I was afraid to give you enough room to push me away," he said. He gave her a little half smile that acknowledged his own vulnerability and held out his hand to her. "You scare me, too, babe. I'm scared to death you'll decide you can get along without me."

She crossed her arms and glared at him, refusing to take his outstretched hand. "If you think you'll get a little slave, you'll be disappointed. I won't pick up after you, I don't like cooking and I won't tolerate dirty clothes strewn all over the place."

A grin began to spread across his face as she talked, a look of almost blinding elation, but he only said mildly, "I'm fairly neat, for a man."

"Not good enough. I heard that qualification."

He sighed. "All right. We'll write it into our wedding vows. I'll keep my clothes picked up, wash the whiskers out of the sink and put the lid back down on the toilet. I'll get up with the kids—"

"Kids?" she asked delicately.

He lifted his brows at her. She stifled a smile. God, dealing with him was exhilarating! "Okay," she said, relenting. "Kids. But not more than two."

"Two sounds about right. Deal?"

She pretended to consider, then said, "Deal," and they solemnly shook hands.

Quinlan sighed with satisfaction, then hauled her into his arms, literally dragging her across the table and knocking her mug of coffee to the floor. Oblivious to the spreading brown puddle, he held her on his lap and kissed her until her knees were weak. When he lifted his head, a big grin creased his face and he said, "By the way, I always know how to bypass my own systems."

She put her hand on his rough jaw and kissed him again. "I know," she said smugly.

Over an hour later, he lifted his head from the pillow and scowled at her. "There's no way you could have known."

"Not for certain, but I suspected." She stretched, feeling lazy and replete. Her entire body throbbed with a pleasant, lingering heat.

He gathered her close and pressed a kiss to the top of her head. "Six months," he grumbled. "And it took a damn blackout to get you to talk to me."

"I feel rather fond of the blackout," she murmured. "Without it, I wouldn't have been forced to spend so much time with you."

"Are you saying we never would have worked it out if it hadn't been for that?"

"I wouldn't have given you the chance to get that close to me," she said, her voice quiet with sincerity. "I wasn't playing games, Tom. I was scared to death of you, and of losing myself again. You never would have had the chance to convince me, if it hadn't been for the blackout."

"Then God bless overloaded power grids," he muttered. "But I'd have gotten to you, one way or another."

"Other than kidnapping, I can't think how," she replied caustically.

He went very still, and the silence made her lift her head to give him a suspicious glare. He tried to look innocent, then gave it up when he saw she wasn't buying it.

"That was what I had planned for the weekend, if you refused to have dinner with me Thursday night," he admitted a bit sheepishly.

"Ah-ha. I *thought* you waylaid me that afternoon."

"A man has to do something when his woman won't give him the time of day," he muttered. "I was desperate."

She said, "It's six-thirty."

A brief flicker of confusion crossed his face; then he glanced at the clock and grinned. "So it is," he said with satisfaction. She had just given him the time of day— and a lot more. With a lithe twist of his powerful body he tumbled her back into the twisted sheets and came down on top of her.

"I love you," he rumbled. "And I still haven't heard the 'yes' I've been waiting for."

"I agreed. We made a deal."

"I know, but I'm a little more traditional than that. Elizabeth Major, will you marry me?"

She hesitated for a second. Eric Landers had lost the power to keep her a victim. "Yes, Tom Quinlan, I certainly will."

He lowered his head to kiss her. When he surfaced, they were both breathing hard and knew it would be a while yet before they got out of bed. He gave the clock another glance. "Around nine," he murmured, "remind me to make a couple of phone calls. I need to cancel the kidnapping plans."

She laughed, and kept laughing until his strong thrust into her body changed the laughter into a soft cry of pleasure, as he turned that relentless focus to the task of bringing them both to the intense ecstasy they found only with each other. She had been so afraid of that part of him, but now she knew it was what made him a man she could depend on for the rest of her life. As she clung to his shoulders, a dim echo of thought floated through her brain: "God bless overloads!"

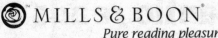

Romantic reads to
Need, Want

...International affairs, seduction and passion guaranteed
10 brand-new books available every month

Pure romance, pure emotion
6 brand-new books available every month

Pulse-raising romance – heart-racing medical drama
6 brand-new books available every month

From Regency England to Ancient Rome, rich, vivid and passionate romance...
6 brand-new books available every month

Scorching hot sexy reads...
4 brand-new books available every month

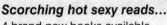

LOOK OUT...

...for this month's special product offer.
It can be found in the envelope containing
your invoice.

**Special offers are exclusively for
Reader Service™ members.**

You will benefit from:

- Free books & discounts
- Free gifts
- Free delivery to your door
- No purchase obligation – 14 day trial
- Free prize draws

THE LIST IS ENDLESS!!

*So what are you waiting for —
take a look* **NOW!**

DM/OFFER